PRAISE FOR DiANN MILLS

DEADLY ENCOUNTER

"Crackling dialogue and heart-stopping plotlines are the hallmarks of Mills's thrillers, and this series launch won't disappoint her many fans. Dealing with issues of murder, domestic terrorism, and airport security, it eerily echoes current events."

LIBRARY JOURNAL

"[Mills] has the ability to sweep you off your feet and into the middle of an adventure in a matter of paragraphs. . . . If you are looking for a little bit of action, romance, intrigue, and domestic terrorism (and a happily ever after!), then this is the book for you."

RADIANT LIT

"Fans of clean romantic suspense will enjoy this well-plotted winner."

PUBLISHERS WEEKLY

DEADLOCK

"DiAnn Mills brings us another magnificent, inspirational thriller in her FBI: Houston series. *Deadlock* is a riveting, fast-paced adventure that will hold you captive from the opening pages to the closing epilogue."

FRESHFICTION.COM

"Mills's newest installment in the FBI: Houston series will keep readers on the edge of their seats. For those who love a good 'who-done-it,' *Deadlock* delivers."

CBA RETAILERS + RESOURCES

"Mills does a superb job building the relationship between the two polar opposite detectives. With some faith overtones, *Deadlock* is an excellent police drama that even mainstream readers would enjoy."

ROMANTIC TIMES

DOUBLE CROSS

"DiAnn Mills always gives us a good thriller, filled with inspirational thoughts, and *Double Cross* is another great one!"

FRESHFICTION.COM

"Tension explodes at every corner within these pages. . . . Mills's writing is transparently crisp, backed up with solid research, filled with believable characters and sparks of romantic chemistry."

NOVELCROSSING.COM

"For the romantic suspense fan, there is plenty of action and twists present. For the inspirational reader, the faith elements fit nicely into the context of the story. . . . The romance is tenderly beautiful, and the ending bittersweet."

ROMANTIC TIMES

FIREWALL

"Mills takes readers on an explosive ride. . . . A story as romantic as it is exciting, *Firewall* will appeal to fans of Dee Henderson's romantic suspense stories."
BOOKLIST

"With an intricate plot involving domestic terrorism that could have been ripped from the headlines, Mills's romantic thriller makes for compelling reading."
LIBRARY JOURNAL

"[A] fast-moving, intricately plotted thriller."
PUBLISHERS WEEKLY

"Mills once again demonstrates her spectacular writing skills in her latest action-packed work. . . . The story moves at a fast pace that will keep readers riveted until the climactic end."
ROMANTIC TIMES

"This book was so fast-paced that I almost got whiplash. . . . Heart-pounding action from the first page . . . didn't stop until nearly the end of the book. If you like romantic suspense, I highly recommend this one."
RADIANT LIT

"Fast-paced and action-packed. . . . DiAnn Mills gives us a real winner with *Firewall*, a captivating and intense story filled with a twisting plot that will have you on the edge of your seat."
FRESHFICTION.COM

DEEP EXTRACTION

DiANN MILLS

DEEP EXTRACTION

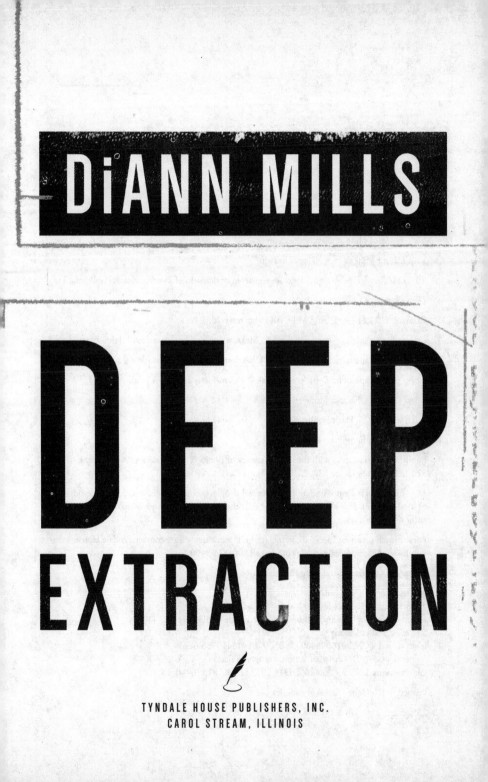

TYNDALE HOUSE PUBLISHERS, INC.
CAROL STREAM, ILLINOIS

Visit Tyndale online at www.tyndale.com.

Visit DiAnn Mills at www.diannmills.com.

TYNDALE and Tyndale's quill logo are registered trademarks of Tyndale House Publishers, Inc.

Deep Extraction

Cover design by Faceout Studio, Tim Green

Interior design by Dean H. Renninger

Edited by Erin E. Smith

Published in association with the literary agency of Books & Such Literary Management, 52 Mission Circle, Suite 122, PMB 170, Santa Rosa, CA 95409.

For information about special discounts for bulk purchases, please contact Tyndale House Publishers at csresponse@tyndale.com or call 800-323-9400.

Library of Congress Cataloging-in-Publication Data

Names: Mills, DiAnn, author.
Title: Deep extraction / DiAnn Mills.
Description: Carol Stream, Illinois : Tyndale House Publishers, Inc., [2017]
   | Series: FBI task force
Identifiers: LCCN 2016048469 | ISBN 9781496410986 (sc)
Subjects: | GSAFD: Christian fiction. | Suspense fiction.
Classification: LCC PS3613.I567 D44 2017 | DDC 813/.6—dc23

Printed in the United States of America

23   22   21   20   19   18   17
 7   6   5   4   3   2   1

TO MY DREAM TEAM
FOR ALL THEIR ENCOURAGEMENT
AND SUPPORT

ACKNOWLEDGMENTS

Shauna A. Dunlap, special agent/media coordinator, Houston FBI—Through every FBI novel, you've graciously answered questions and guided me in the right direction. I appreciate your friendship.

Lynette Eason—Thank you for your friendship and all the fabulous Skype brainstorming sessions!

Beau Egert—Your experience and knowledge in the oil and gas industry helped me create a realistic story.

Julie Garmon—Thanks so much for your willingness to read my stories and give me fabulous feedback.

Dr. Richard Mabry—I couldn't write a single novel without your expertise and experience in the medical field.

Edie Melson—Our long talks and time spent together helped me discover so many things about my characters.

Alycia Morales—Your support and encouragement in the final stages of this book provided insight and the ability to finish on time.

Tom Morrisey—Thank you for sharing your knowledge about weapons and how they work. Over the years of writing, you've never declined my need for help.

Donna Rice, attorney and writer—I appreciate your help in writing the legal sections. Lost without your expertise.

Kathi Wilson—Your real estate assistance gave my characters homes in the best neighborhoods west of Houston.

ANYTHING COULD HAPPEN while the dead slept. Which was why some would say a woman shouldn't tread alone through a cemetery at 2:55 on a Tuesday morning in April. But possible danger had never stopped Houston FBI Special Agent Tori Templeton, especially when her mind marched with determination. Her body refused to give in to rest, but it wasn't a violent crime robbing her of sleep.

The worn path below a black sky ended at Kevin's gravesite. She was here to visit the one person who could help her make sense of a puzzling world.

Tonight, like many nights in the past, she made her way to Kevin's final resting place to talk to him about work, life, problems, and victories. Maybe someday she'd figure out his intrigue with God.

Her brother. Her friend. The one she looked up to and treasured.

Tori didn't stalk a cemetery because of some superstition that he lay beneath a marble stone and could communicate with her. She visited the site because it signified peace. Maybe by a weird osmosis, she'd find what had given Kevin strength. She wanted to believe he lived pain-free with his God. No cancer. No side effects of chemo and radiation. An eternal home with a God he embraced tighter than life. At least he'd claimed those beliefs before he breathed his last.

"Special Agent Templeton?"

At the sound of the voice, a twinge of annoyance filled her spirit. The man greeting her was a friend, except she wanted to be alone. No need to face him. "Yes, Officer Richards."

"Saw your car, thought I'd check on you."

"I'm a creature of habit."

"I noticed. Nothing's stirring, so I'll leave you to your thoughts."

The sadness in his voice drew up a well of compassion, and she turned to him. "Wait. How's your family?" The man walked the graveyard shift—literally—and he might need a listening ear more than she should ponder the existence of a good God in a world plagued with unrest.

"The same. Ups and downs mixed with hardheads and love." He sighed and scanned the area. "Nice night."

A familiar insect's call reached her ears. "We have a choir." She smiled into the shadows, where a light, twenty feet away, illuminated his stocky frame and highlighted his silver-gray hair, giving him a halo effect. She stared above his head at a slice of the moon resting on a canvas of stars.

"Cicadas are to the night as robins are to the day."

"Well stated," she said. "I never pay attention to them until it's dark and quiet." She brushed aside a leaf on Kevin's gravestone. "We haven't talked in over a week. Did your son join the Navy?"

"Yes. A good choice. I pray he learns discipline and respect for himself and others."

He said the *pray* word. Not what she wanted to hear, and she drew in a breath. "Your daughter?"

"Agreed to rehab. Another prayer answered."

Kevin had used the same language, and look where it got him. Was her brother's confidence in a divine being a way to endure the devastation of cancer? A crutch in the midst of excruciating pain? Always the same questions as she searched for the why of tragedies. "How's your wife?"

"Good, thanks. She told me you were welcome to—"

Her phone alerted her to a call. "Excuse me a minute." She yanked it from her shirt pocket and confirmed it was Assistant Special Agent in Charge Ralph Hughes before answering.

"We have a possible homicide," the ASAC for violent crimes said.

Her mind spun into agent mode, her job, the only part of her life where she sensed purpose. "Who and where?"

"Nathan Moore, owner of Moore Oil & Gas, died in his home this evening."

Distress rambled through her, though she did her best to overcome it. She'd known Nathan since college days. "What happened? Why suspect murder?"

"Due to the threats on his life and a call made to his attorney prior to his death," the ASAC said.

"What was said in the call?"

"Moore suspected someone was trying to kill him and getting close."

Tori stared at Kevin's tombstone and recalled the day she and Mom selected the blue-gray granite. Now Nathan's widow faced the same dilemma. "Are we thinking the environmental activists are responsible?" Five days ago, one of Nathan's drill sites had been bombed—possibly part of a retaliation move for winning a lawsuit filed by environmentalists who believed he was illegally dumping backflow water from fracking. But a bombing was unlikely in his home. "Was he gunned down? A break-in?"

"Moore's death appears to have been a heart attack, the result of natural causes. A medical examiner is on it."

"Why?"

"Too coincidental for my take. I want to know who threatened him, and I need you and Max at the Moore residence. He's been notified and will meet you there." He texted her the Moore address at Lake Pointe Estates in the Katy area west of Houston, but she had it memorized.

The call ended and Tori rose to her feet. "Officer Richards, I need to go."

"Sure thing. See you again soon."

"Count on it. Best to you and your family." She hurried to her car while the devastating news played havoc with her mind.

Why hadn't Sally contacted her about Nathan's death? They were closer than sisters, weren't they? Tending to her grieving sons could have her emotionally spent. Even Tori was finding it hard to accept Nathan's death.

She shoved aside personal sentiments that ushered in disbelief. Her investigative skills were needed. The ASAC had assigned her to investigate a potential crime.

Nathan possibly murdered? He had sainthood stamped next to his name. Charity work. Generous donations to worthy causes. Incredible husband and father.

Who could possibly want him dead?

2

COLE WOKE WITH his cell phone blaring in his ears. He snatched it from his nightstand and read the screen: *Sally Moore, 3:22 a.m.* Calls this time of the morning usually meant bad news. "Hey, Sally, what's going on?"

"Nathan's had a heart attack."

He snapped on the lamp. "Is he okay?"

She sobbed quietly. "He's dead. The boys and I said our final good-byes at the hospital. We just got back home a little while ago."

"I'll be there in a few minutes."

"No, please. Your coming isn't a good idea. I wanted you to hear from me before the media announces it."

Alarm zipped to the forefront. "What happened?"

"I found him at home on the floor of his office. Suspected a heart attack, called 911, and tried to revive him. But he was already gone."

"How are the boys taking it?"

5

"In their own way. Jack's quiet, and Lance is verbal."

"None of you should face this without support. Don't you have a girlfriend to call?"

"Being alone is the best way to handle Nathan's death. My dad and stepmom will be here before noon. They'll help make necessary arrangements."

Something was wrong. "What aren't you telling me?"

She released a ragged breath. "When I found him, his phone was inches from his fingers. After calling 911, I checked it and saw his last conversation was with Jacob Farr, his attorney. I returned the call and learned Nathan feared for his life—because of threats from someone. The attorney suggested foul play. He contacted the police, and they're here now."

"Your attorney's actions are appropriate. Any threats need to be investigated. Considering Nathan's high-profile position in the oil and gas industry, the recent bombing at the Texas City site, and the controversy over the court case, law enforcement must be involved. Did Mr. Farr indicate a suspect?"

"I didn't think to ask."

"Where are the officers?"

"In the foyer. I think they're on the phone."

"Where are you?"

"The kitchen."

The hesitancy in her voice pushed him forward. "I don't understand why you want to endure this alone. Are the boys listening?"

"They're upstairs." Her voice broke. "Tonight Nathan said he planned to file for divorce in the morning. I have no idea if he told his attorney, but—"

Cole inwardly groaned. "Sally, that doesn't even sound like him."

"He was like a stranger. Hurling horrible insults at us." She drew in ragged breath, no doubt for control. "When he stormed out of the dining room, I told the boys their dad wasn't himself. I told them I loved Nathan, and he loved us."

"I'm so sorry."

"You've been a wonderful friend, but it's better you keep your distance. I'll call later." She disconnected the call.

Nathan wanted a divorce? And now he was dead? Possibly a homicide? What kind of madness was this?

It was 3:30 a.m. and Cole lay awake with his mind full speed ahead. He stared at the ceiling and listened to the whir of the fan while his thoughts continued to spin. Nathan's death hit Cole hard, as though he'd been punched in the gut. Although his friend's heart condition was no secret, a pacemaker and subsequent follow-up appointments with a cardiologist had given him a thumbs-up on his health. Most people were irrational prior to heart attacks. Their anger levels rose right along with their blood pressure. But Cole had worked out with Nathan yesterday morning, and nothing indicated a health problem—or that his marriage was in jeopardy. He had asked Cole's opinion about securing more bodyguards for his family.

His cell phone rang again. The caller was Nathan and Sally's son Jack, a boy who'd soon reach thirteen years old without a father. Cole hesitated to answer after Sally's warnings, but the situation could have gone further downhill. He responded on the second ring.

"CJ, Mom needs help," Jack said. "Dad died of a heart attack tonight. She told us not to contact anyone, but I don't know why, and I'm scared."

"I'm really sorry about your dad. Nathan was a fine man. Your mother called me a few minutes ago. The future's uncertain, and you're going to miss him. It will take time to work through your grief."

"I'm scared. The FBI's on its way here."

Cole deliberated what he could say to the boy. With the bombing of the drill site last week, he could see the reason for bringing the FBI in. "I'm sure there's an explanation."

"All I know is they suspect murder, like something caused Dad's heart attack. Mom's losing it." The pitch rose in his young voice, not yet starting to change. "Dad must have been sick tonight because he said awful things to Mom and us."

"Jack, I'm sure he didn't mean them."

"The real bad thing is the cops think Mom hurt Dad."

If Jacob Farr told the police Nathan planned to file for divorce . . . "I'm sure you've made a mistake."

"When Dad went off on Mom tonight, he said he wanted a divorce. Lance told me he wouldn't blame Mom if she'd done it."

An alarm hit Cole hard. "Knowing your dad, I'm sure they resolved the issue."

"He turned over a glass at the dinner table, then went to his office."

What a cruel final memory of his father. "Your mother wouldn't hurt your dad."

"I know, but a cop heard Lance say it."

Lance had a habit of speaking out of turn, a bad tendency for an angry fourteen-year-old without a filter on his tongue. "Jack, take a deep breath. Is your brother close by?"

"He's in his room. CJ, we need you here."

Cole didn't want to ignore Sally's request for distance. "Maybe someone else can better help your mom."

"Miss Tori is an FBI agent. I really like her, but her being with us could make things worse. She might ask questions. Make Mom feel worse."

The situation kept plummeting. What else had happened tonight? "Jack—"

"What about me and Lance?" He burst into tears. "Please come."

He wrestled with wanting to comfort the boy and wondering how his presence might look to investigators. "Let me talk to your mother. See if you can calm yourself. I know this is horrible."

A few moments later, Sally answered. "I had no idea Jack had contacted you. Both boys heard the argument."

"Did Nathan apologize?"

"No. His final words to all of us were filled with hate, a side of him I'd never experienced before."

"What do I tell Jack?"

He watched the digital clock on his nightstand move to the next minute.

"Cole," she finally said, "it's only a matter of time before the truth about tonight surfaces. When that happens, you may be questioned simply because you were here. Jack is insistent you come, so you choose. I can't figure out what is best."

What a decision. If he ignored Jack's request, the boy might think Cole didn't care. If he showed up at the Moore home, law enforcement would document it. And then there were the threats on Nathan's life—the Moores could be in danger. Cole trusted the truth. "Tell him I'm on my way. I'll deal with the aftermath. If Jacob Farr testifies about divorce proceedings, time will reveal it."

"All right. I hope you don't regret this." Sally ended the call.

Cole held the phone with his teeth while he pulled on a pair of jeans from the bathroom floor. Cramming the device into his pocket, he yanked on a T-shirt. Sally didn't have the word *vengeful* in her vocabulary. She and Nathan loved each other . . . or so Cole thought.

He grabbed his wallet and keys. The questions and scenarios targeting his mind were symptoms of a career he'd given up, one he couldn't quite shake.

Now he earned his living ensuring the exteriors of people's

homes and businesses were aesthetically pleasing and maintained a green and healthy design. Nothing more. Nothing less. For a brief moment, his thoughts trailed back to the demons stalking him . . .

The shooter stood over him, laughing. *"He's bleeding out. Won't last until the cops get here."*

One thing Cole knew for certain: he would be a friend to the Moores, but he refused to get involved in investigating another murder case.

3

TORI DROVE WEST ON I-I0 toward the Moore home. She wanted to call Sally but held back. How would she handle Tori investigating Nathan's death? The thought of working this case made her ache all over. As if there were a choice in the matter. Unless she gave the ASAC reason to remove her. Claimed conflict of interest . . .

You're an FBI agent. Act like one. Put aside personal feelings and concentrate on learning what happened to Nathan tonight. But how could she? The why of her friend not contacting her about his death hammered at her heart, as though a ghastly revelation might surface, one a friend and special agent shouldn't be told.

The lack of sleep had messed up a logical explanation for why Sally hadn't notified her.

Before leaving the cemetery, she'd downloaded from the FBI's internal website what little info was available about Nathan's death. Now stopped at a traffic light, she scanned the findings. Not much to go on at this point.

Five days ago, a bombing occurred at one of his drill sites, and her partner Max had been consulted on the case due to his past experiences with explosives. No arrests had been made but lots of activity. Some of the radical environmental activists hailed the IED bombing as a step forward in their cause, since a judge ruled in Nathan's favor about the alleged illegal dumping suit.

A truck laid on the horn behind her, and she frowned in the rearview mirror before releasing her foot from the brake. Preoccupation was a side effect of working violent crime.

Max would have insight, and she needed to know what he'd formulated before they entered the Moore home. Facing Sally . . . facing the boys in agent capacity. The thought sickened her no matter how much she tried to force it away. She pulled over with her hazard lights on and pressed in Max's cell phone number.

"I'm nearly there." The familiar gruff voice gave her a moment's relief. Sanity in the midst of turmoil.

"Me too. What are your thoughts?"

"You mean are we looking at a heart attack or a murder?"

"Your opinion first," she said.

"With the call made to his attorney, it's worth an investigation."

"Were there signs of a struggle, bruising, or possibly a bad mix of drugs to induce a heart attack? A look at his stress level will help too."

"We'll find out. You're a bit wired this early in the morning."

"I'm tired, not wired. The victim had a history of heart problems. Has a pacemaker and saw his cardiologist regularly."

"Are you a fan? Where's your source of info?"

Confession time. "I'm a friend of the family."

"Tori, can you work this case objectively?"

Heat rose from her neck. "I'm a professional. My job is my first priority."

"You didn't answer my question."

"It doesn't require a response."

"Has a family member contacted you?"

"No." The question of why Sally hadn't called pressed against her mind. But a few days ago her friend had said Nathan was concerned about activists taking further action. "I know my job."

"All right. We'll discuss your neutrality later." He coughed, a deep, raspy sound that seemed to originate in his toes. Max's health was deteriorating with no explanation. Giving up the cigarettes hadn't done a thing for him.

"Are you all right?" she said.

"Why wouldn't I be? Back to what I was saying. Sally Moore's teenage son implicated his mother."

She cringed. "Are you certain?"

"All I know is whatever the kid said prompted an HPD officer to contact us."

Sounded like hothead Lance had inflicted severe damage. "Anything else I should know before I get there?"

"That's it."

"All right. I'm five minutes out."

"I just parked."

"Wait on me."

"Will do. In view of your relationship to the family, I'll pose the questions."

She opened her mouth to state exactly how she viewed his declaration but decided otherwise. He could be right. No room for emotions . . . just facts. She'd jump in if the situation headed south. "If Sally has misgivings about Nathan's death, she'll tell us."

"Why?"

"It's in her DNA. She loves—or rather, loved—Nathan. She has a nursing background. Would do everything in her power to keep him alive."

"So she's innocent because you know her?"

"I'm giving you her background."

"Are you blind to a suspect's faults?"

"That's absurd. I've known her for years. But I'm an agent investigating a possible homicide. Save your cynicism until after we get the medical examiner's report."

"Okay. But if I detect a problem with you on the case, we'll discuss protocol." He clicked off.

At times, Max's methods ground at her nerves. Great guy and she'd learned tons from him. Yet he had his rough edges, and they were getting rougher. One thing he'd asked hit her hard. Could she work the case objectively? What exactly had Lance said in the presence of a police officer? Had Sally angered her oldest son, so he implicated his mother in a vicious crime? Didn't take much with his volatile temperament. Lance's normal behavior toward his family swung a pendulum between whoever irritated him at the time. When not lashing out, he stayed to himself, sullen and uncommunicative. According to Sally, his bad moods had grown worse in the last six months.

Tori's desire to usher justice into a dangerous and unpredictable world meant weighing the evidence and finding the truth. Turning over rocks that often unearthed dirt. Friendship and loyalty beyond the realms of understanding meant enduring the good and the bad.

Most likely Nathan died naturally of a heart attack. Until proven otherwise, she was simply burning brain cells with what-ifs.

She parked her Charger next to the curb in front of Max's car and slid her purse onto her shoulder before opening her door. Two HPD vehicles with flashing blue-and-red lights lit up the area in front of the Moores' massive white-stone contemporary home. She stepped out of the car. At the cemetery, the star-studded night sky had filled her with awe. Now cloud cover added to her mood, and her emotions ran the gamut.

Max waited by his car, and he was smoking. No wonder the hacking cough persisted. A spot on his lung hadn't deterred the habit. His shirt was tucked in on the left side but not the right and exposed a round middle. His attire didn't meet FBI guidelines. No doubt the ASAC would get wind of it and handle the problem. Right now the two of them had a murder case to investigate.

Max nodded her direction but said nothing. Neither did she. They were both taking in the surroundings and thinking.

They walked to the front door, where they were met by an officer who inspected their creds. He gestured them inside the two-story foyer, where a diamond-shaped chrome-and-crystal chandelier glittered as though mocking the tragedy. The Moore home with its sleek design and stark black-and-white decor had never seemed warm or inviting, and this morning Tori shivered. The chill of death seemed to penetrate her bones.

"Before you speak to the family, Detective Hernandez would like a word with you," the officer said. "Wait here while I inform him."

A plainclothes Hispanic man walked their way from the living area. After introducing himself, he pointed to the kitchen. "The family is upstairs with a friend. Please follow me." Once in the familiar room, the detective continued. "According to Mrs. Moore, she found the body and called 911. Her second call was to Jacob Farr, the victim's attorney. According to Farr, the victim consulted him about hiring two more bodyguards. He feared for himself and his family."

"Where is the victim's phone now?" Max said.

"We have it secured. I'll make sure you have it before I leave."

"Did Mr. Farr suggest a name or service for the alleged protection?" Max said. "Or were suspects mentioned?"

"Negative on both counts."

"When did Mr. Moore contact his attorney?"

The detective pulled a notepad from inside his jacket pocket. "He placed the call at 10:03 last night and ended it at 10:24. Mrs. Moore found him at approximately 10:38. The security monitor shows her entering their bedroom at 9:27. A 911 call came in at 10:40. At 10:45, she contacted the attorney and explained what happened."

Tori internally breathed relief.

"However," Detective Hernandez said, "the master bedroom has a rear exit leading onto a balcony and staircase to the pool level. The cameras show her sitting poolside from 9:33 until 10:00, when she disappeared, and returning to the pool at 10:25, where she remained until 10:36."

Max cleared his throat. "Has Mrs. Moore been questioned about where she went at the unaccounted-for time?"

"Not yet."

Tori bit her tongue to keep from saying Sally was without a doubt innocent. Right? Her training led her in another direction. Let the evidence play out to prove her friend's innocence. "Are you thinking Mrs. Moore might have let someone inside or contributed to the victim's death?"

"Agent Templeton, the victim had bruising on his chest. Whatever caused it could have brought on the heart attack."

She wanted to talk to Sally now. Get these ridiculous accusations clarified. "Mrs. Moore is a registered nurse. Maybe she gave CPR."

Detective Hernandez lifted a brow. "She claimed to have done so. The older boy said his father asked for a divorce tonight."

Impossible. The two were soul mates.

"The kid offered the info?" Max said.

Detective Hernandez shook his head. "An officer overheard it when the two boys were arguing."

"The FBI's been working on the source of a bombing—at one of his drill sites," Max said. "We want to make sure the victim's death is not connected to that crime or the threat on his life. What's Mrs. Moore's emotional state?"

"Very distraught. Cooperative."

"Appreciate all you've done. Before we talk to the family, I'd like to see Mr. Moore's office."

Tori could have led the way, but instead she followed Max and Detective Hernandez to Nathan's office. His cell phone lay in a plastic bag on his desk. She knelt beside an overturned desk lamp. Blood stained the hardwood floor. From an injury or the fall?

"Were photos taken of the body?" Tori said. Since Max had excluded her from asking Sally questions, she could get a few answers from the detective.

"Not here. The paramedics examined him and transported him to the hospital."

"I see blood on the floor. I'm assuming it's Nathan's, but why?"

"Trauma to the head," Detective Hernandez said. "I'm sure the medical examiner will determine the cause."

Tori continued. "Fingerprint sweep?"

"No. Doesn't seem necessary until the official ruling on how the victim died."

She agreed but glanced at Max for his reaction.

"In view of what we've learned, I'd like a sweep and a blood spatter analysis." Max focused on the bookshelves behind Nathan's desk and the desktop, not touching anything, just peering intently. "No one is to enter this room until I give the okay. Have you instructed the family not to enter the crime scene? We can't have anyone tampering with potential evidence."

"We have, and we'll get on the fingerprints ASAP," Detective Hernandez said.

"Shall we talk to Mrs. Moore?"

Detective Hernandez motioned to the foyer. "Up the stairs to the right."

"Is the friend with her male or female?" Max said.

What did Max mean with that cutting question?

"Male. A little too cozy if you ask me."

"Right." Max harrumphed. "A man is found dead by his wife the same day he decides to file for divorce? Looks like a closed case to me. She's hiding something."

Tori hated the stereotypical wife-was-involved allegation. She couldn't contain her anger. "Why don't you hold off on the cuffs until you have cause of death and evidence?"

Max shook his head. "Nathan Moore wouldn't be the first man to die and leave a wealthy widow."

4

AT THE TOP of the wood-and-metal winding steps that led to the Moore media room, Tori took in the familiar surroundings—a mammoth curved TV with super-high-def viewing—Nathan's favorite for year-round sports. Gray textured walls, a white sofa, wood-and-marble square coffee table, accents in blue gray, and floor-to-ceiling windows. How many times had she enjoyed laughter and long talks here with cherished friends?

Sally's pale face served as a grim reminder of the tragedy. Red-rimmed dark-blue eyes met Tori, and her shoulder-length blonde hair was in a makeshift ponytail. Dressed in a pink buttoned shirt and jeans, she held Jack's hand on the sofa. Recessed lighting above them lit Sally's face but dimmed Jack's. Nathan's possible murder and Max's statement that Sally knew more than she'd given HPD shouldn't bother Tori so much, but it did. Because she was a homicide investigator, and the two women had always been there for each other. Could her role with the FBI be a caustic mix?

Standing at the window overlooking the street, a man she didn't recognize observed the agents—three fingers in his jean pocket. Firm jaw. Expressionless. Mid- to late thirties.

Sally rushed into Tori's arms. "I'm so glad you came. I wanted to call about Nathan, but one thing after another kept happening. Who contacted you? Jack?"

For the first time, Tori longed for a simple career. "Neither of the boys called me."

Sally stepped back, her eyes wide. "You're here in agent capacity? I was told the FBI had been contacted, but—"

Tori took her friend's hands. "I'm sorry. We've been briefed on all that's happened. Nathan's death may have been the result of criminal activity." She hated the ordeal for Sally. "This is my partner, Special Agent Max Dublin."

Max nodded. "Sorry for your loss."

Maybe he'd behave himself. When the interview was over, they needed to have a talk. Lately, his mannerisms breached FBI protocol.

"Is Agent Templeton's presence a problem?"

"I suppose better a friend than a stranger. I know you'll get to the bottom of what happened to Nathan. I tried to save him, but my efforts were useless. When the doctor reported he was gone, I called his cardiologist. I want to know what happened and why his pacemaker failed."

Jack bolted from the sofa. "The cops and FBI are Lance's fault."

Sally released Tori's hands and moved to her son. "Your brother's hurting, like you." She focused on Tori. "This is about the threats made on Nathan's life on the heels of the drill site bombing, right? I mean, who listens to a teen grieving the loss of his father?"

Tori captured her gaze. "Your attorney's statement about Nathan fearing for his life and needing to hire additional bodyguards has to be looked into. Add to the mix what Lance said in the presence of the officer, and questions must be asked to find out what happened tonight."

Sally whirled to the nameless man by the window and back to Tori. "That's insane. You heard Lance say he was glad Nathan's gone, but he didn't mean it. Nathan was a wonderful husband and father. You saw him in action."

"Sally, where is Lance?"

"In his room. Do you have to question him?"

"Yes. In a few minutes."

Jack wrapped an arm around his mother's waist. His light-brown eyes matched Nathan's, and he was nearly as tall. "I won't leave you, Mom."

Always the sweet, devoted boy. Reminded her of Kevin at his age.

The man posed by the window joined them and reached out his hand. "Cole Jeffers." The intensity in his eyes held her for a moment. Still no readable emotion. The fresh scent of the outdoors met her senses.

She took his hand firmly. "Special Agent Tori Templeton." Why hadn't she heard his name before? "We haven't met."

"You don't know Cole?" Sally frowned. "He's been a family friend for years."

"I'm the yardman," Cole said.

Odd a yardman had shown up in her friend's dark hour, bearing a name Tori had never heard before. She and Sally talked about everything . . . but not this guy.

Sally dabbed beneath her eyes. "He's taken care of the landscaping for Moore Oil & Gas and our home for a long time. Since he arrived a few minutes ago, he's been a comfort in the midst of our loss." She hesitated. "Maybe Nathan or I referred to him as CJ. That was the boys' nickname."

Relief eased Tori's frazzled mind. She'd heard the name reference but thought CJ was a neighbor. She took in his jeans and T-shirt—muscles that would rival a model's on a weight lifting magazine. Sky-blue eyes and a day-old growth gave him a certain ruggedness. Nothing like Nathan, who always appeared spit polished. A good-looking yardman who arrived shortly after his employer's death? Max was no doubt having a field day with this.

And Tori hated where her suspicions were going.

"Mr. Jeffers, who contacted you?" Tori said, ignoring Max's instructions for him to pose questions.

"Jack called. Asked me to come by. Sally didn't object due to the circumstances."

For Jack or for his mother? And why was Lance in his room alone?

Max coughed. "Mrs. Moore, I'd like to speak to you privately. Without your sons."

Sally blinked. "Will Tori be coming too?"

"Yes, ma'am."

"The kitchen okay?"

"Mom, you need me with you," Jack said.

Max raised his hand. "It's important your sons not be present during the interview. I have matters about tonight to discuss."

"All right. Isn't Tori your partner, or do you have a policy against agents asking friends questions?" Sally rubbed her face. "Whatever you need. I'm too spent to argue." She turned to Jack. "Stay with Cole and away from Lance."

"I'll keep him company," Cole said. "Are you sure about not having an attorney present?"

"Yes. I've nothing to hide. The misunderstanding will soon be cleared up."

Downstairs in the kitchen, an open room with white cabinets, stainless steel appliances, and white stone trim, they sat at a black-and-white round table.

"You have my permission to record anything I say," Sally said. "All I know is my husband suffered a heart attack and died."

Max pressed the Record button on his cell phone. "Your name and address . . ."

For the next several minutes, Tori mentally weighed her friend's responses. No face or throat touching. No hesitation or lack of conversational eye contact. Nothing to indicate deceit. Max's absurd accusations made Tori furious.

"Do you give your consent for us to take your husband's laptop to the FBI for mirror imaging?"

"No. All of his business files are there. I'd need a signed court order."

"All right." He sighed. "What time did you leave your room for the pool?"

"Almost 9:30. The security cameras will show that. You can check them."

"Why were you by the pool alone?"

"Listening to water flow from the landscape rocks relaxes me. Too early to go to bed." She drew in a breath. "Tori can vouch I do this regularly."

Tori slipped out of agent mode. "We've enjoyed the pool and talked there many times. Sometimes Nathan or the boys joined us."

"What about Mr. Jeffers?" Max said.

"Yes. As I said, he's a family friend."

"But Agent Templeton has never met him, and I thought you two were close friends."

"I was unaware of the oversight until a bit ago."

"How convenient. The security monitors show you left the pool at approximately 10:00 and returned to the pool at 10:25. Where did you go?"

She glared at Max, then looked at Tori. "Is this really necessary?"

Tori spoke gentleness into her tone. "I suggest cooperating no matter how offensive the question."

Sally closed her eyes. "I slipped into the laundry room, unloaded towels from the dryer, and folded them. Straightened up the room because the boys had friends over earlier and went swimming. They hadn't picked up their wet things. The towels are on the laundry room counter if you'd like to check, and the wet trunks are in the washer."

Max smiled. "Thank you. Were you aware your husband discussed with his attorney the need for added security here and at his workplace?"

Tori feared her friend would crumble.

"He said added protection would begin today," Sally said. "He'd increased the number from two to four. After the bombing and threats on his life, he was concerned about us."

"Where were they this evening?"

"Home, I assume. Their contract is from 6 a.m. to 9 p.m., unless Nathan wasn't here. He didn't like anyone invading his privacy. But beginning today, the protection would be 24-7. I gave Detective Hernandez their names and the private firm's number."

"Did Nathan voice any extra precautions?"

"Yes. The boys were to give me their whereabouts at all times. They were to attend school functions only, and I wasn't to leave the house without an escort."

"Did he mention a name or names of anyone he suspected?"

"No."

"What about the divorce?'"

Sally inhaled sharply. "He made the announcement after informing us about additional bodyguards."

"Are you saying he looks out for you and his sons, then asks for a divorce?"

"Yes."

"Your response?"

"I protested, of course, but he'd already made the decision," she said.

"When you returned to the house from the pool, what caused you to check on your husband?"

"I told the police I heard a crash. It's in their report. So I went in to find the source."

"Weren't you afraid?"

"We have a solid security system. My first thought was a picture had fallen from the wall."

Max lifted a brow but said nothing. "Then what happened?"

"I searched the downstairs calling out for Nathan until I found him in his office." She wrung her hands. "I . . . I checked his pulse while calling 911 from his cell phone on the floor beside him. When he didn't have a pulse and wasn't breathing, I suspected a heart attack. He'd been under tremendous stress with business matters. Repeated attempts at resuscitation produced nothing." She trembled and seemingly fought for composure. "I then called Jacob Farr and learned more about the threats."

"Why? Were you bored waiting for the ambulance?"

Sally stiffened. "It was the last call Nathan made, and I wanted to know what was said."

"Why?"

Her face reddened. "As our attorney, I thought he might know something that could have led to Nathan's death."

"And?"

Contempt etched her features. "You already confirmed the call, so what more do you want? My husband died tonight, and some are saying he was murdered. I'm upset and grieving." She buried her face in her hands.

"If you're innocent, why didn't you call Tori?"

"Max!" Tori wanted to punch him.

Sally drew in a steadying breath. "Agent Dublin, I've been friends with Tori for years, and your method of conducting an interview is inappropriate by any standards. For your information, I wanted to call her, but I lean on her too much as it is."

"Your husband's death looks like a solid reason to call her." He squinted as though reading her features. "What happened then, Mrs. Moore?"

"Jack and Lance came downstairs in time to see Nathan pushed out into an ambulance. I drove us to the hospital. There a doctor confirmed he'd passed. The boys and I said our good-byes. I contacted Nathan's cardiologist for answers about what happened with his pacemaker. When we arrived home, three police officers and a detective were waiting. They asked me questions and said they were contacting the FBI." She focused on Tori. "I will get through this."

"Believe it," Tori said. "Sal, we have to talk to Lance."

"He's been in his room since Jack gave him a black eye. First time little brother ever stood up for himself."

"Why did they fight?"

"Because of Lance's outburst. I can't fault either boy. Lance simply speaks before thinking about the impact of his words. Jack told him to shut up, and the verbal battle started. Lance pushed him, and Jack punched him. An officer broke it up. I got an ice pack for Lance's eye, and he took off to his room. I tried talking to him, but he refused to open the door. Can we make this short? I'm exhausted."

"Agent Templeton and I will do our best. Why did the younger boy call Mr. Jeffers?"

"How many times do I need to answer the same questions? Cole is a family friend, like an uncle to the boys."

Max cleared his throat. "Mrs. Moore, you thought it was okay for your son to call another man, but not a woman for yourself?"

Sally, be careful. Max will twist your words.

"Jack and Lance needed a man to identify with. If I craved a friend, I'd have contacted Tori."

"But you didn't. So obviously Mr. Jeffers handled your emotional needs too?"

"My attorney will be notified about your unprofessional method of interviewing an innocent woman."

He snorted. "I don't have any more questions." He slid a rock-hard look at Tori. "Do you?"

Tori touched Sally's arm. "Nothing at the moment, except to talk to Lance."

Max scooted back his chair. "I'm ready. The forty-eight-hour rule is ticking away."

Max always had this immediacy thing going—granted, he was right. People had a habit of forgetting or confusing facts within hours after a crime was committed. The three left the kitchen and wound through the dining area to the foyer, up the stairs, past Cole Jeffers and Jack, and to Lance's room.

Sally knocked. "Lance, open the door. Two FBI agents need to talk to you. One of them is Tori."

"I don't want to talk to anybody."

"They need to know why you think I might have hurt your dad."

"My business."

Sally covered her mouth. In the next breath, she arched her shoulders. "Lance Moore, please open the door."

Tori had seen mother and son butt heads before. "Lance, this is Tori. I'm here with my partner. One way or another, we're talking to you."

His vile response wasn't worth repeating.

5

COLE EXCUSED HIMSELF from Jack in the upstairs media room and hurried down the hall to Lance's bedroom. No excuse for the kid's language. Sally and Nathan had spent many a sleepless night over his behavior. Lack of discipline bred rebellion, and rebellion paved the road to criminal activities.

"What are you doing?" Max Dublin reminded him of a Saint Bernard with drooping eyes and jaw. But Cole doubted he was "man's best friend."

"I'm going to use my relationship with Lance to persuade him to open the door." Cole spoke slowly and eyed the agent. "Enough trouble has erupted in this house tonight." He caught Sally's attention.

"I know what you're thinking, Cole," she said. "Lance can be difficult, and he's pushing all of us. I think breaking in the door seems harsh in view of his father's death and law enforcement swarming our home. Besides, privacy is important to a teenager."

"I agree his solitude should be respected, but not when the FBI wants to question him about something he said."

Sally sighed. "Let me talk to him a little longer. He just needs a gentle hand."

"Go away, all of you." Lance tossed more profanity than Cole had heard in the landscaping business. "I have the right to do whatever I want."

She dug her fingers into her palms. Her face was etched with pain . . . and frustration. "Go ahead."

Cole knocked on the door. "Lance, this is CJ. Jack asked me to come by. He told me everything that happened last night."

"Right. Dad's junk tossed at us. I'm still not opening the door."

"I have no choice but to force my way inside." Cole pulled out his pocketknife and picked the lock. Turning the knob, he pointed to the open door for the agents to enter. "Lance, cooperate or you'll make things worse for your family." When the kid spit out a curse word, Cole stepped inside the room ahead of the agents and focused on the teen. Lance held an ice pack over his eye. His actions were more wounded pride than anything else. "This is not just about you. Settle down. For no other reason than your mother's sake."

Lance threw the ice pack at him, but Cole caught it and didn't budge. Oh, the predictability and mystery of teen boys.

"Are you going to punch me?" Lance sneered.

"Jack has the corner on that one," Cole said.

"Why don't you gas up the lawn mower? Seems to be the only thing you know."

"Hey." Cole forced a friendlier tone when he wanted to hurl a few words about the kid's attitude. "Your mother needs your support."

"Now I'm the bad guy?"

"No. You're a young man who lost his father, and there's an investigation that requires your help."

Lance glanced away from those in the room, then turned to Agent Templeton. "My mom would never do anything to hurt my dad. Or anyone. She's too good and kind—always puts us first. Dad told her he wanted a divorce in front of Jack and me. When she told him she loved him and asked if they could talk alone, he said he was done with all of us. Flipped over a glass of iced tea. Then said we were a liability." His eyes narrowed.

Lance's comments failed to exonerate his mother, but he was attempting to be an asset instead of a hindrance.

"Mom, I'm sorry for getting you into trouble." He gave her an awkward hug and stared at Agent Templeton with sad eyes. "Sorry. What else do you need? I can see how you might think he was killed because of the threats and stuff, but I have no clue about any of it."

Tori Templeton's green-gold eyes softened. Hair the color of pecans rested in waves on her shoulders. Definitely gorgeous and in control of the situation with her friends. A draw for him if he was looking.

"Thank you, Lance." Agent Templeton rubbed her left wrist. "We'll have more to go on in a few hours."

"The medical examiner's report?" Lance said.

"Yes." She must have caught Cole staring because she glanced away. "Where's Jack?"

Agent Templeton was a type A personality, in control. Cole took his cue and headed toward the media room. So he'd added extra duties to his typical responsibilities at the Moore house—taking orders from the FBI and babysitting.

"Mr. Jeffers, don't leave until we talk," Special Agent Dublin said.

"Sure." Cole had committed friendship to the Moore family, or he'd be out the door.

Questions hammered at his brain. Why had Nathan contacted his attorney about bodyguards for his family when he planned to leave them? He swung around and retraced his steps to Lance's bedroom. "Agents, have you considered that Nathan's announcement of a divorce could have been a means of protecting his family?"

"Leave the investigation to the professionals," Max Dublin said. "Stick to mowing yards."

6

TORI GLANCED OUT the rear window of the Moores' kitchen. Soon the sun would be rising, glistening. Drying the dew. She wished she could stay. Sally's frail nerves needed a boost, including strength and confidence in her ability to withstand every moment ahead. But Tori had a twofold problem on her hands, and first was how Nathan had died. Although a massive heart attack looked probable, a legitimate threat would prove someone wanted him dead.

When would they receive the medical examiner's and cardiologist's reports?

Tori hoped Nathan *had* died of a heart attack. Overthinking a case could lead to disaster. Ignoring clues meant she wasn't doing her job.

The second problem rested with an unruly teen. Would Lance later decide to blame his mother for his father's death? The teen had grown more rebellious about six months ago, and Nathan's and Sally's efforts seemed to make the matter worse—for some reason he despised his dad.

"It's six thirty," Sally said. "I'll grind some beans for coffee. It'll give me something to do."

"I don't know how much longer we'll be here," Tori said. "The fingerprint and DNA teams can do their jobs without me or Max."

Her friend's shoulders slumped, and the dark circles beneath her eyes could hide a coffin. "Why the extra work? I'm telling you he died of a heart attack. Are you thinking someone was in his office? Upset him to the point of inducing the problem?"

Tori's eyes stung like sand had invaded them. "Just protocol for the investigation. He was threatened, and I want to know by whom. Mr. Jeffers may have a valid argument about Nathan making his absurd announcement to protect you."

"I simply don't understand any of it. The man last night was not the husband and father we loved."

"We should have the initial medical reports soon."

Max coughed. Sounded like his lungs would burst. "I'd like coffee, ma'am, if it's not an imposition."

Sally first handed him a glass of water. She moved across the kitchen to the coffee bar area. Her grace was embedded in her beauty and a draw to all those in her presence. For certain Tori wouldn't brew coffee for anyone who questioned her like he'd done.

Max captured Tori's attention. "We have questions for Mr. Jeffers."

"Send Jack down to me." Sally sprinkled coffee beans into the grinder. "The conversation will disturb him, and I could use the company."

Again Max and Tori climbed the stairs to the second floor. Jack and Cole were playing a video game. Lance was still in his room, probably nursing his ego. "Jack, your mom would like you downstairs while we talk to Mr. Jeffers."

He stopped the game. "He's a friend, Miss Tori. Not an enemy."

She tilted her head. "Of course he's your friend. It's our job to talk to everyone here."

"Even me?"

Max moved in front of her. "Do you have information for us?"

"No. You're a real jerk, know that?" Jack disappeared to the lower level of the home. Cole put the video controller aside and stood to face the agents. Arms at his side. Concentrated eye contact and no visible hostility.

"Mr. Jeffers, how long have you known the Moore family?" Max peered at Cole over his nose.

"About seven years for Nathan and about two and a half for the rest of the family."

"During this time, you became a friend to Mrs. Moore."

"Correction. Nathan and then his wife and their sons."

"Seems strange a businessman and a family of this caliber would call a yardman a friend."

Cole's sky-blue gaze penetrated Max's face. "Guess so. I didn't know friendship required a pedigree."

Max huffed. "Were you here often?"

"Professionally, as often as necessary. Socially when Nathan and Sally invited me."

"Did Mrs. Moore ever invite you without her husband?"

"No. What are you insinuating?" Cole's voice growled low.

"You'd have a lot to gain with Nathan out of the way. A beautiful woman, huge house, all that Moore money could buy."

Cole stared at him before responding. "A well-respected man has died. That's a loss, not a gain."

"Depends. What did you and the victim have in common?"

Cole again used silence, as though he was thinking through each word. "We respected and trusted each other. Enjoyed sports. Exercised in the early hours. I have experience with oil and gas, so he could talk about the business without concern of it leaking to the media."

"Were you aware of the threats on his life?"

"Yes. He confided in me yesterday morning, and I suggested he hire more bodyguards until the matter resolved itself. He was worried about his family."

"Why would he listen to you when you plant flowers for a living?"

"Because I made sense. Because I'm intelligent. Because I'm a friend. Are you finished? Because I have a job to get to."

"Who did you suggest for protection?"

"He already had a service, but I recommended two options: off-duty law enforcement and to contact his attorney for ideas."

"Not yourself?"

"You do have issues, Agent Dublin."

Max hesitated. Tori wasn't used to seeing him back down from a confrontation, but Cole seemed to hold his own. "We need a way to contact you."

Cole flipped a small notepad and pen from his shirt pocket and jotted something. "Mobile number is best." He tore off the slip of paper and handed it to Max.

"Address?"

"Sure." A moment later he returned the paper.

"That's the high end of Cinco Ranch." Max jutted his chin. "A little pricey for minimum wage."

"I manage. Where do you live?"

"I'm asking the questions. Do I need to remind you that you're speaking to a federal agent?"

Cole dragged his tongue over his lips. "I'd like to be with you when you give Sally the report."

"Why?" Max's brows narrowed. "What's your stake?"

"My stake?"

"Yeah. What's in it for you?"

Tori couldn't believe what Max was saying. Why had he turned so antagonistic? Or did she already have a clue?

Cole's face reddened. "Look up the meaning of friendship."

"You have all the answers. Why's that?"

"When your investigation is over, you'll learn I'm not the bad guy."

"Where were you last night?" Max continued.

"With a friend from seven thirty to after midnight."

"Name?"

"Manny Lopez."

Max poised his pen. "One of your yard guys? Does he speak English?"

The animosity between the two men could have been sliced with a butter knife, and she couldn't blame Cole Jeffers. Tori made a decision. Crossing Max got her in trouble every time, but she couldn't let this slide. She faced Cole. "Would you mind joining Jack and Sally until we're finished?"

Cole strode to the staircase. "I'll suggest Jack and I take a walk. The air in here has a stench to it."

Tori waited until the sound of his footsteps faded. Fury at Max's obstinacy seized her. If Cole Jeffers had any facts or evidence to help them with this case, they'd just kissed it good-bye. "Max, since when did treating people like second-class citizens help solve a crime?"

"You're an idiot if you don't see what's going on here. A lonely, rich woman has an affair with the yardman. They're in this together, mark my word."

"And where's your proof? You're not the agent I partnered up with six years ago. That man used his head and not his mouth. He taught me how to work homicide and care about people. Treat them with respect. I know the spot on your lung has you scared. I know you can't give up the cigarettes. I know your daughter isn't speaking to you. I know your wife moved out, and it's tearing you apart. But suck it up 'cause you're doing a lousy job as an agent. Cole Jeffers has an alibi for last night, or did you miss it?" She whirled around and headed downstairs. She'd lost it and didn't care. No excuse for unprofessionalism.

Max didn't say a word, and that was more disconcerting than a face-off. She heard his steps behind her. Now was not the time to mention that his work at the FBI might be the only thing of value he had left.

Tori's and Max's cell phones alerted them to an incoming update: the medical reports. The answer they needed. She read the findings while Max did the same.

Not good. Not good at all.

The cardiologist had spent hours testing Nathan's pacemaker. The device had not malfunctioned but been remotely accessed, causing the heart attack.

Murder. She despised the word.

A life snuffed out of existence. Her ribs ached as though she'd had the wind knocked out of her.

7

TORI TURNED TO MAX, descending the steps behind her. "I have to tell Sally how Nathan died."

"Trust me on this one. She already knows."

Tori swallowed a retort and concentrated on the new information. According to the pacemaker's monitoring report, the breach occurred at approximately 10:32.

By then Sally had returned to the pool, and the boys' trunks and towels were in the laundry area. The security cameras showed her staring and doing nothing at the time of Nathan's death. Tori's blood pressure dropped ten points, then rose again at the thought of Sally hiring a hacker.

The investigation had officially become a violent crime. Remote access to a wireless pacemaker ensured Nathan's cardiologist could make minor adjustments without surgery, but the wrong person gaining access spelled death.

She made her way to the kitchen, where Sally stared out the window facing the patio.

"Sal—" Tori poured gentleness into her words—"are Jack and Cole taking a walk?"

She nodded. "Why?"

"We have the medical report."

She lifted a tearstained face. "Did I hurt Nathan when I administered chest compressions?"

"Not to our knowledge." Tori put an arm around Sally's waist. "Nathan's pacemaker had a malfunction caused by a hacker."

Sally's face blanched. "He was murdered?"

"I'm afraid so, and it happened while you were out at the pool."

She leaned her head on Tori's shoulder. "People loved him. He was generous and kind, a man of integrity." She stiffened. "Find out who took Nathan from us, Tori."

❈

Shortly after 7 a.m., Cole found Sally seated on the back patio overlooking the pool and stone waterfall. He'd learned about the hack into Nathan's pacemaker. If Sally hadn't contacted the cardiologist, the cause of death might never have been labeled murder.

The rhythmic sound of the water would normally have calmed him, but not in the face of tragic circumstances. This was the first chance he'd had to speak with her privately since he'd arrived. The agents were in Nathan's office—doing their investigative work. "Will you be all right until your parents arrive?" He had a landscaping project for a computer company that started yesterday, and he'd signed a contract to oversee the work personally on a daily basis. Any breach of the deal meant his men wouldn't get paid.

"I need to stand strong." She took a sip of coffee, then set the mug down. "Thanks for everything. Kit and Dad will be here by ten. Jacob, our attorney, will be here shortly. Let him deal with Agent Dublin's rudeness."

"Good." The question that propelled fury through his body begged for an answer. "Why would Nathan ask for a divorce? Or is it none of my business?"

She stared at him with watery eyes. "I've wondered the same thing repeatedly, tried to remember a time when he could have inappropriately interpreted something I said or did. I keep drawing a blank. He'd been acting strangely since the bombing. I thought his irritability was due to stress. But to make such a loathsome announcement in front of his sons?"

"Had he been drinking?"

"Not that I could tell, and the medical examiner didn't mention alcohol in his blood. Besides, he couldn't drink with his medications."

"What brought on the argument?"

"Dessert." She picked up her cup of coffee from a small table. "During dinner, he explained the hiring of two more bodyguards for our protection. He wanted us to be careful, said he feared for his family after the bombing and another matter he wasn't ready to discuss. Then he asked Lance if he'd brought up his algebra grade. You know Lance. They quarreled. I tried to calm them. We finished dinner. Jack knew we were having dessert, Nathan's favorite, and offered to help me in the kitchen. He hates it when Lance and his dad are at odds. Anyway, we cut slices of pineapple upside-down cake and carried them to the dining room." She blew the steam from her coffee as if it would make the turmoil evaporate. "Lance and Nathan were shouting, and I asked them to stop. That's when Nathan turned to me and asked for a divorce." She hesitated. "Definitely got quiet. Jack and I served dessert, and I took my seat. I asked Nathan if we could discuss the matter privately. He said no. I told him of my love and requested counseling. He said no again. Lance blew . . . Ugly things were said. My temper took over, and I rather vehemently declared we needed to talk in private."

Cole hated the loss to this family, the shatter of emotions that blindsided them all. "I'm really sorry. He never said a word to me. I'm leaning toward the theory that his decision was to protect you and the boys."

She glanced away as a squirrel ventured closer to the patio and captured her attention. "That would be the man I love, not the out-of-control stranger who left us at the dining table and spent the rest of the evening in his office."

"You didn't talk to him again?"

"I tried, but he locked me out of his office. The door was open, though, when I found him. I want to believe his explosion was all about keeping us safe. Everything happened so fast—the whirlwind trip to the hospital. The police. The boys' horrible fight." Her lips quivered.

"The FBI and HPD will get this resolved."

"But Nathan was murdered, and Tori's partner suspects me. . . . She might too."

"You have an alibi, and that agent's a hothead." The psychological workup of suspects churned every bit of evidence to find the truth. Media would announce the murder to the world. The boys would face other kids' questions.

"Jack wants to stay home from school today," she said. "Doesn't want to leave me. I get it. His way of working through pain is to support me. Lance hasn't left his room, so I assume he doesn't plan to attend either."

Lance had a tendency to consider himself first. That trait could change if he chose to declare war on things that stood between him and his relationships with others.

Sally picked up her cell phone and touched her fingertips to the screen. She burst into tears. "Would you call the school and explain why the boys are home today?"

He took the phone. "This is Cole Jeffers, a close friend of Nathan and Sally Moore. Their sons, Lance and Jack, are enrolled at your school." He explained the tragedy, omitting the term *murder*. "Yes, ma'am. Lance and Jack might return tomorrow, but if anything changes, Mrs. Moore will contact you." He gave Sally a grim smile—the best he could do. "It's handled. I've got to talk to the agents and then get to work."

She covered her mouth, then nodded. "Thanks for everything. I'll contact you later."

"Don't unless you communicate the why first to Agent Templeton."

She stared at him blankly, and he left her alone.

Inside the house, he made his way to Nathan's office. "Agents Templeton and Dublin, I'm leaving now."

Dublin stiffened—apparently annoyed at the interruption—while she laser focused on him. "Jeffers, I'm not finished with you yet."

"You have my contact info." Cole walked to the foyer and opened the front door, welcoming the fresh air.

"I'm thinking you and Mrs. Moore arranged for Mr. Moore's pacemaker to be hacked."

"Look, if you'd take the time to study Nathan's personality, you'd see that something else was going on last night. Your job, Agent Dublin, is to discern the truth, dig deep for motive, and make a professional case against whoever committed this atrocity."

"Pretty fancy words for a yardman."

"Whatever." Cole headed toward his truck. Time to get to the job site and not let Dublin crawl under his skin and stay there.

The spring sunshine warmed his bones: low seventies and perfect weather for planting. Four bodyguards took up positions around the house. The sight gave him momentary relief that Sally and the boys would be safe . . . if the killer wasn't finished.

He unlocked his truck and took a long look at the Moore home. Three acres of precision for every tree, plant, and color according to sun exposure and Houston temps. In the rear stood a monument to a man who didn't enjoy the water: an Olympic-size pool that Cole had spent hours designing to Nathan's specs. The natural-rock formations and waterfall, enhancing the rear of the huge plantation-style home, had attracted cameras from national magazines. Had Nathan understood wealth never arrived hand in hand with peace unless the person accepted the faith aspect? None of the Moores were on that track. Neither were they interested, except maybe Jack.

Nathan lived the life most men never grasped: a lovely and caring wife, two healthy and intelligent sons, this incredible home, a multimillion-dollar business . . . but at least one enemy wanted him dead. Who'd killed him? Hacking into a pacemaker took skill. Either the killer already possessed the ability, or he'd hired the expertise. Nathan had taken precautions to ensure his family was guarded, but the killer didn't need to access his home security system, just a keystroke to his heart.

Cole pushed aside old habits. The FBI and HPD were investigating the cause of death, and they didn't need his help.

They'd learn the truth about him soon enough, a fact Nathan had promised to keep secret from his family until Cole was able to put the past where it belonged and step forward in the confidence he once had in himself and his skills.

8

FROM A WINDOW inside the Moore home, Tori watched Cole drive away in a Ford F-450 Platinum pickup. A little uptown for a yard-man, along with a few other expensive habits—the Montblanc pen used to write his contact info for Max, Lucchese boots, 7 For All Mankind jeans, and an Apple Watch wrapped around his wrist. But no warning flares emerged from his tone or his body language. Simply odd she hadn't seen him before, although Sally had indicated her desire for Tori to meet Nathan's friend. Tori wasn't into sports, and that was apparently what he and Nathan had in common.

Sally valued the man's friendship, and for her sake, Tori wanted to clear their names. Instinct told her Cole Jeffers had something else going on behind his ultrasmooth confidence.

Sally, please let your friendship with Cole being nothing more than that.

Checking the time, she entered the kitchen to wrap things up with her friend and Max. Both were there with Jack.

"Mr. Jeffers left for his job," Tori said.

"He has several landscaping projects going on." Sally sank onto a barstool, her shoulders slumped. "I hope I didn't interfere with his business."

"Anyone can mow a lawn. I'm sure he's more expensive than others." Max coughed from the pit of his stomach.

"He doesn't mow yards and pull weeds," Sally said low. "Cole is a professional."

"I don't trust a yardman who cozies up to a rich man who's now dead. Does he call often?"

"No." She arched her back. If Max didn't ease up, she might bring out her claws. "Are you saying Cole is a suspect?"

"Everyone is guilty in my book until they're proven innocent."

Sally stepped into Max's personal space, her eyes flaring. "Excuse me, but my son is present. Watch your language and your implications. The FBI must have lowered their standards to let you carry a badge."

Tori didn't take the remark personally. She studied his face, drawn with lines far beyond his fifty-one years. Was she right about his abusive attitude? She'd asked him repeatedly the last couple of months about the change, but he refused to offer an explanation. Today she'd witnessed how far south he'd gone. Dare she go to the ASAC? Tattle like an elementary school kid?

"I think we're done here for now." He gave Sally a curt nod. "Mrs. Moore, I guarantee we'll find out who murdered your husband." He handed her his card. "Do not open the door to your husband's office. You already know how to contact Agent Templeton. If you receive any unusual phone calls or feel uneasy, please don't hesitate to call." He studied Jack. "If you or your brother have any new information, I'd appreciate hearing any suspicions."

The doorbell rang.

"Excuse me." Sally's voice rose. "That is most likely my attorney." She disappeared.

Max coughed. Sounded like it came from his toes this time. Why hadn't he given up the cigarettes? Surely he knew they were killing him.

"Young man, do you have anything to hide?"

"Max." Tori touched his sleeve. "Enough. He's a boy, and this is inappropriate."

Sally appeared with a man dressed in a three-piece suit and introduced him to Tori and Max as her and Nathan's attorney. Tori shook the man's hand, but Max merely nodded.

"Jacob, you arrived at just the right time. Agent Dublin requested Jack call him if he had any information about his father's death."

Jacob offered no emotion. "Agent Dublin, you know the law. Mrs. Moore's sons are underage. As attorney for the Moore family, I speak on their behalf during this time of sorrow and grief. You'll not speak to any underage member of this family unless I am present. I also encourage Mrs. Moore to exercise her right to counsel."

Max eyed him. "I'll do my job how I see fit." He turned to Sally. "Mrs. Moore, you're a person of interest. Don't even crawl into your BMW and drive to the River Oaks Shopping Center unless I'm notified. In the meantime, I recommend using discretion in addressing the media."

"I have no intentions of talking to a reporter." Sally set her jaw. "For a man who's supposed to serve the community, you have the manners of a pig."

"Others have said the same, but most of them are behind bars." He huffed as though swallowing a cough and left the house.

Tori gave Sally and Jack a hug. "We'll be in touch. Be safe. I'm so sorry about Max. I've never known him to act like this." But she had, and it must stop.

"Just so you know," Attorney Farr said, "I will report his inappropriate actions to the FBI this morning."

What could Tori say? "I understand."

Sally sighed. "I will also make a call. Is this the behavior of most agents?"

"Not at all." Tori left and joined Max at the curb, so angry she wanted to rip his head off. "I'm assuming we're heading to Moore Oil & Gas?"

He leaned against the driver's side of his car. "Not yet. I'll meet you at the office in about two hours."

"Where are you going?"

His features hardened. "My business."

"Whoa. You're not solo on this case. I'm going with you."

He coughed and clutched his chest. "This is personal. Back off."

Fury laced her words. "What's wrong, Max?" She pointed at the Moore home. "You treated every person in there like trash. They are the victims, not criminals."

"Get a life, Tori. This case is cut-and-dried." He swung away from her as though she'd slapped him. "I don't need to tell you everything that's going on in my life." He opened the door and slid into his car.

Reality check. Max was either on his way to see a lawyer or the doctor. "Do you want me to ride along?"

He slammed the door, but the window was down.

"Doctor or lawyer, Max? This is Tori, your partner." She scrutinized every line on his face. "It's the spot on your lung, isn't it? You have a diagnosis."

"Do what you can from the office. Text me Jeffers's initial

background. Nothing deep unless I see reason to explore it. Rubbed me the wrong way. Sleeping with Sally Moore."

She opened her mouth to refute his callous words, but why? Whatever stalked Max had made him mean and possibly afraid.

Once in her car, she touched the button on the radio for classical music. Low enough to be soothing and not overpower her thinking. With the morning hour, she'd get caught in inbound traffic. Not a bad thing when she needed to process what was behind Max's attitude and the mystery surrounding Nathan's death.

Conflict between Nathan's company and environmentalists was nothing new, necessarily, but the momentum between Moore Oil & Gas and activists had escalated in the past few weeks. Nathan was exonerated in allegations of illegal dumping of backflow water four days before a bomb exploded at a drilling site. Four days later, he lay dead. The facts repeated in her mind. A link to radical activists was worth investigating. Good theory, and one she'd look into at the office—along with a ton of other things.

Could there have been problems in the workplace? A wronged or jealous employee? How could she ID the killer? Did that person wear a designer suit or sweat on an oil rig?

She wanted to believe in Sally's innocence . . . but Cole Jeffers?

Her cell phone beeped with a notice. Stuck in stop-and-go traffic, she snatched it. A background on Cole rolled in. He owned Texas Garden and Landscaping, the largest and most prestigious commercial and residential landscape company in the city. Burst onto the scene about two and a half years ago and continued to rise. Her embarrassment joined forces with stupidity to mix a bitter stew. His designs won national awards. Definitely not a yardman. No need to read more.

She wanted to crawl into a hole and let him mow over her.

Now Nathan's and Cole's friendship made more sense. They were both successful businessmen. The question bombarding her mind was how much did he know about the threats made on Nathan's life? Had the two men quarreled?

Max would look at Cole's profession and conclude he was even more of a suspect. Maybe so.

9

COLE ARRIVED at his office after checking in with the crew on the new landscaping project. The team had completed the preliminaries to raise the elevation at the rear of the complex to complement a new architectural design. A multilevel plan he'd spent six months designing and perfecting. By owning and overseeing his own nursery, he'd developed quality plants that withstood the hot summers while providing a beautiful outdoor setting for his customers. For the past year, he'd maintained the property, provided annual color, and conducted tree services. His team of over a hundred employees and contractors brought skill and expertise to the project. Cole had promised them more money, and this job allowed the salary increases to happen. Yep, he was proud of what he'd accomplished in such a short time. But Cole missed the excitement, the flow of adrenaline.

Landscaping took care of the creative side of his nature, but not the deep satisfaction that came from his former role as a US Marshal.

Nathan's death surfaced memories of what it meant to wear a badge. Could he willingly put his life on the line to keep others safe? The thought quickly dissipated with the memories of why he'd taken a leave of absence from the agency.

He feared the demons who labeled him a coward.

Thoughts of Nathan wouldn't let him go. He was one of the smartest men Cole had ever met. His business savvy had made him a millionaire several times over. From the first day the two men collided in the gym when both reached for the same size weight, they'd hit it off. One morning, Nathan actually listened to why Cole followed Jesus. Nathan didn't ridicule him, just felt he had no reason to accept a sovereign Lord when he already had all he needed. That day Cole vowed to convince him otherwise. Too late now.

Deplorable to see a man's life end so tragically.

He scooted his chair back and stood to survey the property his office overlooked. A stone path led to blooming azaleas and wound around to a tiered fountain that sprayed water thirty feet into the air. At night, the pool became a light show for the public.

Back to work. No more diversions until tasks were checked off his list.

Turning his attention to his computer, he responded to his mother's latest blog on gardening. He laughed at her analogy about how pulling weeds made her a better person. She looked at each one like a weakness in her character. She'd taught him how to prune a rosebush, when to fertilize, and why a balance of soil acidity and drainage gave thriving plants a supercharged boost.

He moved on through his e-mails, deleting and junking far more than he read.

An e-mail from Manny hit his in-box.

Cole, have you thought about reinstatement since we
talked last? It'll soon be three years, and then it might be
too late. I get your leave of absence, but we could use you.
Heck with that. I miss you. Been transporting prisoners,
and I'm ready to get back to running down bad guys. The
old days were the best ones. Let me know you're thinking
about it.

Cole tapped his fingers over the keyboard. To reply or not to
reply. That was the question. . . . He blew out his indecision and
smacked Delete. Not going there even for Manny.

But what about Nathan? Could Cole offer his experience to the
investigation? Weren't knowledge and experience already in place
with HPD and the FBI?

Or was the nudge to reinstate coming from God? Tough call
when Cole feared and yet longed to return to his former career.
What if he froze in the middle of danger? Did his reluctance stem
from his inability to forgive the shooter? The man's sneer stayed
with him constantly.

Truth shattered his argument to stay away from the US Marshals.
He closed his eyes and ended the bitterness eating his heart and soul.

He stared at his cell phone. Snatched it and pressed in Manny's
number.

"Hey, Cole, thinking about joining forces with us again?"

He ran his fingers through his hair. Manny had succeeded in
taking the edge off his raw nerves. "You know what's stopping me."

"The guy who shot you won't escape the law forever."

"So I tell human resources I've had a change of heart?"

"Your words, not mine. If I were you, I'd tell them the job's in
your blood, and you regret ever leaving. You've never stopped being
a US Marshal."

Cole moved to the window. "Right, and I have a scar to prove it." Flashbacks too, but he'd not admit it.

"Still bitter, but you can channel it."

Cole digested his friend's words. "Truth is, a good friend was murdered: Nathan Moore. A hacker tampered with his pacemaker. The FBI and HPD are already on it, but I'm trying to figure out if there's anything I can do to help."

"Is this really Cole Jeffers, a member of the Special Operations Group who's an expert sniper and better at high-risk entries than any SWAT team I've ever seen? All the while working witness protection and prisoner transport? The Cole Jeffers who made Chief Deputy Marshal?"

"I turned down the latter, remember? If I was able to step into a task force with the FBI, could I work the case with a clear head?"

"You worked a task force with them in the past." Manny said. "I remember the case. You were assigned to protect a judge who'd ruled against a chemical company. That company was found guilty of exposing employees to toxic substances that resulted in an explosion. You found evidence that sent the owners of the chemical company to prison."

"Good memory. I worked with the current FBI ASAC, Ralph Hughes, back then. Good man. We keep in touch."

"Then come on back and do what you do best. Making big dollars in business is nothing to sneeze at, but this is where you belong."

"I might be a suspect."

Manny moaned. "What?"

"The victim told his wife he wanted a divorce, and one of her sons asked me to come over early this morning."

"You were there in the thick of the investigation?"

"Yes."

"I thought he was your friend."

"He was. One of the FBI agents implicated me and his wife."

"Any validity in his allegations?"

Cole snorted his irritation. "How long have you known me?"

"Okay. I get it. Christian guys don't normally mess around. Not supposed to, anyway. Needed to ask. You have an alibi and a girlfriend?"

"You must not have had enough caffeine today. You're my alibi, man. Girlfriend, no."

"Right. One out of two isn't bad. Are you coming in today?"

The immediacy settled on him. Either walk away from the US Marshals and abandon a grieving family. Or risk everything to sink time and effort into investigating Nathan's death. Because both were connected. Both shoved him into tenacious mode. But was the plan for him?

"I'll call human resources and see what they have to say."

10

SOON AFTER TORI ARRIVED at the FBI office, she reread the medical examiner's and cardiologist's reports for indications of a struggle before Nathan's death. Clear and straightforward. She reviewed HPD's findings, and they were consistent with Sally's statement. The blood on the floor of Nathan's office matched his type. The security firm and the bodyguards had solid records. Every case was different and every case had similarities. But she'd never worked a case where a killer chose to eliminate a victim by hacking into his pacemaker. What an impersonal way to end a life. Ruthless—like every premeditated murder.

Tori scheduled an appointment with Nathan's cardiologist, a woman with an impeccable reputation as one of the finest surgeons in the country, for early afternoon to learn more about the remote access of the device. The FBI's tech team was working on finding the IP address of the hacker, but cyberpunks knew their way through the endless codes uniquely hidden in cyberspace.

She phoned attorney Jacob Farr using the number Sally had given and identified herself.

"Agent Templeton," Farr said, "I can tell you the following without legal ramifications. Nathan did not give me an organization or name of whom he suspected behind the bombing or personal threats. He informed me about adding bodyguards and requested an appointment for this afternoon to discuss matters of concern."

"And to file for divorce?"

"Further specifics will require a court order."

"You're aware his pacemaker was hacked."

"Yes. Mrs. Moore relayed the unfortunate cause of death earlier this morning."

"Do you have any information to help the FBI?"

"No, ma'am. Not without a court order."

"Thank you for your time." She thought about the call while jotting down a request for a court order. What Jacob Farr didn't say plunged into the territory of a deeper investigation. He also used the plural form of *threat*. Who had the most to gain from Nathan's death? A person or persons who thrived on—

Power.

Money.

Revenge.

Love.

What was it, Nathan? What drove a person to kill you?

A power motive centered on work colleagues or those in competition with Moore Oil & Gas? Tori made a note to interview not only his front office and blue-collar employees but also his competitors. She typed a request to the FIG, Field Intelligence Group, for a list of known offenders in Houston and South Texas who thrived on environmental issues. Max had no doubt read the backgrounds when the bomb squad consulted him about the explosion.

Money drove many people to commit the most horrendous of crimes. Had Nathan deceived or cheated someone? Based on his request for added protection, he had reasons to be fearful.

Revenge involved those who had power and money concerns—everyone from work to personal life.

Love as reason to kill meant a crime of passion, and he'd filed for divorce. Although maybe Cole Jeffers was right, and Nathan's insistence stemmed from wanting to ensure his family was safe. Tori could hope.

She glanced at the time. Nearly two hours had passed since she and Max parted this morning. No communication either. She stared at her cell phone, debating whether to text him. Max had made it clear his whereabouts were none of her business. She hadn't dealt with his actions this morning either. Sighing, she moved on to what could be investigated without him.

Tori phoned Moore Oil & Gas to speak to Nathan's executive assistant, Anita Krantz. Those who worked closely with high-ranking executives were usually a better resource than a wife. Unfortunate but true.

"Ms. Krantz, this is FBI Special Agent Tori Templeton. Are you free to talk?"

"By all means." She gasped lightly. "Is it true Nathan was murdered?"

"Yes. I'm sure all of you are grieving his loss."

"We are. It's unspeakable." Ms. Krantz's voice rang soft, sweet, and Tori remembered the gorgeous platinum blonde with a knockout figure who'd delivered papers to Nathan one night while she visited the Moores. "I called Sally to express my personal condolences. The office will send flowers and arrange for food during the funeral, but I wish we could do more."

"We all want to reach out to the family. Do you have any idea who could have orchestrated his death?"

"He told me EPA radicals had threatened him. And then there's the bombing."

"We'd like to view his files and image the computers."

"We'll need a court order."

Cooperation would have been a perk, but what aspects of a murder investigation were ever easy? "I'll handle the legal paperwork. I thought you might have information aside from business, a person for us to interview."

Obviously the woman was debating offering particulars.

"Ms. Krantz, your words will be held in strict confidence."

The woman sighed. "Please, this did not come from me. . . . Nathan had concluded that Sally no longer loved him, but he loved her. He regretted the situation and what it might mean for his sons. He told me when he was incredibly upset."

Could this possibly be true?

"Does it make sense to you why he'd arrange for additional protection for his wife and sons if he had plans to leave the family?"

"You'd have to know Nathan to comprehend that's the kind of man he was. He'd have her and the boys' best interests at heart."

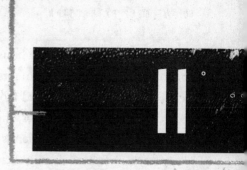

BY ONE THIRTY, Max hadn't returned, and Tori fretted that whatever kept him was medical, like the spot on his lung. Facing an afternoon without her partner meant dreaded paperwork and no face-to-face interviews. His absence was creating a delay in working the case. Not like him to leave her out of the loop. Unless he was working remotely and had made inquiries. Had he completed his own background check and become aware of Cole's business expertise? A more thorough history on "the yardman" seemed in order, but she'd wait until Max contacted her. The fact Sally called Cole instead of Tori when Nathan died bothered her. Was the issue about leaning too much on Tori like Sally had said, or did Tori fear Cole and Sally might be more than friends? After rescheduling the appointment with Nathan's cardiologist, she asked for information on the wireless connection of his pacemaker.

She completed a subpoena request and search warrant affidavit for Nathan's business and personal cell phone and computer devices, then added the entire Moore household. A bit of her felt like a traitor to her friends, but sentiments never solved a crime. Just made her feel like scum. She added Cole Jeffers to the list of cell phone records. Rubbing her temples, she fought a nagging headache that told her the regret for her friends was pounding at her brain.

A freckle on her left wrist seized her attention. Was it darker? It looked bigger too. It could be melanoma. She snatched her cell phone. Less than five minutes later, she had a doctor's appointment tomorrow morning at 7:30. Being overly concerned about her health stalked like a predator. She was so afraid she'd end up with cancer like Mom and Kevin. Maybe Max.

She refused to go there and turned her attention to the cardiologist's report about Nathan's type of pacemaker and its vulnerabilities. Sally had told her Nathan's cardiologist could make changes to the device without surgery.

Tori phoned the tech department and explained the initial findings. "For a hacker to gain access, would this most likely be the fault of the pacemaker's manufacturer or the hospital's equipment?"

"Hospital's equipment. The manufacturer would take every precaution."

"Would you look into it and get back to me?"

She texted Max and coaxed her thoughts into bursting through the walls of her brain. Didn't really matter how the hacker accessed Nathan's pacemaker, except it might lead to the who and why. Although the wireless features could be remotely accessed by those capable of reprogramming the device, Nathan obviously hadn't been concerned about anyone using his lifesaving pacemaker to inflict harm. In this case, death. The man must not have researched the potential downside before making a decision about his health and how that would affect his family. Perhaps he viewed himself as indestructible.

�֍

At two fifteen, Max texted her.

Stay on source of hacker. Won't b in 2day. I called ASAC.

The worst-case scenario blasted her mind. **R u @ home?**

No.

I care, Max. What's wrong?

At MD Anderson. Stage 3A.

Her stomach threatened to rise to the top of her throat. **I can come.**

No. This is my war. U work the case. I know about Jeffers' job.

K. I requested court orders & all devices business and personal w/ Moore family & Cole Jeffers.

Good. I'll call later.

Thoughts about Kevin's suffering with chemo and radiation sped through her mind. **U shouldn't b alone.**

Back off.

What about a medical leave?

This is all I have left. Done. Get 2 work.

She rubbed her temples again. Max's diagnosis wasn't a surprise. She'd seen his steady weight loss followed by the unhealthy gain from steroids and whatever meds the doctors prescribed. But a lung could be replaced. That could save his life. He could continue his days with quality. When she saw him, she'd probe more. If he didn't shut her down.

Her cell buzzed, and she startled. The ASAC. "Yes, sir."

"Max texted me. Said he told you about the medical diagnosis."

"Yes. Not really a shock when he admitted to having a spot on his lung."

"His options aren't optimistic. Only one in five people survive stage 3A cancer."

Her stomach roiled. "I suggested a medical leave."

"He's retiring after this case."

Had Max given up? It didn't sound like the man she knew. "What can I do?"

"Act normal. Understand he's been short-tempered."

"Without a doubt."

"Don't let him get away with it. I told him he must maintain professionalism—his attitude, dress, and methods. He's chosen to finish the investigation, and he's aware that he's walking a thin line."

"I'm assuming complaints have been made."

"Sally Moore filed a report, and Max admitted to his tactics. Are you sure about working this case with your personal interests?"

"Absolutely. My first priority is to find Nathan's killer. I want to believe Mrs. Moore is innocent of any crimes, but my beliefs need proof."

"I'd like to think your outstanding work ethic won't fail you now."

"Yes, sir. I promise you my relationship with Sally Moore will not stand in the way of justice."

"But if it does, I expect you to resign from the case."

"I agree. Max's last words were 'get to work.'"

"I believe it. I'd like to see you in my office about four. Should have your court orders by then, and I have someone for you to meet."

"A new partner?"

"We're not replacing Max unless his treatments leave him incapacitated. We'll talk later."

❈

Cole parked in the visitor area of Houston's FBI offices. His stint earlier today at the US Marshals human resources department made it clear he'd been set up for an expedited return to his former career. Manny must have been busy laying the groundwork, and Nathan's death had fueled Cole to bring in the killer and connect the dots in the recent bombing.

The reinstatement and Cole's desire to return, along with his experience, quickly set things in motion. Earlier in the day, Ralph Hughes, the FBI's ASAC, had contacted the US Marshals office and requested Cole be fast-tracked to join the FBI task force investigating the crimes associated with Moore Oil & Gas. Odd Ralph hadn't contacted Cole first since he knew his status with the Marshals.

A call was made, and here he was meeting with Ralph and about to be introduced to the agents assigned to the case. Again.

How would Special Agents Tori Templeton and Max Dublin react to their prime suspect, a Deputy US Marshal, working with them? Might be entertaining. Might be a nightmare. Not so sure the environment would be conducive to solving a crime. But bringing to justice Nathan's killer and learning who bombed his drill site superseded any ruffled feelings.

Cole cleared the security gate and waited in the lobby for Assistant Special Agent in Charge Ralph Hughes to escort him into the secure area. A bit of déjà vu. He paced. This was where he belonged. Adrenaline no longer dripped but flowed like a waterfall.

"Cole." The man still reminded him of a high school football coach on game day.

"Yes."

"Good to see you again." He reached to shake Cole's hand. "Feels like old times."

"I was just thinking the same thing."

"Makes me wish we were in the field together." Clear eyes behind dark-rimmed glasses met Cole. "Ready to work?"

"Absolutely."

Cole followed him around the corner to the office area and onto an elevator. Once in the ASAC's office, the man settled into his chair. Yep, game day coach—with much higher stakes.

"One of our special agents will not be present this afternoon— Max Dublin. But Tori Templeton will arrive at four."

"Is she aware of the task force?"

"No. There could be a problem with her partner."

Cole maintained an unemotional stance. "In what way?" He knew all too well Dublin's rough mannerisms.

"Medical issues that have the potential of impacting the investigation. He probably won't admit it to you, but he's dealing with lung cancer."

No excuse for Dublin's rudeness, but definitely an explanation. "Got it. Is Agent Templeton aware of his medical problems?"

"Yes, as of today. He's currently at MD Anderson receiving treatment."

A knock on the door and a recognizable woman's voice indicated Tori Templeton had arrived. Hughes welcomed her to take a seat beside Cole.

He stood. No smile until he read her reaction.

She blinked, then quickly regained her composure. Any chances to make a good impression vanished.

"I don't understand," she said.

"Agent Templeton, I'd like for you to meet Deputy Marshal Cole Jeffers. He served on a task force with the FBI about eight years ago when I was in the field. In fact, we worked together. Cole will be working with you and Agent Dublin on the Moore case. This includes the bombing and the murder."

No flash of surprise. He had to admit she was quick on her feet. A pro.

"I apologize for any misleading this morning," Cole said. "In truth, I was reinstated in the US Marshals this afternoon after a leave of absence."

"And I requested him for the task force," the ASAC said. "Cole won't disappoint you."

"A man of many hats." She smiled through an icy glare. "From yardman to business owner to Deputy US Marshal all in one day."

"Again I apologize. I'd like to think we could work together."

The ASAC lifted his chin. "Is there animosity I should be aware of?"

"No, sir," she said. "Deputy Marshal Jeffers and I both have an investment in this case. We're friends of Nathan Moore and his family."

"That relationship is a big reason why I'm here." Cole ushered sincerity into his words. "I'm committed to finding Nathan's killer and whoever bombed his drill site."

"All right. If you're ready, we can discuss the current findings." Hughes lifted a brow over his glasses. "Agent Templeton, I'll send you Cole's background. I'm sure it will dissipate any misgivings in your mind."

She sat on the edge of her chair. "I would appreciate the information."

Cole cringed at the thought of how she'd interpret his law enforcement career . . . and how he'd resigned after . . . Maybe that part had been omitted.

ASAC Hughes continued. "Agent Templeton, there are three reasons why I requested Cole be added to the case. He has experience working on an oil rig, what can go wrong and the temperature of the workers. Secondly, he and I worked on a case together several years ago—an oil rig bombing and a murder. The third reason is his friendship with Nathan Moore. He'll have valuable insight into the habits and personality of the victim. Your role as a friend to Sally

Moore can be just as important as long as you and Cole remain objective. Are we in agreement?"

Both responded positively.

"Good. I have the report on the Moore oil rig bombing, and the EPA has been cleared. But that doesn't mean activists didn't take matters into their own hands."

Cole nodded.

"I'll send the updates to your phones. Currently we have the court order to mirror image Nathan Moore's business and attorney's files. The judge expedited matters in light of the bombing and the alleged threats on Moore's life. The order also includes imaging those devices for the entire family. In the morning, a CART—" he glanced at Cole—"Computer Analysis Response Team, a group of agents and professional support employees who are trained in digital forensics, will be at the Moore office to handle the process. The Moores' attorney, Jacob Farr, has agreed to cooperate, but he also tossed the attorney-client privilege card. Tori, you have training and experience with CART, so I suggest you and Cole image the devices at the Moore home." He handed Tori a document. "Here's a copy of the court order."

She turned to Cole. "I'll pick up a tool kit for the Moores. Shall we handle the personal mirror imaging after our meeting here? Follow up with the team in the morning at Nathan's office?"

"Perfect."

"My partner will most likely join us tomorrow," she said.

The ASAC leaned forward. "Cole and I already discussed the situation, but I didn't tell him this is Agent Dublin's last case. However, professionalism is a priority."

"I see," she said. The ASAC was aware of how Sally had been treated.

"One more thing—he doesn't know about the task force. I'll handle it before I leave the office."

"A question." Agent Templeton glared at Cole, not that he blamed her. Cole felt the distinct wall, built with distrust and suspicion. One he'd erected in the early hours of the day and one he'd need to tear down to work with her effectively. "Are you a former cop?"

"Marine. Why?"

"US Marshals are usually a bit gritty. Trying to figure out what to expect. A little advice here," Agent Templeton said. "Don't bring up the cancer to Max. His attitude is already pushing our buttons."

"Advice noted." He'd handle Max in his own way.

12

LATE TUESDAY AFTERNOON, Albert Weiman rang the doorbell of the home belonging to Nathan and Sally Moore. The widow needed to know how sorry he was for her husband's untimely death. How had this happened? The situation perplexed him . . . needled at his conscience. He crunched on a breath mint so she wouldn't be able to tell he'd been drinking.

As Sally came to the door, he squared his shoulders and mustered congeniality into his tone. "Good afternoon, Mrs. Moore. I'm no doubt a stranger to you. My name is Albert Weiman. You knew my son, Erik, in college. May I come in?"

The delicate blonde smiled. No makeup and yet extremely attractive as he remembered. She opened the door, but instead of inviting him inside, she stood on the porch. Her gaze took in a bodyguard not far from where they stood.

"Yes, I remember Erik, and you and I have met."

"I'd like to offer my condolences on behalf of my son in the death of your husband."

"Thank you. How is Erik?"

Albert wanted to shout, scream. Instead, he fixed a grim smile. "Unfortunately confined to a wheelchair, but we haven't given up on finding a treatment."

Shock spread across her face. "I'm sorry. I didn't know he was ill."

Nathan had been informed . . . and could have helped. "Multiple sclerosis. Progressive relapsing."

"My sincere sympathy, Mr. Weiman." Her shoulders fell as though the news saddened her. "Not sure if you remember I'm a nurse. Isn't he responding to medication?"

"A year ago corticosteroids reduced the nerve inflammation in his brain and spinal cord. The drugs are no longer effective."

"How sad Erik's condition is worsening. How are his spirits?"

"A combination of pain and weakness has pushed him into severe depression. I'm his caretaker." Albert stiffened and ordered his emotions to stop reacting. "I'm not here to discuss my son's MS. Erik asked me to speak to you, and would have done so in person if physically able."

Her features softened. "Please tell him I appreciate his concern."

What a great actress. "When the boys were younger, Nathan spent quite a bit of time at our house." He fought real tears for his precious son. "I still think of them as boys."

"Yes, I remember their friendship." Her fingers pressed against her knuckles. "When was the last time you saw my husband?"

"I guess four or five months ago. He looked well. How are your sons doing?"

She blinked. "Each in his own way."

"Sorrow can invoke unusual behavior. Please let them know I was here. I'll be going. If there's anything I can do for you, please don't hesitate to contact me." He pulled a folded piece of paper from his pocket. "Here's my cell phone and e-mail. Sometimes when we're upset, talking to a stranger makes us feel better."

She took the offered paper. "Thank you for stopping by."

"Have service arrangements been made?"

"The funeral is Friday, to give the authorities adequate time to complete the autopsy and for family and friends to arrive from out of town." She dabbed beneath her eyes.

"I'll be there. How can I ensure you're okay?"

"I have a good support group." She hesitated. "I'd like to be informed of Erik's condition. Let me give you my cell number."

He quickly lifted a notepad and pen from his shirt pocket and jotted down the information. "I'm glad Nathan provided well for you. If he can't be here, then continuing in your lifestyle must be a comfort."

"He always took care of us. His family came before every business decision. I'm thankful for the heritage he left his sons."

Albert swallowed his desperation. Nathan's death meant Erik had no future.

13

FOR THE SECOND TIME in less than twenty-four hours, Tori drove her Charger to the Moore home. She refused to ride with Cole in his ultraexpensive truck. Stupidity marched across her mind, did an about-face, and marched again. Why hadn't she run a full report on him at the time he appeared ultra-confident, ultra-egotistical, and ultra-yardman?

According to his background, he gave the Avengers and other superheroes a run for their money.

She had no choice but to apologize and swallow her pride. Clear the air. Work the case. Caressing wounded pride meant she gave her worst to the investigation. She parked her car at the same place along the curb as early this morning. Yawning, she grabbed her purse and tool kit. If she could still function, she'd pay Max a visit later on and provide an update. Hopefully get him to open up about the seriousness of his cancer and find out if his family had been told. Probably not.

Cole waited at the curb with his laptop. He looked far too good for a man she was upset with. Broad shoulders. Those incredible sky-blue eyes. And he wore jeans like . . . *Never mind, Tori. Put on your professional badge.*

She waved and joined him. "Before we go inside, I want to say something."

He grinned. "Do I need to step back?"

Had he paid for those perfectly white teeth? "You aren't making this easy."

"I'm not? Let me alleviate your angst."

Tori snorted, so unladylike. But since when did she worry about impressions? "Angst?"

"Yep. I told you I was a yardman. Said nothing while you and your partner dragged me through the trenches. I own a landscaping business, but with Nathan's death, I've decided to be reinstated in my former career. As you said earlier, all in one day."

Still confident in his own shoes. "I'm embarrassed. Your career doesn't define who you are or your value as a human being, but I allowed it." She took a breath. "I'm very sorry." And she meant it.

"It's okay. I led you astray."

She reddened at the thought of him steering her in an . . . inappropriate direction. "Are you always this—?"

"Arrogant? Witty? Charming?"

He had the scruffy beard thing going too. She pointed to the front door of the Moore home. "Seriously, how do we work amicably?"

"I'll try harder to cooperate. The disadvantage is we're close to Sally and the boys. We care about them. And we're going to uncover the killer's motivation. Could be ugly."

"As in we might not like what we find?"

"Are you prepared to learn the truth no matter what the cost, even if it's Sally's friendship?"

Sally and Nathan lived as community examples of good citizens and parents. Her stomach took a dip. Bringing the truth to the surface came with a price, and she'd chosen to pay it a long time ago. "Neither of us wants to discover any kind of a scandal about Nathan or Sally. But no matter what we uncover, I can handle it."

"Special Agent Templeton—"

"Tori."

"Okay, I think it would be better if you lead out. Sally knows we're here to image their personal devices. I called her on the way and told her about the task force. Nathan knew about my prior stint with the US Marshals, but she had no idea. She indicated I'd deceived her. Not sure my apology sufficed or she understood why."

"I don't understand either."

He appeared to think through his answer. "My last case left me doubting why I was ever in law enforcement."

He didn't elaborate further. Maybe she'd learn more later.

Why hadn't she thought of alerting Sally to their visit? Self-absorption and preoccupation about Max added to the list of her current flaws. "Would she prefer strangers to work Nathan's murder? I understand how she might feel that way."

"It will be tough at times. Remember what she said this morning. She'd rather have a friend investigating the case. Lance will use this as another excuse to buck the system, in this instance his mother and law enforcement. Not sure about Jack."

"Lance can be extremely difficult," Tori said.

"Is it teenage rebellion, or does he have a solid reason for his hostility? Nathan and I talked about him often. No matter what Nathan tried to do or say, Lance always kicked it back in his face.

No sign of drugs. Friends are top-notch. Grades are so-so. No current girlfriend."

"Would he open up to you now you're investigating the case?"

"Hard to say."

Tori observed the man beside her. "You genuinely care about them, don't you?"

"I do. Every aspect of their lives affects me. I'm a Christian, and the only person I'd made any headway with regarding faith is Jack."

Sounded like Kevin. "My brother believed. A lot of good faith did him." A twinge of irritation sounded in her words.

"Past tense? What happened?"

"Died of cancer two years ago."

"I'm sorry for your loss."

She rubbed her left wrist, and uneasiness crept up from the soles of her feet. She should have left the faith thing alone. An awkward silence added another obstacle between them.

"Shall we get our job done before it's midnight?" she finally said. "Those inside will wonder what we're doing out here. Besides, I want to see Max when we're finished."

He walked toward the front door. "I want to tag along when you see Max."

She scrambled to keep up. "Why?"

"We got off to a bad start. Need to fix it. Justice is our goal here, not personality conflicts."

What kind of man was Cole Jeffers? Deputy Marshal extraordinaire? A Bible-thumper? Complexity and rugged good looks could drive a woman to distraction. But the Christianity thing made her want to run.

14

COLE AND TORI followed Sally into the kitchen. He recognized her stepmother and dad, Kit and Wes Brent, and Tori greeted them too. Sally still wore the same clothes from early this morning. Ruffled hair. Red-rimmed eyes. Valuing the Moores as a family had its advantages and disadvantages. As much as he wanted to prove Sally's innocence, he needed to take his own advice about being an investigator and truth seeker. This could get ugly before arrests were made. Airing dirty laundry meant relationships were weakened. Possibly destroyed.

Caring Jack was in the thick of the adults. A shoulder for his mother. Cole seized his thoughts. Jack shouldn't ignore his grief. Putting it off meant the recovery period would stretch into other areas of his life. Jack and Nathan had spent quality time together, and those moments were now memories.

"Where's Lance?" Cole said.

"In his bedroom. He hasn't emerged since this morning." Sally poured herself a glass of water. "I brought him lunch and dinner. He took the tray but refused to talk."

"That's not healthy."

"He'll come around," she said, while her eyes glistened with pain. "I'll try again later." She faced her parents. "Tori and Cole are here to examine every device in the house."

Her dad eyed Tori, then Cole. "What are you talking about?"

Cole remembered her dad's often-surly attitude. "We're copying all the information from the family's electronics."

"Do you have a court order?" he said.

"Tori has it."

"I want to see the judge's signature."

Sally nodded at Tori, and she pulled the paper from her purse and gave it to Wes.

"Here you are."

Sally took it from his grasp. "They are here to do a job, and we will not interfere."

"Glad Cole and Tori are on this." Jack breathed out a hint of stress. "Something was definitely off when Dad told Mom he wanted a divorce."

"What?" Wes pounded the kitchen table, his white hair and high cheekbones giving him a fierce look. "Why didn't you tell us he'd lost his mind? How long has this been going on?"

Sally touched his arm. "Dad, I'm dealing with his death and unknowns prior to it. Not sure how I can form the words, but we can talk later while Tori and Cole are busy."

"Is the media aware of his ludicrous intention?"

Cole held his breath. Sally's dad had anger issues, and enduring one of his tirades didn't sit well.

"I don't think so," Sally said, "or we'd've heard by now. I have no clue who knows what happened, except the boys, our attorney, a few police officers, another FBI agent, and of course Tori and Cole."

Kit hooked her arm through Wes's. "Let's discuss this with your daughter outside." She glanced at Jack, mirroring a mom look Cole had seen from Sally. "In private."

"Sure. I'll do homework here in the kitchen."

"We need every device in the home," Tori said. "That means smartphones, iPads, notebooks, computers."

Sally directed them toward the dining room. "I gathered all I could find and put them on the table."

Cole entered the room ahead of Tori. The three-foot rectangular crystal chandelier glittered over a pile of technology. "Neither Lance's laptop nor his iPhone are here," he said. The familiar devices with the maroon A&M emblems must be with the teen.

Sally crossed her arms over her chest. "He wouldn't give them up."

"Does he know Tori and I are assigned to the case?"

"No. When I attempted to tell him, he turned up the volume on his music. I thought about your not telling me about the US Marshals, and I'm okay. You have your reasons, and right now I need friends. But I thought the US Marshals were in charge of witness protection and prisoner transportation."

"One of our other responsibilities is working as a task force with other law enforcement agencies. Houston's ASAC and I worked a case some years ago involving the bombing of an oil rig, which resulted in a death."

"I see. The more I think about it, I'm relieved the investigation includes two dear friends."

"Appreciate it. I'll talk to Lance." The teen was playing a toddler's game.

"Cole seems to know how to get his attention," Tori said. "Both of us will do our best to calm him down."

He respected Tori's input. Working with her, he saw success rising to the top, but her sidekick gave him doubts. Right along with Lance's lack of cooperation.

Tori and Cole waited until the adults made their way to the patio area. "Can we tackle the hard stuff first?" he said.

"You're reading my mind. Shall we take a battlefront with Lance?"

He chuckled to relieve the tension. "I'll lead the way. Once Lance learns about my previous role in law enforcement, I'm afraid his trust level will hit rock bottom."

She shook her head and started toward the landing. "Deputy Marshal Jeffers, do you have a strategy?"

"I'm going to ask for his help. Does he know anything that could point to the killer or a motive?"

"With the way he felt about Nathan, why would he help? From what we've seen, he hasn't shed a tear, only nursed a black eye and used bad language." She glanced away. "Family relationships are never what they seem."

"Right. Neither of us likes the downside of this."

They mounted the stairs and moved down the hall to Lance's room. Cole hoped this encounter wouldn't have any resemblance to this morning's. He knocked. "This is CJ. We need to talk."

No response.

Cole tried again. "Tori's with me—we're investigating your dad's death together."

"FBI must be hard up. Go mow a yard."

The comment rubbed him wrong. "Lance, what you don't know about me is I'm a Deputy US Marshal."

"What?"

"I'll be glad to explain but not with a door between us. Tori and I have a court order. So it's either one of us or law enforcement who don't care anything about you. Your devices are needed, but more importantly, Tori and I are requesting your help in getting to the bottom of this."

"Like what?"

"I'm counting to three. If you don't open this door, it'll be a repeat of this morning." Cole glanced at Tori and shook his head. "One. Two."

"All right." The door opened. The bruise around Lance's eye had deepened to an ugly blue-black, worse than this morning. Clothes were strewn from one corner of the room to the next, a new development from earlier in the day.

"What is this US Marshal—?" Lance spit out curses as though he were describing toppings for a pizza.

Pick and choose your battles, Cole. "Sit down, if you can find a place, and I'll give you the quick story."

Lance glared but then found an empty spot on his bed. Cole and Tori lifted junk from two chairs and did the same.

"Over two and a half years ago, I was a US Marshal. Sniper expertise. While transporting a witness to a safe house, we were attacked and I took a bullet to the stomach. The bad guy got away. I didn't handle it well and took a leave of absence. Lately I've been thinking about going back. Your dad's murder helped me make the decision. This afternoon I was officially reinstated. I worked a task force with the FBI some years ago, and that's where Tori and I come in."

"Did my dad know about your past?"

"Yes. I asked him to keep it to himself. Personal reasons until I dealt with why I'd left."

"So you and Tori are on the case. What about her partner, the old guy with the bad cough and attitude to match?"

Lance had a lot of room to talk. "Him too. But just us tonight."

The teen wore a permanent scowl. "You're going to take my stuff whether I like it or not?"

"We're not taking anything, Lance." Tori spoke for the first time. "We're imaging them."

"Thought I had rights."

"You do." Her voice sounded soothing but firm. "Unless those items are required for an investigation. I know you and your dad had your differences, but don't you want his murder solved?"

He stared at her. A slight nibble to his lip.

"Lance," she said, "are you withholding evidence?"

"Yes," he whispered. "I had good reasons to hate Dad. Not for anyone to kill him, but I might know why."

"Is the information on your laptop?"

He shook his head, stood, and reached into his pocket, wrapping his fingers around something. "I downloaded everything on Dad's computer a few months ago after we had a blowup." He handed a thumb drive to Tori. "You and CJ need to see it. Makes me sick."

15

COLE INSERTED the flash drive into his own laptop and sat beside Lance on the messy bed. Whatever they were about to see discredited Nathan. "Weren't these files password protected?"

"Yes. Or so Dad thought. His computer was off-limits and for business use only. Took it back and forth with him to work. He used fingerprint entry security, but I still got into his devices."

"How?" The moment Cole posed the question, he had the answer. "You copied his fingerprint."

"Pretty easy, actually. Got the idea in my computer class about biometrics a few months ago. At the time, gaining access pumped me more than reading all the files, until after he blew up at Mom and let Jack and me know how we were a burden. Guess the idea of being right about him wasn't really what I wanted to find."

Cole and Tori viewed the screen. Business data. Geology reports. Statistical analysis from various drilling sites. Fracking information, including types of fluids needed and the amount of sand. Pressures used to pump fluid and sand. Comparison of high and low pricing for the last several years. Nothing incriminating. "What did you find?"

"Boring stuff until last night. Click on Geology Reports 2014."

Cole opened the folder. "Several subfiles here."

"VermontMtg14."

Disgust punched Cole the moment the file was open. Nathan and a blonde woman together in Vermont. Taking in the fall with changing leaves. Smiles. Kisses. Repulsive. Porn. No wonder Lance hadn't slept.

"Dad's executive assistant," Lance said. Cole had recognized her. "Looks like she managed a few other duties on her off hours."

"Anita Krantz," Tori said, her voice edged with turmoil.

"My mom has cooked dinner for her. Gone shopping and played tennis with her. All the while Dad was lying and . . ."

Again Cole chose to pick his battles with the teen about his language. If the profanity continued, he'd intervene. Lance hurt in the pit of him, and his way of expressing it was honesty and bluntness. Condemning his choice of words now would only isolate Cole from ever making a solid friend and opening the door to a Father who wouldn't disappoint him. He clicked on Nathan's calendar.

"I did that too." Lance rubbed his jean leg. "A business meeting. Legit."

Tori stood and paced the room, stepping over books, papers, empty plates, and junk. "Lance, could this have been a one-time affair?"

According to ASAC Hughes, Tori had spoken with Ms. Krantz today and apparently found no red flags. Cole would discuss the conversation with her when Lance wasn't around.

"Miss Tori, there are other pics with dates in the file. Why would Dad keep this trash? He wasn't stupid. Everything on a computer can be found." Lance's shoulders arched. "How could he do this to Mom? No wonder he wanted a divorce."

To soothe his own guilt and shame.

"I'm so sorry," Tori said. "No wonder you're on emotional overload."

"Yeah. Easier to be the smart-mouthed kid than deal with the truth about my scum of a dad."

Sympathy for Lance swept through Cole. "Showing us these files took guts." He grasped the teen's shoulder. "And I'll never forget you took a punch to keep your mom and brother from learning what you discovered."

He blinked. "Sorta like a black eye of truth."

"I'd call it love," Tori said. "Cole and I will handle this delicately and attempt to keep your dad's indiscretion from getting out."

Lance's eyes fired. "But you can't promise?"

"No," she said. "If we learn incriminating information because of these photos, then other people will find out."

"Dad wiped his computer clean before he died," Lance said. "I checked today when Mom thought I was in my room. The meeting stuff is still there, but not the pics. No reason for anyone to find them or dig deeper. I hope he deleted them to protect Mom and not his girlfriend."

"But they are evidence," Cole said.

Lance swallowed hard. "Protecting Mom and Jack is what matters to me."

Cole wanted to shield all of them, but it wouldn't happen. "We're looking at a situation that none of us understands. When we're able to weave all the facts together, then the whys will be clearer. Until then, we keep searching and analyzing everything we find."

"The 'we' means you and Miss Tori and the old guy, right? 'Cause this will destroy Mom."

"You're not responsible—"

"You don't understand. I'm the man of the house now. It's my job to keep my family safe. Mom and Jack never questioned anything about Dad. He's their hero, the guy who—until the night he died—said and did all the right things. Finding out Dad isn't perfect will hurt them so badly they might never get over it."

"What about you?" Tori said.

"Not sure right now. He talked about that woman in front of Mom like she was a saint. I heard him ask Mom to take her to lunch. It's impossible to remember good times when those things are in my mind."

Cole knew tossing out the one question that had to be asked was like pitching acid on an open wound. "Lance, my job is to find a credible trail in a labyrinth of clues leading to your dad's killer. You despised what you learned about him. He disappointed—"

"If you're about to ask me if I had anything to do with his death, the answer's no." He dug his fingers into his palms. "After what he said to us, I wanted him to leave. Get as far from us as possible. Not dead."

"You may be asked the same question again by another investigator."

His fingers remained tight. Lance was keeping something to himself. "I figured so." He stiffened as though summoning courage to withstand whatever lay ahead. "Right now I have to help Mom and Jack get through the funeral. She wants to pull out photos, make us look like a happy family."

"Protecting those we love is honorable. But your mom and Jack are stronger than you think. I'm at the top of the list in wanting them not to discover what happened with Ms. Krantz. Yet if it goes public, those of us who care for you will be right here."

He covered his face. "I keep seeing those pics of Dad and her.

I hate him. All his self-righteous charity work and making himself look so good. What a liar."

Cole seized the opportunity. "Forgive him. It's the only way I know to put it behind you and be a better man. Someday you'll have a family of your own. You'll want them to love and trust you as you do them. As long as there's bitterness in your heart, your relationships with others will suffer."

"But how do I get past it right now? Stomach's tied up in knots. I'm so mad. This is just wrong."

The condition of his room demonstrated Lance's anger. "Each new day will get easier. Here's what happened to me. . . ." Cole told him about the shooting that stole his career for too long. "It wasn't until I forgave the shooter that I could open my mind to going back to the US Marshals."

Lance rubbed his eyes. "When this is over, will you tell me what it was like? I mean, how you handled the anger and stuff?"

"Sure." He patted the teen on the back. Too much of a burden for a fourteen-year-old. "Right now Tori and I need to get busy. See if you can sleep tonight."

Lance removed the thumb drive and handed it to Cole. "I'll try. Thanks for keeping my secret. Not sure how I'm going to explain my black eye at school."

"A big guy like you doesn't have to say a thing. The truth doesn't hurt either. Joke about it and say, 'My shrimp of a brother slipped a punch in.'"

Cole and Tori finished with Lance's devices and left him alone. An hour later, they said their good-byes to those downstairs and walked to the curb.

"It's 8:43." Tori dragged her finger over her left wrist. "Do we pay a visit to the model in Nathan's photos?"

"I'm ready. We need to get this settled. Did you hurt your wrist?"

"Oh no. Habit, I guess. Do you want Anita Krantz's home address?"

Once he saw where the woman lived, a condo inside the Loop, he turned to Tori. "Why not drop off your car at the FBI office, and I'll drive. On the way, we can pick up a sandwich."

Her stomach protested loudly its lack of dinner.

"Or we can go separately," he said. "Though we could talk."

"Probably a good idea so we can discuss Nathan's extracurricular activities and whatever we learn from his mistress."

"I want to make sure those images weren't Photoshopped."

Tori stopped at her car. "I wish they were computer generated, but I'm guessing those pics are the real thing."

"This will get worse before it gets better."

"I know." She snapped the words like a crack of gunfire. "On the way to the office, I'll give her a call."

"How well do you know her?"

"We've been introduced, and I've been there when she dropped by to see Nathan."

"Since you spoke with her today, why not lead out in the interview?"

"Aren't you afraid I'll shoot her?"

"Not in the least. I have both your backs. I'm furious with Nathan, and I'm sure the two concealed their rendezvous from high-profile staff. Did he ask Sally for a divorce to free himself from the marriage, or was he protecting his family from a person or persons who wanted them dead?"

"Or both. A scorned woman is nothing to mess with."

"Anita or Sally?"

She didn't answer. Neither was he so sure he wanted to hear it.

16

ANITA KRANTZ HADN'T BALKED at the late hour for Tori and Cole's interview. She wore an apron, and classical music played in the background. Weird. Strangely psychotic in Tori's opinion.

"We've met at the Moores'," Tori said, attempting to shake off her animosity toward Nathan's mistress and seek answers to Anita's and his relationship. Tori handled the introductions. "This is Deputy US Marshal Cole Jeffers."

Anita reached out to shake his hand. Exquisite nails in a fashionable French manicure. A classic beauty, as Tori's mom would say, with high cheekbones and flawless skin. "Nathan spoke highly of you."

She positioned petits fours in pastel shades of green, yellow, and pink on a crystal plate. She pulled pale-yellow napkins from a drawer and folded them into triangles. A sprig of mint and crystal demitasse cups set the stage for what appeared to be a ladies' party. She wiped her hands on a dainty towel and placed it perfectly beside the sink.

She carried the tray of petits fours into an adjoining living area and set it on the coffee table. The room held all the furnishings of a Victorian era . . . except the owner's moral ethics when it came to extracurricular activities.

Had this woman lost her mind? Serving party food at an FBI interview? Tori had called her less than twenty minutes ago.

Tori could take no more of the hospitable charm. "Ms. Krantz, we aren't here to socialize." She studied Anita's smile, a bit forced— the woman failed to mask her fear.

"Oh, I totally understand. Give me just a minute. I want to ensure my guests are comfortable." With a soft sigh, she retraced her steps to bring a tray of coffee and a pair of crystal cream and sugar containers. After rearranging the display, she sat primly. Her hands trembled. "Your call gave me a few minutes to prepare for your visit."

Like deleting files and images from your own devices? "We aren't guests. Although I appreciate your efforts." Tori focused on Cole. "Marshal Jeffers and I are part of an FBI task force to bring Nathan's killer to justice and also learn who bombed the oil rig."

"Please, sit down." She gestured to a high-back chair and a green brocade love seat.

Tori took the chair and Cole the small sofa. "Marshal Jeffers and I have a few questions. He and Nathan were good friends."

Anita's blue eyes clouded. Naturally she'd mourn her boss's death, but this was more. "I assume you were able to obtain a court order for Nathan's business files."

"Yes, a team will be there first thing in the morning. Our visit is about your relationship with Nathan. Ms. Krantz, is there anything you'd like to tell us?"

Again the woman appeared perfectly poised. "Nathan exhibited the utmost professionalism of anyone I've ever met. We all should emulate his manner of dealing with critical situations."

"Were you two also friends aside from business?"

"Yes." She wiped invisible dust from her slacks. "He chatted about the two of you."

"What else did you discuss with him?"

"Business dealings mostly."

"We have evidence that you and Nathan were having an affair," Tori said.

Krantz startled. "Nathan loved his wife. He was devoted to her, his sons, and—"

"Were you involved with him?"

She dabbed beneath her eyes, her exterior crumbling. "Nathan Moore was my employer. We had a professional relationship. Where did you hear such preposterous claims?"

"What about Vermont in 2014?"

"I'll look at my calendar, but I remember a few years back a fracking symposium took place there. Nathan pioneered many of the techniques used in the process."

Cole cleared his throat. "Excellent memory, Ms. Krantz."

"An executive assistant prides herself in remembering pertinent information."

"Sounds like a statement from an employee's handbook. Why haven't you answered Special Agent Templeton's question?" Cole's voice left an uncomfortable silence in its wake.

"A fabrication doesn't deserve a response." A distinct coldness settled in her eyes, and for the first time, Tori saw a woman in control, not one emotionally distraught.

"We're here to discern the truth," Tori said. "We have incriminating photos taken in Vermont in 2014. The question is, had you two maintained the affair?" She allowed silence to continue weighing heavily in the room. Nothing more needed to be said. She relaxed and stared at Anita Krantz.

Moments ticked by. Cole must have played this game before because he hadn't budged an inch or uttered a sound.

Ms. Krantz stood. "We're finished here."

"Not exactly," Cole said. "We have enough evidence to arrest you."

"For what?" Her voice rose.

"The murder of Nathan Moore," Cole said. "Looks like a simple case to me. You two had a spat, and that spells murder. What do you think, Tori? I have my cuffs."

"Please," Anita said. "I'm innocent."

"I have another theory." Tori settled back in the chair. "A woman's angry that her lover won't leave his wife, so she kills him. If she can't have him, no one will."

Tears spilled over Anita's cheeks. "I have no idea who killed Nathan. All I know is someone threatened him and his family."

"You were involved with him," Cole said.

"Yes," she whispered.

"How long?"

"Since February 2012. I knew about the pics, but Nathan said he'd destroyed them."

"Did he plan to leave his wife?"

"Not to my knowledge. He loved her. I was there and convenient." She glanced away, then returned to him. "I mean, he cared for me, but he loved Sally. He never gave me any hope or indication otherwise."

"But you loved him." Tori inched closer to the truth. Anita had motive as old as time.

"Is there evidence on your personal or business computer vital to this case?"

She swallowed hard. "No."

"Can we image your device here?"

Her eyes flared. "Not without a search warrant. Besides, all you'll find are personal things and family photos. Work information stays at Moore Oil & Gas."

Tori couldn't fault her for exercising her legal rights. "We'll get right on it. Were you aware Nathan would be killed last night in his home?"

"Absolutely not. I repeat: I have no clue who killed him. Call my sister. I was with her and her family for dinner. We watched a movie until after eleven."

Tori saw the anguish in her face. "Ms. Krantz, I see you're hurting. You loved a man and had to keep your relationship quiet. Now he's gone, and you're grieving. There's no one you can talk to or share your misery with."

The woman sobbed. "I promised him I'd never breathe a word about us. Reality is, I like Sally, and his kids are great."

Tori pushed aside her growing contempt for Nathan and Anita. She thought she knew the man, and the idea of his infidelity made her blood boil. "Our investigation will point to your involvement, and others will likely learn about you and Nathan."

"Is there a way to conceal it?"

"That would be an obstruction of justice," Tori said.

"Ms. Krantz," Cole said, "you are a person of interest. In short, don't leave Houston without contacting Special Agent Templeton or me."

"Yes, sir."

"During the course of our investigation, if you have additional information, please contact one of us."

"I will. How did you find out about the affair?"

"Don't worry about where we got the evidence, but we have it."

17

IN THE DARKNESS of Houston's busy residential streets, lit by oncoming vehicles and strategically placed streetlights, Cole drove with Tori beside him. As it neared midnight, he longed to stretch out anywhere and get some sleep. But working a critical case meant postponing life until those responsible for the drill site bombing and Nathan's murder were apprehended. Ms. Krantz's demeanor broke the mold on covering up the life of a mistress. She presented herself as too perfect and proper while the pics of her and Nathan revealed more than Cole wanted to remember. The hammering at his internal workings refused to let the discrepancy rest. He'd figure out what was gnawing at his gut.

First things first. Time to fix the bad start with Max Dublin, even if it meant eating a little humble pie. Cole could have told the agents from the start their assumptions about his friendship with the Moores was off-kilter. Didn't seem important at the time to correct them.

Tori yawned.

"Would you rather I talk to Max alone?"

She laughed lightly. "He'd blow a hole right through your heart, then drag you inside to claim home invasion."

"I manage to trigger his killer instinct. Has he always been a cantankerous man? Is it the cancer?"

"Appears to be the cancer. The illness hit him blindside. Like many of us in law enforcement, we think we're invincible. He's a tough agent, yet detailed and compassionate when a situation calls for it. His approach to Sally and the boys was not the Max Dublin who taught me how to investigate violent crime. A bulldog when it comes to bringing in bad guys. But not bitter and . . . shoving others away. His wife left him, and his adult kids insist his commitment to the FBI is more important than his family. Those were his words back when he used to confide in me."

Cole had seen the crusty attitude of remorse and pity too many times. "Are they right?"

"Probably so. He told me he never learned how to balance the job and family."

"As a single man, I can see the problem. Not impossible to rectify if he chooses to fix it."

"Might be too late for Max. Not sure where I'd fall. Depends on the opportunity presented."

Opportunity seemed like a strange word to use. No ring on her finger, but she could want a family. He nearly started to probe further but changed his mind. No point being accused of prying into her personal life. More important was the ability to gain her confidence. "Nathan has been gone twenty-four hours. What I've learned about him makes me wonder if I knew him at all."

"I met him in college when he started dating Sally. Never dreamed he'd cheat on her."

Cole dodged an SUV swerving in and out of traffic on the interstate at breakneck speed. "Came as a shock to me too. Sometimes when a man reaches the top of his game, he looks for ways to channel his drive. Anita Krantz was there and obviously willing. The imaging of Moore Oil & Gas devices tomorrow could reveal more about Nathan's business dealings. But the affair has my attention."

"Anita or Sally?"

"With Anita pretending to be prim and proper?"

"Cole, I don't believe Sally is capable of murder."

"Me either. But we have a bombing that needs to be investigated."

Tori pointed to an intersection. "Here, then turn left at the light. Second street on the left, fourth house on the right."

After parking in the driveway, they approached the front door together. The night air refreshed Cole, shoving clarity into his blood. A single lamp shone through a thin curtain of the agent's home as though he was expecting them.

Tori knocked on the door. "Max, it's Tori. Can we talk?"

"Why?" His gruff voice ended any pleasantries of the peaceful evening.

"I have Deputy Marshal Cole Jeffers with me."

"Can't it wait until morning?" He sounded weak too.

"We have an update on the case. Information you'll want to hear and process."

"Good call," Cole said, barely above a whisper. "He needs a reason to fight."

"I have cancer, Jeffers. I'm not deaf or stupid. And don't think your relationship with the ASAC impresses me."

Cole laughed. "If you'll let us in, I'll apologize for this morning."

"Which means we're best friends? Hell will freeze over first."

"I have an ice pick."

The door clicked from the inside. "It's open, smart mouth."

Tori stepped in with Cole behind her. What he could see of the home resembled Lance's room. Except the house reeked of cigarette smoke, stale beer, and the pungent stench of vomit. Max must have hit bottom and decided to hibernate, and his pasty skin made him look like warmed-over death.

"No need to sit. Y'all won't be staying." He lifted a can of Bud to his lips.

"Think I will." Cole shoved newspapers onto the floor. "Whether you like it or not, we're working together. Now do you want to know what Tori and I learned tonight, or are you going to sit here and drink yourself into a stupor?"

Tori inhaled sharply. Obviously she preferred the kid glove treatment.

"I'm better than you on your worst day."

"Prove it to me."

Max coughed. Sad in far too many ways to count.

"We acquired sensitive information about Nathan from his oldest son, Lance," Tori said. "He hacked into his dad's computer."

Max lifted a brow.

She continued to tell him about the photos and their interview with Anita Krantz.

Max rubbed his whiskered jaw. "A jealous lover is one thing, but it doesn't explain bombing the oil rig unless she was trying to prove a point."

"We're tracking the same path with her," Cole said. "She was playing a role tonight, hiding her and Nathan's affair until we nailed the truth. I'm trying to figure her out."

Max sneered. "Let me know how using your brain works for you."

Tori shot Max a hint of disgust. "We want to protect Sally and Jack from the truth."

"They'll find out soon enough. Why not give them the pretty story now?"

"We chose not to," she said. "No point in dumping more dirt into their lives."

"And you think they'll handle it any easier later?" Max took another long drink. "Anything else?"

"Yes," Cole said, questioning the logic of this late-night visit. "Are we going to work together as a team?"

"Gonna tell on me if I'm a bad boy? One of you already complained to the ASAC."

"It wasn't me," Cole said. "I believe in confronting problems head-on."

"I didn't either," Tori added. "Sally Moore placed the complaint. She told you it would happen."

"She's weak and afraid of what I'll learn. 'Specially about her and ol' Jeffers."

Cole considered Max's testy nature, as though the man were a child craving boundaries. "Max, I'm not your whipping boy. You can take your self-pity and pride and stay right here and drink yourself to death. I don't care." He stood. "Or you can sober up and do the one thing you know best. A real man would want to leave a heroic legacy for his family, not a bill for housekeeping and extermination services." He glanced around at the filth. "I'll be at the FBI office at 7:45 in the morning." He left the house.

Ten minutes later, Tori climbed into the passenger side of the truck and slammed the door. "You were harsh. Totally uncalled for. He's dying of cancer and all alone."

"Didn't you tell me the latter was his own fault?"

"Your comments aren't what he needs right now."

"And a six-pack is?"

"Sympathetic understanding that coaxes him out of his mood works best. I should know after six years with him."

"Then go right back inside and hand him a blanket and a pacifier. See if numbing his brain lengthens his life." He started the engine, and neither spoke on the drive back to the FBI office. Running interference for Special Agent Max Dublin on an FBI task force wasn't in the job description.

A call came into Cole's phone. Lance. The kid should be asleep. He snatched it. "Hey, what's going on?"

"Someone threw a rock and broke the living room window. No one's hurt, but it had a note tied to it. Said, 'I know the truth.'"

"Where's your mom?" He pressed Speaker.

"She's talking to the cops. Didn't want to call you 'cause she said you and Tori needed your rest."

"We're on our way." He dropped his phone into the console. "The temperature just got hotter."

✻

Cole and Tori found the Moore home swarming with HPD officers. Flashing lights again brought attention to the family. Inside, Lance, Jack, Kit, and Wes gathered in the kitchen. Sally was speaking with Detective Hernandez. The man had been there about twenty-four hours ago, and now a return trip. The detective's hardened features from the previous encounter had been replaced with a gentler tone.

"Mrs. Moore, I'm sorry for the chaos invading your home," Detective Hernandez said.

"It's okay. I understand." Sally lifted her gaze to Cole and Tori. "I didn't want to bother you."

"Our job is here," Cole said and greeted Detective Hernandez. "I neglected to mention my former role as a US Marshal when we spoke previously. Since this morning, I've been reinstated and am now working with the FBI regarding Mr. Moore's death."

"I . . . I see. Then you'll be receiving our report on what happened here this evening."

"Yes, sir. One of Mrs. Moore's sons contacted me about the rock and note."

With latex gloves, Detective Hernandez handed him a piece of paper. It read as Lance indicated. Cole returned it. "I'll call tomorrow for the fingerprint check and handwriting analysis."

"Okay. Looks like we're finished here." Detective Hernandez excused himself.

Once the officers left, Cole studied Sally. "Are you all right?"

"Yes, sure."

Tori gave her a hug.

"I have a question, Cole," Wes said, making his way across the kitchen. He frowned, his normal look. "I have a concern about this whole crime and murder situation. It looks to me like Kit's and my lives could be in peril. What's your take?"

Peril? What about his daughter and grandsons? "Your daughter has bodyguards, just as Nathan requested prior to his death."

"I'm concerned about Kit," Wes said. "She's frail."

A flicker of anger sparked in Sally's eyes. "Dad, you don't need to stay. For that matter, I can handle the funeral on my own."

Lance huffed. "Let me get this straight, Grandpa." Sarcasm whipped around the room. "So your wife is more important than your daughter?"

"It's complicated, son," Wes said.

Lance shook his head. "I'm not your son. You made yourself real clear."

Everyone in the room was bone tired, and Cole had no problem being a mediator. "Sally is working with law enforcement to ensure the protection of everyone in this house."

"Beginning immediately, I'll have the boys tutored at home until this is settled."

"Mom," Lance said, wrapping his arm around her waist, "I'm going to help you and Jack through this. You don't need an old man who's afraid of his own shadow."

Cole sucked in his irritation. "How about everyone head to bed? Tori and I will stay a little longer to check the house's windows and other points of entry." He glanced at Tori, who agreed.

Another long night.

18

TORI'S DOCTOR'S APPOINTMENT came too early Wednesday morning for her weary body and overstimulated mind. Three hours' sleep and two cups of coffee should have perked her up. Now, sitting on the doctor's examining table, she craved four more hours and an IV of caffeine. To stay awake, she concentrated on each known detail of Nathan's death.

Murdered by someone who'd hacked his pacemaker.

Shared with his attorney concern for himself and his family's safety.

Claimed he wanted out of his marriage and family.

Involved with Anita Krantz.

Logic said the crimes had to link back to the oil rig bombing and winning the EPA case. And whoever hated him wasn't finished yet. Why toss a rock through Sally's window except to shake her up—a tactic that worked.

The doctor entered the room and took her hand. "Tori, how's my favorite FBI agent?"

She offered a smile, although frowning best suited her. "Good. Busy. Always chasing bad guys."

He grinned. "Rather you than me. How can I help you this morning, other than suggest more sleep?"

"I have a mole on my left wrist that's darker and growing."

He inspected her wrist. "Tori, there's nothing to be alarmed about. It's a freckle."

"Are you sure?"

"A second opinion is always your choice."

How many times had they shared the same conversation? She glanced at the blood pressure cuff, a tissue box, the glass jar of cotton balls, and back to her doctor. "I'm embarrassed . . . as usual." Contempt for herself made the situation worse.

He crossed his arms over his chest. "There's no need to feel uncomfortable. I want to help you through this."

What he didn't say was it began after Kevin's death. "It's part of the grieving process. I can handle it on my own."

"I disagree, Tori. This is about fear, not grief. I see what it's doing to you."

"I'm not a hypochondriac."

"And I'm not diagnosing you with it. What I'm saying is your dread of cancer has you preoccupied."

"The last time we spoke about the problem, I saw a psychologist." Tori hadn't wanted it on her record, so she didn't use a recommendation from the FBI. "She suggested I talk to you about an antidepressant. But I'm not depressed, and I haven't gone back."

He uncrossed his arms. "Okay. But you're here this morning, you were here two weeks ago, and two weeks before that." Compassion oozed from his eyes, and she grew hot with humiliation. "All stemming from the same fear. Family health history has a tendency to paralyze you."

She drew in a breath and held it. He was blunt and right.

"Would you like the name of another psychologist?"

"Not yet."

He wrote on a prescription pad. "If you change your mind, here's the name of a friend. Goes to my church. He's a listener."

Not another one of those believer types. He'd want to pray with her, make sure her soul had *bound for heaven* stamped on it.

Her doctor left her alone in the silence, so quiet her ears throbbed. She'd get past the worry of cancer invading her life. The big C had taken her brother, but Mom was nearing the six-year mark free from breast cancer. Family stats were a nightmare, but Tori should never have allowed it to turn her into a pathetic woman preoccupied with freckles, nonexistent lumps, and headaches resulting from stress—not malignant tumors. She was made of stronger stuff, and she despised those who were all wrapped up in themselves. Reaching deep inside, she vowed no more doctor visits. No more sleepless nights. If she contracted cancer, she'd develop a big C of her own—courage.

Within the hour, she and Cole were in the FBI's break room, waiting for Max. Cole had nailed him hard last night, hitting him in the pride zone. With the mood he'd exhibited lately, he might have requested to be taken off the case. Planned to drink away his remaining days.

She refused to shove Max away when he was struggling with too many issues. Friendships were like marriage vows—for better or worse, in sickness and in health. With his family out of the picture, he had no one but her to see him through to the end.

"Max won't be here." Tossing a dagger at Cole crossed her mind. "You destroyed what little incentive he had left."

"We'll see." Cole threw a paper cup into the trash. "Is he normally on time?"

Unlike most of her colleagues, Cole added cream to his coffee.

Wimp. She swallowed her inconsiderate thoughts. Taking her sour mood out on a man's coffee preference was just plain wrong. "No, he's punctual. If anything, early. My point."

Cole sat back, way too confident. "Tori, how long are you going to disapprove of my method of getting him out of his funk?"

"Glad I'm so transparent."

"Like glass. If I'm right, he'll march through that door ready to bring our bad guy to his knees."

She gave him a sideways glare. "You're wrong. You belittled him. Besides, I've worked with Max for a long time."

"Wanna bet lunch?"

"You're on, and—"

Max burst through the door like an angry bull. "Traffic is one huge bottleneck coming into town." He swore. "What's first? Running down Moore's files? Squeezing Anita Krantz into a confession? Contacting HPD about the fingerprints on that rock and fingerprint analysis? Taking a drive to the oil rig, seeing if any of those guys have a clue about who killed their boss?"

Cole covered a grin. "Steak and shrimp."

"In your dreams," she said.

"What?" Max's voice thundered.

"Nothing," Cole said. "Glad you're here. Let's do all of it."

Max shook his fist at him. "For the record, if you ever mention self-pity or pride again, I'll blow a hole through your face."

Tori offered a broad smile with "I told you so" emanating from her eyes.

"Good. I won't unless you show up with breath that would kill a horse."

It pained her to recognize Cole had taken the right approach with Max, but she'd not admit it. Lunch would be on the run, burger and fries—if they were lucky.

"Let's take the yardman's fancy, extended-cab truck, make calls on the way to the Texas City area. Depending on what we learn, head over to the offices of Moore Oil & Gas, snoop around, and see who our victim was doing business with." Max held up a finger. "Tori, bring a copy of the court transcripts from the EPA suit and the initial bombing report. I want to take another look at the backgrounds on those involved and bring you two up to snuff about the bombing. I also want a list of all the Moores' friends, including their sons'."

"I've been involved with the boys' school and sports activities," Cole said. "Investigating their angle works for me."

Max shook his head. "Tori and I have this. You can drive unless we find a yard to mow."

"As a member of the task force, the lone Deputy US Marshal has skills to contribute and expedite the case," Tori said. "My vote's Moore Oil & Gas first on our agenda."

"Experience trumps every time."

Cole let him finish. "Anita Krantz probably didn't sleep last night with the knowledge she's a person of interest, and we've asked for a search warrant to image her personal devices. Seeing us first thing could crack her plaster."

Tori listened while the two shoved their egos into the conversation.

Cole won.

TORI FASTENED HER seat belt in the rear seat of Cole's truck. Before the truck pulled onto Highway 290, she'd posed her question to Max. "So you were consulted on the bombing case because of your past work in that division. What went on in the meeting and afterward?"

"I accompanied the team to the drill site to find the source of the IED. While the men there were questioned, I went over every inch of the place with two other agents. Nothing found at the crime scene indicated who or motivation. The bomb's components could have been purchased at Lowe's or Home Depot."

"Backgrounds on the Moore employees indicate the majority of infractions are drunk and disorderly," Tori said.

"Right, but one man did time for armed robbery. He was on duty the night of the bombing and received second-degree burns, was treated and sent home. Although it possibly eliminates him as a likely suspect, I'd like to find out how the victim got along with the rest of the crew."

Max's agent mode lightened Tori's tension, at least temporarily. "Any bombs in the system with the same signature?"

"No. Nothing conclusive. I sent the full report to both of you earlier this morning."

"Interesting the pipe bomb detonated in the wee hours of the morning in an area that caused only a few injuries," Cole said, passing an SUV. "An obvious threat to Nathan for him to do something. It's all muddy until we receive more info."

"Isn't muddy to me." Max stifled a cough. "Sally Moore or Anita Krantz thought they'd planned the perfect crime."

"Still have to prove it," Cole said. "Rethinking Nathan's threats. Was there a note or a recording of what was said to him? Or are the cell phone records all we have to go on?"

Max scrolled through his phone. "According to Moore's attorney, Nathan received a text stating he deserved to be killed for what he'd done. It came right after he won the EPA suit, and he assumed someone there was upset with him. Then another text arrived earlier the day he was killed stating the best way to get a man's attention was to destroy his family. Either woman could have easily sent the texts. Both came from the same burner phone and prompted him to hire more bodyguards. Again, you two have the reports. I'm convinced the second text was worded to toss off any guilt from the killer."

Max turned to Tori. "Send a request to the FIG. See if Anita Krantz has any relatives employed on that rig or any of Moore's holdings. She was previously married too. We want names, employment, and whereabouts of the ex."

Cole interrupted. "We have a list of men with criminal records working at the drill site, and they've been cleared. But what about a list of those who weren't working during the bombing? Add men who had problems with other employees. And former military."

"Know what?" Max said. "Yardman's gonna help us pull the weeds out of this case."

❊

Cole, along with Tori and Max, entered the executive suite Nathan had shared with Anita Krantz on the fifth floor of Moore Oil & Gas. Ultramodern, chrome, glass, gray marble—similar to his home. Framed quotes of John D. Rockefeller occupied one wall. Floor-to-ceiling glass revealed all the happenings in the suite. Two white leather chairs and a matching sofa.

Cole remembered what Nathan had said about the design. *"The glass walls derail any gossip about me and my executive assistant being alone behind closed doors. No one will ever accuse me of conducting myself in an inappropriate manner."*

Nathan, you lied to me and how many others? If the man were alive, Cole might punch him.

The downhill revelation about Nathan's character further deepened Cole's agitation. The who, why, and a suspicion about Anita Krantz kept him focused.

Anita rose from behind her glass-topped desk and greeted them. Poised, professional, and pale. The three *P*s didn't quite fit under the label of "innocent." A short red skirt and four-inch heels added fuel to what she'd done.

"Good morning, Ms. Krantz," Cole said. "I'd like to introduce you to Special Agent Max Dublin. The three of us are working the Moore case together."

She glanced at Max, her gaze turning to scrutiny. "FBI agents arrived about thirty minutes ago with a court order to view business files and devices." Little emotion passed over her smooth face, much like last night, except for sympathy-driven dynamics. She continued. "Your people have a big job sorting through personnel, financials, and various records. This won't be a small project. But I understand it's necessary to bring the killer to justice."

"We can handle the details."

"I'd like to talk to those agents, Ms. Krantz. I have my own agenda," Max said. "Could you point me in their direction?"

"I can show you where they're working."

Max lifted a brow at Tori and Cole. "I want to see who's running the show with Moore out of the picture."

"We have the list of executives," Tori said. "I'll accompany you."

"No thanks. I'm good."

From the look on Max's face, Cole suspected he was going off the grid. The executives would not put up with any resemblance of his interrogation tactics from yesterday.

"I'll be back when I'm finished," Max said. "Interviewing Ms. Krantz will skyrocket my blood pressure."

Anita whirled into his path. "Then you're too old for the job." She shifted and led the way down the hall.

Cole watched the pair disappear. The woman's moods were like a light switch.

Tori made her way to a credenza, where photos of the Moore family spread the six-foot length of the piece. "The last time I was here, Sally and I stopped in after having lunch. Anita and Nathan were in a meeting where everyone could see."

"My last visit was three days ago." Cole glanced around, then back to her. "What's your impression of Krantz this morning?"

"Calculated and emotional. I'm sure she's interested in finding out what's in her boss's files and if anything implicates her."

"That will take a while. I have a hunch," he said.

Her green eyes questioned him. "What?"

Krantz returned from escorting Max before he could respond. She clutched her stomach. Last night, when she exhibited the gesture, he'd thought the emotional conversation had made her physically ill. What else did she hide or fear?

"We'd like to see Nathan's office," Cole said. "Is it locked?"

"I opened it, his desk, credenza, and closet when the other agents arrived. Nathan kept few items in paper form in his office. Agents are searching through those in another area. I'll show you inside."

"I've been here before." Tori walked to a closed door behind Anita's desk, opened it, and stepped inside.

Cole joined her, and they each slipped on a pair of gloves. Later on a team would sweep the office and image his computers. He pulled open desk drawers while Tori searched the credenza.

"Everything looks in order." She opened the closet. "Nathan was OCD when it came to organization."

"His locker at the club had things labeled." He stood. "If he were to hide something, it wouldn't be here where anyone could find it. If he had an idea who wanted him dead, then why not tell his attorney?"

Tori pointed to another door. "Do you know about the bedroom?"

"No."

"When the office building was constructed, Sally insisted Nathan have a bedroom there. Too many nights he didn't arrive home until well after midnight. She fretted about his drive home. Worried about an accident. Then one night he was robbed in the parking garage of the old complex, and he gave in to adding the room. Sally chose the interior and picked out the furnishings."

The affair with Anita . . . "I want to take a look."

The door was locked, and Cole waited while Tori retrieved the key from Anita. The bedroom, a project designed by his wife, ensured the affair was easy for Nathan to manage.

A few moments later, Tori returned. "I saw the room right after

Sally finished with the decorating. Forgot about it until we walked in." She inserted the key and gestured for Cole to step inside.

A lamp on a nightstand lit the approximately fourteen-by-sixteen bedroom containing a king-size leather sleigh bed covered with a gray duvet. A bistro globe chandelier hung over it and a glass- and chrome-encased bar. The bathroom had a similar design.

Cole flipped on the overhead lighting, illuminating the probable rendezvous point. The floors were dark-cherry hardwood—Nathan's favorite, as the upstairs of his home displayed.

"This makes me sick," Tori said. "I wonder what else I can find." She made her way to the bathroom while he scrutinized every corner of the room.

The closet door caught his attention, and he opened it. Instantly a light flashed on, revealing a man's suit, jeans, and two shirts. He picked up a black garment bag and unzipped it. Red see-through lingerie that didn't belong to Nathan.

"Tori, has Sally ever spent time with Nathan here?"

"I don't think so," she called from the bathroom. "Why?"

He heard her footsteps across the wooden floors. She stood in front of the closet and sighed. "Sally never wears red. Hates it. A conversation we need to have with Anita."

A truckload of disgust hit him. *Nathan, what were you thinking?*

They made their way back to the outer office with the glass walls. Anita sat behind her desk, peering at the computer screen. She looked up and smiled through ultra-red lipstick. "Finished already?"

"We have a couple of questions for you," he said.

Anita's business line buzzed an incoming call. She raised her finger to stop his speaking and answered the phone.

"I'll be back in a moment," Tori said to him. "Don't start without me."

He nodded.

20

TORI ENTERED ANITA KRANTZ'S private ladies' room to compose herself. Concern for Sally raged through her heart. Anita had admitted to an affair, but seeing the evidence shook her. For a moment she questioned her ability to perform her responsibilities as a violent crime investigator. Her training supposedly prepared her for job hiccups and disconcerting information.

Max had been right. Working a case where she had personal stakes might spell disaster for the investigation and her career. Her emotions circled in the winds of contempt and disbelief. Especially when she'd cared for Nathan, a man she'd believed held the trophy for husband and father of the year. When Kevin died, Nathan had lingered at the funeral home, stood by her, and encouraged her healing. Although he wasn't a Christian, Nathan had urged her to seek Kevin's God.

She studied the brown-and-tan Italian tile and the rubbed bronze chandelier with its amber glow of light. Leaning against a variegated stone wall in light-earth tones, she laced her fingers at her waist and stared into the mirror. With the length of time she'd been gone, Cole would think she was ill.

Tori Templeton, friend to Sally Moore and a special agent. She viewed herself in multiple roles, but the one most important was to get to the bottom of the murder and bombing. Putting aside those things she wished she didn't know, one fact remained: Nathan had a double standard of ethics. Unlike him, Tori knew truth always trumped personal gain.

She took refuge against the wall with her hands behind her and breathed in and out. *You can do this, Tori.* Her fingertips touched something that gave way, and she turned to examine the small object further. It was painted the same color as the brown tile. She pressed it, and a panel door slid back into the wall leading to Nathan's bedroom. Seamless in the wall. No one would have detected a hidden doorway.

Her contempt for Nathan and Anita mounted like plaque on unbrushed teeth. Nothing but decay and holes.

But job commitment came first, and she texted Cole and Max.

I've found an entrance to Nathan's office bedroom from Anita's bathroom. Join me. Bring her with u.

Within moments, the shuffling of feet met her ears. "Come on in." She turned to see Max with Cole and Anita behind him.

Max stepped into the bedroom. "Ms. Krantz, you and Moore sure knew how to throw a party."

The crass remark caused Tori to hurl him a dangerous glare. She started to give him her sentiments, but what good would it do to lose her temper? Sally's betrayal had taken place here . . . many times. The secret entrance to Nathan's bedroom had sucker punched her. "The bedroom was not a secret, but I'd like Anita to explain the hidden entrance from her bathroom."

The familiar hesitancy and the moistening of lips. "It is what it is."

Tori focused on Cole. "Would you take her statement?"

Cole met Tori's gaze with caring, and although she appreciated his concern, she grasped the reality of her job and held on tightly. She gave her attention to Max. "After Cole and I examined Nathan's office, we discovered something else." She moved to the bedroom closet and revealed the garment bag with the lingerie.

"Anita, is this yours?"

Her brows narrowed. "I've already confessed to an affair."

How would Sally feel about Nathan using her suggestion as a lovers' nest? Had Sally known what he'd done and arranged his death? Tori hoped not.

"Ms. Krantz," Cole said, "I suggest we continue this discussion in the waiting area. I'd like to record it for future reference."

"I'm not so sure that's in my best interest." Anita tapped her foot. "What else is there for me to say? Do you want dates, times?"

If Anita lawyered up, her statement would be on hold.

Cole stepped forward. "I understand the stress with Nathan's death and what it means to you personally and to the company. We can talk in the waiting area, where it's comfortable."

Anita appeared to debate her decision, then followed him out of the room.

Tori watched them leave. She'd *liked* Anita at one time. "I'm going to request our team question the staff about the affair. Discreetly."

"Tori." Max's gentle tone caught her unaware. "Can you continue with this case?"

She well understood the implication of his question. "I have to or I'll never be able to work violent crime again. I'll be back as soon as I talk to the agents. One of my concerns is who else was privy to what went on here? I want answers now."

"We all do."

She drew in a cleansing breath. "Thanks, Max. I have a job to do."

One where there's no room for personal emotions.

❋

Cole observed Anita seated across from him in a white leather chair. Pale. Trembling and holding her arm over her stomach. Tori and Max found their way to the sofa.

"I have a couple more questions," he said.

"I'll do my best with dates of when Nathan and I were together."

"Good. Thank you. I understand there's a medical clinic on the third floor staffed with a doctor and nurse."

"Correct. It's available for all employees."

"Our court order doesn't include medical records from the company's clinic," he said. "Did Nathan ever use the services here?"

"Not to my knowledge. I'm fairly certain he used his personal physician."

"What about you?"

"Yes. It's convenient not only for me, but for everyone under the Moore umbrella."

"You use the clinic exclusively?"

She hesitated. "Why?"

"It occurred to me we should request a court order for those records."

"Why, when Nathan didn't use the clinic?"

"I mean you."

She shivered, her shoulders narrowing. "You're not making sense."

Cole held her attention. Fear creased her smooth features. "I have two sisters, and I've been around them when they were pregnant.

I noticed you hold your stomach when upsetting questions are raised. Today, as the three of us entered the office, you touched your stomach again. It could be a habit . . . or an unconscious means of protecting an unborn child."

Her eyes widened. "Mr. Jeffers—"

"Ms. Krantz, are you pregnant?"

As though paralyzed, she stared at him.

"Ms. Krantz, are you pregnant with Nathan Moore's child?"

"Yes." Tears streamed down her cheeks.

"Was he aware?"

She swallowed hard. "No. I found out three weeks ago. Couldn't tell him. Neither the right words nor the timing."

"Did you think he'd leave Sally for you?"

"His family meant too much to him. I was . . . convenient." She brushed away a tear. "I was willing and lonely. That's not an excuse. But the truth."

"If you had no intentions of telling him, what were your plans?"

"To move home to Portland. My parents are there. Nothing's changed. Never thought I'd be a mother. It's a strange feeling. Overwhelming. But I'm making progress." She shook her head. "This isn't about me but who killed Nathan."

"When were you going to inform Nathan of his child?"

"Never. He loved Sally, not me. How many ways must I explain it?"

"Ms. Krantz," Cole said, "with this new information, you've just added fuel to the fire."

The coolness returned, as though Anita turned her emotions from hot to cold with the blink of an eye. "I had nothing to do with the murder of Nathan Moore, the father of my child and a man I loved. There's no evidence to arrest me."

"You're right," Tori said. "But we'll keep digging, and we'll find out who killed Nathan."

"My resignation is on my computer."

"Did you compose the letter before or after he was murdered?"

"Before. My parents have been aware of my situation for two weeks. Nathan knew of my decision to resign but not the reason."

"And he didn't ask you to reconsider?"

Anita shook her head and reached for a tissue.

Cole analyzed the facade of the desperate woman before him. Who was the real victim here?

21

TORI FUMED and attempted to concentrate on Max, and Cole wrapped things up with Anita in the waiting area. The chief executive officers denied any knowledge of their esteemed owner having an affair. She hadn't mentioned Krantz's name. No need because they'd find out soon enough. One trait Tori had seen in Nathan—he kept his distance from employees, no individual socializing outside of the office. Big events, like charity golf tournaments and a reserved box for Astros and Texans games, included the best of food and entertainment. But that was it. Repeatedly she'd heard him say the only friend he needed was Sally, the love of his life. Odd he'd formed an alliance with Cole.

Anita's pregnancy shouldn't have shaken her, but Nathan had requested Sally have her tubes tied because he was thrilled with the boys and felt their family was complete. Daughters-in-law and granddaughters would come later.

What a jerk.

Nathan might not have known about his unborn child, but he was cognizant of how his affair reflected on his marriage. Did he think he could keep it secret forever? An affair was traumatic, but a love child threatened to destroy his whole family.

Cole spoke to Anita, who sat with her long legs crossed and her skirt a bit high. "As you were informed previously, do not leave town. You are a critical witness in our ongoing investigation, and we may uncover some important evidence in the company's records."

"You will find nothing anywhere to implicate me in Nathan's murder. I'm only guilty of loving him." She arched her back. "Sally should have kept better tabs on him."

The real Anita Krantz?

Max blew out steam. "The man is dead. You have motive. Have a pleasant morning, Ms. Krantz."

Cole, Max, and Tori made their way to the elevator. Cole pushed the down arrow and they stood silently.

Max's flushed face was an improvement over the colorless one earlier this morning. His attitude needed rehab. He spoke low. "The time spent here wasn't a waste. That woman has reason to be afraid. The executives have greed dribbling from their pores, and we're fools to believe they were ignorant of the affair. I've already requested backgrounds on the top six. The team is gathering other employee history, but I requested information about who was up for promotion, notes from meetings, and financials for all the staff. A big order, but everything helps. Who had the most to gain from his death besides Sally Moore and Anita Krantz?"

That was Max Dublin with his game on. "Far too many," Tori said. "Lust in all areas makes strange bedfellows."

The elevator door opened and the three stepped inside. Nothing was said for fear of possible listening devices in the elevator. They exited on the first floor of the complex and headed out to Cole's truck. At his truck, Tori took the bench seat behind the passenger side. Cocoa-brown leather trimmed in brass. Custom order. A cup holder held her cold coffee from earlier.

"I have to tell Sally what we've learned before the day's over," Tori said.

"I'm right there with you," Cole said. "We owe her the truth before she hears from another source."

"I gave my word to Lance to help shelter his mom from the truth. Not sure what I was—"

"Why?" Max spit out an expletive. "Our job isn't to shield her from the inevitable. And then there's the issue of her being a suspect."

"Hey," Cole said, "our job is to serve the community, and that means sincerity and concern for every person who has been victimized. Today is a fact-finding mission in hopes we'll have more answers by tonight."

Max huffed. "Stupid when we already have two women to bring in and press for a confession."

"Not on my watch until we have evidence," Cole said. "If my understanding of the law is stupid, deal with it."

Tori was in no mood to listen to arguing. "Stop it, you two. I've had enough."

"Maybe you need to resign from the case. Want me to make a recommendation?"

"That works both ways, partner."

"She's right," Cole said. "Nothing is solved arguing. So we're heading to Texas City?"

"You bet. Those roughnecks will tell us exactly what they thought of Moore and who'd want him dead. When I was there about the bombing, they wanted to help, mad about those who'd gotten hurt. Rumor mill runs hot and strong. Might take a few beers to get 'em to loosen up. Leave it to me. None of them were killed in the explosion—peculiar, don't you think? Unless a few of them were in on it too."

Tori ignored him. "He paid his employees well and provided excellent benefits. He sent a six months' supply of Pampers to every baby born, offered college scholarships based on grades, and attended all employee weddings and funerals. Promotions came from within, and he shared profits with every worker."

"Fat chance those employees were disgruntled," Cole said.

"Depends," Max said. "Never know what makes a man angry enough to kill."

Tori took over the discussion again. "We're looking at a complex man who played the role of devoted husband and father, lover, entrepreneur, exceptional employer, and friend to Cole and me. He lived a complicated life, and we're starting to unravel it."

"I'm all for Sally Moore as the killer." Max followed up his words with a cough that she thought would never end. Tori stayed quiet until he could speak again. "My years of experience tell me she's our strongest suspect. Think about it. Krantz wouldn't want the victim dead. A baby gives her leverage for him to leave his wife. At the very least, make a handsome settlement. The Moore woman arranged the bombing and the hacker, just like I told you all along."

Tori's head throbbed. "Krantz also had motive with Nathan refusing to leave Sally and the prospect of raising a child alone."

"Truth is, we're dealing with speculation," Cole said. "Nothing more. The more we dig, the closer we'll get. Assumptions don't solve a case—important to help theorize, but in the end you might be chasing an empty trail."

"You don't have my experience." Max wouldn't let up.

"We're looking for a man's killer, a person who had knowledge of his medical condition," Tori said. "The announcement went public when he had a heart attack and the surgical procedure resulting in the pacemaker."

Max swore, and she was tired of hearing it. "You two refuse to see the obvious."

Tori forged ahead. "I'm not denying both women are persons of interest. Either one could have done the crime. Or neither. The killer sees the act as justified, and Nathan had it coming. Whatever he did to push the killer's buttons meant he committed the unredeemable, the worst of immoral acts that could no longer be ignored. I'm looking at this from a woman's point of view, and both have issues which could have resulted in murder. But if I hold strong on this theory, then why bomb the oil rig?"

"Cover-up," Max said. "Or an accomplice. A woman easily charges into the arms of another man when she thinks she's been wronged or can do better. I—"

"Please." Tori's voice rose. "Neither Sally Moore nor Anita Krantz is your wife. Cut the personal injury stuff and stay on task."

Max turned and threw visual bullets her direction. "Prove me wrong. Those women could have planned it together. A huge hormone overload. Hired out their dirty work." He held up his phone. "Requesting a surveillance team on them."

Tori valued brainstorming and teamwork, but Max pushed both means of solving the crimes into a hole where he was always right. Her phone chimed with an update from the ASAC. "Watching them is wise. You could be right about Sally or Anita Krantz. But we have to investigate all the angles. Right now we've got a new lead, so a little effort to focus would be appreciated." Max needed to add counseling to his chemo and radiation.

Cole caught her attention in the rearview mirror. A hint of admiration in his sky-blue eyes. In her present mood, he should be careful or she might unload on him.

ALBERT WRAPPED ERIK'S leftover hot ham and cheese sandwich in foil. He'd about run out of ways to keep his son alive, and bribes no longer did the trick. Erik had taken a few bites at lunch, but not enough for a grown man or a small child. Used to be, he'd eat two sandwiches. Now Erik forced nutrition into his body only to please his dad. The doctor suggested pureeing all of his meals, but who could eat such slop?

He stared outside, not planning to pull the weeds from the flower beds but devising means to get his son to eat. To survive. To live.

Until Nathan's death, Albert had clung to hope. He must devise a new plan, but his mind spun with doubt and regret.

He slid two dirty plates into the dishwasher. Erik had given up, and why not? His relapses had grown worse, sinking him deeper into depression that nudged him toward suicide. The MS steadily took his life like a flesh-devouring piranha. A diagnosis of progressive relapsing multiple sclerosis offered no hope for quality of life. No chance of improvement for a man who once competed in distance running and ran a company.

Albert heeded the advice of Franc Lawd, a nurse who'd become his friend, and made sure no medications or sharp objects were within his son's reach. Good friends were hard to come by, but he had two fine ones.

Medical advances in Germany claimed a new drug forced remission of the disease in 75 percent of cases. But the FDA refused to approve it without further testing, stating the side effects of potential stroke made the medication too much of a health risk. The treatment in Germany required the patient to remain hospitalized for six weeks in order to receive four doses. An insurmountable amount of money, nearly 1.5 million dollars, far more than Albert's pitiful assets, which had dwindled with Erik's care and in trying to force Nathan's hand. Beyond selling his soul, Albert no longer had options, except for one. If Erik could hold on and if the law would rectify an eighteen-year-old crime, he had a chance to live.

He crept into Erik's room. His son was staring at the ceiling. "Dad, I can't go on much longer. Neither can you. I see you aging by the day. Put me in a nursing home before you collapse."

"I've taken care of you since you were in diapers."

"Almost there again." He reached for a plastic cup containing water, took a drink, and ducked his chin so the liquid had no opportunity to trickle into his lungs. "When you saw Sally, how'd she look?"

Albert considered saying she'd lost her trim shape and her hair had fallen out, but she might visit Erik. "Hasn't changed a bit. Still the blue-eyed beauty I met years ago."

His son smiled with gaunt features and closed his eyes for a moment as though remembering. "Her sons, do they resemble her or Nathan?"

"I didn't see them."

"I'm sure they got the best of both worlds."

Acid rose in Albert's gut. "How can you say that when Nathan stole your life from you?"

"Doesn't matter anymore." He dragged his tongue over his lips. "Thanks for passing along my condolences." Erik started to say something but stopped for a moment. "Dad, think I'll take a nap . . . and dream about the old days."

While Erik slept, Albert's thoughts moved from one aspect of his son's life to another. Idle hours often caused his mind to dwell on how Erik could have spent his life without MS. A wife and children sounded like paradise. Other men Albert's age bragged about what a grandkid did or said. Attended sports events and dance recitals. Albert could only live through their stories.

Although doctors hadn't proved what caused MS, Albert blamed Nathan. The dead man had pushed enough stress into Erik's life to send his son into autoimmune disease—or whatever the experts were classifying MS as these days. Yes, it was Nathan's fault, and the reality nudged Albert until he became a predator.

He switched on the radio—anything to keep his mind off what Nathan Moore had done to Erik.

"Update on the death of Nathan Moore, owner of Moore Oil & Gas. Moore was murdered Monday night when a fatal heart attack took his life. Authorities learned his death was due to an adjustment to his pacemaker, done by a hack into the hospital's equipment. No arrests have been made, but law enforcement have two persons of interest.

"Evidence indicates Moore led another life that is just now surfacing. The benefactor of many charities, scholarships, and worthy causes had maintained a five-year affair with his executive assistant, Anita Krantz. Although it hasn't been confirmed, our sources claim Ms. Krantz is pregnant with his child."

The newscast ended, and Albert paced the floor. How could he hate a man and regret his death at the same time? He wanted to feel the sweet satisfaction of justice served. But he was angry.

Time to pay the bereaved widow another visit. Be a grandpa to Lance and Jack. Let her cry on his shoulder while he demonstrated concern for her plight. Find out who her friends were and play the ultimate sympathizer. Then he'd tell her about treatment for Erik.

He'd sit back and watch the Moore family ask to help. Sally was no fool—Nathan had told her how he made his millions. The truth must be hidden in the depths of Moore's paperwork. Perhaps his will. Maybe Albert should consult a lawyer.

When the dust settled, Erik would be a rich man and a recipient of Germany's medical discovery.

23

THE FAMILIAR SOUND of water pouring into a drilling rig pipe transported Cole back to working alongside Dad. Being a roughneck had filled him with pride and taught him the value of backbreaking gratification in a job well done. Before daylight, he and Dad would slap on hard hats and pull on steel-toed boots. The day could be eight or twelve hours long. Didn't matter. Just sweat and good times with great memories. Calluses and sore muscles laid the groundwork for country western music lyrics and a round of beers. Never worked so hard in his life.

At the Moore Oil & Gas drill site, construction on the area that had been bombed was well under way. Another week, and the roughnecks would be working a full crew. The bomber had no intentions of hurting anyone or the bomb's components would have done more damage.

A possible threat for what happened to Nathan.

Cole shielded his eyes from the sun and stared up at the metal platform. One man hosed down a drill pipe. The pipe rose from deep within the ground, and one guy was helping two men release a clamp, fasten a shield, and dump drilling mud. The process would begin again, this time going deeper. The screech of the plunging drill and the uneven hum of machinery reminded Cole of moments he could never recapture except in memories.

Dad retired from a rig, but he never tired of telling stories about the days when a well came in strong—or when a rig blew and the men lost control of the well, some never living to tell about the tragedies.

When a break was called, Max moved like a politician among the crew, shaking hands and making his way toward the drill pusher, the one man responsible for every crew member. But those guys knew an outsider when they saw one, and Max wore gray slacks, a dark sports jacket, a shiny visitor helmet, new safety glasses, and an air of arrogance.

Tori stayed back while Cole joined him. "I don't need your help," Max said. "I've met these guys. They know me."

"Then talk to your ASAC's lead, Preston Ustach. Not a man who could be responsible."

Max stopped, then walked toward Ustach and requested they talk in private. He nodded and they walked about twenty feet away. "Heard you told an FBI agent that you might have evidence about the bombing."

The derrickhand was blond and resembled a Texan linebacker. "Sir, I'm not sure my information is accurate. I won't give a name without proof on my side."

"Let the professionals investigate the crime. You stick to the rig."

Ustach's face flared. "Looks like your work hasn't found the bomber or Mr. Moore's killer." He made his way back to his bud, a driller they'd met a few minutes earlier.

"He knows something." Max gritted his teeth.

"If he does, you're the last person he'll tell." Cole questioned if he could work this task force with the man. Max's poor health had become a loose excuse for his attitude.

Cole swung his attention to Ustach and his bud. They were talking privately. The driller was obviously mocking Max. Ustach sized up Tori. She stood back from the men and observed Max, no doubt listening to conversations, studying mannerisms, and processing what they'd learned about Nathan Moore. Or maybe not. Her scrutiny could be a cover-up for the men to approach her. She turned to Ustach and smiled, a curve of her lips that Cole hadn't seen before. Ustach stepped beside her. His smile said more than a passing interest. Wouldn't be the first time a fascinating woman extracted information out of a man. The driller joined them, with the same obvious interest in Tori.

He gulped. *Whoa, Cole, has the green-eyed monster drop-kicked your heart?*

Cole hesitated. Let Tori do her stuff. She could whip those guys into shape if they ventured out of line. He scanned the area away from Max and Tori, ensuring every angle of the site had eyes. Doing his job to make sure everyone was protected.

A few moments later, one of the men with Tori broke into a loud laugh, and Cole convinced himself she needed a deputy US Marshal, so he made his way there.

"You with the FBI?" said the driller, a small man, wiry and arms loaded with ink.

"No. Deputy US Marshal."

He shook Cole's hand. "Jose Aznar. Moore was a good man. Paid us well and took interest in our work problems. Don't suppose you'd know anything about the oil business."

"My dad worked on a platform, and I helped him in the summers during high school and college. Loved every minute of it. But I heard the complaints too."

Ustach stuck his hands in his pockets. "Just telling the lady here how much we appreciated Nathan Moore. A finer man never owned a rig. He'd come to the site, grab a helmet, and pitch in to help. Stay until the job was done. That's the kind of man he was. Whoever messed with his pacemaker deserves to be dead."

Cole shifted his weight to one leg. "We were friends. Can't imagine why someone would kill him."

"His wife and I have known each other since college days. Like us, the family is devastated." Did Tori's voice sound sweeter in talking to these guys? "We all have more than a personal stake in getting to the bottom of this."

Ustach shook his head. "I told an FBI investigator that I only recall one man who didn't like him, and he wasn't employed here."

"You mean the reporter caught snooping around?" Aznar said. "The guy who got thrown off the site?"

"He wasn't a reporter. But that's who I mean."

"I remember 'im." Aznar snorted. "I heard the EPA paid him. Then they lost the lawsuit. Served them right for attacking a good man and spreading lies."

Cole filed every word away. "What did the guy say to the crew?"

"Wanted to know about Moore as a boss," Ustach said. "Had his own agenda. Claimed his son worked for him on another rig, then got killed in an accident. Never heard the story before. We guessed it was a pack of lies aimed to get one of us to say something against Moore."

"Do you have a name?" Tori swept back her dark hair in a flirty motion.

Ustach nudged her shoulder. "Yes, ma'am. Franc Lawd, first name with a *c*. He wrote it down for me in case I remembered something."

Had Ustach been an informant for Nathan?

Tori turned to Cole. "Why don't you run a background on Lawd while I chat with these fine gentlemen."

Cole grinned at the men. "This gal packs, so I'd be careful if I were you."

"She's too cute to be dangerous." Ustach did a redneck assessment, a head-to-toe scan with an appreciative smile. "She looks harmless. Stick around, honey, and we'll have dinner later on."

"My boyfriend might not be too happy, and I don't have a ride back to Houston."

"Who's gonna tell him? You're safe with me, and I'll get you home when you're good and ready." He hesitated and seriousness entered his eyes. "A guy doesn't meet a smart and pretty girl like you very often."

Cole walked to a secluded spot and requested the background on Franc Lawd. He wanted to be there while Tori talked to the two men, but it might interfere with her method of interviewing.

Who was he fooling? He respected her role in the task force. She was tough while feminine, and she had eyes that resonated with depth and intelligence. But he had a green side when it came to her. She laughed and he whirled around for just one more look.

An explosion of blood and tissue burst onto the front of Tori. Ustach fell backward, a shock of red on his chest. Tori shoved Aznar to the ground.

A split-second paralysis hit Cole. Shaking off his fear of the past, he lunged toward the scene. "Everybody down!"

Another shot fired, and a man about twenty feet away grabbed his shoulder.

24

TORI DREW HER WEAPON while searching for signs of the shooter. Two shots. No more fire. She rolled off Aznar and crawled to Ustach. Empty eyes met her, open and lifeless. A hole in his heart. "Please. Don't give up," she whispered.

Aznar handed her his T-shirt, and she pressed it against Ustach's chest. He knelt on the other side of Ustach. "Hey, man, you're gonna be okay."

She touched the man's neck for a pulse. Nothing. His lips held no semblance of air.

She listened for a heartbeat, but only silence met her. Not the way a good man should die. She looked into Aznar's face, wrenched in grief. "He's gone. I'm sorry."

"How did this happen?" His words broke.

What could she say? Canned responses were useless, so she took Aznar's hand. She'd been there before . . . staring into the eyes of a victim. Her gaze swung to the man who'd been injured. A shoulder wound. With the help of two men, he walked her way.

Ustach had been shot through the heart, while the other man cradled his shoulder. Realization flowed through her. A sniper seldom missed. Only a fool would label this a random shooting. Ustach had been targeted. What did the man know that got him killed?

"Tori, are you all right?" Cole's words shattered her thoughts.

He grimaced and bent to her side. His thumb traced over her left cheek. "Want to make sure that's not yours."

The blood from when she attempted to find a heartbeat. "I'm okay. Angry. This was a hit."

"I agree." He gripped Aznar's shoulder while Tori kept her hand firmly around his. "911 is on the way. Max called for backup." His eyes narrowed. "I'm going after the shooter."

"Wait until help gets here."

"Not while a killer gets away."

"Take your truck."

Before she could protest further, he hurried to his vehicle and headed east in the direction of the shot's trajectory. She focused on Preston Ustach. Blood and death. Anger swirled against the killer, and she fought hard to keep her thoughts away from raw emotions.

✼

Cole raced across the flat level of sparse grasses following motorcycle tracks leading to the road. A few trees could have hidden the sniper.

A man killed on his watch.

Cole had frozen. . . . Did anyone notice? When the bullet hit Ustach's chest, he'd been transported back to being shot and left for dead. But he'd found the courage to do his job. *Thank You, God.*

He'd not forget today.

He sped to the area where the shot had originated, approximately 820 yards away. Nearing a lone oak, he noted crumpled grass the length of a man. About six feet. Tread marks of a motorcycle. The indentations of a rifle and bipod aimed at the rig. Spent casings from an M110. Where had the sniper gone once he reached the road?

Dust kicked up in the distance. Cole gunned the gas to where the sniper had disappeared. The field emptied onto a dust-covered road. Two sets of fresh motorcycle tracks traveled right and left, dirt flying in both directions. Identical treads. A setup for a kill and to confuse law enforcement.

Blowing out his frustration, he whirled his truck around to document the crime scene.

Near the roughnecks and Tori, Max was bent over in a coughing spasm. Cole's concern leveled on a man who'd been assassinated and the woman who watched it happen.

Tori stood, her face, jacket, and blouse stained in blood, phone to her ear, and her weapon drawn. All the while she looked around as if the shooter might appear again. Aznar bent at the dead man's side. The toolpusher close by. The others formed a semicircle around Ustach, including the wounded man clutching his shoulder. Most of the men's experiences with death came from accidents and illnesses, not murder.

Tori slipped her phone into her pocket seconds before Cole reached her. She trembled slightly, but he'd not mention it.

"Find anything?" she said.

"Signs of the shooter about a half mile away. At the dirt road were indications of two bikes to throw us. They went in opposite directions. Took pics at the sniper's nest, but only one set of tracks there. Bullet casings from an M110."

Worry etched on her face. "Someone was afraid of what Ustach would tell us."

Sirens drew closer.

Cole joined Aznar beside the body. The man was pressing his thumb to his eyes with one hand and swiping at his nose with the other. "I'm really sorry."

"Preston wanted to do his part in finding Moore's killer," Aznar said. "This is how he paid for it. The shooter rode a bike?"

"Yes. Seen any around here?"

"All the time."

"Did Lawd have one?"

"No. A pickup."

Cole made a mental note to check DMV records on Lawd. "Had Mr. Ustach ever mentioned anyone threatening him?"

Aznar shook his head. "Get your hands on Franc Lawd. If you don't, we will."

"We'll find whoever's responsible and make sure justice is served. Is there family for Mr. Ustach whom we can notify?"

The man took a heaving breath. "His mother lives outside Texas City. She's a widow. I'll be leavin' to see her once the ambulance's here."

"I'd like to ride along with you."

"Why?" He narrowed a distrustful glare.

"Because no one should have to tell a mother her son's dead."

"A couple of other guys will want to go, but you're welcome."

Cole thanked him. "I want to tell her I'm not stopping until I find out who did this to her son."

25

TORI HANDED MAX the plastic bag containing her bloody jacket, blouse, and pants. One of the men from the rig had phoned his wife and made arrangements for her to drive by Walmart for jeans and a T-shirt. Tori gladly accepted them, reflecting a moment on the kindness of good people.

"Sure you're all right?" Max squinted in the sun.

"I'm doing my best. Sorta hard when a sniper takes out a man standing beside me." Wearing clothes spotted with a dead man's blood had fogged her mind, shaken her. She slipped off plastic gloves and dropped them inside the bag.

Max sealed it, then handed her a bottle of water. "One of the men thought you might need this."

She uncapped it and took a drink. What should have tasted refreshing hit the bottom of her stomach and threatened to come back up.

"You're green," he said. "Another woman would be on a stretcher."

"I'm giving it serious consideration."

He gave her a sideways smile. "I have a few more men to interview. Should get it done before Jeffers returns from sympathy duty."

Disgust had hit its limit. "Number one, I have the skill set to interview, and I'm still your partner. Number two, exhibiting a human trait doesn't make him less of a man."

"Point taken."

She hoisted her shoulder bag. "You should have gone with him. I'm capable of taking care of myself."

He frowned. "Suit yourself."

For what seemed like the hundredth time, she scanned the area where the sheriff's department and agents now swarmed. Concentrating on her job and not the impact of a man's violent death made sense, if she could follow through. Later she'd break down. "Have they found anything?"

"Not any more than Cole." Max nodded at the rig's security camera. "We caught the aftermath, flat good that does."

She pointed to the five men near Cole's truck waiting for an interview. "What have the other men given you to follow up on?"

"Very little. It's recorded. We'll pull it together later. The two who went with Cole and Aznar might know more, which could be why they were in a hurry to visit Ustach's mother."

"Once we're back at the office, we'll look at backgrounds—priors, military. The victim was the only name that came to our attention. He had info about the bombing, but what about the second man who was shot? Before the ambulance left with him, he claimed not to have seen a thing." A flash of the bullet entering Ustach's chest sickened her. "I want to talk to Franc Lawd. See if he knows anything. Cole requested a background on him before the shooting."

"He texted me while you were changing," Max said. "Said he'd send Lawd's report as soon as he received it. I'd rather it had gone through our office instead of the US Marshals."

She was too whipped to argue with him and turned toward Cole's truck. "Those men have stood there long enough."

Shortly after the interviews concluded, Cole returned from notifying Preston Ustach's mother about her son's death. He drove Aznar's Jeep. Two other men who'd ridden with him walked back to the rig. Cole's features were stoic. She'd been there, wanting to offer comfort when nothing would bring back a loved one. Guilt made them all angry and full of shame, even though the fault lay with the sniper.

"I didn't hear or see anything to raise suspicion," he said. "Two of the men cried like babies. Aznar stayed with Ustach's mother until her daughter arrived."

"How's the mother?"

"In shock. I suggest we talk to her tomorrow. Right now she's having trouble processing one breath to the next."

She despised senseless death. They made the rounds to the agents, sheriff's deputies, and US Marshals sweeping the area. Media reporters were on the scene too, and she'd rather not get tangled up with what happened when she hadn't figured it out herself.

As they made their way to Cole's truck, his phone buzzed. He read the message before giving them his attention. "Lawd's record."

"What did you learn?" she said.

"He has no priors. Army background—medical corps. A nurse at St. Luke's downtown. Lives in Texas City. Divorced. No kids. Not even a speeding ticket. He did find a way to get past the security guard here and questioned some of the men about Nathan's business practices. Used the bogus story about having a son killed at one of Moore's sites. Escorted off. No charges filed. No affiliation with any environmental activists."

"What's your gut telling you?" Max said.

Thanks, Max. About time you showed Cole a little respect.

"Not sure yet. But I want to know the reason he gained access to this particular drill site. Who are his friends? What do his coworkers say about him? Financials? What about paying him a visit? He works the day shift and should be home by now."

"Good call," Max said.

"Glad I met your approval."

Tori opened the rear door of Cole's truck. Exhaustion hit her, but the weariness was stress. She recognized the symptoms and would deal with it when the day ended. Having the backseat to herself sounded good. She rested against the leather while willing the throb at the base of her neck to vanish so she could think. His truck rode smooth, and soon the drone of the wheels lulled her toward sleep. Max's coughing jarred her awake, and the longer his death rattle ricocheted off the sides of the truck, the more she mourned for what stage 3A cancer meant. Why were those close to her plagued by the big C? Worse yet, was she a death magnet?

Definitely stress working overtime.

When Max's spasms ended, she focused on what they'd learned at the oil rig. The first victim had been a friend who'd betrayed his family and others who'd trusted him. The second tragedy with Preston Ustach added another body to this case.

"What did the pair of roughnecks tell you?" Max said. "They cozied up real tight before Ustach was shot."

The insinuation irritated her, but she quickly blamed her reaction on the headache. "Actually, they were perfect gentlemen. A little lonely, that's all. They're wanting Nathan's killer found, and like us, they believe his death is linked to the bombing." She opened her purse for a couple of Tylenol.

Max rubbed his chin. "Ustach's background cleared. But let's go back a few years. Might be something there."

Tori swallowed the two Tylenol dry and snatched her phone. "I will."

Max banged the side of the truck. "Gotta pull over. Gonna be sick."

Cole swung his truck onto the right shoulder, spitting stones in the wake. Before he ground the vehicle to a halt, Max opened the door and vomited.

She wanted to help her partner, but he'd never allow it. Cole laid a couple of napkins from Sonic on the passenger seat. He opened his door with a bottle of water in his hand, jogged around the front of the cab, and handed it to Max. Neither man said a word, while the special agent who'd solved one violent crime after another for Houston's FBI fell prey to his decaying body. The only way she could honor Max was to do her job. She made the request to review the extensive background on Ustach while Max fought to control his body's violent reaction to what was supposed to lengthen his life.

Moments later, the two men climbed back into the truck. Max thanked him. "Don't know what's going to kill me first, the cancer or the chemo and radiation."

"I'm praying for you," Cole said. "God can put that cancer into remission."

Max moaned. "Are you a pew-jumper?"

"I'm a Christian."

"What have I done to get a yardman who's a US Marshal and a Bible-thumper?"

Cole chuckled. "You got lucky. Think about it: Do you want a Christian behind the Glock or a US Marshal who likes to get his hands dirty? Actually, you got both." He pulled his truck onto the interstate.

"We'd better be heading to Lawd's place," Max said. "No stops at a church or watering hole to get baptized."

"Want me to belt out a few bars of 'Shall We Gather at the River?'"

"Spare me. Got enough of that as a kid."

Tori's cell phone buzzed with an incoming call. The screen read *Sally* and she answered.

"Tori, why didn't you tell me?" Each word was punctuated with anger.

A dreaded chill crept up her spine. "What are you referring to?"

"Why do the people I care about lie to me? The news is all over the media." Sally's voice grew shriller. "Nathan was having an affair. He told me he loved me every day."

By not informing her friend, Tori had created a chasm between them that might never be repaired. "Tell me what you heard."

"Does it really matter? As a friend, I deserved to hear it from you first. Not a sound bite from a reporter. How long were you aware of his affair? Have you confirmed she's pregnant?" Sobs broke her words.

"Sally, I'll be there tonight and we'll talk."

"I don't need you. My parents are here, and they promised not to keep anything from me. And for the record, I loved Nathan."

"You're upset." Her response was lame.

"You have no idea how I feel. I've been betrayed by my husband, his assistant, and my best friend. Who knows? Cole is probably deceiving me too, since he neglected to tell me about his job with the US Marshals. Can you imagine the nightmare this leaves for Lance and Jack? How are they going to face their friends—the ugly things that'll be said? They will have to live with their father's duplicity for the rest of their lives. And did I mention a little brother or sister? How endearing. Maybe the baby will have Nathan's eyes. I despise what all of you have done to what's left of this family."

The phone clicked in Tori's ear. What had she done to her best friend?

26

COLE SIZED UP FRANC LAWD—about five foot ten with lightly tanned skin. He was dressed in blue scrubs and leaning against the doorway of his second-floor apartment. "Tell me one more time who you are and why you're here."

Three teens gawked from about twenty feet away, their phones aimed at the agents. Probably using Periscope. Cole took long strides to the girls and boy. "This is official government business. I suggest you take yourselves to another area."

"Free country," a dark-haired Hispanic girl said. She looked about fifteen.

"True. But do you want the repercussions of interfering with a federal investigation? Are your parents ready to pick you up in juvie?"

Tori touched his arm. "Cole, she isn't—"

"I'm not FBI," he said to Tori. "Miss, I suggest you leave."

The girl opened her mouth, then quickly shut it and walked away with her friends.

One more time Cole introduced himself, Tori, and Max to the suspect.

Lawd beckoned with his fingers. "IDs please. Make it fast 'cause I have things to do." His black hair had strands of gray and was worn in a foot-long ponytail. He looked to be in his early forties.

They showed their creds and Cole took over. "We understand you were escorted off a drill site near Texas City belonging to Moore Oil & Gas."

"What of it?"

"We'd like to come in and discuss it."

He closed the door behind him. "Anything you have to say can happen right here. No way are you getting inside my home." He appeared to notice Tori. "Not even the pretty brunette."

"I'm harmless," she said. "All we have are questions." Her words landed like honey.

"All right. What do you need to know?"

"We heard a story about your son being killed on Moore property?" Cole said.

"I have no idea what you're talking about. I don't have a son."

Max stepped in front of Lawd, nose to nose. Lawd's was crooked. "The deputy Marshal requested information, and you got smart. Now I'm asking and I don't take lip from anybody."

Cole hid his amusement. Max sounded like Dirty Harry.

Lawd moved aside, his back against the door. "I was curious about what went on there. So I found a way past security and asked a few questions."

Max smiled. "Thank you, sir. Marshal Jeffers, Mr. Lawd is ready to talk."

"Whoa. Do I need my attorney?" Lawd said.

Cole took his cue. They needed answers, not a suspect who law-yered up. "Sir, not unless you have something to hide or are afraid for your life."

He pressed his lips together. "Nothing to hide or fear to the best of my knowledge."

Cole slid a silent invitation to Tori for her to take over. "Thank you, sir. I really appreciate your taking the time with us. How did you manage to get on the site? When we arrived, the security guard wanted everything but our blood types."

He shrugged. "A roughneck let me slip him a hundred-dollar bill."

"Name? The guy must have had pull."

"Didn't ask."

"Would you mind describing him?"

Lawd snorted. "Dirty. Hard hat. Gloves. Needed a shower. Guess that fits all of them."

Cole ignored his last comment and let Tori keep going.

"What was the purpose of your visit?" she said.

"To see what happened when the public wasn't looking."

"You accused Nathan Moore of being responsible for your son's death and asked questions about his character. What was the reason?"

Lawd snorted. "That story is a lie. I was upset with my job and thought I'd check out the possibilities of working closer to home. Wanted to see if the owner was a jerk."

"So you requested information about the way Moore conducted business."

"Right. I heard he paid good benefits. Must not have been enough because he's dead and so is another guy."

Tori pressed her lips together hard, and Cole took it as a sign she wanted to back off. "Not many nurses on an oil rig."

"A smart man keeps his options open."

"Where were you on March 30, 2:50 a.m., when the drill site was bombed?"

"With a friend."

"Name?"

"Can't remember right now. But when I do, I'll contact you. Strange thing about law enforcement types. You intimidate a man until he can't think."

Cole hated the thought of Lawd shutting down. "Do you own a motorcycle?"

"Too dangerous. I've seen enough twisted bodies when they're put down."

"What about a rifle, specifically an M110?"

"If you're asking if I own one, the answer's no. A tragedy in the making. Don't hunt either. You'll find no weapons registered to me."

But he might have one in his possession. "Where were you at approximately one o'clock this afternoon?"

"In the middle of an appendectomy on a twelve-year-old boy. Saved his life if you're interested. Are we finished?"

"Just about, sir."

"That rig was bombed and you haven't made your arrest quota. According to the latest news, a man was shot there today and another man killed. I suggest you look elsewhere for a bomber and killer instead of bothering law-'biding citizens."

"You're a smart man. But none of us said a thing about the drill site bombing or Nathan Moore's death," Cole said. "Did you pull the trigger or hit the right keystroke to end Moore's life?"

Lawd glanced at his feet before responding. "I have no reason to commit any crimes. I'm in the medical field, which means I do my best to save lives, not take them. And for the record, this little Q and A is concluded without my lawyer." He opened the door, stepped in, and latched it behind him.

Cole rapped on the door. "Mr. Lawd, I suggest contacting your lawyer soon because we're not finished. We'll be in contact."

27

ALBERT FLIPPED THROUGH THE CHANNELS on the TV in Erik's room. The same old programming, even with the addition of cable. Erik's food grew cold while his son slept. Tonight he'd pureed chicken noodle soup, but it would need to be rewarmed when his son wakened.

His phone rang and he checked the sender. Franc. Good. He could use a diversion. "Hey, what's going on?"

"The FBI just paid me a visit."

Albert glanced to make sure Erik still slept. "Why?"

"A man at the rig was shot and killed today. The media is calling it a sniper. Since I'd done some snooping around, they suspected me."

"You were working, right?"

"Yeah. But I didn't like them poking in my business. They asked questions about Nathan. Wanted to know about my interest in him and the business."

Albert closed his eyes to focus on the conversation. "What did you tell them?"

"Made up a story. A pathetic one."

"Your alibi has you covered for the bombing and Nathan's death."

"Albert, I agreed to help you dig up dirt about Nathan, to help you get the money for Erik's care, but this has gone far enough. The man's dead. There's nothing more you or I can do."

"But someone is destroying Erik's legacy."

"Putting my life on the line is not worth 10 percent of the money you thought Nathan would pay. Especially when there is no money, and people are getting killed."

Franc wanted out, and Albert couldn't blame him. "I'm not giving up."

"Then you'll have to do it without me. I'm your friend, but I'm not ending up on a cold slab."

Albert sighed. "All right. I understand."

He ended the call and stared at Erik. Nathan had deadly enemies, and this trouble at Moore Oil & Gas had bit a chunk off of the money owed Erik.

28

AFTER SEVEN THAT EVENING, Tori paced the floor of her apartment. Texting Sally hadn't done a bit of good, and contacting Lance or Jack seemed unethical considering their ages. But doing nothing went against everything she valued about resolving conflict. Her and Sally's relationship, their sisterhood, needed to be restored. From past experiences, Tori knew the longer Sally delayed in talking through a disagreement, the more the problem would fester. Not since their college days had Tori seen Sally so angry. Back then it was about accepting Nathan's marriage proposal three months after she and Erik had broken up. When Tori questioned the decision, Sally claimed jealousy, which had never been the case. Then and now, Tori's attempts to protect her friend had exploded in her face.

Staring at her phone and willing it to ring made the urgency worse. Her other option played out in her mind. Showing up at Sally's front door. If Tori confronted her face-to-face, would that invite disaster? Certainly Sally had changed her method of dealing with controversy since being a twenty-year-old.

Her doorbell rang before she could pick an option. A huge part of her wanted the person to be Sally, but a glance through the peephole showed Cole outside her door. Whatever did he want? He had a charm that was undeniably a distraction, and right now she needed wisdom about how to deal with her best friend, not an invitation to explore her feelings for an irresistible man. When he knocked again, she opened it.

"You didn't get enough of me today?" That might not have been the best opener.

He grinned, beautiful white teeth. "Of course not. Can I come in?"

She hesitated. He could have a new development, one that shouldn't be shared in the hallway of her apartment building. "I suppose so."

"What about my delightful personality is most irresistible?"

Couldn't help the giggle escaping her lips. "Umm. Probably your ability to leap tall buildings in a single bound."

"Good one." He glanced around her apartment. "Looks like you."

"How so?"

"A light-colored sofa. Gold and green pillows that match your eyes, and a coffee table on wheels, like a wagon. Shows you're creative."

Warmth crawled up her neck and settled in her cheeks. Great. He'd gloat over it. "What brings you here?"

"I have a request."

"Hope it's easy 'cause the day has me brain-dead."

He sobered. "Thought we could take a ride over to Sally's. See if we can talk her down off the ledge."

"Have you been reading my mind?"

"Is that a yes?"

She picked up her purse and cell phone. "I'll drive."

"I expected no less. The little red Charger it is."

On the way, they chatted about the weather and Max's and Cole's teen years making a buck at a drill site. Tori found it easy to banter with him, and driving gave her the sense of control she desperately craved.

"You've known Sally since college days?" he said.

"We roomed together. That's when she met Nathan."

"Ever any indication of him cheating on her?"

She shook her head. "A whirlwind relationship, but he always appeared devoted to her and the boys. Of course, now we know the truth. What about your friendship with him?"

"I thought good. Never saw it coming. He was the master of deceit. I feel like a fool, not even suspecting his . . . choices."

The situation weighed on her heart like a huge boulder. "How do we convince Sally of our sincerity? Because of our jobs, she's convinced we deceived her."

"Truthfully, Tori, I feel stupid that I didn't see it."

Misery was supposed to love company, but knowing Nathan had fooled so many people didn't make her feel any better. "Me too. I realize sometimes men with power and money look for the next conquest, but I never thought it applied to Nathan."

"Our conversations were about business, Sally, and the boys." He paused. "I hadn't told you or Max this, but Nathan asked if I'd be interested in dating Anita. Said she was a fine woman, and we were well suited for each other."

"Jerk. All the while, he was . . ."

"Covering his tracks."

"Sounds better than what I was thinking. If he really didn't care for Anita and she was aware of it, then she has motive. But if Sally found out, she could have arranged it." Tori's stomach lurched with her own words.

"I want to think Sally is too obvious a suspect."

"Then there's Lawd. He's hiding something. Call it woman's intuition. Plus he had no reason to be on the rig."

"We'll see what the surveillance team finds. He's shady, but that doesn't pin murder on him."

Soon afterward, Tori and Cole stood on the Moores' front porch, waiting for Sally to open the door. Lance answered it. He stiffened at the sight of them and started to slam it, but Cole caught it with the toe of his boot. "Hold on. We aren't the bad guys."

"How do you figure? Who else would have gone to the media?" Lance set his jaw. "The news is killing Mom and Jack."

"I have no idea who leaked this. But Tori and I are your friends, and right now all of you need a support team. Someone bombed your dad's drill site, threatened him, and followed through with murder. Today another man was murdered who must have had knowledge about the crimes. What we're learning is as big a shock to us as it is to you. We have to pool our findings and end the upheaval. An investigation takes time, and it won't be over tonight or tomorrow."

Lance set his jaw. "I hate him."

"Tori and I understand. This is painful. Makes us angry. We want the truth now."

"I've been thinking . . . What if all we've learned is a crazy scheme to destroy Dad's reputation?" Lance leaned against the doorjamb. "Except I'm not a fool. He said those horrible things. He had the pics on his computer."

"Lance, do you want the truth or do you want to live with what you think you know? Which is it?"

Lance sighed with the weight of facing the world's evil without a weapon. He opened the door. "Mom's in the living room with Grandma and Grandpa. Jack's there too."

"Thanks," Cole said. "We'll solve this case and arrest the people responsible. I promise."

At the sight of Tori and Cole, Sally rose from the sofa, her eyes wide. "Didn't I make myself clear today? Lance, what were you thinking?"

Tori moved toward her. "We persuaded him to let us in. Don't you see, by staying away, how it looks like we contacted the media?"

Her dad stood. "You two have made my daughter's life a public spectacle. Because of your lack of good judgment, her and her sons' futures are in ruins, shattered by your thoughtless actions."

Tori recognized the closed portal of anger, and Mr. Brent staggered dangerously close. She eyed him, sympathizing with his ire. "You're wrong—very wrong—in your accusations. I'd never abuse my friendship with your daughter by exploiting a tragedy." She gave Sally her full attention. "My job is to find Nathan's killer, not to hurt any of you with what's been uncovered in the investigation."

"But I'm a suspect. Are you using me now?"

"No."

"Mom," Lance said, his voice strangely quiet. "If someone can hack Dad's pacemaker, that person can also find other things about him. Maybe those people who lost the lawsuit wanted to get even. Or maybe it's like the news said, and Anita Krantz had him killed. What about the man killed on the oil rig when CJ and Tori were there?" He folded her into an embrace, a rare sight. "We'll get through tomorrow and the next day. Then we'll move on. We have to be strong. You and Jack can grieve on the inside, but we have to fight on the outside."

Sally cried in his arms for several minutes before drawing back and lifting her chin. "You knew about your dad and his assistant."

Lance hesitated. When he started to speak, she shook her head. "I don't need to be shielded from the truth. But I love you for trying to protect me and your brother."

His eyes pooled. "Mom, I heard you crying last night, and I'm sorry you're hurt. I haven't been much of a son, but I'm stepping up to the plate now. You and Jack need me, and I won't let you down."

"Whoa." Jack's voice was strained, as though realization startled him. "You knew about Dad when we argued, and you still let me say rude stuff and everything. Sorry I punched you." He encircled his mom and brother.

"Sure, Bro. No problem."

So sad it took a death to strengthen what was left of the Moore family. Yet Lance's determination offered the help Sally and Jack needed.

"Sally, can Cole and I talk to you privately?" Tori said. Critical questions required putting her personal feelings aside.

"Nathan's office okay?"

"Sure." Tori and Cole followed her down the hall to the room where it all began. She shut the door, and they all stood.

Thinking like an investigator challenged Tori's every instinct when it came to Sally. If this weren't her dearest friend, she'd be in the same position as Max. He believed in Sally's guilt. Tori wanted the truth . . . and to learn her dear friend was innocent.

"Please, whatever this is about, get it over with," her friend said.

"I have to do this," Tori said. "It's my job. Did you arrange for the bombing of the oil rig and Nathan's murder?"

She pounded her fist on the desk. "How dare you even suggest I'd commit such atrocious crimes?"

"Calm down, please. I don't like asking these questions any more than you like hearing them."

Sally swung her anger at Cole and Tori. "I thought having friends to help me through the most devastating moment of my life was a good idea. How wrong I've been."

Tori wished she couldn't see the anguish in her eyes. "Do you want us to resign from the case so you can deal with strangers?"

"How many times are you going to ask the same question?" Sally buried her face in her hands. "I loved Nathan. I had nothing to do with his murder. I'm a widow who's learned her husband was unfaithful."

"Then you must comprehend the seriousness of why we had to have this conversation." Tori kept her voice even, firm. "Your responses are documented. Consider this a formality, not an accusation. If I were sick, you'd ask me how I felt and check my vitals. We're no different here. We need to check the temperature of this case, give you a clean bill of innocence."

Sally touched Tori's arm. "I am innocent." She turned to Cole. "I know both of you have reservations, but you'll find I'm not involved."

"We want to prove it beyond any doubt," Cole said. "That means we must ask hard questions."

"Promise me you'll tell me everything from now on. I can't handle learning things from the media."

Tori sensed her own weariness. "We'll do our best."

Sally closed her eyes and pressed her lips together. "I'm angry about the affair, and I ache because Nathan is gone. My sons are the most important thing in my life, and I'm not strong enough to take care of them."

"Lance and Jack need you," Tori whispered. "That looks like a good place to begin."

Sally glanced toward the room where her sons waited. "I'm going to start now."

Time for Tori and Cole to make their exit so the family could pull together. They said their good-byes and walked toward the door.

"Tori, Cole," Sally said. "If you didn't call the media, then who's responsible?"

A second flash of reality hit her. Max hadn't been himself . . . made some poor decisions lately. She wanted to be wrong, terribly wrong.

29

NEARING MIDNIGHT and Cole's body refused to give in to sleep. He wanted to deliberate the facts and push around the evidence. He crawled out of bed and sat at his laptop. Scrolling through the app store, he found one kids used for brainstorming school projects. He could draw circles, move them around, and connect them with lines. The US Marshals had the technology to explore evidence strategically, except he'd been out of the loop too long. Tomorrow he'd make an inquiry—update his tech savvy. The issues were now.

Sally Moore, Anita Krantz, and Franc Lawd held top billing as persons of interest.

In a red bubble, he typed in Nathan's name.

Sally seemed the most unlikely, unless she had the ability to hide her feelings and actions like her husband. He placed her name in a blue bubble with the word *betrayed* and drew a line to Nathan.

Anita Krantz was being tailed as a person of interest. Her

background showed a two-year marriage over ten years ago to a man who resided in New Mexico—remarried with four children. Anita's record was clean except for a speeding ticket in 2010. Cole placed her name in a blue bubble and typed *vindictive? pregnant* inside it.

The third blue bubble belonged to Franc Lawd. His interest in the Texas City drill site hadn't been determined nor whether he had motive to hack into Nathan's pacemaker. His Army background was spotless. Solid alibi during the sniper shooting. Cole typed *shady* in the bubble.

A nagging thought pinched his brain, a suspicion he hoped sprang from lack of sleep. If Lance had the know-how to bypass his father's security-protected computer, then he could have hacked into the devices. Terrible thought. But there nonetheless. The many confrontations with Nathan surfaced, how the youth's spiteful words and behavior had tested Nathan's and Sally's patience. With his dad out of the picture, Lance could play man of the house, and his mother's honor would remain intact. He'd never been in trouble outside of home, and his friends were good kids. Cole prayed to be wrong. He placed Lance's name inside a blue bubble with the words *wounded and immature*. Still, it'd be short of impossible for Lance to bomb the oil rig. He'd been in school during the crime. Cole relaxed slightly.

Then there was Jack, the sweet boy who adored his mother. Cole placed his name in another blue bubble, but there was really nothing to deliberate. Never gave Nathan or Sally an ounce of trouble, so he typed *caring and devoted*.

Nathan, you had everything. Why ruin your family and your repu-tation for one dirty weekend after another?

Cole typed in what they'd verified about the names in blue circles. The reason was critical, but the suspect most likely had deep psychological issues, ones that had festered over time. Sally and

Anita both fit that category. He was beginning to sound like Max. The brainstorming report looked sterile, cold, and unsympathetic.

Two separate crimes working against Nathan?

He read through the reports on the pipe bomb used at the drill site before Nathan's death. Although the investigation and further analysis showed the components could have been bought anywhere, he hoped a detail had slipped their attention.

Nothing. No fingerprints. No model numbers that led to a buyer. No signature matching other bombings. He made a note to widen the signature match search parameters.

A text sailed into his cell phone from Tori.

Thinking & need help.

Why aren't u asleep?

Same reason u aren't.

What's up?

Think I know who leaked 2 the media.

Who?

Call me.

Three days ago, he hadn't met Tori Templeton, and now they were in constant communication. She answered on the first ring.

"Fairly certain Max made the call," she said. "With the way his mind works, he'd justify releasing details of Nathan's affair."

"Here I thought Lance might have confided in one of his friends. Why do I think there's more you're about to tell me?"

"Have you checked the latest media report?"

"Not for about twenty minutes. What's going on?"

"Our names came up as part of a task force with Max, and he's the lead."

Cole groaned. "Excuse me while I pin a bull's-eye on my chest for the killer." He thought about the agent he wanted to respect. "He's decided the killer is Sally or Anita. Reasoning isn't far off, except he wants to stamp guilty without evidence. He obviously made the call before we talked to Lawd or the media would have wind of his interview too." Then it hit Cole. "He wants to go out with *hero* etched on his tombstone."

"Exactly. Max is acting on impulse, wanting to end his career with a huge punch. The only positive is the media is shoving the blame on the women, while the real killer laughs and relaxes."

Cole walked to the fridge for a Coke. "Giving us time to hunt him or her down."

"An edge anyway. I wish you'd known Max a couple of years ago. Spot-on in every case."

"Tori, this is what we signed up for—facing a killer and the barrel end of a weapon." He remembered one of his dad's sayings. "You heard me say Dad worked on an oil platform. Good money, but my mother was always afraid for him. He told her, 'A pilot who signs up to fly through the eye of a storm doesn't complain about turbulence.'"

"A wise man. Is he still living?"

"Retired and busy in Florida. Almost have to make an appointment with him and Mom to visit."

"Thanks. I needed a reminder of why I signed up for the FBI. For me it's the constant pursuit of keeping others safe through exposing criminals. What about you?"

"We have similar goals. Back to our case." Had Sally shared anything about Lance with Tori? "What's your take on Lance?"

"At first a little nervous about what we might find, but if his school reports are any indication, he's clear."

"His computer skills bother me."

"I know what you're thinking. If he could gain access into Nathan's laptop, then he could hack into his father's other devices."

Cole allowed silence to speak for him.

"I'll call Sally in the morning. See what I can find out."

"Are you sure? Because I can handle it."

"I volunteered."

The finality in her tone told him to back off. "Where are you with what we've uncovered?"

"For the record, I believe Anita Krantz is innocent. Nathan's charm matched his brilliance. Especially with women. I saw how he mesmerized Sally when she was dating another man, Nathan's best friend. Nathan convinced her this guy didn't love her like he did." Tori paused. "At the time he came to me in tears about his love for her. I thought I heard sincerity and told Sally about his visit, and I've never doubted his love until now. There was a time I thought he pushed for a wedding date, but that was my only reservation. My point is, I can see how he charmed Anita into being his mistress."

Cole read into the crisp tone of her voice. "Had he approached you?"

"Not in the way I sensed a problem. When my brother died, he counseled me. I appreciated his caring mannerisms, but when he asked if I wanted to talk over dinner, I refused. Told Sally, and she said he'd asked her opinion about it first. Never thought much more of it until now."

Cole sensed again his own attraction to the dark-haired beauty talking to him. The continuing doubts about a man he'd called friend bothered him tremendously. He pushed them aside. Answers would unfold, and he'd weigh in as an investigator who wore his game day shirt, like the ASAC. "All right. What about dealing with Max? If you're right about him alerting the media, I have reservations about working with him."

A deafening silence met him for a long moment. "Me too. One of us could be killed. I'll confront him first thing in the morning. I'll handle this interview. Max and I have been partners too long for me to let this slide. Cancer is no excuse to deliberately put others at risk, and he's already been warned."

"What about breakfast first? I can meet you at the office around six thirty and go from there."

"To talk the case and Max?"

"And eat."

She laughed lightly, and he enjoyed the musical sound. "Okay. See you then. Good night." The phone clicked in his ear.

He looked forward to having Tori to himself.

30

TORI WALKED the worn path to Kevin's grave. Calming night sounds soothed her heart, as they always did, and the blackness of night wrapped her in a cloak of peace. She stopped and closed her eyes, allowing herself to relive a distant memory from when she was nine and Kevin had treated her to ice cream.

"What flavor for you today, Princess Tori?"

"Vanilla." She giggled.

"Are you ever going to expand your horizons to taste the flavors of the kingdom?"

"Never, Sir Kevin." She took his hand. "With vanilla, I can add fruit or candy or syrup. Whatever I want to make it special."

Inside the shop, he chose three scoops of various flavors, and she ordered her favorite. Kevin pointed to a small round table for two in a corner. "What fairy tale suits you today, Princess Tori?"

She loved the way he told stories. His voice rose and fell according to the character and action, and he knew just when to pause or make a face. Once seated with her dish of vanilla ice cream drenched in pineapple syrup, she touched her chin with her finger. "I think Noah."

He lifted a brow as if he was surprised, though it was a common request. "Why? It's not a fairy tale."

"I love the way the animals were different, and God loved them all."

Tonight she could hear Kevin roaring like a lion and neighing like a horse. But her reason for selecting the story then and recalling it now revolved around her brother's idea that God loved every creature whether it used four legs or two, crawled on the ground, flew with the wind, or swam in the sea. How they looked or survived had no bearing. This was the God Kevin wanted her to find. And tonight she felt closer. Logic told her the overwhelming professional and personal messes in her life demanded an explanation. While deep inside, she craved something to wrap her tightly and never let go.

Was it foolishness, or had she begun to inch toward answers, toward finding God?

"Special Agent Templeton?"

She smiled and gazed into the familiar face of Officer Richards, his silver-gray hair highlighted by the streetlamp. "It's about time you called me Tori."

"I will, and for the record, Officer Richards sounds archaic."

"Can't do it. My mother would thrash me for not respecting your wisdom."

"At least you stayed away from calling me old."

She stood and hugged him, a first. "How are you? Your family?"

"Coasting. Son claims he's glad to be in the Navy. Talks of one day being a SEAL. Daughter can't see us until she's had two more weeks in rehab. Wife and I are enjoying the empty nest. Like being newlyweds again."

"Progress is important."

"And you?" he said.

"Working Nathan Moore's murder case and the bombing of his oil rig."

"Been following the news reports. Be careful. He sure has surprised a lot of folks."

"True. The investigation has us uncovering one revelation after another. And his wife is my best friend."

"I'm sorry. How is Mrs. Moore?"

"Dealing."

"That can be moment by moment." He wasn't a stranger to the heartache of family disappointments. "I'll leave you to your time with Kevin."

"Any sage advice before you go?" Silence enveloped them.

"Things are rarely only as they seem. Your case, the people in your life, even your thoughts and fears have a purpose. Good night, Miss Tori."

❈

Early the following day, Tori waved at Cole from the FBI office security entrance. She'd finally fallen asleep in the early hours of the morning, and when the alarm jarred her from peaceful oblivion, she'd wanted to throw it. The first thing that popped into her mind was breakfast with Cole. A sweet twinge of excitement followed. Whew, the man sent distraction whirling through her at the mention of his name. Or his voice. Perceptive and intuitive. Rugged good looks. Too many disturbances for one single woman. Was he seeing anyone?

Now she fast approached the man. He walked with a swagger that should be outlawed. "Morning," he said. "Hungry?"

Her pulse sped. "Starved. Where are we headed?"

"A breakfast café not too far from here, a mom-and-pop restaurant. Omelets, pancakes, and endless cups of coffee. You name it."

"Sounds healthier than my usual Venti Starbucks, which I haven't had yet, and a promise to start the day better tomorrow."

He swung a look her way that caused her to shiver to her toes. "The downside is falling asleep on the job."

Be professional . . . not distracted. "Did you see we have the court order to image Anita Krantz's personal devices?"

"Yep. A team will handle it later this morning."

Cole drove to the café, and they made small talk about lack of sleep. Until caffeine was locked and loaded into her body, she wasn't ready to discuss pressing matters—the bombing, two murders, and Max.

The moment Cole opened the door to the restaurant, the scent of bacon and eggs wafted around her, definitely intoxicating.

"Can we work here all day?" she said.

"I wish. They have to-go coffee, so we can keep fueled."

They scooted into a booth, and the server took their orders—omelets, sausage, bacon, fruit, and grits. She preferred grits with honey, but he swore the benefits of cheese and hot sauce. Too bad they weren't just friends sharing a meal instead of investigators. Tonight she'd sleep and stop this nonsense thinking.

"Are you dating anyone?" Cole said while they waited for their food.

Her stomach did a hip-hop dance. "Not currently. Why?"

"The obvious." He winked. "Am I in trouble?"

"Haven't decided. Is candid a prerequisite for a US Marshal?"

"I'll make sure it is."

She smiled and took a sip of coffee. "I'll think about it. Give me a reason why I'd want to date you after the case is over."

"Aside from my compelling good looks, wit, and charm?"

"You forgot ego."

He straightened his shoulders. "I'm a nice guy. Great friend. Loyal—"

"So's a cocker spaniel."

A grin spread over his face. "I'm giving you my excellent qualities first. Honestly, my experience with women slides downhill when I have to break a date because of work."

She'd been there too many times, until she decided the FBI and relationships were a disaster. "Typical of our jobs."

"My faith is important to me, and I know you attend church. Nathan told me."

Kevin, must you haunt me in death? "I haven't made a decision about God yet." The curious look on his face moved her to explain. "When my brother was dying, he made me promise to find God. That's why I'm in church, sorta regular."

"Many of us have taken the same quest."

She thanked the young man serving their food. Once he disappeared, she gazed into Cole's eyes. Not really sure what to think of this strange man. "You make it sound like a medieval journey."

"There's nothing old-fashioned or primitive about faith in God."

An uncomfortable chill left her with an ill feeling, the same feeling she'd experienced with Kevin when he talked about the God stuff. Hours ago, she wanted to learn more on her own. Not discuss it with anyone. "It's not my intention to be disrespectful of anyone's religion. Neither am I the type of person to jump on board a belief without first examining and analyzing every detail. Until then, the idea of God as Creator is a theory, which is totally different from faith." She held up her hand. "Faith is an acceptance of things without proof. But I need tangible evidence, the same way Max does in proving Sally's innocence." She closed her eyes and stared at her plate. "Guess you heard more than you bargained for."

Cole picked up his fork. "Those who doubt the most find the strongest faith. I'm still interested in Tori Templeton and her views about God."

"How did we get on this theological discussion?"

He poked a generous amount of eggs into his mouth. She took a lesser bite. "I asked if you were dating anyone," he said. "Headed uphill after that."

Tori nearly choked. "Remind me to call you when my life turns into a nightmare. I could use the optimism."

"I will. We needed breakfast conversation. What's the plan with Max?"

This she could handle. "He's violated our partnership and placed our lives in jeopardy."

"You're positive he leaked the info."

She nodded. "Ninety percent. He won't lie. His irrational way of thinking could have alienated us from Sally and the boys. As it is, our trust will need to be earned, and time is crucial."

Cole studied her. "You asked for an opportunity to handle the situation. But if we aren't able to control his behavior, I'll take matters into my own hands. You realize that, don't you?"

"Unfortunately I do." Tori pushed back her plate and wished she'd opted for a Starbucks Venti—alone.

The sound of texts broke the uncomfortable silence.

Cole read from his phone. "The wounded man from yesterday has a clean record. Only been working for Moore a few weeks. He said the men liked Ustach. All he knew. The additional background check on Preston Ustach came back clean."

A second report slid into their phones. She blew out her relief. "This is one I wanted to see, the results of staff interviews at Moore Oil & Gas."

They read the findings.

"Loyalty at its finest," Cole said. "Not a single disparaging comment." He looked at her with those amazing sky-blue eyes. Enough to cause a woman to forget her job.

"We have to be missing something."

"We'll dig deeper until evidence surfaces. Seriously, the consensus is the execs, office personnel, and janitors were aware that Nathan sometimes spent the night at the office, but all denied a woman kept him company."

"He probably flipped for happy hour on a regular basis to show his good-guy status." Her mind drifted to what the secret bedroom entailed. Fury danced across her senses. If she didn't put aside her animosity for Nathan, she'd be accused of not conducting a fair investigation.

No one had the right to take another person's life. Murder was a vicious crime, and while motivations could be understood, even create sympathy, it was still against the law.

Hopelessness did a number on her, but she recognized it and finished her coffee. Today would be different. First she'd talk to Sally and subtly ask about Jack's and Lance's schoolwork. Then she'd handle the matter with Max and make progress on the case.

31

TORI RELEASED A PENT-UP SIGH and set her cell phone on her desk before focusing on Cole standing in her doorway. "Sally says the boys are doing okay with the tutor. Miss their friends. I asked about them falling behind in classes that require a lab or in sports, and . . ." She folded her hands. "I feel like a weasel manipulating a conversation to get info about Lance."

"Was there another way?" he said.

"Not without raising Sally's suspicions. Anyway, she finally mentioned Lance's computer class and how the tutor was good for him because Lance enjoyed the one-on-one teaching. I wish it exonerated him, but it doesn't."

"We'll have to keep our eyes open."

Max arrived at the office forty-three minutes late. Tori spotted him in the hallway. His shoulders were slumped, and he seemed thinner. Was that possible from one day to the next?

"He's here," she said to Cole. "For his sake, I'd better be wrong." She cringed. "He should be in bed."

"Tori, how he looks will only get worse."

Flashes of Kevin's battle with cancer . . . A miserable memory. "I know. But he has to be held accountable. Stay here in case he contradicts me later."

Cole stepped aside so Max could pull a chair to Tori's desk. Wordlessly, the older man lowered himself onto it. "I spoke to Detective Hernandez, the HPD officer we met at the Moore home. He thinks we should have arrested Sally Moore. I despise being thought of as inept."

"Good morning," she said.

"Not today." His pale face alarmed her.

"We have no evidence to arrest Sally, and I have a question," she said. "Who leaked our findings to the media regarding confidential information about the Moore case? And our names as part of the task force?"

He snorted. "What does it matter? We need community support."

She refused to curb the antagonism pouring into her words. "I figured it was you. What were you thinking, Max? You gave details Cole and I assured Lance wouldn't be released unless absolutely necessary and certainly not without informing Sally and Jack first."

His eyebrows knit like tangled yarn. "I made the call for the good of the case."

"By breaking the trust of a teen?" She jammed her finger into his chest. "Then you give our names as the investigators? Oh, big guy, now you're the lead? That sounds impressive." She caught herself before her temper reached an irretrievable level. "You can have your honorable funeral, but the rest of us intend to work smart."

"Big deal." Max swore with gut-scraping force. "I'm the senior agent here."

"Only by age. Trust me, I'm going to the ASAC with this. You're working like a snot-nosed rookie."

"My last case, remember? He won't say a word."

Tori's neck flushed hot and color spiraled up. "Really? That's not true, and you know it. You're in stage 3 and that's still beatable."

"Right." Max's phone alerted him to a text. "There he is now. Did you file a complaint?"

"I didn't have to. Your call to the media received a lot of attention."

"Pardon me while I straighten this out." He slowly stood. "If I'm tossed off this case because of you, Tori, I have enough friends here who'll make your life miserable."

"I have no doubt." Her future with the FBI didn't rest on Max. Or were his friends higher up the ladder willing to squash her career? The thought shouldn't disturb her, but who was she fooling?

As Max disappeared down the hall, Cole lifted a cup of office coffee to his lips. "What's the bottom line here?"

The day had just begun, and already her mood hit zero. Wasn't Cole's fault. "The FBI is incredibly compassionate and generous when it comes to illnesses. I've known them to have blood drives and fund-raisers in hardship cases. Max could be encouraged to take sick leave or get a medical mandate where he'd have restricted duties and still receive his pay." She sighed. The fixer-upper in her wanted him well and working without problems. "Another option is a nonagent position. My guess is the ASAC will counsel him for his unprofessional manner or refer him to the Employee Assistance Program and the psychologist there."

"A few times yesterday I thought he was making progress."

"He's an angry shell about to explode." She offered a grim smile. "The FBI will get it worked out." *Get a grip.* "What about an interview at the hospital where Franc Lawd works?"

"Sure. I want to talk to Lance and Jack once they're finished with tutoring. As much as I like them, and the school states there aren't any problems, I want to make sure they aren't hiding anything."

She glanced at her watch. "If Max isn't back in thirty minutes, we can go without him."

"Are you willing to pay the piper?"

"I'm sitting here when there's a murderer on the streets."

Twenty-nine minutes later, Max made his way down the hall. No emotion on his face, only the pale-gray color of impending death.

"We're burning investigation time," he said. "I'm ready to end this case."

In what way, Max? But she resisted asking.

✿

Cole listened to the director of human resources at St. Luke's list Franc Lawd's commendable traits. "He's one of our most dedicated nurses." The director opened a file before her. "Conscientious and respected for his methods of care and comfort for each patient." She closed the document. "We have nothing in our records to discredit Mr. Lawd."

"Any problems with other employees?" Cole said. Tori and Max sat on either side of him, squashed like pickles in a jar.

"Not to my knowledge. If a problem existed, I'd be informed."

"What about friends?"

"Franc is quiet, introverted. Stays to himself."

"Absenteeism?"

"No, sir." She typed into her computer and peered at the screen. "He hasn't missed a day of work in over two years." She lifted her head and smiled, a little too sweetly. "He's here today."

Cole turned to Tori and Max. "Do you have further questions?"

Max rubbed his jaw. "He always works days?"

"Yes, seven to three."

Lawd had claimed to be with a friend when the rig was bombed and when Nathan was killed. If the surveillance team on him was unsuccessful in finding a link to the crimes, this interview had been pointless. If evidence didn't turn up soon, the label of *inept* would describe the task force.

They thanked the director and left the hospital. Lawd had a solid alibi for the murder of Preston Ustach, but Cole hadn't checked his name off the list yet. Tori appeared absorbed in her thoughts, as though filtering the interview through her own database.

"You're quiet," Cole said once they were in his truck.

"We're missing facts, and I don't like it. Makes me a bit feisty."

"What's new?" Max said. "Okay, I have a few things to say, and it's not easy. But if I don't unload now, it won't happen. ASAC could have put me out to pasture this morning, but he's given me another chance. You know the drill. This is my last case. Blah, blah. Short story is I'm not the man I used to be. I hurt. Can't breathe. Proved to myself at the oil rig that I can't run. Just want to die. Meaner than sin. I'm not a nice guy. Maybe never was. But I want to work this case. Another screwup and I'll be pulled off duty permanently. Best way for me to finish strong is for both of you to lead out. I have no patience or sympathy with anyone."

What a mouthful. From what he knew about Max, that was the closest Cole and Tori would ever get to an apology. "What is the next step in your cancer treatment?"

Max stiffened. "No more chemo or radiation after I'm done with this round. Why puke my guts out and have my insides burned? What quality is that?"

Tori touched his arm. "Don't you want to lengthen your life?"

"The meds already make me sick. I'm about to quit the treatments."

"I'll help you through this," Tori said. "You don't have to face cancer by yourself."

"Don't give me that stuff. Hate pity. Just help me not get thrown off this last case. What do you say, yardman?"

Cole lifted a brow, tired of Max's remarks. "Yardman?"

"Jeffers sound better?"

"I prefer Cole."

"I'll try to remember. An—"

Their cells alerted them to a notification. "What do we have, Max?" Cole said.

"Report in on Nathan Moore's personal and work cell phones. Business calls show several to Anita Krantz. Figures. Others appear work related, but the FIG is tracking each one, date and time. Personal call records show a few to the Krantz woman. One suspicious incoming number shows up five times since the oil rig bombing leading up to his death, placed by a burner phone. The FIG has the location—all downtown."

"By any chance near St. Luke's?" Tori said. "That would give us basis for a search warrant. Franc Lawd is shady, hiding something."

"Give me a moment." Max coughed.

Cole hated to hear him, knowing it came with a vicious countdown.

"According to the report, the burner was located within a three-block radius of St. Luke's. Tori, looks like we should go after a search warrant."

Cole knew a devious mind covered his tracks. "He's smart enough not to keep the makings of a pipe bomb in his apartment or any link to hacking Nathan's pacemaker. Our best bet may be taking down his alibi. But things just don't make sense. Why would a nurse with no history of EPA activism be involved in a bombing or murder?"

32

ALBERT DIPPED A CHOCOLATE BUTTERMILK DONUT into a cup of coffee rich with cream while his son endured physical therapy. Albert had tried to watch Erik attempt the painful movements, but the anguish on his face proved more than Albert could handle. Ironically, he filled his stomach with donuts and coffee instead of becoming sick listening to Erik's cries of defeat. A raspberry-filled beckoned him from the display case. Indulging in a third donut as a reward for confirming Special Agent Tori Templeton's address was due him. He'd figured out a few things in his senior years, and one was surfing the Internet to find an address. Early in the morning, he'd have a caretaker look after Erik while he did some snooping. See about a special surprise for Tori Templeton. The woman had been friends with Nathan and Sally since college days, and she might figure things out.

The two men who showed up with her at the Moores' home

were investigators too. He'd learned their names from the media, and finding their addresses wouldn't be hard. Then he'd figure out what to do with them. Sally didn't need smart friends to spoil his plans while Erik's life swirled down the toilet.

His cell phone rang with the first few bars of the Bee Gees singing "Stayin' Alive." Erik said the song was his, so Albert changed his ringtone to please him. What benefit were the lyrics for a man too young to die? Albert recognized the number as Walt Hanna's and answered on the second ring.

"Aren't we finished?" he said, tired of dealing with this guy.

"I've been watching the news and thinking. Feds are crawling all over this, and I need to protect myself. Talking to the FBI may be in my best interest."

Albert glanced around at the busy bakery and walked outside, leaving his coffee and donut. "You were paid eight grand and I didn't give you the okay."

"Facts are facts, old man. You hired me to kill a man, and he's dead."

Albert froze. He'd tried to avoid thinking about this. "Bank's closed."

"How do you figure?"

"We made a deal."

"How much is it worth for me to keep my mouth shut?"

Albert swallowed his ire. "Look, punk, if I go down, you and I will be in matching cells."

"I have my plea memorized. You paid me to help you with your computer. I had no idea what I was doing."

"With your record? I've seen the charges."

A sardonic laugh erupted. "Try it. Wanna bet how it turns out? I need another ten grand."

"Don't think so."

"Your son is half-dead. Wouldn't take much to finish him off. Tell you what—I'll give you twenty-four hours to empty your bank account of ten big bills. I'll be in touch."

He ended the call.

Albert stole a look around him. The punk didn't have murder in his blood . . . only a love of money. His excuse for hacking Nathan's pacemaker was flimsy at best, but taking chances wasn't part of Albert's game. He snorted. Idiot. In fact . . . An idea formed.

With a hard shake of his nerves, he returned to the café. His coffee and partially eaten donut still at his table. Erik had another hour left of PT.

Back to normal. Been looking after his son since his wife left them when Erik was six months old. Never understood why when she acted so devoted to both of them. Didn't matter now. He cared for his son like he was a baby again. Fed him. Diapered him. One day after another. Instead of anticipating a growing child, he dreaded each new day, as it moved them closer to the date on Erik's death certificate.

Hanna's phone number was in Albert's contact list, a burner phone according to him. Hacking skills were the only brains he had. Arrogance hit the top rung. Albert had met him a year ago on his postal route, just before retirement. The guy had been sitting on his front porch, working on his laptop. Claimed he'd just lost his job because his computer skills were above his boss's.

"What are your plans?" Albert said.

"Hack into the company's secure files and spread the info to the world."

"Can you do that?"

"Sure."

Albert filed the information into his brain until he needed it. Sitting alone, humor rumbled through him and a few people stared. Albert didn't care. He texted the man who thought he had intelligence.

I know where u live. Still got that new Toyota?

A response sailed into his phone.

We aren't done, old man.

He finished his donut and gulped his coffee before driving to the man's address. He surveyed the one-story brick home. The front door opened, and a red-haired woman stepped out with a little girl about four years old. Albert snapped photos of both, then texted them. That would end the threats.

Albert had brilliance hidden beneath his old-man facade. He'd grease the axle on this wheel to his benefit.

33

AFTER LUNCH, Cole grabbed his laptop and took up residence in an FBI interview room to pore over the case's data. Tori and Max used their cell phones to keep up on details, but he preferred a bigger screen. Knowing they were receiving the same reports, he scheduled a meeting in his makeshift office. Tori texted she'd be a few minutes late.

Max shuffled into the interview room in the middle of a coughing fit. The man would collapse before admitting defeat. When he gained control, blood stained a tissue. After tossing it in the trash, he covered it with paper. "Help me out here. Tori isn't to know about this."

"You have my word. How are you going to keep it from her?" He leaned toward Max and motioned for him to wipe his mouth. Blood had trickled from the right corner.

"I have my ways." He tossed another tissue into the trash. This time Cole covered it. "She won't watch me suffer like her brother."

"He died of cancer a couple of years ago?"

"Right." Max slumped into a chair. "Before that her mother had breast cancer and was a few years out in remission when Kevin didn't make it. Look out for her, will you? She takes too many chances. Seems like her fear of cancer is bigger than taking on an angry cartel." He half smiled. "Tori's more of a daughter than my own. She's a good agent, a real team player." He shook his head. "I remember about a year ago, we were working a lead on a crazed killer who had made his way into the tunnel system downtown. She chased him while screaming at people to get out of the way. He grabbed a female hostage from one of the stores, and our girl talked him down. She turned those green eyes into liquid charm. No one got hurt."

"But your case isn't hopeless. You've got a lot of fight in you."

"Tori said the same thing."

The inner workings of Tori Templeton. Her doubts about faith held stronger ground, while they discounted her need for a Lord who loved her unconditionally. Cole wrestled with telling Max how he felt about her, the soft and vulnerable woman hidden beneath a dedicated investigator's exterior. But she bustled down the hall, ending any confessions.

"Sorry I'm late," she said. "Had calls. Took one from Sally. She needed a sounding board with media bothering her and the funeral tomorrow. So where do we begin?"

Cole gestured for her to take charge. "I'd say at the beginning. Go for it."

Her eyes shone with thanks, and he was reminded of how much she meant to him. "Attorney Jacob Farr's files give no indication of pending lawsuits or questionable activities. Neither did he have a name or names as to who Nathan might think was responsible. He'd arranged the extra bodyguards for his family but not himself.

If he had some underhanded business dealings going on, Farr was not aware. The reading of the will is Tuesday morning." She lifted her chin. "Why protect his family, those he planned to abandon, and not himself? I think there's a huge part of this yet to uncover. Nathan is not the man I thought I knew, but he wasn't the devil either."

Cole offered more information. "The court transcript from the lawsuit is straightforward. An anonymous call to the EPA claimed Nathan was illegally dumping backflow water. Proven false. End of discussion. But Nathan suspected activists were behind the threats. Nothing has turned up there yet, but I want to talk to a couple on the list." He wanted to review every name, read every question and answer.

Max unwrapped a stick of gum and popped it into his mouth. "When I started working the bombing, first thing on the agenda were activists in Texas and the Gulf region. When the investigation turned up zilch, we looked at the entire country. Although plenty would like to take the credit, we had no proof. Nathan Moore's murdered, and our only hope of an informant is killed. I have an idea, a bit of a far shot. Tori, can you get the FIG to widen the search for persons who are not just protesting environmental issues, but antigovernment and anti–big business too? The list will keep us busy, but we're missing something."

"On it." She typed an e-mail for the request, then rubbed her left wrist.

Cole scrolled through the documents on his laptop. "Do we have anything from the imaging of Anita Krantz's personal devices?"

Max turned his head to cough before speaking. "Tori and I have the report. I'll forward the findings. Sorry you weren't copied."

A new Max? "Information we can use?"

"Possibly," Tori said. "But nothing connected to the hack. Some texts indicate power lunches and late-night rendezvous points with the distinction of 'after the others leave.' References to 'our office.' She sent an e-mail informing Nathan that Preston Ustach wanted a meeting regarding a potential problem at the Texas City drill site, and Nathan told her to set it up."

"Was she present during the session?" Cole said.

"No. She confirmed Preston and Nathan met at the office twice—on the Friday before the bombing and again the afternoon before he was killed, but she was not privy to what transpired. Security camera footage backs up the first time stamp, but not the second. I phoned her, and she claimed Nathan hadn't confided in her. If there's a follow-up paper trail, we haven't found it. Is she cooperating or covering up? Both men are dead."

Cole typed into his laptop. "Next question is about Ustach. Would he have shared with anyone what he didn't tell us or the agents who investigated the bombing?"

"We can begin with his mother." Max pulled out another stick of gum. "Hate this stuff. Rather have a cigarette."

The words tumbled out of Cole's mouth before he could stop them. "My granddad used to call cigarettes nails in a man's coffin." He held up his hand. "I'm done with the lecture. Let's get back to what we're doing. Nathan's personal cell had a few flags—late-night calls to Anita Krantz and several from untraceable numbers, one with a geo-stamp of Krantz's address. Whoever's seeking his attention preferred contacting him between the hours of 12:30 and 3:30 a.m. Those were traced to a burner phone."

Tori took over. "When I talked to Sally a few minutes ago, I asked her about the calls. She said Nathan told her they were from men at the drill sites, and he always took them outside their bedroom."

"Dead end there unless the caller switches to phoning Sally," Max said. "Add to your request for the security footage at Moore

Oil & Gas to include every person who came in and out over the last four months."

"Another thing," Tori said, "and it's on our list. I had a background completed on the protection company hired to guard the Moore home. Every employee comes highly recommended. Strict guidelines, and the ones working now for Sally have an impressive record."

"Cole—" Max swallowed hard as though stifling a cough— "remind me of what you and Nathan talked about that last morning?"

"Hiring additional bodyguards because he and his family had been threatened. His concern lay with his family. He didn't reveal the wording of the texts or the calls. He just said, 'Another threat.' According to Nathan, when he attempted to reply, no one answered."

"What else did he say?"

Cole had relived their conversation at the gym a dozen times, searching for a clue to his death. "I suggested he send Sally and the boys out of town until the matter was resolved. Nathan said no. He'd worry more about them away. Just before we headed to the showers, he took a phone call, said it was the office." He focused on the cell records listed on his laptop screen. "Looks like Anita made the call."

"No surprises there." Max turned to Tori. "What else do we have?"

She scrolled through her phone. "Must be our lucky day, or unlucky depending on what we can pull from these cell phone records."

Cole hadn't exonerated Anita Krantz, but he'd been wrong before. "Does Anita have any link to the EPA?"

Tori spoke up. "None that we've noted, nor to any activists."

Cole read his notes, thinking. "Lawd's attorney hasn't released the name of his alibi. Do you suppose he had to lay the groundwork?"

Tori massaged her neck muscles. "The man we met was not the same man the director of St. Luke's HR described."

"No ring on the director's left hand," Max said. "Did a little probing. My cousin works at the hospital, says Lawd is popular with the women. Not quiet or a loner."

"Did you ask if he dated the director?" Cole said.

"Yep. My cuz said not to her knowledge."

"Most of his coworkers are women," Tori said. "I found him nauseating and lacking in character."

Cole leaned back in his chair. "I have a name linked to an activist that I want to check out. Then there's Franc Lawd or Anita Krantz. Someone is funding these crimes." He drummed his fingers on his laptop. "I'm going to call Mrs. Ustach, see if there's anything she's remembered."

"Can I?" Tori said. "She might find talking to a woman easier than a man."

"Sure." He wrote her number on a slip of paper and handed it to her.

"Mrs. Ustach, this is Special Agent Tori Templeton from Houston's FBI. I'm working with US Marshal Cole Jeffers, whom you met the day of your son's death. We are so sorry about your loss, and we want to find the person who's done this. Do you mind if I put this call on speakerphone?" Tori smiled into the phone and pressed Speaker after the woman agreed. She laid her phone on the table between them.

"Are you alone?" Tori's tone offered compassion.

"No, ma'am. My daughter's here. She just made coffee. I'd offer you a cup if you were here."

Tori tilted her head. "Thank you. Call me Tori, please. How are you doing today?"

"Confused. Angry. Sad. How could God do this to my family? We've all served Him faithfully."

The woeful tone of Mrs. Ustach's voice yanked at Cole's heart.

"We'll find out who's behind the crimes committed against your family."

The woman sighed. "But it won't bring Preston back. I keep looking at the photos, football awards, sweet pictures he drew when he was a boy, all the cards he gave me on special occasions, and the gifts. It's comforting even though I'm crying."

"You have wonderful memories. Those will help in your sorrow."

Cole wanted to take Tori's hand, but not with Max there. Listening to Mrs. Ustach reveal her gut-wrenching emotions was part of the job . . . unfortunately.

"I lost my brother two years ago," Tori said. "And when sadness threatens to overtake me, I remember the good times. You can do that too."

"I've always heard there is something very wrong about a child passing before a parent. Oh, to have taken the bullet instead of my precious boy."

Tori blinked back tears. "I talked to him for a while just before it happened. He had a quick smile. Handsome too."

"Preston looked like his dad. Never could resist that smile. He was a charmer."

"He asked me to dinner."

"He'd have taken you someplace nice. Gotten all dressed up. Worn a jacket. Shined his boots."

"Tell me your favorite story," Tori whispered.

"Are you sure?"

"Yes, please."

"Preston was eleven years old and playing baseball. He hadn't hit his growth spurt yet and spent a lot of time on the bench. He refused to give up. Practiced with his dad until he had his catchin' down good and could slam a ball hard. He kept pestering the coach to put him in. It was the bottom of the last inning and his team was down four runs. No hope at all. The coach told Preston to send the ball into glory. And he did. He hit the first ball pitched to him and smacked it out of the field. After that the coach let him bat all the time. Called my Preston his glory-hitter."

Tori glanced at Cole, her eyes watery and red. "Thank you. It's a lovely story. Mrs. Ustach, had he mentioned anything about the oil rig bombing or being in danger?"

"At the time I didn't think anything about his comments. Preston was always on the side of the folks who were hurting, and he hated the idea of what happened at the drill site. And Mr. Moore's death. He said he suspected a man who'd gotten past security. The man lied about something Mr. Moore had done and asked a lot of questions about the company. Preston escorted him off and told him never to come back."

Franc Lawd. But he had an alibi.

"Did your son give the man's name?"

"No. Refused to talk about it once he saw I was scared for him, but he said the FBI were on it. They'd get it handled and for me not to worry." She sighed. "I'm no fool. He had proof and was killed for it."

"Did Preston have lots of friends there?"

"That's hard to say. Preston liked everybody, but he only buddied up to Jose Aznar. That dear man is so upset. I asked him if he knew anything that could help you folks, but he said no."

Cole wanted another conversation with Aznar.

"Did he ever mention a man by the name of Franc Lawd?"

"No. I'm sorry."

"Mrs. Ustach, you've been a big help by talking to us. I promise you, we will find out who has done this to your family."

"Honey, nothing will bring my Preston back. I know where my boy's at, and he's a glory-hitter in heaven. But whoever's done these awful things needs to be stopped. That's you and your friends' job."

34

ALBERT EASED ONTO a worn chair in Erik's small bedroom. Before his son got sick, Albert had used the room as an office to pay bills and keep his finances in order. He wanted Erik in the master bedroom, but he refused.

In the shadows, Erik's face looked gray and frightfully thin.

"Anything I can get you? Ice chips? Some soup?"

His son glanced at the window. "I'm good, Dad. Feel decent today." He scooted himself up in the bed. "Would you mind opening the blinds? Feels like a tomb in here."

Albert blinked back a tear and stumbled on his way to the window.

"You're drinking a lot. I smell it on you constantly."

"Just a little to soothe my nerves."

"My fault. You need something to help you through this. Sorry to have mentioned it."

Albert sighed. "It's all right." He adjusted the light filtering into the room. "That okay?"

"Perfect. You know, I've been thinking about Nathan. We had some good times growing up. Miss him. Sure hate what happened."

Albert stuck his hands in his pockets. "I don't remember anything worth holding on to about the man."

"Dad, sit by me. Let's talk about this. Nathan's gone, and I hate the bitterness in you."

Albert nodded and found his old spot on the chair. "What do you want me to say?"

Erik closed his eyes. "That you forgive him. I have."

"Not sure I can put aside the past."

"Think about it, will you? I don't want my life to end knowing you're bitter about Nathan. I've let go."

Albert swallowed hard. The nagging thought persisted . . . the one keeping him up at night. He'd contracted Hanna to hack the pacemaker, but then he realized Nathan's death wouldn't solve a thing. In fact, it made matters worse. While Nathan was alive, Albert could continue to talk to him, make him see his negligence was sending Erik to an early grave. All Albert wanted was the money owed to his son to pay for the treatments in Germany.

"Dad, Nathan left a widow and two sons. The situation is sad for Sally but even worse for those boys who won't have a father. I've always had you, and they will have no one."

"I'll think about it."

A chill swept through him again. Could he have been drunk and given the go-ahead to execute the hack—execute Nathan—and not remember?

35

AT FIVE THIRTY THURSDAY EVENING, Cole and Tori were walking to the parking lot with Max. A long day of reading reports, discussing them, and ordering interviews and backgrounds. Cole had spent time on the EPA activist theory, talking to the investigative team who'd worked it—including Max—and come up dry.

"I want to interview Dale Bentley about the bombing. He's not on the FBI list but on my personal one. A few years ago, I arrested him in a bombing case involving a state representative. Did eighteen months."

"Why?" Max stopped on the pavement.

"May be a long shot—"

"If you don't mind, I'll let you handle the business this evening. I need a good night's sleep."

"No problem. Sleep hard, and we'll work in the morning."

"Text me a pic of the confession." He laughed, but it sounded forced.

"What can I do?" Tori said. "Need me to pick up dinner?"

"I'm not an invalid." Max's voice held the familiar growl. "Just get the job done. End this mess." He slowly walked to his car.

"How do we convince him that he needs more treatment?" Tori said.

"Wish I knew. Are you going with me?"

"Oh yes. Your long shot might be an ace."

He smiled. "I'll drive. Once we're finished, I want to talk to the Moores, show them pics of Franc Lawd, Preston Ustach, and the wounded man. Possibly Bentley. We'll see how the interview goes."

Cole parked his truck at the apartment complex where Bentley lived. The building needed a paint job, broken windows replaced, and six dump trucks on duty for eight hours to haul away the junk. Drug dealers negotiated while smoking the disgustingly sweet stench of pot in the midst of filthy children who reeked of urine and lack of parenting.

"Did Bentley work alone in the past?" Tori said.

"Had a partner, but he died in the takedown."

"What else?"

"Originally from Phoenix. Moved here fourteen years ago. In and out of jail for drugs. Suspected in the murder of a dealer from Honduras. He talks smack when it comes to government interference in his lifestyle. Goes by Big D. The rig's IED is similar to his signature." Cole opened the truck door and Tori followed.

They climbed steps to a second-floor apartment where Bentley was talking to three other guys—all drinking beer. Could be a problem in the interview.

"Dale Bentley," Cole said, flashing his badge.

"We've met." He took a long drink and squeezed the can before tossing it over the railing. A real powerhouse. "Need to make your quota, Mr. US Marshal?"

"FBI Special Agent Templeton and I need to ask you a few questions."

Bentley glared down his long nose. Brow and ear piercings gave him the . . . stereotypical look. "Whatcha want?"

"We're investigating a bombing and two murders connected to Moore Oil & Gas."

"Don't waste your time talkin' to me. I've been out of town until this afternoon. You're lucky. Just unloaded my stuff."

"Where have you been?"

"Phoenix. My mother died."

"Sorry to hear that. When did you leave Houston?"

"Three weeks ago. Had to take care of business with my mother."

"Who can I contact there for verification?"

He gave Cole a name and phone number. Bentley smiled at Tori. "You're hot, girl. Come on back without the cowboy, and you can welcome me home. We could have a good time. The door's unlocked."

"I'll remember the invitation."

❊

Cole and Tori entered the Moore home. He wished he had better news, but the more they explored the crimes, the higher the body count.

Sally escorted them to the kitchen, where the boys were talking with their grandparents. Although the facade was in place, distrust streaked her eyes. He couldn't blame her. Everything about a man she'd loved had crumbled.

"You two okay?" Lance said. "Heard the latest about the shooting in Texas City." The teen had experienced too much tragedy. "It keeps getting worse."

Cole hid his exhaustion. "We're on it. Like you, Tori and I want arrests made." He greeted Kit and Wes. Distrust there too.

"Would you like iced tea, coffee?" Sally said, her tone absent of hospitality.

Tori seemingly ignored the emotional ice between them and hugged her. "No. We won't stay long. Thought you'd like to hear about our findings."

"All of them?"

"No, Sal, only what we can relay." Tori scanned those present. "No reason any of you shouldn't hear this."

"Sit down." Sally pointed stiffly to the empty chairs at the table.

Cole and Tori obliged, and he began. "Cell phone records indicate several texts and calls to Nathan's personal phone came from a burner. We assumed this before requesting the report. Nothing on your devices raised a red flag."

"What about Anita?" Sally said.

"Still under investigation. To date, we have no evidence implicating her in the crimes. I'm concerned about your welfare—of the whole family, including Kit and Wes. After what's happened in Texas City, the consensus is the people responsible for the crimes are not taking chances on being identified."

Wes cleared his throat. "What are you suggesting? The bodyguards Sally hired are stationed 24-7 outside the house. They ID all those coming and going. The boys and Sally don't go anywhere without them. They keep a log and monitor Kit's and my business too."

"I'm not comfortable with the risk assessment. Once Tori and I are finished here this evening, I'd like for you to consider witness protection until this is over."

"With the US Marshals?" Sally said. "Cole, we haven't been

threatened to the point I want to leave my home. I appreciate the suggestion, but not yet. I have Nathan's funeral arrangements. If we receive any threats, then I'll agree to the boys. But I'm not going anywhere until my husband is buried."

"The killer won't send you his schedule or make it convenient for you. How would you feel if something happened to one of the boys?"

"The bodyguards are sufficient. They have military backgrounds. We have taken precautions to ensure our safety." Sally's voice rose. "Boys, what are your thoughts?"

"No," Lance and Jack echoed.

He sighed, wanting to get them all as far away from Houston as possible. "You're still under suspicion, and refusing additional protection might not look favorable. Those who believe you're guilty will use your stand against you."

She lifted a brow and her blue eyes emitted anger. "I'm fully aware of my status."

Cole sighed. He wanted proof to exonerate her. "I understand. If taking advantage of a federal program is out of the question until after the funeral, then you should consider further precautions."

"Like what?" Sally dug her fingers into her palms. "Are you insinuating I'm shirking my responsibilities?"

"I'm a friend who doesn't want another crime hitting this household."

Sally rallied the boys' attention. "Your current tutoring will continue until arrests are made. You are not permitted to leave the house. Understood?"

The boys nodded.

"And if you choose to leave, then you're looking at me shipping you out of state. I want your lives to be as normal as possible, but if I learn about your trying anything, sneaking out, then it's over."

Cole used his phone to display pics of Lawd, Ustach, Bentley, and the wounded man. He handed it to Sally. "Do you recognize any of these people?"

"The blond man is the one I recognize from the news as being killed yesterday. But I've never seen the others." She passed the phone to Lance, who glanced at it, then gave it to Jack.

Neither boy had seen the men before.

"Boys, what are your friends saying about this?"

"It's bad, CJ," Jack mumbled. "Bully stuff. Don't want to talk about it."

Cole studied Lance. "How are you handling it?"

"Trying to ignore them." He jutted his jaw. "Being home stops me from getting into a fight. But I know who they are."

Some kids wore cruelty like a suit of armor. "Do you have any information that can help us make arrests?"

The older boy peered at his mother.

"Lance, answer Cole. No more secrets in this house."

Lance squirmed, confirming Cole's suspicion. "I went through Dad's trash sometimes. His habit was to shred it last thing at night, so while he and Jack did the homework bonding thing, I'd take a look."

What? "Why didn't you come forth with this sooner?"

His gaze fell to the table and then to his mother. "Dad's gone. Just wanted all of us to get past it."

Wouldn't do a bit of good by tearing into Lance. "What did you find?"

He rose from the table. "They're in my room. I'll get them."

While they waited for Lance, Sally squared off with Jack. "Are you keeping anything from Cole or me?"

"No, Mom. Promise. Sure see why Lance was always mad at Dad."

Cole held his comments until the older boy returned. "Before I look at what you have, here's a question. Did you ever confront your dad about any of the things you suspected?"

Tossing two crumpled pieces of paper onto the table, Lance sank into a chair. "Read these, then I'll answer your question. I got the one on the left after the bombing. The second one the night he died. Pulled it from his office before the police arrived. He hadn't run his trash through the shredder yet."

Cole smoothed out the papers. Both had been typed. He picked up the earlier one.

"Read them aloud." Sally's voice hit a high pitch.

"All right," Cole said. "'Do what is right before it's too late.'" He laid it on the table and read the second one. "'I gave you many chances. You think you and your family are safe. Wrong. Now deal with the consequences.'" He stared into Lance's face. "I'll need to take these, have them analyzed."

Lance rubbed his temples. "Figured so."

Cole folded the papers and gave them to Tori. She pulled a plastic bag from her purse and dropped them inside.

"Why did you hold on to them?" Cole said to Lance.

"The first one didn't bother me. Thought it was a prank. By the time I read the second one, Dad was already dead. I was afraid Mom had done it and wanted to protect her. In answer to your other question . . . No, I didn't ask Dad about his stuff."

"And you didn't find envelopes?"

"No, sir. I was always in a hurry."

Sally moaned. "Son, do you have more secrets? Because if you're withholding information, you're also protecting the killer."

Lance whitened. "No, Mom. I swear. Nothing else. I want Dad's killer found. Really. I want our lives back."

Cole would like to shake this stubborn family. "One more incident, and I'll insist on witness protection."

"Okay." Sally's lined face showed she understood the seriousness. "As much as I value my privacy, I'll request two of the bodyguards be inside the house at all times . . . just in case. And that means a total of eight bodyguards will know my business. I'll live with it. At least they work long shifts, so more people won't be involved."

How much more could this family take?

36

TORI OPENED HER EYES AT 5:55 A.M. The doorbell rang again. Never good in the life of a special agent who worked violent crime. Grabbing her robe, she slipped her arms inside while racing to the door. She peered through the peephole. An older man with glasses smiled. Gray hair and spider eyebrows gave him a comical look, but not enough appeal to open the door. He seemed familiar, but she failed to recall from where.

"What do you want?"

"My name's Albert Weiman. You attended college with my son, Erik. I'd like to talk to you about Sally Moore."

"I remember Erik. Why are you here so early in the morning, and what does this have to do with Sally?"

"She gave me your address when I expressed—"

"She wouldn't give anyone my address without my permission."

"But she did. I apologize for the early hour. This is the only time I have while my son's with his caretaker."

Tori rested against the door. "Are you referring to Erik?"

"Yes. He has MS. In bad shape."

She studied him more carefully. "Again I ask, why are you here?"

"Erik asked that I give you his condolences for Nathan's death personally. He said the two of you had dated before you were engaged to Nathan."

"Erik and I?"

"Yes."

Erik had dated Sally until Nathan showed up on the scene. "That's not true."

Albert rubbed his face. "You are Tori Templeton?"

"Yes."

"And you're a nurse? Work at Methodist Hospital?"

The man was delusional. Sally had worked prior to Lance's birth, but at a doctor's office. Now pity washed over her. "I'm not in the medical field. Sally is the RN."

"I must have the wrong person. Erik said he'd seen you at physical therapy."

"No, sir. You have me confused with someone else."

"Okay. Sorry. I'll tell Erik you didn't want to hear from him. Neither do you remember him."

"I didn't say either of those things." To think she could have slept awhile longer.

"Can I come in and talk?"

"No. Can I call someone to escort you home?"

"I'm not crazy, Miss Templeton. I simply wanted to personally express my sympathies. If you'll let me in, we can talk."

His last statement triggered her alarm button. "Sir, I suggest you return home." Tori said nothing else.

The older man shook his head and disappeared.

The conversation vexed her. Was Erik really suffering from MS?

If that were true, she'd want to see him for friendship's sake. But how did Albert Weiman find her? Definitely a question for Sally.

She showered and drove to meet her mother at the Starbucks near the FBI office for their weekly, civil mother-daughter time. Mentally labeling it as civil was Tori's way of soft-pedaling Mom's constant prying into her business. But after viewing Lance and Sally last night, Tori had resolved to do a better job with their relationship. The two had DNA in common and shared a last name. Plus, they were survivors of the Templeton family, and the glue kept them from verbally destroying each other.

Arriving first, Tori purchased her Venti black and Mom's grande skinny mocha with soy milk and a glass of water. She secured a table and sat where she'd see Mom enter and anyone else who came through the front door. Her thoughts turned to the two notes in her purse. As soon as she made it to the office, she'd send them to the lab.

She doubted if much could be lifted or if any DNA could be traced, but it was worth a try.

Promptly at 6:55, the striking middle-aged woman, known as Valerie to her friends, waved at Tori. Mom's figure rivaled most thirty-year-olds', and she'd inherited genes that kept her skin flawless. Tori's skin hadn't gotten to the point where she'd show the telltale signs of age, but she hoped for the best. Both had dark wavy hair and the same green-gold eyes.

Mom wore jeans and three-inch heels. Nicely.

Tori wore a navy-blue pantsuit and sensible shoes for the day's work—and Nathan's funeral.

Something was terribly wrong with the picture—Tori should be the cute and fashionable one, not old and out-of-date.

Grow up, Tori.

When she wasn't being immature and jealous of Mom's good looks, she admired her mother's optimism and unending stamina. Kevin had said they were alike, and he'd been right. They both journeyed from one crusade to the next with their type A personalities and love of people. Tori stood and gave Mom a real hug and spent a few extra seconds silently letting her know how much she loved her.

"Are you tired, dear?" Mom's smile deepened her dimples as they sat at the table. "Are you certain helping to solve Nathan Moore's murder is a good idea for you? The years you've spent with the family have to make the case difficult. I mean, are you stressed?"

"Sort of. It's complicated." She cringed. "I forgot you hate that phrase."

"Drives me insane, and I certifiably don't have far to go." She took a sip of water. "'It's complicated' says either I'm too stupid to figure it out, or I'm not in the inner circle for privy information."

Not a great way to start their time together. "Sorry. I can't talk about the particulars."

"Oh, I know the FBI has specific protocols." She tilted her head. "My concern is for you and the pressure of work and friends suffering with tragedies. And don't get me going on the danger." She swiped beneath her eyes. "Now I'm sorry. I keep thinking about the man killed at the oil rig . . . the pic of you covered in blood. The FBI should offer coping skills for those who care for a special agent."

Mom's words melted her pride. "Thanks. I'll be all right. This hasn't been an easy ride, and I imagine it'll get bumpier."

"I'll change clothes and be at the funeral this morning."

"Sally will need all the support she can get." Tori rubbed her left wrist.

"Dear, have you hurt yourself?"

"No. Just habit."

"Are you sure? Can I see?"

"Really. I'm good."

"Your forehead is wrinkled. What are you not telling me?"

Tori inhaled deeply and ushered in patience. "Along with the case, Max is in stage 3A. His lung."

Mom startled. "Is he undergoing treatment?"

"He refuses. You know how stubborn he can be."

"I'm aware of stubbornness." Mom sighed. "But it's not incurable. You and I understand the hole of pain and despair."

Opening up to Mom meant taking a huge risk with her own emotions. Still, why hold back when their relationship could be stronger?

"Feels like I'm always there." The plague of the big C—needing courage when it came to cancer.

Mom glanced away only to return with watery eyes. "Victoria, I've seen you beat yourself up since I was diagnosed and then Kevin. He was more than your big brother, the gentle giant you adored—"

"Mom."

She held up her hand. "Let me finish, please. I see the fear in your eyes every time you get a cold, a headache, or a mark on your skin. You can't live when you're afraid of dying."

Tori drew in the sharp reminder of her weakness. "Are you saying I'm preoccupied with my health?"

"Are you?"

"You make me sound . . . sick, and I resent it."

Mom reached for Tori's hand. "You're my strong, determined, beautiful daughter. You battle violent crimes and help keep people safe. You're bold and daring except in one area, and that's cancer."

Tori opened her mouth to speak, but the lump stopped her. "I've got to go. I'll . . . call."

She snatched her purse and hurried toward the door. If Mom saw the constant dread, then who else did? But the accusation was true. Tori would rather face a dozen armed men than a diagnosis of one more loved one with cancer . . . or herself. She rushed past the line of those ordering coffee and out to the parking lot. Touching her car door, she heard the familiar chirp and would soon be at work, a haven from facing the truth about herself.

"Tori."

She whirled around to her mother offering the coffee she'd left behind. "I love you. Behind your worry is the ability to overcome it. Reach to your core. You can do this."

Shame hit her for treating her mother without respect. "Thanks, Mom. I've been thinking. When this case is over, why don't you and I take a long weekend together? Stay at a nice resort, get massages and manicures and pedis."

"I'd love it."

Tori kissed her cheek and slid into her car. "I'm working on the problem."

"You're a survivor, Victoria. We both are."

Tori entered the office area at 7:35. Max and Cole stood in the hallway. Both men had their impassive faces going, which meant they hadn't discussed anything more than the weather.

"Glad you two are early." She took a sip of coffee and allowed the caffeine to energize her body. "I'm leaving at eight thirty to attend Nathan's funeral, but what can I do until then?"

"The funeral's at ten." Max eyed her with his typical annoyance. "Why so early?"

She assumed he'd balk at her announcement. "I intend to support my best friend. Truth is, I might be gone until the afternoon."

Cole picked up the conversation. "I'll be at the church at nine fifteen, unless I receive a call that I'm needed sooner."

"You're a pallbearer?" Max said.

"Yes."

Max slammed a file against his palm. "You two are wasting valuable time."

"Paperwork should fill your hours." Tori fought the words she wanted to fling at him and his lousy attitude. "Who knows? Our bad guy might be at the funeral. Moore Oil & Gas shut down for the day. While the person is gloating, Cole and I can make an arrest. We'll be able to help Sally bury her husband and stop the killer at the same time."

37

TORI ARRIVED at the Moore home at the same time the caterers were unloading food and supplies for the luncheon following the funeral—courtesy of Moore Oil & Gas. Sally must have seen her park because she met Tori on the driveway. Impeccably dressed in designer black and simple gold accessories, only her eyes, red and swollen, betrayed her. She fell into Tori's arms, silently weeping.

"I thought I could handle this morning without breaking down, but I can't. Nathan hurt me and still I love him. Miss him every minute of the day."

Tori held her tightly, despising the turmoil in Sally's life. "You've loved him since the day you met him. I wish I could make this all go away."

"Tell me you believe in my innocence." She sobbed. "I have to know you believe in my innocence."

What could Tori say? That she desperately wanted Sally exonerated? But too many investigators viewed Sally as more than a person of interest.

Sally stiffened and pulled back. "Now I'm sorry. You have a job, and finding Nathan's killer has priority." She blinked.

"You are more than my friend. My sister," Tori said. "I want you happy and at peace."

Sally nodded. "Some moments catch me off guard and I'm frightened for my sons and how this whole thing will scar them."

"Have you thought more about witness protection?"

"Only if there is trouble. Honestly, we're not a threat to anyone. No reason to run."

Tori refused to argue. "What do your parents suggest?"

"Dad is taking Kit home after the funeral. He says it's not safe for her to stay."

They were cowards. "Is he returning?"

Sally paused. "No. The evidence about Nathan's character and the crimes at the oil rig have caused his blood pressure to rise, and Kit is supposedly frail."

"What about taking the boys with them?"

"Lance and Jack make them nervous."

"I'm sorry."

"It's all right. The boys and I will persevere until you and Cole end the nightmare."

Tori wrapped her arm around Sally's waist. "It can't happen soon enough. I wish I could give you details, but I can't. It's a puzzle, and while it looks devastating to you right now, some of the pieces are sliding into unusual places."

This would be a long day.

❈

Cole glanced at the time before taking off for Nathan's funeral. "Max, just got a report on Dale Bentley. He was in jail in Phoenix during the crimes."

"Just cross his name off the list and move on."

But he was tired of running down empty trails. "What have we missed on this case? Who made sure Preston Ustach never talked?"

"Do you remember anything unusual about the men he talked to, anything said when you went to see Mrs. Ustach?"

Cole replayed the trip to the drill site earlier in the week when Ustach lost his life to a sniper. Ustach had stayed to himself except for Jose Aznar. Later Cole went with three roughnecks to tell Mrs. Ustach that her son had been killed. Aznar had shed tears and comforted the grieving mother, vowed revenge. The other two men who accompanied Cole and Aznar were emotional and caring. Hard to believe any of those three could be behind a murder.

Aznar had texted someone on the way. At the Ustach home, he'd requested to see this friend's bedroom, said he wanted to spend a few minutes there alone. How had Cole not seen it? "Let's bring in Jose Aznar for questioning. Run prints on him too."

"I thought he was a weasel."

Cole studied him. "You might be right."

38

ALBERT DROVE to the huge nondenominational church for Nathan Moore's funeral, a service he looked forward to attending. The marquee outside the church brought on a snicker. *All were welcome.*

A nondenominational church for a nonspiritual man.

Albert had arranged for a nurse, a woman who specialized in home health care for MS victims. He preferred Franc, the nurse from St. Luke's, but he worked the day shift. The nurse hired for the day would sit with Erik until around nine tonight while Albert and his longtime friend James finished dinner and shared a much-needed talk. The nurse had his phone number in case of an emergency, yet pangs of conscience assaulted him for leaving Erik. Once everything legally had taken place, his son's health would be restored. Until then, Albert had to stay fixed on the future.

Tori Templeton hadn't given him an opportunity to use the chloroform in a fatal dose. He feared she'd stumble onto something and destroy any hope of Erik getting the money owed him. Albert had driven to her apartment in a rental car, dodged the security cameras, and worn a hoodie until he got to her door. But the FBI agent stayed in her apartment. He thought for sure she'd let him in. No compassion for an old man who showed signs of dementia. Later tonight he'd come up with another solution to get rid of her. After all, if he'd been drunk and ordered Nathan's death, he needed to protect himself and Erik. His son's request to get rid of the bitterness stomped across Albert's mind, but forgiveness came at a price, one he wasn't willing to pay.

Deputy US Marshal Cole Jeffers, who'd been Nathan's friend, would be harder to eliminate. Not impossible, just took more planning. Max Dublin, the lead man, stayed away from the Moore home. Dublin didn't bother him like the other two who doggedly worked the murder case.

Inside, the room reeked of sickeningly sweet flowers, overpowering perfume, and far too many people sandwiched into one space. Nearly made him sick with his claustrophobic tendencies. Sally Moore should have limited those attending the visitation and funeral. But nobody asked for his opinion.

A keyboard set replicated an organ and filled the room with religious music Albert faintly recognized. The funeral dirge sounded as phony as the dead man. A dark-suited usher handed him an order of service that opened in the shape of a gate. The only entrance Nathan found when he faced death was hot and fiery. Albert noted the family requested guests contribute to the American Heart Association. Good call since Nathan's heart had rotted years ago.

A colorful photo of Nathan was arranged near the casket with other photos of him and his family. Liar. Cheater. The accolades made Albert physically ill, and he was there explicitly to gain energy from the mourners.

He forced sorrow into his demeanor and stared at the casket.

Comments of how handsome, young, and the incredible loss met Albert's ears.

You played and you lost, Nathan. I gave you one chance after another until you insulted my son beyond redemption. He did an internal knee jerk. What good was Nathan's death?

Templeton seemed surprised to see him. She acknowledged Albert as though nothing had transpired this morning.

The US Marshal working with her was one of the pallbearers. According to the order of service, the others bearing the load of the dead man were Moore Oil & Gas executives.

Anita Krantz arrived just before the service started—he recognized her from the media. She sat in the rear of the church, but as if on cue, Sally turned to observe her. How did she feel about her husband's mistress attending his funeral? A bit ironic. By now everyone in the room realized the man they loved was disgusting. Thank you, media. Somehow Albert endured the PowerPoint presentation of the loving family man and successful business executive. A pastor gave the eulogy, praises for a worthless man. No one from the family spoke. Not even Tori Templeton or Cole Jeffers. Their agencies must not permit an investigator to speak on behalf of a victim. At the closing hymn, Albert left the church. He'd considered joining the others for the graveside service until he realized he had a voice mail from Erik's nurse.

Trembling, he contacted her, but his fears were a false alarm. She only wanted to report his son was sleeping peacefully.

After treating himself to shrimp and jalapeño grits at a popular seafood restaurant, he headed to a 1:30 appointment with an attorney, a man he'd researched online as being successful in a well-known firm, having recently won a case against a doctor for malpractice. By now Nathan Moore's files should have revealed his deception. What puzzled Albert was why he hadn't been notified of Erik's funds. Unless Moore's attorney concealed the information.

Albert found a parking lot downtown near the attorney's office and cursed the cost. Even the underdog made his buck. He emerged from his twelve-year-old Toyota and drew in the rancid smell of downtown. Stale, like old socks mixed with alcoholics who drank their lunch and caffeine addicts who scrambled into coffee shops like roaches heading for the dark. The tattered homeless mixed with three-piece suits and short skirts, hotfooting it to moneymaking destinations, breathing in exhaust fumes, and listening to whatever was going on in their earbuds. He could unload a .38 on himself, and no one would hear, notice, or care.

Life's potholes had turned him into a cynical old man. He'd change soon.

He crossed the street and stared up at the stone-and-glass building housing the firm with the answers. The next hour would cost him plenty, not just dollars but the heartache of exposing what had been done to his son. Still, hope shone like a beacon. He had to keep believing it. His wallet held a twenty-dollar bill, his driver's license, and a maxed-out Visa. Everything had gone to the hacker. The jerk wouldn't get another penny for more reasons than Albert cared to list.

Inside the black-and-gray marble-floored building, he took the elevator to the eighth floor. What if the attorney required payment up front? If so, he'd ask for a senior discount or better yet a pro bono offer due to Erik's condition. Stiffening his shoulders, he opened the door to the attorney's office.

A matronly receptionist with a tattoo of a red rose on her neck escorted him to an office where a young black man dressed in a tailor-made suit greeted him.

Albert took a seat and played the role of the bereaved old man, which didn't require much acting. "My name is Albert Weiman, and I'm here on behalf of my son, Erik, who is dying of advanced progressive relapsing MS. We've been awaiting approval from the FDA for a drug that has been used successfully in Europe. Except time is running out. Our last chance at surviving the disease is for him to make a trip to Germany for treatment." He bored a sorrowful gaze into the attorney's dark eyes. The young man in turn offered a sad smile, which boosted Albert's endeavors. "I know there's nothing you can do regarding my son's deteriorating health. The funds to accomplish remission are tied up in a situation that occurred nearly twenty years ago involving my son and the late Nathan Moore. They were business partners."

The attorney pulled out a legal pad and pen. "You said Nathan Moore?"

"Yes, sir. He owned Moore Oil & Gas. His funeral was this morning. Erik and Nathan were friends throughout high school and college. Peculiar friendship when they were constant rivals academically and even with sports. They both obtained geology degrees and planned to be partners. Erik developed a means of fracking that was not only environmentally safe but also economical. It created more fractures, more spiderwebs to give greater coverage than what was done at the time. Nathan stole the patent and dissolved any further discussion of a partnership. If you study the method Moore Oil & Gas uses, you'll see it's Erik's design. That's how Nathan became a multimillionaire." Albert thought better of mentioning how Nathan took Sally away from Erik.

The attorney pressed his lips together, reminding Albert of a man hungry for fame. And that's what Albert was banking on. "Do you have proof?" the attorney said.

"I have Erik's original development of the method. It's dated. Nathan would have the same documentation in his files."

The attorney leaned back in his chair. "Have you or your son discussed the business arrangement with legal counsel in the past?"

"Erik refused. I talked to Nathan a few months ago. Requested he financially take care of what was due my son." He aimed his frustration at the attorney. "Nathan threw me out of his office. Said I didn't have a legal leg to stand on, and his documentation was patented and binding."

"Mr. Weiman, this has the potential of being a costly venture. My firm would request a ten-thousand-dollar retainer to pursue the allegations."

"Even with Erik's original paperwork?"

"Depends if he filed the papers with a patent or copyright office."

Defeatism was a terrible foe, and Albert sensed it weighing like an iron yoke. "The paperwork never proceeded beyond Erik's possession."

"Then we're looking at a lengthy court battle. How would you like to go further?"

Albert stood. He ached all over, and he had no fight left in him to maintain his disillusion. "Sir, you're a feeble excuse for a human. A man comes to you for help, and you ignore him when his son's life is at stake."

"I'm terribly sorry, but our firm doesn't do pro bono work. I recommend legal aid."

Albert's blood pressure spiked. "A down-and-out free lawyer doesn't have the skills to win this case. Pardon me for bothering you this afternoon."

When Nathan had denied owing Erik anything, Albert found a way to punish him. The attorney just sealed the fate of Sally Moore and her teenage sons. He would get the money due Erik, no matter what it took.

39

AFTER NATHAN'S FUNERAL, Cole met Manny at his landscaping business. The projects were under the supervision of a capable man, but overseeing the business was still Cole's responsibility. Once the project manager had the specifications and scheduling down, Cole would relinquish much of his control.

"Having you on an FBI task force isn't how I envisioned you back in the program," Manny said.

Cole propped his feet on the desk. "I'm okay with it. Nathan's death sent me back to where I belonged, and I'm glad to be a part of the team."

"How are the FBI partners?"

Cole considered a dose of complaining, but it would get back to the other Marshals, so he feigned a grin. "A team from violent crime. We're making progress. You've heard it all. Uncovering more about Nathan than I wanted to know. But anyway, Max used to work the bomb squad, and Tori is a solid member of the task force. A real go-getter."

"What are you not saying? Is she out to prove her skills are better than a man's? Problems with husband and kids?"

"Not at all. She's single, and she's fine."

"Fine as in you can investigate together or fine as in she's a looker?" Manny chuckled. "That's it. She has you distracted."

"Did I say she was attractive?"

"Sure. It was in the way you said her name. What's up with that?"

"Nothing, Manny. I like the way she handles herself, and she has a terrific track record. If—and I say *if*—I considered asking her out, it wouldn't happen until the case is solved. Not sure about her faith." Cole had purposely omitted his and Tori's discussion at the restaurant.

"No need."

"What?"

"No reason to date her before you find out about her faith because you see her twelve hours a day. Lacy and I have always said it would take a woman as tough as you are to shove you into a wedding vow."

"Shove? As if marriage is a downhill slope on a pair of skis?"

"So you're thinking about this woman a lot?" Manny acted as if he had insight into Cole's love life.

"Conversation ended. I have questions for you on a professional level."

Manny pulled his phone from his pocket and started to type. "At your service."

"I'm looking for a person or persons in our records who have connections with Moore Oil & Gas. Could be in prison, someone in the judicial system, etc. A solid informant. There's something going on with this case that has flown over my head. Between you and me, when arrests are made, Nathan's family will need counseling for a long time. With his affair and the woman's pregnancy, a can of worms is the least of my worries."

"Are you sure staying on the task force is a smart investment of your time and energy?"

"I'm committed. Plus, Tori and Sally Moore have been close friends since college."

Manny shook his head. "How is Tori handling that?"

"Like me. We're determined to uncover the truth, no matter how much we despise it."

"What about the other agent?"

Cole toyed with how much to say, but Manny could be trusted. "This is personal, okay? Max is a buffer."

"What do you mean? The friendship you and Tori have with the Moores is interfering with your objectivity?"

"Not exactly. He keeps Tori and me on our toes. Max is battling lung cancer. He claims this is his last case, but I think he has more strength than that. And this stays between us. I'd appreciate your putting an unspoken request on your prayer chain."

"Sure." Manny grimaced. "Tough one. I'll do all I can. Tomorrow, I have prison transport, so give me a couple of days. I have a cousin in prison. Got himself in a cartel and killed a man. Doing life. Operating from the inside. His wife is our informant, and she's given us leads on a couple of cases. On the surface, she's visiting him and playing the role of a caring wife. I'll check with her."

"One more thing: see if the name Jose Aznar means anything. His background cleared, but I'm curious."

"On my list."

"Thanks. Are you up for burgers and fries? I'm buying. I'd like to catch up on Lacy and the kids."

Manny grabbed his cap from Cole's desk. "Great. Little Manny is playing T-ball, and . . ."

40

LATE FRIDAY AFTERNOON, Cole joined Max at the FBI office. Tori was with Sally and might not return for the remainder of the day. The funeral had been emotional, and guests lingered at the Moore home long after the luncheon.

Cole and Max met with the tech agents to examine security camera footage from the Moore Oil & Gas complex. They'd used their equipment to pull the surveillance videos directly from the recorders, preserving the footage in its original state.

A tech agent navigated to the correct footage. "Our instructions were to check for three persons—Preston Ustach, Franc Lawd, and Jose Aznar. Early this morning the request to capture all images of Anita Krantz was made."

Max narrowed his gaze at the tech. "What have you got?" He dragged a chair beside the computer screen, but Cole remained standing.

The tech clicked on an image of Ustach entering the building alone the day before the drill site bombing. Time stamp of 4:30 p.m., which meant he'd finished work before his arrival. "Hallway images show him getting on an elevator and off on the fifth floor. He entered Nathan Moore's executive suite and left the building thirty-five minutes later."

"Did Nathan learn something from Ustach?" Cole said. "I'm contacting Krantz now to see what she has to say about the visit." He pressed in her number and initiated the speakerphone. "Ms. Krantz, this is US Marshal Cole Jeffers. Agent Dublin and I are viewing security footage from Moore Oil & Gas. We have a couple of questions. With your permission, we'd like to record our conversation."

"You have my permission. Anything to get me off your suspect list."

"Preston Ustach met with Nathan the day before the bombing."

"Yes, and the afternoon before his death. I told you that previously."

"The second visit is not in the security footage," Cole said. "Neither is Ustach listed on the guest register."

Nothing but silence.

"Ms. Krantz, is there something you'd like to tell us?"

"I'm at a loss for words. What I can say is Nathan must have requested someone delete the images and the man's name from the list of visitors entering the building. But he didn't tell me."

"Why wouldn't he want a record of Mr. Ustach's offer of information?"

"I honestly don't know. But maybe Mr. Ustach had an idea of who'd bombed the rig."

Was Krantz covering up something? Or had Nathan received important info from Ustach and eliminated any trace of the meeting? "You stated in a previous interview that you weren't privy to any of the conversations."

"Correct. I remember the afternoon of Nathan's death, Mr. Ustach seemed troubled. Nathan had me escort him to the suite's observation deck, where there are no cameras or recording devices. I had an upset stomach and went home soon afterward."

"Is there a reason you failed to mention this in previous interviews?"

"Honestly, I'm a hormonal mess, stemming from his death and my pregnancy."

Innocent or attempting to keep a few steps ahead of the investigation? "Is there anything else you can remember that might be pertinent?" When she said no, he ended the call and turned to Max. "Two dead men went to their graves with evidence."

"She knows more. I can tell it in her voice."

Max irritated him, but he could be the spokesperson of wisdom. "Then put together more questions for her."

"Trust me, I will." Max peered at the screen. "Any images of the others?" he said to the tech agent.

"Nothing. We've isolated Anita Krantz to those where she's in the company of another person." He positioned several images of Krantz for them to view. "We've identified her with Nathan Moore, coworkers, guests of the business, and Preston Ustach."

Max broke into a coughing spasm and left the room. Cole requested the tech agent enlarge the image of Anita and Ustach and roll the video. The pair met in the lobby and rode the elevator to the fifth floor. Cole studied the images for the next hour, but none of the others flashed a possible warning.

He sent Krantz's interview to Max and Tori. Two things he'd assessed from Ustach—he'd gotten too close to the bomber and possibly Nathan's killer, and he'd died for it. His funeral was tomorrow. Cole texted Tori.

Want 2 go with me 2 Ustach's funeral tomorrow morning?

Yes. How about a visit 2 the oil rig? The security guard was on duty the day of the bombing and the sniper attack.

Reading my thoughts?

Need 2 end this case.

How r Sally & boys?

Up & down. Not leaving until later.

Kit & Wes gone?

Yes.

His opinion of the couple leaving their daughter when life was shattering around her wasn't complimentary. Abandonment fit the bill.

Ok. Pick u up @ 7:30 a.m. @ FBI office.

Cole slid his phone beside his laptop. He'd wrap things up here and head to the Moores', where he could see her in person. The same bodyguards had worked for Nathan since the EPA suit, and they'd been questioned and cleared. But a nagging thought persisted. Difficult to work around people and not hear things, and he was banking on one of them giving him more info.

Outside the Moore home, the bodyguards held two positions, front and back of the huge home, two people inside and two outside. Cole made his way to the man at the front. He stood legs apart, dressed in jeans and a blue cotton shirt.

"Marshal Jeffers, how can I help you?"

"I assume you've always been stationed in this spot."

"Yes, sir." His eyes never left the perimeter of his detail.

"I've done protection duty for judges and witness protection. Kept me on alert and my fingers not far from my weapon."

"Yes, sir."

"I heard personal things and comments that could have been used in a court of law."

"Sir, nothing's been overheard on my watch that could solve Mr. Moore's murder."

"Thank you. Have you seen or heard matters that concern you for their safety?"

He appeared to deliberate the request. "Talk to my colleague at the rear of the home."

Cole found the tall woman pleasant but quiet. He made small talk before asking the same questions as with the other guard.

"My job is to protect people, not to gossip." Large brown eyes bored into his.

"Look at the situation this way. What you know could bring a killer to justice and prevent others from being hurt."

She squinted. "Marshal Jeffers, I've thought about that very thing . . . often."

He waited while she glanced away, then back to him.

"Mr. Moore took calls outside, which corresponded to my afternoon and evening shift. On the night of his death, approximately 7:20 p.m., he made a call. He never referred to the person by name or gave any indication whether it was a man or woman. I stood in the shadows, and I doubt he knew I overheard the conversation."

This occurred after asking Sally for a divorce and leaving the dinner table. The call must have been made on a burner because it wasn't registered on the Moores' cell phones.

"He said he detested what he'd done to Sally and the boys. His flight was booked for the next afternoon, and he'd take care of business from there. Nothing more was said. Except . . ."

"What?"

She blew out her hesitation. "He dropped the phone on the patio and stomped on it. Several times. Then he picked up the pieces and walked them across the street to where the neighbors had trash bins ready for the morning pickup. He tossed them there."

Just like Lance, she'd withheld information. "Why hasn't this information come forward before now?"

"I'm in the middle of a divorce that's leading to a custody battle. No excuse, except my mind is on personal matters. Been thinking about what happened to Mr. Moore and the investigation. My conscience got the best of me. I may lose my job over this, but the truth still needs to be said."

"Thank you." Cole excused himself and spoke to the two bodyguards inside the home. Neither of them had information. He returned to the patio and contacted his sources about Nathan's flight. Tori saw him from inside the kitchen and waved. He returned the gesture.

Who had Nathan called? If he'd contacted Anita Krantz, would he have shared his concern over hurting Sally and the boys?

Fifteen minutes later, the report sailed into his cell phone.

Nathan had been booked on a flight to London out of IAH Airport. One-way. Who had he called?

41

ALBERT ENTERED the Chili's restaurant where he'd meet James for dinner, their habit whenever his friend was in town. The two had been friends since James stopped Albert's mail truck years ago and asked for directions. They started talking and the rest was years of good times. James was already seated at their normal booth near the bar. Good, because Albert wanted to drink and talk. His friend rose to meet him, his tan jacket and navy pants indicating he'd come from an event.

A server approached and placed two cocktail napkins on the table.

"What are you drinking?" James said. "The usual?"

Albert nodded and ordered a beer.

"A Sprite for me." James silenced his phone.

"Nothing stronger this evening?"

"I'll pass. Have to lecture early in the morning. Need to be alert." He ran his fingers through thick white hair.

"Disappointing, considering I've already had two."

James grinned. "Next time. Are you in the mood for a rack of ribs?"

"Definitely." The day was supposed to have rejuvenated him. Instead he wanted to forget.

His friend rested his arm on the table. "Once we order, you'll have to tell me what's been going on."

Apprehension seized him. "What do you mean? With Erik?"

"No, I check in with the hospital every day. I'll see him while I'm in town. I mean you wanted Nathan dead, and that's what happened."

Albert's mind jumped to panic mode. "I'll get to that discussion after another drink."

"No problem," James said. "You look like you need to relax."

"Thanks for all the advice you've given and payment toward Erik's medical bills. James, you're closer to me than a brother. I can never repay all you've done for my boy. Since Erik was a toddler, you've helped me with him." Would James still be his friend when Erik breathed his last?

"My privilege." James straightened.

The server brought their drinks, and they placed their food orders.

James picked up the conversation. "I'm worried about you. You told me a few months back your plans for the man who'd ruined Erik's life. How you wanted him dead and had arranged for Walt Hanna to hack his pacemaker. Are you being careful?"

Albert swallowed a lump in his throat. "I told you what I intended to do?"

"You sure did. We were right here. Been drinking for a few hours. You even gave me the day and time. You had been talking about how Nathan must pay for what he did to Erik."

Albert fed caution into his brain. He'd have to be more careful.

Trusting James was a given, but Albert had little control of his mouth when he was drinking. "The problem is I wanted money for my son's care, not revenge that resulted in murder."

"Too late now."

"Well, it happened. Funeral was today. Thought you might be there to send Nathan off in style."

"I had a speaking engagement. Besides, I might have been guilty of smiling too much. In any event, I'm proud of you. Glad it worked out. Nathan destroyed Erik's life, and you brought justice to the matter."

"According to an attorney I saw this afternoon, without proof of Erik filing the appropriate paperwork, my son is still in a precarious situation. He'd take the case but the upfront money is ridiculous." He shook his head. "Who am I fooling? I'm back to where I started."

"Looks like the FBI and US Marshals are investigating every aspect of his death and business practices," James said. "The media reports discredit his impeccable reputation. The proof will surface."

"Maybe so, but Erik's running out of time, and I spent my last penny on the hacker. The house is mortgaged. My retirement's gone." This wasn't his friend's battle. "I'm sorry. No need to unload on you."

James paused while the server placed their salads before them. He thanked the young man and turned to Albert. "I despise the evil Nathan did to Erik and you. If I had the cash, I'd fund the attorney. My wife watches every penny I spend of her money, and she's reluctant to part with any more for Erik."

"I'd never come to you for money. Hope I didn't interfere with your marriage or come across like a beggar."

"Of course not. Surely there's an alternate plan, another angle to look at the problem."

Albert contemplated his options. "I refuse to give up when the money is sitting in the Moore family accounts."

"I figured you bombed the oil rig."

He lifted a brow. Another crime he didn't remember? "Not me."

"You're an ingenious man. I'm sure an idea will rise from the momentary setback." James leveled his butter knife at Albert. "And it is only a minor setback. Don't give up."

"You already know about Nathan's demise. Suggestions for this next go-round?"

"Extract the money from Sally Moore. She stands to inherit millions."

"Do you think that because she once dated Erik she'd hand over what's owed to him? You're crazy, James. She has to be aware of how it ended between Nathan and Erik."

"Maybe, maybe not. Nathan was devious, the master of deceit. My point is he's gone, and legal action appears worthless."

Albert studied his old friend's face, the man who'd been like a brother to him. He'd think through his options. "When I visited her, she appeared surprised about Erik's illness. I can turn this around, and I have a plan to accomplish it."

"You do whatever it takes." James motioned to Albert's empty glass. "Have another drink. Our ribs will be here any sec."

An hour and a half later, long after Albert stopped counting the beers, he and James made their way into the night air, which should have sobered him up a little. Tonight he didn't care. Numbing his brain to Erik's illness was always welcome. To make matters worse, depression had settled when he failed to focus on a way to force Sally Moore to relinquish some of her money. James declared revenge was sweet, but all Albert tasted was defeat.

James helped him into a taxi and gave the driver his address. He'd follow with Albert's car, and the taxi driver would make a round trip. The drill had become rote.

42

SATURDAY MORNING, Cole met Tori at the FBI office before he drove them to Kenny & Ziggy's on Post Oak for breakfast. Another working weekend. Eight o'clock and the restaurant was bustling with activity and smelled like he'd just stepped into heaven. He'd been up since before six, pondering facts and statements, searching the Internet, and requesting reports. The biggest question revolved around Nathan's plans to leave Houston. Was the trip permanent? How did he intend to inform Sally? Where did Anita Krantz fit?

He and Tori were seated. She ordered challah French toast with a side order of blueberries, and he chose a Western omelet. He drank deep of the coffee, willing his head to clear the fog.

"You're quiet this morning." Tori rested her chin on her palm.

He stared at her. She had this beautiful, sweet glow about her. Nice to think it was because of him. "I'm going to unload. I'm puzzled, angry, confused, and downright determined. And the latest is who did Nathan call on that phone he destroyed?"

She covered her mouth, but he saw her upturned lips. "Thanks for making me smile. All week, you've made the pressure of this case a little easier."

He'd take that and dive into the day with or without coffee. He chose to voice his apprehension. "The real Nathan was not the man I respected."

"Sally used similar words. I regretted the promise we made to her the moment you told me about his London trip. I don't want to tell her everything we learn. But on the other hand, I'm glad we're not keeping anything from her. I'm also puzzled, angry, confused, and downright determined."

"How'd she handle the London news?" Tori had taken on that task while Cole looked through Nathan's office.

"I'd say incredulously. That's when she insisted she was married to a stranger and questioned why he hadn't told her about the trip. She also said he'd been to London in September regarding the possibility of opening a second office and negotiating for oil wells in the North Sea." She rubbed her left wrist. "I've made a decision."

"And?"

"I'm moving in with her tonight until this is over. She needs a sounding board, and I have the fortitude to handle it. I know Sally, and she'll spend every idle second thinking about Nathan's trip to London."

He hesitated, forming his words. "What if you learn she's guilty?"

"I'll make the arrest and do my job."

"Do you have any idea what you're saying?"

"Neither you nor I were aware of the real Nathan Moore. If Sally has been lying to us, I'd rather be the one to discover it."

He gazed into Tori's amazing green eyes. Weariness had to stalk her, but she didn't show it. "Who takes care of you?"

She gave him a flirty half twist of her head. "Have you been talking to my mother?"

"No. Is she as gorgeous and smart as you?"

"More so." She shook her head. "Mom's a cancer survivor. She's brave and not afraid to tackle a challenge."

"Like mother, like daughter."

"I've been told that before, which is why we often disagree."

Who is looking out for the hurt in your eyes? Who eases your worry of cancer? "I have a game for us."

"I hate to lose." She took a sip of coffee.

"No losers in this. Fear time. I give you my biggest all-time nightmare situation, and then you give me yours."

She gave him a sideways glance.

"We play until our food gets here, then we talk case. I'll go first."

She waved at him to begin.

A twinge of do-you-really-want-to-dig-deep? hit him. Except turning back had *coward* branded on it. "Mine is a repeat of what happened leading up to my resignation from the US Marshals. Part of it you know. I was transporting a key witness in a case where a cartel leader had been charged with three counts of murder." He sighed. "I made the arrest. On the way to trial, a car cut off the armed car behind me. An SUV slammed into the side of my vehicle and spun us around. Doors opened and masked shooters came out firing. They killed the man I was transporting, another Marshal, and shot me in the stomach, narrowly missing vital organs. I remember lying there in the street and watching my own blood pour from my body." He moistened his lips. "And I was afraid of dying alone."

Her face shone warm with compassion. "What a nasty nightmare."

Should he tell her his faith made the flashbacks easier to bear? Not yet because she'd run. "Your turn."

She glanced to the kitchen, where a server would emerge with their food.

"Hey, I spilled my guts."

"All right." She took a drink of water. "I can't believe I'm telling you this. My dad left us when I was two. Disappeared into the unknown, and I've never tried to find him. My brother, Kevin, took care of me while Mom worked to support us. After I graduated from college, Mom was diagnosed with breast cancer. When she's three years out cancer-free, my brother is diagnosed with the big C. He never hit the remission stage. Now I'm afraid. Afraid . . ."

"Someone else you love will contract cancer."

"Yes." Visible emotion swept over her face. "A little fearful for myself too."

Max had told him about her phobia, but for her to admit it was incredible. "You're brave."

She blinked. "We're playing a game."

"I'd like to make a deal. When I wake up in a cold sweat because I'm bleeding out on a street with no one around, I want to know I can call you."

"Of course. We're friends, and I want to help."

"The deal works both ways. When you're afraid cancer is about to strike a friend or yourself, you contact me."

Her eyebrows narrowed. "Why?"

He opened his arms. "To help each other. Be better people. Everyone creates what he fears."

"Are you always philosophical?"

"You bring out the best in me."

The server placed their food platters before them. He bowed his head and silently thanked God for the meal. He dug into his omelet without looking at her.

"Your request may not be possible after we're finished with the task force," she said. "We'll both have new cases."

"So we'll work on it until then." He pointed to her French toast. "I'm regretting what I ordered."

She used her hand to cover her plate. "I don't share my food."

He gave his best little-boy hurt look. "I'll share mine."

"Nope. Sorry. Another topic, please."

He'd brought up the fear thing, and now he'd keep his word by discussing the case. "I searched way into the night for information about Nathan opening another office in London. I found he'd signed a lease on a flat and opened a bank account for himself and Moore Oil & Gas. He rented an office and hired staff."

"We have agents on the ground who can run down details. It doesn't mean he'd decided on a permanent move."

"Why keep the trip secret from his family, his mistress, and business executives? The background on Anita Krantz verifies her plans to move to Portland. Was he tired of the race—work, family, the affair? Was there another woman? A business venture with partners to expand his business with less risk? Falling oil prices is a downside for anyone in the industry. Then again, London is a money capital for investors. Or had he taken the only steps he could to protect his family from a predator?"

"Cole, when we find out his reasons for not informing anyone about the trip, then we stand a better chance of learning who killed him and why."

He pulled a pen from his shirt pocket and grabbed a napkin. "How many people have motive?"

She tilted her head, an expression he'd come to recognize, in such a short while, as her means of processing info. "Start a list. Lots of people have motive."

"My point, Tori. From Houston to London, from women to environmental activists, we have no idea who murdered Nathan. All we can do is dig through the life of a man we called a friend.

Franc Lawd smells like trouble. Preston Ustach discovered something. Anita Krantz could be lying. We want to believe Sally is innocent, but that could blow up in our faces. Lance is a lit fuse and despised his dad. Jack apparently wears a halo. The roughnecks appear loyal, though we've uncovered a few with criminal records. People lie and can be bought, especially when it comes to money, power, and vengeance."

43

TORI SIPPED HER TO-GO COFFEE from Kenny & Ziggy's while Cole drove south on I-45 to Texas City. Traffic refrained from bumper-to-bumper mode while most people slept. Great thought when her schedule cleared. After Preston Ustach's funeral, she'd change into jeans, a T-shirt, and tennis shoes. Then they'd do a little snooping. The oil rig had closed for the day due to the death, like they'd done for Nathan.

"Know why I like your truck?" she said.

"The hunk driving it?"

Cole and his wit. "No. It's the height. I can see all around. Comfy too. But I bet my Charger can take you on open ground."

He chuckled. "I'm a sucker for a race. I have the perfect spot. It'll be our celebration ride."

"Weep and mourn, Cole." She slipped off her shoes and wiggled her toes. "What is it about the US Marshals that attracted you?"

"An interest in protecting the judicial process of our country. My parents had a family friend, a congressman, who was often threatened because of his decisions. At times he sent his family out of the state."

She valued his commitment to protect the innocent. "You were insistent Sally and the boys leave town."

"Right, and I really wish she'd taken my advice. Anyway, I looked into the Marshal Service and its other areas of expertise. I saw protecting witnesses was another area where mistakes meant death. Combine those interests with a redneck cowboy who liked to shoot, be a hero, and just passed his bar exam, and out rolled Deputy US Marshal Cole Jeffers."

"Impressive record. You've taken a few risks."

"Hmm. So have you. We have the gene that defies common sense."

"You mentioned Nathan's death pushed you into a reinstatement." Tori craved knowing more about his life. Never mind why because that frightened her as much as the big C.

"Yes, and one of the Marshals is a good friend, Manny Lopez. He'd been after me to come back for a long time, and I couldn't ignore the nudge in my spirit or let it go."

Max had asked if Manny was a yardman, spoke English. The memory embarrassed her. "Tell me more—I mean, the wanting to return but hesitating. I'm not nosy, just curious."

"Right. You find me so irresistible that you have to know everything."

"Please." She dragged out the word and stared out the window so he wouldn't see he'd been right.

"All right. I missed the work of being a part of the national police. Kept up with what was going on through Manny. A judge in Dallas had been threatened, and US Marshals were assigned.

Two prisoners escaped at Huntsville and US Marshals were on it. I wanted to be there."

"What areas have you worked?"

"Is this going into a report?"

"We're getting to know each other."

"I'll remember that. Okay, I've worked within the investigative operations, witness security, and prisoner transport. The end."

"Huge stretch from the Marshals to landscaping."

He palmed the steering wheel. "Blame my mom for that. She forced me to endure hours of lectures on soil, plants, fertilizer, design, you name it. When I needed a second career, landscaping came naturally."

"Have you checked me out?" She groaned. "Delete my question."

"I have. Homecoming queen. Prom queen. Head cheerleader. Lettered as a pitcher in softball. Class president junior and senior year of high school. Majored in law enforcement at the University of Texas. Top of the class. Expert marksmanship."

She raised her hand. "How'd you know about the high school stuff?"

"I'm good at what I do. By the way, is tomorrow your Sunday for church?"

She saw the path this was headed. "It is. Are you inviting me?"

"Thinking about it. Not sure you can handle two days in a row of my incredible charisma."

What he didn't know was she'd welcome the time with him.

They drove into Texas City and easily found the church where the Ustach funeral would be held. Her carefree persona changed the moment they saw the parking lot filled with vehicles, mostly pick-ups. Yesterday, she'd attended Nathan's service, and today Preston Ustach's. Back-to-back grim affairs. And the killer could be among the mourners.

"What are the chances of the same person or persons attending the funerals?"

"Like us?" He stared at a family mounting the steps to the church. "That's why we're here."

People young and old crowded the building. She and Cole signed the guest book and took a place along the back wall. Tori glanced at a framed photo of the man who'd asked her to dinner. So much of life ahead of him and then murdered. Cole appeared to observe those filling the pews, nodding as they passed. She recognized some of the men from the rig but didn't see Jose Aznar. Two of the executives from Moore Oil & Gas paid their respects and took a seat in a middle pew. Preston's mother sat in the front row in a black suit. Many embraced her, supporting her.

When Kevin had died, Sally and Nathan were with Tori and her mom every step of the way.

She hated funerals. She despised killers more.

The music began, a mournful song titled "Life's Railway to Heaven." A woman sang in a clear and passionate tone. "Life is like a mountain railway, with an engineer that's brave; we must make the run successful, from the cradle to the grave; watch the curves, the fills, the tunnels; never falter, never fail; keep your hands upon the throttle, and your eyes upon the rail."

Tori tuned out the rest of the words to the song. She'd handled Nathan's funeral better without the religious stuff to make her feel uncomfortable. After all, she was there to study those in attendance.

At the close of the last hymn, Cole took her hand—strong. She didn't mind. In a way, they were playing a role this morning. He lingered at the guest book, and she read each name. He turned the page. A few were familiar from the oil rig, but none from Nathan's funeral except the executives. Cole squeezed her hand, and she looked into his sky-blue eyes. A weak moment and she'd lose herself in the depth of those pools or in his strong arms. Working with Cole brought out the best in her . . . as well as other things she found hard to accept. She released his hand.

"We paid our respects to a good man," he whispered. "His mother and sister saw we were here."

Outside, a soft breeze played with a curl on her neck, and the sun touched warm on her face. Seemed wrong the day could be so beautiful when those inside the church were laying a good man to rest.

Cole's voice broke her brief respite. "There'll be a guard at the rig. He's expecting us."

"The same man who was on duty when Lawd showed up?"

"Yes. Maybe he's remembered something about him."

Tori waited to speak until they passed a small crowd from the funeral. "Lawd bothers me. He lied to gain access to the site but we have no clue why. The surveillance team will have a report on him before the day's over."

"If he's the mastermind, he'll not be seen doing anything that would send us back to him."

"No one's foolproof."

He opened the truck door for her, and she climbed in. "When's the last time you caught up on your sleep?"

"That bad? For the record, you look like a zombie."

He grinned and closed the door and made his way to the driver's side. Once on the road, he turned to her. "Is tonight when you move in with the Moores?"

She nodded. "Doubt I'll catch up on sleep there either."

"What are your plans?"

"We're going through everything Nathan owned. Although that's been completed by one of our teams, he could have hidden things in obscure places. Nothing at his office or safe-deposit boxes has revealed anything amiss."

"With what we learned about his London trip, the investigation will take longer than we anticipated."

"As in Max will have a tough time finishing the case." She feared he wouldn't endure another week unless he made the choice to survive. "Wish he'd agree to more chemo."

"Are you friends with his wife?"

"Both treated me like family. I regret what tore her and Max apart, but it's too late now."

"Maybe not. Is she aware of his diagnosis?"

"Where have I been, Cole?" Guilt riddled her. "Why haven't I contacted her, told her how seriously ill he is?"

"What if she knows and doesn't care?"

She lifted her chin. "I'll take the risk. On the way back to Houston, I'll call her."

He smiled. "Compassion is one of the reasons you're a great agent. I noted it when you talked to Mrs. Ustach."

"Not always, as I just confessed to not calling Max's wife."

Cole stared at his rearview mirror. "We're being followed."

She noted the vehicle gaining on them. "It's a van, possibly a cargo type. Can't tell from this angle." She jotted down the license plate number.

He turned down a country road, taking a left, another left, then a right, and another right. Definitely a cargo van. A half mile later he announced they'd lost the tail. He drove on another two miles, then took a series of turns that eventually brought them back to the drill site.

"Want to speculate on who was following us?" she said. "No generic 'all those who don't want us to find them.'"

"Send the license plate through the FIG just in case."

"Already done, partner."

A single battered Ford was parked near the security entrance. They greeted the older guard at the gate and presented their IDs.

"Sir," Cole began, "do you recall anything the night of the bombing or the day of the shootings that raises suspicion?"

"Are you sayin' I wasn't doing my job?"

"Not at all. Sometimes we remember details after the fact."

The man's drawn face told Tori he blamed himself. She touched Cole's arm. "Sir, no one's blaming you," she said.

"Thanks. I pride myself in keeping my eyes open. Haven't seen or recollected a thing."

Cole reached through the truck's window and shook his hand. "Mind if we look around?"

"Go ahead. No one's around."

Cole parked near the rig and they exited. "In my experience, the bad guy often returns to the scene of the crime. Either to admire his work or make sure he didn't leave any evidence."

"Investigators have been thorough. What are you expecting to find? I get it. We're going to look at where the bomb went off and walk the path of the sniper."

"The one detail bothering me is the bomber could have set it off during the day and taken men out. He could've also set the IED in a place that destroyed more of the rig."

"Maybe he tried and someone saw him, like Preston Ustach."

"Who in turn went to Nathan and got himself killed. But why wound a second man when Ustach was the target?"

She sighed, taking in the surroundings. "To throw us off the motivation?"

"Makes me wonder if we're looking at separate crimes that crossed paths."

"Try proving it." A nearby shed caught her attention. Flies

swarmed around the door and she pointed to it. "What's stored there?"

"The other day it had a padlock. But I don't see one now." Cole walked toward the shed and she followed.

He opened the metal door, and they both peered inside.

Jose Aznar had been shot in the chest, his mouth clamped shut with a staple gun.

44

"CALL IT IN, TORI."

As she reached for her phone, Cole bent over Aznar's body. Suddenly rifle fire cracked the air. They whirled around.

The cargo van they'd seen earlier raced past the guard gate and toward them. A rifle from the passenger side unloaded again.

The nightmare flash hit him hard. The shooter standing over him, watching him bleed out.

Not this time! Amid heavy gunfire, Cole raced with Tori to the truck. The van slid to a stop next to them in a screech of brakes and a cloud of dust. Weapons pulled, Cole and Tori took cover on the driver's side and crouched behind the tires. Three black-hooded men poured from the rear, and two from the side door in a roar of fire. Five plus the driver against two. Bad odds.

A firefight edging closer to a disastrous outcome.

Bullets whizzed in both directions. How long could they hold off these guys? The men fired repeatedly into his truck using high-powered large-caliber weapons that sounded like M60s.

"Cover me," he called to Tori. Opening the driver's side, he grabbed an AR-15 from under his seat. They needed rifle power, more than their pistols and his hunting knife in the glove box.

Tori rose from her folded position and fired. A shooter fell against the truck bed less than six feet away and slid down, leaving a trail of blood. She shoved a magazine into her Glock as another shooter moved closer. Cole aimed and fired at a slight man moving toward her, sending him backward. Cole spun to his left and put a bullet into another man's ribs. Shooters poured more fire while others grabbed the downed men and pulled them into the van.

The acrid scent of blood assaulted his nostrils, and if he didn't control the memory, he'd be useless.

Help me.

The shooters inched closer, like animals surrounding a kill.

Cole snapped to attention and leveled his rifle.

The odds were still against them. A shout ordered the shooters back inside the van. They hadn't given up, so what was the plan?

Gut-wrenching dread crawled up his spine.

Tori shot out their front passenger tire. The van moved ahead several yards, bouncing on its rim. It stopped, and what looked like a Barrett M82A1 emerged. The .50 caliber rifle fired an armor-piercing round that, while ineffective against modern tank armor, could penetrate a well casing or the piping on a platform.

The oil rig would blow like a volcano.

A streak of light flew toward the drill site.

Cole grabbed Tori's hand and they raced away from his truck, his body shielding her side. Bullets whistled, following their every step. A sharp sting hit his shoulder, and he stumbled. "Keep going, Tori. I'll hold them off."

"Fat chance." She returned fire. "I'm not leaving you. Get on your feet or I'll drag you."

He leveled energy into his body and obliged while firing at the cargo van. "You're one stubborn agent."

The roar of the explosion sent them scrambling, and the force hurled them airborne and to the ground while the van sped away in a cloud of gunpowder. An inferno burst into his senses and darkness overcame him.

45

TORI PACED the emergency visitor area of Galveston's UT Medical Branch while a team hovered over Cole. The bustle of activity heightened her stress, reminding her of the times Kevin and Mom struggled with medical issues. Shouldn't she have word soon about Cole? Nearly an hour had passed since they were brought in—him near death and her with scrapes, bruises, and wearing his blood. His treatment continued while she'd received stitches in her right arm below her elbow.

The image of the left side of his burned and battered body wouldn't leave her. He'd been shot in the upper left shoulder before the explosion sent them flying. Even in his war-torn condition, he'd shielded her from serious harm. His sacrifice and the question of his recovery caused her to wonder what more she could have done.

Though her ears had rung like a dinner bell from the explosion, she'd heard him moan and call her name just before his body succumbed to unconsciousness. At the time, she viewed it as a blessing because he couldn't feel the agony. The pounding in her head must have dulled her thinking, though, because she'd kissed him and begged him to hold on. That's when she realized her heart had fallen prey to Deputy US Marshal Cole Jeffers, something she believed would never happen.

Thankfully the van didn't return—the shooters must have thought the agents were dead.

She'd ridden in the ambulance that transported him, and he'd not wakened in the ten-mile drive to the hospital. Who were the shooters? With their black hoods and only the size of their bodies as an identifying factor, she had little means of assisting law enforcement. Crossing her arms, she concentrated on the parking lot. Bad guys with an agenda could take out a lot of people while searching for her and Cole. Today raised the stakes big-time for the task force. What had Preston Ustach and Jose Aznar discovered? Were she and Cole close to identifying the killers? Was that why they'd been attacked?

But nothing fit, and she despised being inept.

The injured shooters would require medical attention. Every doc-in-a-box and medical facility in the area had been alerted the moment she entered the ambulance with Cole. She'd texted the ASAC with all she remembered. No one, absolutely no one, would hurt the innocent on her watch.

Her attention turned once more to the ER doors leading outside. A police officer guarded the entry, and several were posted around the various entrances, but the men who'd tried to kill Cole and her possessed heavy firepower.

Her cell rang: Max. He'd texted twenty minutes earlier when the doctor was stitching her up. At the time, she'd typed back about the firefight at the oil rig site and Cole's serious condition. Max must be antsy.

"Hey, I'm in the ER waiting room while they work on Cole." Her voice shook, and she regretted the display of weakness. "Not sure if he's gained consciousness. He also took a nasty blow to the head. Lost too much blood in my opinion."

"What about you?"

"I'm okay."

"Tori, I asked a question."

"Stitches in my lower right arm. Some bruises. A bump on the head from the same piece of metal that hit Cole."

"What happened out there?"

"We found Jose Aznar's body in a shed. Seconds later we were attacked by shooters driving a white cargo van. One of them used what looked like a Barrett M82A1 on the oil rig. From the light, I'm saying they had magnesium compound in the tracers. I got the license plate and gave it to the ASAC."

"A visual?"

"They were hooded. Dressed in black. Didn't leave a business card."

Silence met her, then, "Do you have any idea how lucky you two are?"

She hadn't gotten past the shock to consider anything but Cole's injuries. "A paramedic mentioned it. We were about forty yards away when the well blew."

"I'm on my way."

"Max, you're in no shape to drive. I'll be fine. The ASAC is en route."

"Didn't say I was driving."

"Are you taking a bus?"

"Cut the sarcasm. Janie's driving. I called her when I got the news. She just pulled into the driveway. See you in a few."

Janie? How good to see her again, even if the circumstances

stank. Max and his wife would have over an hour to talk on the way here.

Mom . . . Tori pressed in the number and waited for her mother to answer, hoping the news came first from Tori and not the media.

Mom picked up on the second ring. "How's your weekend?"

"Oh, I've spent easier days. Are you at home or out?"

"Home. Honey, what's wrong?"

"Cole and I were attacked in the Texas City area. I wanted to tell you before the media announced it."

"Where are you?"

"The ER of the University of Texas Medical Branch in Galveston."

"How badly are you hurt?"

Tori explained her minor injuries and Cole's condition.

"He's the deputy Marshal you told me about?" Mom said.

"Yes. A good man. He saved my life."

"My purse and keys are walking to the door."

"Mom, stay where you are. I have no idea the extent of Cole's battered body."

"This is your mother, and I'm locking up the house now."

"Hold on for a minute. I can't stop you from coming, but would you call Sally? She shouldn't find out about this on the news."

"Yes, of course."

Tori observed the strangers around her. Some wept. Others talked in hushed voices. A woman rocked an infant. "I do want to see you."

"Oh, honey. That means so much. I'm hanging up now. I'll contact Sally and will see you soon. You know how I feel about talking and driving."

Tori brushed away a tear. Where was her tough-girl FBI agent persona? She dropped her phone into her purse and leaned against the door overlooking the parking lot. Dizzy. Disoriented. If the bad guys shoved their way through the ER doors, she wouldn't have enough sense to shoot back. Inhaling, she closed her eyes. A bed sounded good, but she needed to be alert. A doctor had said Cole was in serious but stable condition. The thought frightened her. How long before the doctor reported back to her?

Cole was a decent man. He had Kevin's good qualities and more—a solid investigator, one whom she admired, respected, and might learn to love. He'd confessed his interest . . .

She and Cole had talked about fear . . . his nightmare and her disease phobia. Today trumped both. She fought to stay awake, especially with the bump on her head. Rubbing her face, she willed away the beating to her body. Too bad there wasn't a pill for logic.

"Ms. Templeton?"

She peered into the face of Dr. Nguyen, the doctor she'd talked to earlier, a petite Asian woman. Her brown eyes emitted confidence.

"How is Cole?"

"Let's sit down and talk." The doctor pointed to an empty area of the visitors' waiting room.

Once seated, Dr. Nguyen smiled, a gesture Tori feared accompanied bad news. "As you may have already realized, Mr. Jeffers lost a considerable amount of blood prior to his arrival. We prefer a patient to build up his own blood as long as he's not in shock. I made a call that the borderline shock and his physical condition eliminated the need for packed cells, and he's responding positively. He regained consciousness in the ER, so we stabilized his airway, breathing, and circulation. We've drawn blood, and until we have the hemoglobin/hematocrit report, we're giving him an IV to support his blood pressure. A cursory physical exam and neurologic evaluation revealed no red flags. That's good, Ms. Templeton. Currently he's having an MRI scan of his head to look for subdural or epidural hematomas—bleeding on the brain. Also X-rays of his left shoulder, ribs, and back. He's tender in some areas, and I want to make sure there aren't any fractures. Assuming those areas are okay, we'll suture his head wound. I've contacted an orthopedic surgeon to explore and debride—"

"What is that?"

"I'm sorry. Debridement is when foreign tissue is removed from a damaged area."

A definition Tori hoped she never heard again.

"Assuming no bone damage, the ortho surgeon will close the wound and put him in a sling."

"Would you say he's still in serious but stable condition?"

"Yes. We'll know more after test results."

Tori trembled and she breathed deeply to control it. "Providing test results and your other procedures go according to plan, what will be the treatment after surgery?"

"If all goes well, he'll be kept at least overnight for observation—vital signs and a neuro check for late symptoms after the blow to the head. His length of stay is difficult to determine at this point."

"I appreciate your explanation."

Dr. Nguyen excused herself, leaving Tori feeling very alone and scared.

If a God truly existed, now was the time for Him to show up. Step through the ER door and wave His magic wand to heal Cole, end the crime spree, and cuff the ones responsible. *What do You want from me? Every Sunday attendance until the day I die? Daily Bible reading?*

A flash of her promise to Kevin . . . The times spent at his grave . . . The moments in her sporadic church attendance when something made sense. Kevin spoke as audibly as if he were standing beside her.

"Sis, don't test God or bargain with Him. Just trust in who He is."

Tori sank onto a chair and buried her face in her hands. Trust was what she had in her job and her skills. Stepping outside her safety net scared her beyond comprehension. Could she even embrace an invisible God? What came of relinquishing control? Kevin claimed peace and a life that began here and existed long after her body turned to dust.

The truth punched her hard. If her way of living hadn't calmed her restless heart, perhaps it was time to accept the intangible. Kevin called Him the Creator of the universe, the God who never slept, and the Author of life.

Yes, God. Whatever this means, I'm on Your side. Please help Cole live through this. I now have faith in what I've thought was a myth. You, Jesus, and the Holy Spirit working to keep me alive . . . and unconditionally loved.

46

TORI'S INJURED ARM THROBBED—the pain meds were supposed to keep the agony under control, but not yet. A strange feeling had swept over her. One she couldn't describe but definitely a supernatural assurance that the ugly happenings would be resolved.

Dozing off, she relived the attack . . . The man who'd shot Cole had laughed at his fallen body. The shooter had raised his weapon to take her out too, but she'd gotten him in the head. Nothing for her to gloat over, just a memory that would live with her forever.

"Ms. Templeton."

She recognized the voice of Dr. Nguyen. Through blinding pain, she opened her eyes to the doctor. "Yes. How is he?"

"Awake and asking for you." The woman smiled. "Insistent, as a matter of fact. He'd like a word before we take him into surgery."

Tori struggled to her feet, and the doctor steadied her. "Be careful, or you'll be in the bed next to him."

"I'm okay. Really. Is there anything else you can tell me?"

"So far, we haven't detected further problems or injuries. Three of his ribs are broken, but we won't have an idea about the damage done to his shoulder until we're in there and the orthopedic surgeon can see what's going on. He'll have scarring from the gunshot and burned area, but a good plastic surgeon can do wonders. Come on back, and you can see him. I'll be with you."

Tori blinked a few times to gain control. *Thank You, God.*

Behind the enclosed area, Cole lay with an IV dripping life-saving fluids into his body. The massive swelling and bruising on his face appeared worse under the bright lights. Stitches on his left temple were an angry red, a sharp contrast to the blue and purple. She took his hand, and he opened his eyes.

"You look awful," he whispered.

"Should've seen the other guy." She bent over the bed. "Hey, you had a close call."

"Plural. *We.*"

"But you drew the short stick. How are you feeling?"

"Haven't decided yet. Mad is right up at the top."

"The ASAC and Max are on their way. Even my mom."

He dragged his tongue over cracked and bleeding lips. "Party." He swallowed hard. "Would you contact my parents? Go light on 'em. Hate for them to hear about this on the news."

"I'd be glad to. I memorized the license plate to the van." She took his hand in hers and wrote on his palm. "Better than any hottie's phone number."

"Hurts to laugh."

"I'm trying my best to keep you entertained."

A nurse opened the drape. "Mr. Jeffers, we'll be taking you shortly to surgery. Any questions or concerns?"

"Just get it done," he managed.

Dr. Nguyen checked his eyes. "What did a big, strapping US Marshal do to make those guys so angry?"

"Stole their girlfriend."

The doctor swung to Tori. "You?"

Tori rolled her eyes like a sixteen-year-old—purposely. "I'm an FBI agent. We're working a case together. I have no idea what he's talking about." She hid her mirth, not sure why when they'd both nearly been candidates for a mortician. "Must be whatever's flowing from his IV."

Dr. Nguyen shook her finger at him. "I might have to cut back on the meds."

Two men in blue scrubs swung back the drape and assisted Cole onto a stretcher.

"I'll be back when you're fixed as good as new," Tori said.

He closed his eyes. "Thanks."

Tori returned to the waiting area, where ASAC Hughes was speaking to an ER nurse. She recognized two FBI agents beside the police officer positioned at the ER door.

The ASAC joined her. "How's he doing?"

"Awake. Hurting. He was just taken to surgery." She relayed his condition.

The ASAC pointed to the seating area. "You're pale as a ghost, Tori. Let's sit down."

They chose an isolated area. She wanted to sleep, badly. "Back to your question. Cole and I left Houston early this morning to attend Preston Ustach's funeral and check out who was in attendance." Tori explained the tail leading up to the firefight. "They either placed a tracker on Cole's truck while we were in church or waited for us to leave the funeral and followed us."

"His vehicle was totaled in the explosion."

She recalled the security guard, a retired man who teased Cole about the pretty girl beside him. "The only witness bled out while I waited for the ambulance." She jammed strength into her words. "Cole told me in so many words that we signed up for whatever it takes to end a crime. It's our job."

"We all enlisted for the same thing. But we still hurt and bleed like anyone else. Take a look in the mirror. I'm sure you feel the same. Let me arrange a ride home."

"Not yet. I'm sticking around until Cole's out of surgery." In truth, she had no plans to leave until Cole was discharged.

He frowned. "Is Max aware of the attack?"

"Janie is driving him here."

"Good news in that arena." His cell rang. "This is a report from our guys at the explosion. I'll be right back." He headed to the ER doors.

Until ASAC Hughes returned, she'd rest. He'd bombard her with questions, and she'd have her own. Right now, she wanted to hear the investigators' initial findings. Then stick with Cole until the doctor determined how to proceed. Oh, the dread of dealing further with the ASAC, Mom, Max, and even Janie. She'd rather sit at Cole's bedside, alone. For that matter, how would the two of them go forward—with the case and her bewildering attraction to him?

Today they proved working together professionally had its perks: he had her back and she had his. Literally. Cole had sheltered her from the onslaught of bullets, and she'd never forget the price he paid.

The ASAC stepped back inside and sat beside her. The familiar lines across his brow told her the intel wasn't good. Before he could speak, she garnered his attention. "What have they found?"

"The van was deserted on a side road. Stolen. Sweeping it now. Blood everywhere. Towing it in." He stuck his hands in his pockets. "We ID'd the dead men."

"Would I recognize them?"

"Hermanos de Pistoleros. Have a reputation for hiring out their services."

"The Pistol Brothers." Guns for hire. Her gaze swept to the interior hospital doors leading to patient care. "Has the public been notified?"

"The PIO released the news to every TV, radio, and online media source."

"Which means they'll be here, and I'm not in the mood to dodge them."

"No need to. I got you covered. Agents and police officers are posted at each entrance and the parking lot. If the Hermanos de Pistoleros bring friends, we have the firepower to stop them." He sighed. "Jose Aznar's cousin is a member of the gang. I want to know where he fit."

47

THE LAST THING Cole wanted to hear was the doctor requesting at least one overnight stay for observation. "Doctor, I have a hard head. No reason for me to drive everyone here nuts."

Dr. Nguyen smiled. "You have a concussion and a slight fever. Furthermore, you could exhibit neurological symptoms that would need to be addressed immediately. We have no idea how your tumble affected the rest of your body."

He tried to demonstrate a trait of humor. "Tumble? Never thought of being chased and shot at as gymnastics."

"Admit him," ASAC Hughes said. "My agents have to be in top physical condition."

"I'm a US Marshal."

"On loan to me." The ASAC tapped the doctor's clipboard. "Admit him." He focused on Cole. "I'll make sure you have protection. By the way, while you wait for your room, visitors are here with Tori."

Although she'd mentioned company on its way, Cole wasn't in the mood for pleasantries. "Better not be a reporter or a troop of Boy Scouts."

"Neither. Max and his wife. Tori's mother."

He groaned. "I hope they have a piñata. Hey, what about my truck and the shooters?"

"Tori can fill you in. While you're lying in bed, I suggest searching online for new wheels."

No surprise there. "Any other good news?"

"I'll keep you posted. Don't worry about coming in on Monday—"

"I'll be there."

He shook his head. "Highly unlikely. But I'm glad you survived the attack. Sorta reminded me of us years ago."

A slight smile surfaced, despite the pain. "If you'd been there, we'd have them arrested by now."

"According to Tori, you made hero status." ASAC Hughes left, giving Cole a few precious moments to put on his optimistic face.

The drape opened and Tori entered first, followed by a striking woman who strongly resembled her, another woman with white hair and no wrinkles, and Max, whose face held more lines than yesterday.

"This is the visitor detail," Tori said. "Cole, this is my mom, Valerie Templeton." The woman waved. "And this is Janie Dublin, Max's wife."

Mrs. Dublin stepped forward and took his hand. "Thank you for putting up with my husband. He can be a handful."

He liked the woman.

"And thanks for putting up with my daughter," Valerie said. "I heard you held your own with her, and that means she's met her match."

Okay, he liked her too. He'd be civil. Turning to Tori, he posed the most important question. "ASAC Hughes claims you have all the information from the shooting. What have you learned?"

"I can fill you in on some of it. The van was abandoned. Towed back to the office."

"Okay. Who's after us?"

"Hermanos de Pistoleros."

The name sounded familiar, but his foggy mind refused to yank it to the surface. "Other than Brotherhood of Latin Gunmen, I'm lost."

"Hispanic prison gang founded in the eighties," Max said. "Independent contractors. Have a tat of a snake running up the left side of their arms. The big question is who hired them."

"Now I remember," Cole said. "Blame the drugs."

"Y'all scare me," Valerie said. "Tori lives this life, but she spares me the inside scoop."

"Twenty-four years of it, and I'll never get used to the danger." Max's wife glanced at her husband. Her compassionate look told Cole her fears referred more to his health than being an agent.

"You're one tough hombre," Max said. "By all rights, you both should be dead."

"Max," Tori said.

"Yeah."

"Had to be God."

Janie nodded. "Without a doubt."

Max was silent. What would it take for him to see he needed God too?

"We need to let this man rest." Janie hooked her arm through Max's.

"Yeah, give Cole and Tori time alone. Let them flirt in private."

Cole stifled the urge to grin.

Less than ten minutes later, the group left him to rest. Truth known, he was exhausted and the steady drip into his veins made him sleepy. He woke an hour later when a nurse helped him roll over onto a stretcher and pushed him toward his suite for the night.

�֍

When Cole opened his eyes, Tori was sleeping in a chair close beside him. She had her hair pulled back with a clip, but a few curls flowed around her face. How peaceful she looked, with the faint light over his bed accenting her beauty. He noted the bandage on her arm. It had to hurt, and still she was there with him. He could get used to her company.

A distant memory crossed his mind, but it must have been a dream.

He managed to wrap his fingers around his phone on the night-stand and pressed in Manny's number. His friend answered on the first ring. Once they got past the catching up, Cole dug into the reason for his call.

"Remember you told me about your cousin in prison?" Cole said.

"Might get parole in ten years. What'cha need?"

"Earlier Tori and I found Jose Aznar's body in a shed at the rig. Hermanos de Pistoleros used me and Tori for target practice this morning. We left three bodies behind. I want to know who paid them. It's linked to Nathan Moore's murder, Preston Ustach, and now two explosions at the same drill site. And Aznar's cousin is a member of the gang."

"Just heard about the firefight and the explosion, but names weren't released. Should have known you were in the middle of it. Were either of you hurt?"

"Tori has a few stitches on her arm and a minor head injury. I'm okay. At the hospital in Galveston waiting to hear from the doctor."

"Close call. I'll light a candle for you at Mass in the morning."

"Thanks. As soon as you have the names, give me a call. Day or night."

"I'll see if I can get hold of my cousin's wife now."

Cole ended the call but kept the phone in his hand and closed his eyes.

"You neglected to tell Manny how seriously you were wounded or that the doctor is keeping you overnight."

He refused to open his eyes and see the scolding in those green depths. "The doctor could review my test results and change her mind."

"Wouldn't put any money on your theory. Agents are outside your door, and I'm sleeping in this chair tonight with my Glock in my shoulder bag."

He blew out his frustration. "You've got to be kidding. How about I take the chair, and you take the bed?"

"Do I hear a bit of male chauvinism?"

"Yes."

"Honesty is the first step toward recovery."

"What am I going to do with you?" If he could have kicked himself, he would have. This wasn't the situation to confess his ever-growing feelings.

She examined the amount of fluid in his IV. "Is that honesty or anger?"

Her softened tone told him what his heart wanted to hear. "Both," he said. "By any chance did you kiss me at the drill site?"

She would not look at him. "We were in the middle of trying to stay alive."

"Not then. Later."

"Really, Cole. Do I look like the kissy-face type?"

Actually she did, but he'd drop it for now. "What have we uncovered that has the bad guys upset?"

"If they were following Preston Ustach, they might think he revealed critical info before he died. We're snooping around. Makes them nervous."

"Do you have any idea the amount of money funding these crimes?" Cole said. "Two explosions at the drill site, Nathan's hacker, a sniper for Ustach, and a hired gang to take us out. What they're hoping to gain must be huge."

"Control of Moore Oil & Gas? Who is running operations now?"

"We'll learn who's in control at the reading of the will."

"Right," she said. "Tuesday. Sally's in line to inherit millions, but who runs the company remains to be seen. None of his immediate officers indicate they have an idea. All appear to be confused and waiting."

"Are you sure the history on his execs has gone deep enough?" He rubbed his face. "If one or more of them is orchestrating the crimes, the very assets making money are being destroyed."

"You're right, Cole. Money is the motivator here. Someone has millions of dollars in their sights."

"We're a smart team. We'll figure it out." The effort to carry on a conversation weighed on him.

Her gaze turned tender. "For the record, if you ever play hero again, try to protect me like I'm a girl with no skills, I'll personally unload my weapon on you."

"As a graduate of the US Marshals' gladiator academy, I might have found my match."

"You have."

He tried to hide the smile, and not because it hurt to move his lips. "Got it, Special Agent Templeton."

"One more thing. God and I have the best friend thing going."

He'd take another bullet to hear her repeat the claim. "What happened? Did you think I was going to die on you?"

"Right, and then I'd have to finish the case with Max."

He settled back against the pillow. "I'm glad. This is better than church."

"Thanks." She pointed to the phone. "Tell me about your call just now."

"An informant for the US Marshals Service might be able to give us a name." He explained Manny's connection. "As soon as I have info, I'll let you know. My turn. What went on after I passed out?"

"Nothing exciting. Just a lot of heat. I phoned 911. Checked on the security guard, but he was gone." She lifted her chin. "I sat beside you and dabbed at the blood on your head and talked."

"What did you say?"

"Mostly how mad I was that you'd been hurt. Ordered you to keep breathing and not bleed out."

"I listened." His eyes grew heavy again. "If my phone rings, would you answer?"

"Sure. Cole, we will stop those guys . . . before they try again."

"I know we wounded a couple of them, and they'll have to risk getting medical attention. Hopefully something results from that. We're closer to answers, or we wouldn't have been in their sights today." His speech had worn him out.

"Why don't you sleep?"

He raised his hand, the one with the IV. "In a minute. Once I'm out of here, I want to talk to Mrs. Aznar."

48

TORI WOKE from a sound sleep to a phone ringing. Her neck ached from the awkward position in the hospital chair. She glanced at the nightstand and saw the screen light up on Cole's cell phone with *Manny*. Groggy and the pain in her head like a jackhammer, she listened to it ring one more time while struggling to reach it. Cole slept through it.

"Cole Jeffers's phone."

"This is Manny Lopez, a friend. Is Cole available?"

"Asleep at the moment."

"Are you a nurse?"

She smiled in the darkness. "No. FBI Special Agent Tori Templeton. My nursing skills are sadly lacking. He said you might call."

"He told me about you. How is he? For that matter, how are you?"

"I'll survive, and Cole will be okay in a few days. I'm glad the doctor admitted him."

"Sounds like he got the bad end of an ugly stick."

"And was beaten with it. The test results are good, which means he'll probably be cut loose in the morning."

"Knowing Cole, he'll be out looking for the gang who did this. When he wakes up, would you tell him I talked to my friend?"

Curiosity would drive her crazy. "Can't you give me the info? We're partners."

"Yeah. I suppose I could."

"I'm awake," Cole said. "Is it Manny?"

"Yes." She pressed Speaker while flipping on the light. "We have Cole with us now."

The two men tossed a few bantering remarks before getting back to why Manny had called.

"Tonight's conversations with my informant confused me about the Moore case," Manny said. "I haven't put it all together in my head, but I'll help any way I can."

What did Manny mean?

"Who ordered Tori and me eliminated?" Cole said, more alert than she expected.

"A man but no name. The only clue to his identity was he spoke perfect English. My informant will continue looking. The thing is if the Hermanos de Pistoleros were hired for the hit and they failed, they didn't get paid."

"Their reputation and cash flow are at stake." Cole glanced at Tori. "They're minus a few men too."

"I'll update you the moment I have something."

"Thanks."

"Pleasure meeting you, Tori." Manny clicked off.

Cole rested against the pillow. "Are you up to sending a request to the ASAC?"

She pulled her phone from her purse and typed. "If you keep hanging out with the FBI, you might find yourself at Quantico."

"No thanks."

"Cole, I don't think we're going to find a thing unless there's another red flag with Jose Aznar or Nathan's trip to London."

"I hate hospitals."

She ignored him and scrolled through her phone for updates. A report hit her radar. "This came in around 3:10 p.m. yesterday. We were probably napping and didn't hear it."

"Read it to me, unless you're not into clerical duties." He chuckled.

She raised a brow. "How do you manage to stay up in the middle of trying to figure out who killed Nathan and all the other crimes?"

"It's the steady drip of sweet stuff flowing through me."

"I want some." She moved her chair a little closer to the bed. "Here's the latest from London. Nathan invested heavily in oil rigs in the North Sea. No partners in the deal." She glanced up. "It makes sense for him to have an office and flat there, though he could also handle the business in the States remotely."

"Who did he purchase the wells from?"

"A German corporation, and the company checked out."

"What about the flat there? Did the agreement mention a woman?"

"No. We could request security footage from the area."

"Request back to September when Sally stated he flew to London. Has she talked much about the reading of the will?"

"There'll likely be surprises, and I want to offer support."

"Should I accompany you? If Nathan made arrangements to financially take care of Anita Krantz, Sally could use both of us."

She studied him, wounded and still thinking about their friend. "I'll ask her."

He looked at the time. "It's 4:32. Can we get a little sleep before we dive into this again?"

"You're hurting, aren't you?"

"I'm not alone. Your face is drawn like your head's about to explode. But requesting pain meds means I'll be in a haze until noon."

"Just in case, Marshal Jeffers, where's your weapon?"

"In my muscles, Special Agent Templeton. Where's yours?"

"My purse is at my feet." She released her hair clip. "But I have a weapon in my hand."

"What?"

She displayed what the hair clip actually contained. "It has six tools—large flat-head screwdriver, small flat-head screwdriver, serrated cutter, 5/16" wrench, a small ruler, and keeps my hair in place." She snapped off the light. "Good night, Cole."

49

SUNDAY BEFORE 10 A.M., a two-man team of FBI agents drove Tori and Cole to their homes. She anticipated a Hermanos de Pistoleros attack, but no one appeared. The stress kept her adrenaline flowing, and her hand wrapped around her Glock. And something new to her arsenal—prayer.

Agents were in place at Cole's home. Janie and Max planned to stay until Manny and his wife arrived. Cole protested, but when Janie asked where he kept his duct tape, he gave in. Then she offered to make a pot of chili and jalapeño corn bread. Tori promised to check in—which also met his disapproval. But she knew he'd sleep the moment he swallowed a few pain pills.

Two agents escorted Tori to her apartment. They searched each room. Finding nothing, they left to guard her apartment from the parking lot. The question penetrating her skull, along with the incessant hammering, kept her pondering. In her desire to keep Sally safe, would she put her friends in danger?

In her living room, she closed the blinds, forcing her injured arm to do part of the work. For some reason, the rock thrown through the Moore window came to mind. The Moores had their own stalkers too. Better she act as an additional bodyguard inside the house than do nothing. With that conclusion, she packed for a few days and requested the agents to continue watching her apartment. Within minutes, the exhaustion from the previous day and the lack of sleep the night before coaxed her into a nap.

She wakened with a need to phone Cole. Manny answered the phone, stating Cole was still asleep. She left a message for her hero to rest and contact her when he wakened.

Once at the Moores', she unpacked her belongings in the guest room. Sally helped after making more than one comment about how tired Tori looked.

"Are you sure you can sleep here? The mattress is a bit hard." Sally opened a drawer and tucked in pajamas. "My bed is comfy. You could sleep there, and I'll take this one."

The idea of sleeping where Nathan had laid his head seemed morbid. "This is perfect." She hugged her friend's waist. "Thanks for caring. Hey, I nearly forgot this, but did Albert Weiman ask you for my address?"

"No. He visited here to express his condolences. Do you remember Erik? According to Albert, he's suffering with MS."

"Albert showed up at my door before six one morning."

"I think he's grieving Erik's illness. And I smelled alcohol on his breath."

Tori finished putting her clothes in drawers and the closet. "Do we have things to do tonight?"

"I've dreaded the task since I woke this morning. Going through Nathan's closet and personal items is depressing to say the least. Frankly, I'm afraid we'll find more evidence of his betrayal."

Tori hated to see her friend this miserable. "Nathan has surprised us with his activities, but he was killed by someone who had no right to take his life. That person deserves to be tried in a court of law. Whoever threatened you and your sons will be found. Because if he isn't stopped, he'll continue."

"Thanks for using the term *he*. Makes me feel better, like I've been scratched off the suspect list."

"You've been deleted from mine. I'd like nothing better than to make an arrest. Even more so is to see you and the boys safe until it's settled."

"I understand. Lance and Jack are my life. I'll do whatever it takes to protect them . . . except run from our home. Surely it will be over soon." She stepped from Tori's hold and closed the bedroom door. "I know I had things planned for tonight, but I keep thinking about Nathan's office in London. Should I tell the boys first?"

"By all means. You don't want them learning anything new from the media or other kids."

"I'm going to do it now."

"Want me along for moral support?" Tori said.

Sally nodded. "I'll find Lance and Jack, then meet you in the media room."

A short while later, Sally informed her sons of Nathan's second office and his trip plans.

"And you knew nothing about this?" Lance's face held no trace of emotion, making him difficult to read until he rubbed the back of his neck. Frustration raged in him.

"He'd mentioned a second office but nothing definite."

"Mom, do you have any idea what it means if it's proven you were aware?"

"Yes. It means I could have motive to murder your dad. But we don't know if he planned to live there permanently."

Jack rushed to his feet. "Can't Aunt Tori speak up for you?"

"I suppose. The problem—"

"So what are we supposed to do now?" Lance said. "We have been threatened, and you could be charged with murder. What then? A foster home?"

Tori bit back a retort. It wasn't about Lance.

Sally paled. "My parents would never let that happen."

Lance snorted, typical. "Oh, great. Kit and Wes to the rescue. Old people telling us what to do. I had enough of their interference when they were here. Really, Mom. They aren't coming back until it's no longer 'dangerous' and this family's name is splattered clean, which means never."

She rose from the sofa, her manicured nails digging into her palms. "Then how should we move forward, Lance?"

His face scrunched with agony. "I'm sorry. Promised myself I wouldn't go off on you. I wish I had answers, to make everything right."

"You've been doing good," Jack said. "A great brother."

Sally glanced at Tori, then back to Lance and Jack. "I . . . can't take much more." She swiped beneath her eye and left the room, leaving Lance speechless.

Tori moved beside him and laid her hand on his shoulder. "Lance, go to your mother and make amends. Hold her. Talk to her. You need to be united in love and support."

He straightened and disappeared down the steps.

50

SUNDAY AFTERNOON, Cole woke to the heavenly smell of chili and corn bread and the hacking sound of Max coughing. Life and its reminders of the mountains and valleys. He hoped Janie could talk some sense into the man.

Cole hurt all over, but he was alive and healing. A vindictive spirit had attached to his heart. The Hermanos de Pistoleros had nearly killed Tori and him. Who was paying them? He wanted to make the arrest.

Max stood in the doorway. "How are you feeling?"

"Furious at whoever is responsible for these crimes. Furious at myself for not figuring it out. Furious at this body that it isn't what it used to be."

He grinned. "Good. 'Cause I'm in the mood to talk."

"Not before he eats," Janie called.

"I can do both." Cole sensed optimism creeping into his brain.

"A man who can multitask," she said. "Rare."

"Don't forget it. I can be scary. Maybe not today."

Her laughter was sweet. No wonder Max acted more human around her. He positioned a chair at Cole's bedside. "I recorded Tori's account of what happened." Max pointed to his phone. "Mind taking a listen while you're eating?"

"Great idea."

A few moments later, Janie brought in a heaping bowl of chili that made Cole's taste buds go crazy. A huge hunk of corn bread dripping in butter and a steaming mug of coffee added to the feast. Janie left them alone while he ate and listened. Obviously Tori had plenty to offer about what happened after the explosion when he'd been knocked unconscious. She regretted the death of the security guard—another innocent victim.

When the recording concluded and the food had disappeared, he turned to Max, who was champing at the bit to talk. A little amusing.

"Anything to add or seen differently?" Max said.

"I counted six men in the van, and three are dead. All identified as members of the Hermanos de Pistoleros?"

"Yes. Law enforcement are running down leads to pick them up for questioning. So far, none have been located."

"A good friend of mine from the US Marshals has an informant. He found out the person calling the shots is male. What I can't figure out is why the gang didn't attempt to get us while I was in the hospital or on the way here."

"Been thinking about it. Agents are posted outside your door, and Tori has protection at the Moores', but we both know how that can go south. So are they waiting for an opportunity, hiding out until the timing's right? Doubt they've been paid since you two are alive."

Cole finished the last of his coffee. "The mastermind hired them, and he's not happy."

"Or she."

"We'll see. Can you get my laptop? I think better when I have a screen in front of me." Cole motioned to the top of his dresser, and Max retrieved it. "Do we have reports on Nathan's business dealings in Europe?"

"Just legal documents. The sellers are legit, wanted to unload their oil rigs, and Nathan bought them. The attorney on file is Liam Canters, located in London. Canters's background is clean. We have the addresses of the new office, flat, and bank in London. Tori requested camera footage."

Max snapped his fingers. "Learned the call Nathan made outside his home on the eve of his death was to Liam Canters. The man admitted it when questioned by our people in London."

"Nathan must have been friends with him to share personal information." Cole closed his eyes as a stab of pain swept through his body. "I want to know who gains the most from his death—the million-dollar question."

The doorbell rang and he saw the time. "Manny and Lacy are here. You and Janie are officially off the caretaker role. Thanks for being here. You two are a great team."

"We used to be. I'd like to think we could be again."

"Is she pushing more treatments?"

Max blew out his irritation. "Like a mule. But any extra time with her . . ."

"I'm on your side."

Max shook his head. "I know it, even when I can be meaner than a skunk."

Cole stayed awake the remainder of the day, deliberating facts and fighting the aftereffects of Saturday's attack. Manny and Lacy had arrived in separate cars. In a couple of hours, she could return to their children. Manny hadn't uncovered anything—yet. Exhaustion and pain meds sent Cole to sleep.

Gunfire jarred him awake. His clock read 10:00.

"Stay put," Manny growled from outside Cole's bedroom. "You'll get us both killed."

Cole ignored him and grabbed his Glock from the nightstand. "My house, and they're after me."

By the time Cole made it to the foyer, it was pitch-black.

Another exchange of gunfire alerted him to someone inside. Too close.

He fought to clear his head. Calling out to Manny would give away where Cole stood in the shadows.

Movement to the far left caught his attention.

"Cole, look out!" Manny's voice came from the right.

He dropped to the floor, and a bullet flew past. He fired to the left, a grunt and thud telling him a man was down.

The front door burst open and agents raced in. Someone flipped on a light.

"Cole," Manny said. "You all right?"

"Yeah." Cole moved to the downed man, who was closer to him than the agents or Manny. A jab of white-hot pain hit him hard as though the adrenaline had temporarily masked his body's condition. Bending to the man who was bleeding out from the stomach, Cole felt for a pulse. Faint. "He's alive."

One of the agents requested an ambulance.

The man wore a black hoodie matching the attackers from the previous day. Cole pulled it off . . . A Hispanic with a tattoo of a snake running up his left shoulder, a Hermanos de Pistoleros. "Who sent you?" Cole said in Spanish.

The man groaned, and Cole repeated his request in Spanish and English. He leaned closer to discern a faint whisper.

"Pra . . ."

"What? Who?" Cole said, but the man had breathed his last.

51

MONDAY MORNING, Cole pried himself out of bed and made it to the office by 8:48 a.m. Having an FBI agent escort him inside the building was downright embarrassing. He plodded along like an old man, stopping to rest far too often. Last night's break-in had caused him to use muscles that needed to heal. Agents had seen a truck speeding away with at least two other shooters. License plates were from a stolen vehicle, a habit for the gang. Another dead man, and his last utterance was puzzling. The *pra* sound didn't sound like Krantz, Lawd, Sally Moore, the execs, or anyone else. For all Cole knew, the man could have been calling out to a loved one.

Cole craved sleep and his shoulder was a mass of fiery pain, but caffeine offered a jolt. His whole body had taken a beating. Where were the days when he managed an all-night stakeout, got into a fistfight, and didn't flinch driving to work the next day? The tail end of his thirties hit a man hard, and this morning his body confirmed it. Max would have a field day.

Sitting in the interview room, temporarily his office, he concentrated on Nathan, the man no one seemed to know. He'd arranged his life to suit himself, every detail manipulated for his purposes. The first incident that surfaced was the affair with Anita Krantz and the photos taken in Vermont. Later, while his new office building was being designed, Sally insisted on his adding a bedroom for those late nights when she worried about him driving home. Nathan initially refused but, after he was robbed, agreed to her wishes.

Robbed.

HPD would have a report of the crime.

He phoned Detective Hernandez. "Would you have the records of a robbery involving Nathan Moore in October 2013?"

"Give me a few to pull it up."

Cole closed his eyes. Numbing meds weren't an option, which was why he had to be working.

"Got it," Hernandez said. "Send it to you?"

"Yes. First tell me what happened."

"Nathan Moore called 911 at 11:45 on the night of October 16. He'd been held up at gunpoint in the garage of his office. The previous building, not the new one. His wallet and a few credit cards were missing, along with five hundred dollars cash. An artist's sketch led us to a man by the name of Vince Greene, who'd been arrested six months prior for a DUI. None of Moore's possessions were recovered, but Moore refused to press charges."

"Why?"

"Good question."

"Do you know where I could find Greene?"

"No. No arrests since then."

"All right. Thanks." Cole swung his laptop into action. He contacted the US Marshals and requested a history on Vince Greene. Tori and Max would have used the FIG, but they weren't there.

Tori was in the ASAC's office reviewing her report about Saturday's incident, and Max had an early morning doctor's appointment and should arrive shortly.

After reading e-mails, Cole checked in with Manny for any updates. Nothing.

How did the trip to London fit into Nathan's murder? Sally claimed no knowledge of those plans, but was she telling the truth? True, someone had tossed a rock through her window, but a carefully planned murder took into consideration every detail. He ran his fingers through his hair. *Admit it, Cole.* Though the odds continued to stack up against Sally, his gut told him she had nothing to do with it.

Another reason he wanted to be at the reading of the will. Had Nathan provided for his mistress? For that matter, was Anita Krantz aware of the London venture?

He got Anita on the phone. When she answered, he identified himself.

"I recognized your voice. How are you feeling?"

"Better than Saturday."

"Shouldn't you be resting and letting someone else conduct the investigation?"

"Appreciate the concern. But I can't turn calendars off when a case hits. It's get the job done before more innocent people are hurt. I won't take much of your time, but I have a question."

"All right." The reluctance in her voice told him she wanted this over.

"Were you aware Nathan planned to leave for London the day after he was murdered?"

"Since he's gone, does it matter?"

"Ms. Krantz?"

"He told me about the trip and said he was telling Sally that night. Planned to be gone four days. I assumed he was conducting business with a German company."

"He'd already purchased oil rigs in the North Sea. No partners. Rented office space, hired staff, purchased a flat."

She sobbed, but he refused to be duped. "I don't understand what he was doing."

"How could he have made the transactions without your knowledge?"

"I suppose Jacob Farr handled it."

"Actually Liam Canters in London is the attorney on record. Is the name familiar?"

"No, sir."

"Let me get the facts straight, Ms. Krantz. You'd had an affair with Nathan Moore since 2012, but you were not privy to his decision to open a second office?"

"Correct." Her voice trembled. "Was Sally aware?"

"No."

"Then don't bother me."

If Nathan were alive, Krantz would have motive to kill him—unless she was lying now. "How do you feel about the new information?"

"Nathan's business. I resigned, or have you forgotten?"

"Thanks for your time." He ended the call and sent texts to Tori and Max.

Cole's next move was a look at the timeline of incidents. He started a new file after realizing that the brainstorming bubbles had been a waste of time due to the intricacy of evidence and those involved.

1. Nathan gets involved with Anita Krantz. Office bedroom added to his plans for new site after robbery.
2. EPA files suit and loses.

3. Nathan receives threatening phone calls and texts.

4. Drill site bombed in Texas City.

5. Preston Ustach has information regarding bombing.

6. Anita Krantz pregnant. Resigns from Moore Oil & Gas.

7. Nathan killed when pacemaker is hacked.

8. Rock thrown through Moores' home window.

9. Ustach murdered by sniper.

10. Nathan's second office in London verified.

11. Jose Aznar found dead at rig site.

12. Tori and Cole in firefight with Hermanos de Pistoleros.

13. Cole attacked at his home by the same gang.

Max walked into the interview room and sat across from Cole. "Are you sure you need to be here?"

"That's priceless, considering."

"Feeling okay. Things in my life are looking up."

Max and Janie must be talking. Cole breathed in and sensed the need for a couple of Aleve. "I have a hunch about our case."

"Sally Moore may be our killer?"

"Hope not. What if we're looking at two separate crimes?"

"I think you're fishing in shallow water."

Cole would ponder his idea while continuing to view the crimes from all sides. "Max, where are you on this? We need to weed out the truth."

Max smiled, no doubt remembering the remark he'd made about Cole pulling the weeds in this case. "Two things could split this case wide open—the reading of the will and the security footage from London. The company Moore kept there, either male or female, has the potential of shoving facts into the case. By the way, Sally's financials are in order, although every account was jointly held with her husband."

"Let's say she's Nathan's killer or funded all the crimes—where's her bankroll?"

"Overseas account."

"But we've done the research, and nothing surfaced. I have a difficult time believing she's devious."

"You didn't think her husband was either."

Irritating when other people were right. "Dig deeper, see if that's a possibility."

Tori walked into the room. "What's a possibility?"

"That Sally could be devious."

She slid onto a chair. "I hope not."

"Cole here thinks we could be looking at two separate cases— the bombing and other crimes related to the oil rig and Nathan Moore's murder."

She crossed her arms and stared at Max. "I disagree. The crimes *are* related, which says to me one person is calling the shots, someone who has the money and skills to make it happen. Only a coincidence would bring their occurrences within a few days of each other."

The MO of Nathan's death did not fit the violence seen in Texas City. "It's a theory. Period," Cole said. "But beyond that, I want to talk to Mrs. Aznar this morning. She may know what we need to end these crimes no matter how they were done."

"I agree she needs an interview," Tori said. "But not the two separate crimes theory. The pain meds are fogging your brain."

"Over-the-counter ones, not heavy-duty. What else do you have for us?"

She smiled. "The techs are still on the London aspect, but they haven't found any red flags."

Max got her attention. "Do any of the reports about Moore's calls incorporate the London transactions?"

"No. Which brings us back to why he chose to leave Anita and his executives out of the London office decision. To the best of our knowledge, he'd not broken the law. A few moral codes, but nothing that would give him jail time." She turned to Cole. "Was Anita upset when you asked her about the trip?"

"She did the burst into tears thing." A stab of pain raced through his wounded shoulder, and he held his breath until it subsided. "In her background, do we have any acting? High school or college? And I want a DNA test to make sure Nathan is the father of her child."

Max nodded. "I still think she's waist-deep in this."

"As I said before, we need evidence." Cole typed one-handed on his laptop. "Who are her friends? The surveillance team indicated she was a loner, but her position required more of a social personality." Anita was probably just a woman used and spit out like Sally.

"Then let's find out for sure." Tori glanced at her watch. "Anything else before we talk to Mrs. Aznar?"

"Yes," Cole said. He relayed what Detective Hernandez had told him about Nathan's robbery and the man behind it. "I have an address where Vince Greene works as a mechanic."

Max had a coughing spell, but once he stopped, he said, "Where are you going with this?"

"I'd rather wait until we talk to Greene."

An update sailed into their phones, info about Jose Aznar's murder investigation. Neither Aznar's cousin César Vega nor any members of the Hermanos de Pistoleros had been located.

"Aznar was executed," Cole said. "No tattoo, so he wasn't a member. I suspect he set up Ustach, but that's speculation unless Mrs. Aznar gives us insight."

Max displayed his keys. "I'm driving."

"No thanks," Tori said. "You two old warhorses can't be trusted behind the wheel."

Cole refused to relinquish the possibility of separate crimes. It stayed fixed in his mind, and he intended to ride it out—even if he was an old warhorse.

52

TORI DROVE the two men first to a mechanic's shop near Houston Baptist University. She parked outside the garage entrance and settled back in the seat.

"Why is this stop important to you?" she said to Cole.

"If it proves, one more time, Nathan lied, then we have another lead to investigate. Possibly another person of interest."

"Good call." Max opened the passenger door in the front seat. "I'm behind you."

Cole might be right on this one.

Greene was the head mechanic, an African American in his fifties. Trim build. Bald. Cole introduced the three and asked to speak to him privately.

Greene eyed them. "What's this about?"

"Nathan Moore."

He sighed and led the way to a cramped office that left Cole and

Max standing. Greene squeezed in behind a metal desk to a chair, and Tori took a seat in front of him.

"Look, I got in trouble with Moore some years ago. Nothing since then. I saw he was killed, and I'm real sorry. He gave me a second chance at life, and I never forgot it."

"We know," Cole said. "Can you tell us what happened the night you robbed him?"

"Not much there." He shrugged. "He came off the elevator and I held him up before he got to his car. Took a couple of credit cards and five hundred dollars cash. Mr. Moore felt sorry for me and didn't press charges."

Just like Detective Hernandez had told Cole.

"Did Mr. Moore talk to you after that?"

"Asked me to help him out once. Didn't want his wife to know. I owed him for what he'd done." He scratched the back of his neck.

"Doing what?"

"Had me follow his son, Lance. Thought he might be running with a bad crowd. Been giving him trouble. But after three weeks, I told him I was wasting my time. Good kid."

"Back to the robbery. Is there anything you'd like to tell us about Mr. Moore?"

Greene moistened his lips. "Guess it don't matter no more since Mr. Moore's gone." He peered into Cole's face. "I didn't tell the truth about what happened. I'm not a thief."

"Mr. Greene." Cole softened his tone. "Did Mr. Moore pay you to stage a robbery for the five hundred dollars in his wallet?"

Tori counted ten seconds. The thought of how Nathan misrepresented so many things was despicable, but unfortunately with all they'd uncovered about Nathan . . .

"Yes. I used to work for the Mercedes place where he brought his car. One day he asked me if I wanted to earn some extra money. I said yes, and we struck up a deal. He made up the part about a gun. I don't even own one. Of course, I hadn't planned on losing my job but I've been here a long time now."

"Did Mr. Moore give you a reason for the staged robbery?" Cole said.

"No, sir. But I figured it out when I heard him talking on the phone."

"What did you hear?"

"Told his girlfriend he'd taken care of his wife finding out about them. He laughed. Said something about 'another one of my crazy stunts.'"

"Was he ever in the company of anyone else when you saw him?"

"Sometimes when he dropped off his car, a tall blonde was with him. He called her Ann, I think. But our conversations were private."

Obviously Anita Krantz.

Cole thanked Greene, and they piled into the car to head toward the Texas City area, where Jose Aznar's widow lived.

Max started the conversation beside her. "Who was Nathan Moore? The charitable millionaire, family man, and friend? Or a deceiver, liar, control mongrel?"

"Wish we knew," Tori said.

Cole piped up. "He was an only child. Given everything. His parents taught him to make money and keep it. Unaffectionate. He said their lack of caring scarred him emotionally. Even that could have been a lie for Sally or Anita to be sensitive to his needs."

She glanced in the rearview mirror at Cole. His face was scrunched, his eyes closed while he spoke. "Take about three of whatever you're using to kill the pain. You look awful. We'll have more info once we have answers about Krantz, talk to Aznar's wife, learn the contents of the will, and view the London footage."

Max took a drink of water. "Even with a note to speed up matters, the paternity testing will take one to two days, providing Krantz doesn't object. If it goes to court, then we're looking at a huge delay."

"If she refuses," Cole said. "Then chances are the baby isn't Nathan's. Then again . . . I've been wrong before."

Tori listened while she drove. *Nathan, who killed you—and why?*

❊

Tori noted Jose Aznar's widow, a petite woman with dark hair and olive skin, lived in a well-kept mobile home park in Texas City. Her English contained a Hispanic accent. Her reddened eyes and the way she clutched a baby girl to her chest confirmed her heartache. Tori made the introductions, and the four sat in the living area. Her parents waited in the kitchen, but Jose's widow refused to relinquish the baby.

"Mrs. Aznar, we are so sorry for your loss." Tori reached out and touched the young woman's hand wrapped around her child. "We will find out who did this, but we need help. Can you answer a few questions?"

She gave a thin smile through her tears and nodded.

"Your baby girl is beautiful." Tori meant every word. Lovely dark hair and huge brown eyes veiled in thick lashes.

"Thank you. Her name is Sofía." She blinked. "We were so happy, and he loved his job at the drill site."

"We believe he was the target of the Hermanos de Pistoleros. Had he mentioned being afraid or said anything about the gang?"

"No."

"I understand his cousin is a member of the gang."

She nibbled on her lower lip and nodded.

"Did the cousin spend much time with your husband?"

"A little."

Tori touched the young woman's arm. "We believe the Hermanos de Pistoleros killed your husband. That means his cousin. We think this is César Vega."

"Yes, ma'am."

"Do you know where he is or any of the gang?"

"I don't know anything."

"Did he ever meet with his cousin?"

She nodded.

"Where did Jose meet with César?"

"He never told me." The young woman trembled.

"We know these men are very bad, and we can protect you."

She lifted a tearstained face. "I can't tell what I don't know."

Tori would try a new angle. "What about Jose's relationship with Preston Ustach?"

"He and Preston were *amigos*—friends. When Preston was killed, Jose took it hard. He couldn't sleep. Shaky. Drank too much. Wouldn't talk to me."

"He want you to come to California with us," the older man in the kitchen said. "Jose say he afraid for you and Sofía."

The young woman turned to the man. "I will move back home with you, *Papá*. I promise."

Tori caught the man's attention. "Were you aware of threats?"

"Only what I said, ma'am. We just arrived here to help our daughter through the next few days."

Tori thanked him. "Who were Jose's friends?"

"The men at work."

Tori, Cole, and Max expressed their condolences, gave Mrs. Aznar their cards, and left the grieving family.

Had Jose and Preston learned about a scheme that got them killed? Or had Jose laid the groundwork for Preston to be murdered and then outlived his usefulness?

53

TORI WATCHED SALLY dip pieces of tenderized chicken into egg batter for Monday's dinner. Lance and Jack loved her fried chicken, mashed potatoes, and gravy. Tonight, Cole would join them. Although Tori enjoyed being with him, she could have easily slipped into her pajamas and eaten dry cereal in bed.

"It's time I prioritize my emotions and think about the boys," Sally said. "Cooking is just the beginning. When Nathan was alive, we had family outings, vacations, movie nights." She stopped, her back to Tori. "Was it all an act? He said he loved us. I never doubted him. I never refused him. So why Anita? Who was this man who deceived me repeatedly?"

Earlier, Tori had told her about Vince Greene. "Cole said something today, and I wanted to see if you have the answer. Did Anita ever mention being involved with drama in high school or college?"

Sally turned to study her. "No. Are you suggesting she's putting on an act?"

"Maybe. We're looking into it."

"Might have been a good reason for Nathan to choose her."

Tori moved to her side. "Dwell on the good memories because if you torture yourself with unanswered questions, bitterness will destroy you."

Sally squeezed egg batter and bread crumbs against her palms. "I hate him for the lies, for his last words to Lance and Jack, and for cheating on me with a woman I called a friend. It haunts me day and night. All the so-called family times will never erase the treachery."

"Listen to me. If you don't move on, Nathan succeeds in controlling you even in death. Because control is the bottom line here. Are you ready to be strong and lead this family?"

"I loved him, and it hurts. I want to hide in my room and believe he'll be home and all will be okay."

Tori drew her into a gentle embrace. "I'm so sorry."

"My hands are messy."

"I don't care." This whole case was messy.

After several moments of sobbing, Sally drew back. "I'll be stronger. I can do this." She stared at the raw meat. "A good reason to make the boys' favorite meal. Nathan despised it. I—" Her cell phone rang, interrupting whatever she planned to say next. She looked at the screen. "I don't recognize the number, but it could be important."

"I can handle it."

"No thanks." Sally wiped her hands on a paper towel and greeted the caller. "Hello." She covered her heart. "What do you mean? . . . I understand."

Tori snapped her attention to her friend. Sally trembled, eyes wide.

"I can't get that much cash in two days' time. It's all tied up in assets and the legal formalities of my husband's death."

Tori grasped her attention and mouthed, "Keep the caller talking." She pressed in a request for the FBI to trace the call.

"I'll do exactly as you say. Why are you doing this?" Sally set the phone on the counter. "He hung up," she whispered. "He demanded two million dollars in cash or he'd kill Lance and Jack."

"Did he give you a drop point?"

"No. Said he'd let me know."

Tori grabbed Sally's shoulders. "The boys are upstairs. You have bodyguards and I'm here. The caller doesn't have them—it's a cheap threat."

"He said if I told the FBI, I'd regret it." She raced from the kitchen. Tori followed her up the winding staircase.

"Lance! Jack!" Sally's voice rose near hysteria.

The two appeared from the media room. "What's wrong, Mom?" Jack said.

"Better sit down," Tori said. "Your mother just received a call requesting money or you two would be hurt. But the caller has no idea the power of Houston's law enforcement task force."

"We have Dad's guns," Lance said. "Jack and I know how to use them."

"Under no circumstances," Sally said, her voice now even. "They are locked up, and I'm the only one who has the key. Our horror will not get either of you hurt needlessly."

"Trust me and all those working to end these crimes," Tori said. "The one responsible is getting bolder, which means mistakes are bound to happen."

"Doing nothing makes me feel like a coward." Lance clenched his fists. "The three of us have to stand together."

"We are and will." Sally took the boys' hands. "Clear heads and doing exactly what Tori and Cole tell us is the best decision we can make."

Tori smiled at the tender scene, but she feared what the bad guys could do before they were apprehended.

✤

While driving to the Moore home in a rental car, Cole mulled over Sally's predicament. One episode after another had threatened her and the boys—and made the task force look like the JV team. The caller had used a burner phone. The task force could have traced the call if the person had stayed on the line. The idea of failing Sally and the boys attacked him hard.

Cole crossed the Hermanos de Pistoleros from his mental list of caller suspects. They didn't deal in idle threats. They would have issued enough firepower to take out the bodyguards—or at least attempt to. His theory of two separate crimes lingered. The Hermanos weren't hackers but guns for hire. Hacking Nathan's pacemaker took a special skill set.

This case had two criminals working simultaneously. But how did he prove it when he hadn't been able to make an arrest? How many men had their fingers in every situation connected to the crimes? Had he lost all manner of reason or was he on to something?

Tori, Max, and Cole were smarter than these guys. What had they missed?

He wanted answers now, but the theories slamming against his brain took time to investigate. Already Anita Krantz was back-pedaling the paternity test, wanted to discuss it with her attorney. Which told Cole her baby didn't belong to Nathan. What was the deal there? Had Anita really told Nathan about the pregnancy so he'd include her in his will while she had plans to eliminate him? Would she work with someone to bomb a drill site and a gang to murder him? Her financials indicated nothing out of the ordinary.

Or was Cole simply trying to slide pieces into place and ignore the pain in his body?

Before he arrived at the Moore home, security footage from London hit his in-box. He pulled the rental into the parking area of a convenience store and viewed the report and images. The dates were from the previous September. Nathan had entered a bank in the city alone. While there, he established a presence for a new oil and gas company called Lance Jack Oil & Gas. Cole startled. Nathan had named his new company after his sons?

Playing the footage, he watched Nathan leave the bank with a man identified as a vice president. They returned two hours later. Cole scanned the report, knowing he, Tori, and Max needed dedicated time to analyze it. He swiped through the video frames, pausing when Nathan appeared late at night with a woman, a brunette, her identity hidden from the security camera. A name was mentioned in the report, a woman for hire. The remaining images held nothing incriminating.

Anita Krantz had access to everything in Nathan's business and personal life. Time to visit her again and hope she didn't lawyer up. If she was aware that Nathan had other affairs while refusing to leave Sally, she had motive for murder.

After dinner, Cole and Tori rode in his rental to Anita Krantz's condo, but he let her drive. Tori had arranged for extra inside protection for the Moores while she was gone.

"Have you considered the times we've interviewed her at night?" he said.

"Has to mean something, but my body is too tired to figure it out. I'll sleep on it."

He chuckled, unable to stop the wheels from turning inside his head. "I know this looks like a spurned woman arranged the murder of her lover, and my gut tells me she knows more than she's admitting."

"Refusing to take the DNA test is a biggie," Tori said. "It's practically an admittance that Nathan isn't the father when noninvasive prenatal paternity is available."

"Would it even matter if he's named her in his will?"

"True. The damage's done with the affair. We'll find out in the morning." She frowned. "You're hurting. I saw it all evening."

"I'll take meds when I get home. I'm tired of chasing these guys. Used to making an arrest in three days. Anyway, how are you?"

"I'm okay," she said, but he saw the weariness.

Cole would have reached across the seat and taken her hand if she hadn't needed it to drive. "For the record. You did kiss me."

"I thought you were dying. You know, a send-off."

"Next time, I want to be awake."

Her eyes stayed fixed on the road ahead. "In your dreams."

At the Krantz condo, Anita stood in the doorway, one hand on the door. "We have nothing to discuss. Asking for the test to prove Nathan is the father of my baby will not make it happen."

"Why?" Cole said softly. "We'll get a court order and eventually learn the truth."

"It's ridiculous. Of course it's Nathan's baby."

"Then why the hesitation?"

She stiffened. "We're finished without my lawyer."

54

TUESDAY MORNING, Tori switched her phone to vibrate when she entered Jacob Farr's office. Once seated, she studied Nathan's attorney. He avoided eye contact with her and stared directly at Sally, which left Tori a bit apprehensive about the proceedings. Was he nervous? Why? In any event, Tori would listen to every word. In Sally's fragile condition, her friend could easily miss a detail.

Jacob Farr folded his hands over top a file. "How are we doing, Mrs. Moore?"

He had two strikes against him using the word *we*.

"As best as can be expected."

"Please, let me again offer my condolences." He reached for a box of tissues and placed it in the center of his desk.

"Thank you," Sally said. "I've not seen the will. Neither have I false illusions about its contents."

He studied her a moment. "Mrs. Moore, I regret your husband's untimely death. Nathan was a good friend and client. I hope the authorities are able to find who disrupted your and your sons' lives with this tragedy. Nathan updated his will a year ago to name a new executor. The executor declined to join us this morning."

"Who is the person?"

"Anita Krantz."

Sally gasped, and Tori took her hand. "I see. My husband had a peculiar way of forming alliances. Since he chose to make plans about the distribution of his assets without me, should I brace myself?"

"Ms. Krantz's responsibilities are to ensure the estate is administered in a timely fashion, public notices filed, all debts paid, and distributions made according to instructions left by your husband. She has been asked to complete the tasks in accord with statutory requirements. You won't find many surprises."

Sally stopped him with the wave of her hand. "A question here. Was Anita previously aware of her role as executor?"

He sighed. "She claims not to have prior knowledge, and I have no proof otherwise. Nathan was insistent the contents remain undisclosed until the time of his death. Shall we continue?"

"Mr. Farr—" Sally arched her back—"I simply want to know the provisions made for my sons."

"I understand. In addition to their college funds, Nathan provided that trusts be established for Lance Wesley Moore and Jack Nathan Moore. The trusts will be funded with four million dollars each, accessible when the boys attain age twenty-five, provided they are competent and able to manage their own affairs. Until then, your sons, as beneficiaries of their individual trusts, and with the approval of the trustee, may make certain withdrawals of funds. These are limited to additional education, living, wedding, or start-up business expenses, for example, and they must meet conditions set forth in the documents. I can read over those terms in detail, if you like, or you may simply take a copy of the document home to read at your leisure."

"Who is named as the trustee?"

"Your husband named you as a cotrustee acting along with Chase Bank, or a bank of your choosing within guidelines set forth in the document. The bank can be changed at any time per your decision, but there must always be a professional cotrustee acting together with you. This is for both your and your sons' protection, Mrs. Moore. We don't know what the future holds, and you may find it helpful to have an uninterested third party involved should either of your children wish to withdraw monies in the future."

Tori relaxed slightly. She glanced at her left wrist. How odd— she couldn't remember touching it since she chose to follow God. Sally's voice pulled her to the present.

"And I can contact you with questions?" The edge to her friend's voice had disappeared.

"By all means, feel free to consult with me. The operation of Moore Oil & Gas in the United States and international holdings are solely yours, as well as day-to-day operations and—"

"Did you say the international holdings?"

"Yes. Unbeknownst to me until the FBI brought it to my attention were the purchases in the North Sea. Nathan was confident in your ability to maintain and build the corporation and has named two vice presidents who will mentor you."

"What about Ms. Krantz?" Sally said.

"She's been awarded 10 percent of the stock."

Nathan, your family came first even though I question many of your actions. No mention of another child, either.

"Is there a contingent plan?"

"In the event of your refusal or inability to direct the company, Lance and Jack would take over. If they were not of age, the court would decide who'd manage the operation until Lance reached age twenty-one."

Sally nodded.

"One more item," Mr. Farr said. "Nathan has a document to be delivered to you two days after the reading of his will. He arranged this after the bombing of his drill site. You will need to be home this coming Thursday afternoon after three o'clock in order to sign for it."

Sally released Tori's hand and reached for a tissue on the desk. "Thank you, Mr. Farr. I'm pleased with how my husband arranged for our care."

Within twenty minutes, the two women left the attorney's office. Tori pulled her cell phone from her purse and unsilenced it. She texted Cole and Max.

Nathan appointed Krantz as executor & gave her 10% of company.

Do u have a copy of will?

Yes. Will drop it by office after taking Sally home.

In the elevator, Tori turned to her friend. "Are you okay?"

"I will be."

"I wish I could spend time with you, but this is requalifying day with firearms, tactics, and other skills."

"Standing on my own two feet is a prerequisite to raising my sons."

They exited the elevator and walked wordlessly to the parking lot.

"Nathan provided well for you and the boys," Tori said, disarming the alarm on her Charger.

Sally slid into the passenger side. "I'm not happy Anita is executor, but too many other things could have gone wrong, especially with the boys. I'm amazed Nathan had the confidence in me to run Moore Oil & Gas. I've always welcomed a challenge, and learning the business is definitely an undertaking. I'm thinking the document to be delivered on Thursday is about my running the business."

"You're a smart woman. You'll figure it all out." Tori drove toward the parking lot exit. In the rearview mirror, she detected the two bodyguards directly behind them.

Sally massaged her neck. "Nathan, who killed you? I really don't think it was Anita. We . . . we used to talk about him, his perfectionism and workaholic tendencies. But I was wrong about my husband and very well wrong about her. You've told me everything, right? Anita's refusal to have the paternity testing, Nathan's dealings in London, Vince Greene, all of it?"

"All I can. We're moving closer." She'd not tell Sally about the London footage with the unidentified woman.

What had Nathan arranged for Sally to see after his death? A clue to his killer? More of his immoral activities? Other children?

✳

Late morning, Cole sat in his makeshift office with Max and read through a copy of Nathan's will. The document was straightforward with nothing unexpected, except for Anita's share of Moore Oil & Gas and her role as executor.

"I've been thinking about Krantz and Franc Lawd." Max rubbed his jaw. "Sorta out there, but both of them are part of this case. I can feel it."

"Tori and I stopped in to see her last night about the paternity test, but she lawyered up. Another reason we need the DNA."

"Do you think she'd go for Lawd?"

"When she had Nathan Moore?" Cole deliberated the matter. "The situation would get sticky if she turned up pregnant with Lawd's baby."

"It could implicate both of them in murder." Max pressed his lips together. "Honestly, I can't figure out how the crimes in Texas City are related."

"Two separate crimes. Nathan was killed through technology. The Hermanos de Pistoleros are paid assassins, violent."

"No. That isn't the answer either. We've missed the obvious. I bet when we find one of the Hermanos de Pistoleros, we'll get answers."

"Neither Lawd nor Krantz have the money to pay a gang. Plus, murders and bombings only served to destroy Moore Oil & Gas. Not a smart move." Cole pushed his thoughts into words. "I suggest pressing Krantz. One minute she offers cooperation, and the next she's backpedaling."

Max broke into a coughing spasm, and while he recovered, Cole pulled up Anita's background. Motivation was always birthed in life experiences.

"Hey, Max, Anita was part of the drama team in high school and college. She could pull off the part of a wounded woman."

His cell phone rang, and he snatched it the moment Manny's name hit the screen. Once his friend finished with the how-are-you-feeling? remarks, he dug into the case. "I talked to my informant."

"Bring it on."

"The Hermanos de Pistoleros were hired to create trouble on the rig. Possibly Aznar was working with them and Ustach figured it out. Aznar wanted out, but the gang threatened his family."

"Sounds like his usefulness ran out."

"My thoughts too. Anyway, the gang members hang out at a bar in Galveston. I have to be someplace later on, but I'll see what I can dig up there."

"Thanks. Any other names for us to follow up on?"

"No."

"What about the person who hired them?"

"Male. That's all I was able to learn."

"And it helps." Too many inquiries could cost the informant's life. "Appreciate your getting back to me." Cole relayed the conversation to Max.

"What about the bar in Galveston?"

"It's not a place you and I can go. Our white faces would shine like headlights. Manny will dig a little and get back to us."

"Good thing I have a doctor's appointment, or I'd be in Krantz's face." Max coughed long and hard, like his lungs were filled with gravel.

"You needed a lung yesterday."

"I'm ready to have it yanked out and live a while longer. Janie is going with me to see the doctor after work today. She's persuaded me to have a pneumonectomy." He grabbed a tissue from a box. Without looking, Cole surmised there was blood.

"I'll go through the surgery for her," Max said, "even if it only gives me a couple of months."

"She loves you."

"We've been together over thirty years. She's willing to give me another chance after I messed up our marriage. Don't ever make the same mistake I did. Family has to come first. Nothing else matters at the end of the day."

The closest Max had come to being a friend. "Try church. Will give you a new perspective. By the way, I'll be there when you have surgery."

"I won't have a clue. They'll have me asleep." He opened the door and stepped out.

The quiet moved Cole to concentrate on what he believed. Krantz and Lawd were both lying. Vince Greene might know more than he'd admitted too.

55

SUNSET MET TORI in undulating billows of pink and purple as she drove back to Sally's home after requalifying. Her thoughts were rooted in unsolved crimes and unanswered questions. Right now, wisdom in how to proceed sounded good. Cole insisted Anita Krantz was hiding something, and Franc Lawd's reason for visiting the oil rig before the bombing was connected. She'd go along with it and see how it played out.

Once she parked her car in the Moore garage, she found Sally on the patio in a lounge chair, her chin resting on knees drawn to her chest.

"How are you doing?" Tori eased into a lounge chair beside her.

Dark circles dug beneath her eyes. "Lost in a nightmare. The same one night and day. I'm being chased, and I'm running, but those who offer sanctuary are in the middle of a black forest. I'm afraid to venture either way."

"I'm so sorry."

"I thought the reading of the will would be a mental exercise in composure, but it grew worse." She looked sideways at Tori. "This isn't a time to lecture me about being strong. I'm hanging on by a thread."

"I'm your friend. Ready to listen and help."

"How do you keep the pace of an agent and endure the flow of tragedies?"

"It's my purpose in life. Although it's often difficult and at times dangerous, I've never thought of working in any other career."

"Nursing had its down days and stress, but I was never afraid for those I love or myself. Tori, I've spent hours this afternoon trying to look at the crimes from your point of view, and I see how I could look guilty with what's been uncovered about Nathan's activities. Thank you for believing in me, supporting me through all the roller-coaster emotions. You're the best sister-friend I could ever have. I just want to learn the truth."

"Me too, and soon." Tori remembered the night Lance revealed the contents of Nathan's computer. She and Cole had attempted to convince Lance that his mother could be strong. "You're brave, Sally. Whoever's responsible will not succeed. Don't let the coward see your fear."

"If not for Lance and Jack, I'd dissolve into a puddle of misery."

"Sally, do you remember the promise I made to Kevin?"

"The God thing?"

"Yes. I've found what he treasured more than life."

Sally's blue eyes stared back in disbelief. "You're kidding, right? In the middle of constant threats to our lives, and you decide God is real? Tori, you've lost it. Where's your logic?"

"How else would you explain Cole's and my survival?"

Her face reddened. "A God who loves also causes death and destruction? No thanks. You can grasp on to a crutch if you want, but don't expect me to limp through life with a holier-than-thou attitude. I have two boys to raise without a father. He was murdered, or have you forgotten? And the business I inherited is plagued with bombings and murders." Sally's voice grew louder with each phrase. "Can't count on my parents. They're afraid. And you want me to do the God thing?"

Tori searched for the right words. "I need hope for tomorrow and the next day. This is what I've found."

"Good for you." Sally swung her legs over the lounge chair. "Time I did something about dinner." Tears flowed over her face. She whirled around. Tori rose to comfort her, but Sally pushed her away. "I'm all right."

Her fragile friend was about to bottom out.

❈

Cole woke to his cell phone blaring in his ears. He snatched it. Manny. 11:15 p.m.

"Yeah, Manny. What do you have?"

"I'm on my way there with Jose Aznar's widow."

"What? Why—?"

"I'll explain when I get there. About an hour out. Gotta watch the road, make sure I don't have a tail." Manny hung up.

Wide-awake, Cole pressed in Tori's number. She answered on the second ring, and he explained Manny's call.

"I'm on my way," she said.

"No, Tori. I'll call the moment I have information."

Cole paced his foyer, sipping coffee and waiting on Manny and Mrs. Aznar. Exactly fifty-one minutes after his call, the headlights of Manny's truck shone in his driveway. Cole peered through the window to see his friend and the petite woman move toward the front door.

He refrained from snapping on the lights before he opened the front door. Manny quickly ushered the young woman inside.

"Follow me to my office," he said. They walked down the hall and to the left, where he shut the blinds before turning on a light. The first thing he saw was Mrs. Aznar's bruised and battered face.

"Please sit down." He motioned to a recliner. "What happened?"

She eased onto the chair, obviously in pain. "Earlier tonight I went to see César Vega at his house. I asked if he and the Hermanos de Pistoleros had killed my husband and Preston. César was drinking and got mad. Told me I could end up the same way. Did this to me. When he was finished, he left in his truck. I walked home and got Jose's gun. Then went to the bar."

"How did you know César would be there?"

"It was a place Jose said he hung out."

Cole hated the beating the young woman had taken. "Why did you risk your life to confront this man?"

"Because I had to do something. I wanted to kill him. My Sofía will never know her father. Jose was not a bad man."

Cole glanced at Manny. "How did you find her?"

"I was at the bar watching César when she showed up and accused him of murdering Jose. Waved a gun in his face. I pretended to be a friend and pulled her outside. He was too drunk to question it."

"What about the baby?"

A tear trickled down Mrs. Aznar's cheek. "She's safe with my parents. They left yesterday for California and took her with them."

"What else can you tell me?" Cole said. "We have to stop the Hermanos de Pistoleros before more people are killed."

"When I was on the floor at César's house, nearly unconscious, I heard him make a call. He said, 'Tell the man that Austin is not beyond our reach. The law's after us, and he'll go down too. Just 'cause he's white and rich don't mean his blood isn't red.' I kept my eyes closed. Then he left."

"Where does César live?" Cole said.

"I told Mr. Manny already."

Manny handed her a tissue, and she wiped the blood from her mouth. "The place was empty," he said. "I ordered a sweep. Found his truck abandoned."

Where was Cole's mind? "I'll get a wet cloth and a bottle of water."

"Wait," Manny said. "I'm needed on another case. Can she stay here tonight until we can arrange a safe place for her tomorrow?"

"Sure."

"I'll get the water and cloth. You stay with her." Manny disappeared down the hallway.

"Mrs. Aznar, you're lucky to be alive."

She sobbed. "I know. Is your wife here?"

"I don't have a wife. You mean my partner, Tori?"

She nodded. "I'd like to talk to her."

Cole pulled his phone from his jean pocket and pressed in Tori's number. "Hey, we have a situation here. Can you drive over? And bring clothes for Mrs. Aznar."

56

TORI HAD READ Cole's text before she left home.

She's asleep. Badly beaten by Jose's cuz. Wants 2 talk 2 u.

That was twenty minutes ago. Tori couldn't get answers fast enough. She remembered the lovely young woman with the beautiful baby. Was the child with her? Did she have information that would lead to arrests? Tori watched her speed because her foot was dancing on the gas pedal with the adrenaline speeding through her body.

She parked in Cole's driveway promptly at 1:25. Outside lighting illuminated the front area of the tan-colored stone two-story home with a circular drive and cedar double-door entry. The beauty stole her breath. Cedar shutters gave it a definite Texas flair. She knocked on the door instead of ringing the bell, while admiring the artistry in the landscaping—color, plants, symmetrical design. If only these were better circumstances.

He'd accused her of kissing him after they were attacked, and she hadn't denied it. Given the opportunity, she'd take another and another. Yes, he was extremely good-looking, had a definite rugged appeal and sky-blue eyes that could sweep her away. Putting the physical aside, as the outer appearance attributes would fade with time, she was drawn to his heart. Cole Jeffers took the trophy with Kevin as brilliant and compassionate. A tough combo. He'd claimed interest in her—many times. She had no gauge to measure if he was serious. Yet she hoped so.

And she definitely couldn't get him out of her head and heart.

The door opened. Cole wore a grim smile and jeans that weren't bought at Walmart and fit just right. He invited her inside.

Yes, if only this were a social call.

"Thanks." He took the tote bag filled with things for Mrs. Aznar. They might be a little big, but they were clean. "I made coffee."

She sniffed. "I smell it."

"Ethiopian blend."

"A hint of fruit. I'd say strawberry, orange . . ."

He faced her. "That's it?" he said.

"Ruby red grapefruit?"

"Yes." He frowned. "I'm sorry about the hour."

"It's our job."

He studied her for a moment. "Follow me to the kitchen, and I'll get us both a cup. Got a feeling this will be a long night."

In the midst of chaos, dare she take a few minutes to figure out her feelings for Cole?

She took in the white cabinetry, distressed white brick backsplash, stainless steel appliances, gray-and-white granite countertops, and a bay window breakfast nook with an antique oak table. She longed to see the view into the backyard, envisioning a landscaped design worthy of a photo shoot. Perhaps in the daylight . . . someday.

"This is a delicious kitchen," she said, running her fingers across the granite on a huge island with gray barstools.

"Thanks. The only things I use are the fridge, coffeemaker, and microwave." He opened a cabinet and pulled out two huge mugs. He poured them each a cup of the brew and handed one to her.

He stood so close she could smell his intoxicating, woodsy scent blended with the coffee in his hand. "Did you do the landscaping for your home?"

He nodded.

"You are one talented man, but I see your heart is with the US Marshals."

"I've missed the challenge and the satisfaction of law enforcement."

"Thanks for having my back."

"Same here. We're a good team."

Sensing color rising in her face, she struggled to change the subject. "Your home is huge. Do you mind me asking how large?"

"Forty-five hundred square feet."

"For one man?"

"I plan to one day fill it with kids."

"Your poor wife."

"She'll want kids too. Are you applying for the job?"

She warmed, and his full lips turned upward. She'd thought about it—more than once.

"Your face is a cute shade of pink." He leaned forward, coffee still in hand. He kissed her lightly, feathery soft, gently inviting her response, and she kissed him back. With her mind whirling, she stepped back.

"I won't have to ask if you kissed me." He planted another one on her nose. "I'll remember."

"Me too." Awkward.

His smoldering eyes captured her. "Where are we going?"

What dare she say? "Can we table 'we' until this case is over?"

He chuckled. "We could be a dangerous duo."

"We already are."

She ignored the implication. Time to handle why she was there. "I suppose you should fill me in about Mrs. Aznar. Does she need medical attention?"

"No. They're mostly bruises. She asked for you. Thought we were a husband and wife team."

Tori slid him a sideways glance. "But you corrected her. Was she sexually assaulted?"

"No, ma'am." Mrs. Aznar stood in the kitchen, her left eye a purple mass, her swollen lips seeping blood. "I just feel better talking to a woman."

"I brought you clothes."

"Thank you. I want to shower later if it's okay. Can I have a cup of coffee before we talk?"

Mrs. Aznar repeated what she'd relayed to Cole and Manny hours before. The investigation hadn't taken them to Austin. Where were the missing pieces?

Tori reached across the table and touched the young woman's arm. "Is there anything your husband, Preston Ustach, or César Vega may have said that could help us?"

She slowly nodded while staring into her cup. "After Mr. Moore was killed, Preston and Jose were at our trailer. Preston said the person who'd killed Mr. Moore had computer knowledge, but he also believed the Hermanos de Pistoleros were behind it."

"Did he say why?"

"A few days before the bombing, he saw some of them on motorcycles." She shrugged. "They were on a road near the rig."

"Are you saying Preston wasn't aware Jose's cousin was part of the gang?"

"No. After Preston left, Jose said he was ashamed of César. Didn't want anyone at work to know they were related. I asked more questions, but he started drinking and told me to shut up. Said he'd made awful mistakes. Wanted me to leave and take Sofía to my parents'. I refused. The next day Preston was killed. Jose . . . he cried like a baby." Mrs. Aznar wept. "Then someone killed him. Had to be César."

Cole scooted back his chair and stood. "The gang doesn't have computer skills. Most of them barely finished the eighth grade. They're violent hired guns. Our mastermind could be from Austin."

Tori looked at him. "One person pulling the strings on both crimes or separate crimes . . . like you've expressed before. But I'm not buying it. Who despised Nathan enough to destroy both him and his company? We have to find César Vega."

57

WEDNESDAY MORNING, shortly after seven, Tori and Cole drove to a women's shelter and made sure Mrs. Aznar would be taken care of before leaving to join her family in California. A BOLO was issued for César Vega.

While Max was at the doctor's office, Tori and Cole drove to the garage where Vince Greene worked.

"Are you sure you left nothing out about Mrs. Aznar?" she said, compassion building for the woman.

"You have it all. Every time I think about the beating Vega gave her, I want to find him myself."

"I'm a step ahead of you on that one. He could have killed her."

"How's Sally?"

"Tried talking to her about God, but the conversation didn't go anywhere. Can't blame her with all she's been through."

"We can only love on her and not give up."

Tori pushed ahead. "I've noticed something about myself. My left wrist, the one I rub out of habit?"

"Yes."

"It's a freckle, but in my mind it's melanoma. I thought with my new faith, the concern would dissipate, but it hasn't happened."

"I noticed you hadn't been touching it as much. God doesn't have a time limit. We have much to discuss and explore."

She stared out the windshield. "Our fears or us?"

"Aren't they one and the same?"

She laughed lightly to shake off the nervousness. "Considering I wanted nothing to do with you or God, I guess you're right. I look forward to the future, but I'd rather face a firing squad."

He shot her an irresistible grin. "I've got your back."

At the mechanic's shop, Greene stomped toward them from behind a '67 Mustang. "Why are you bothering me again? Because unless you're here to tell me Nathan Moore's killer's been arrested, you can keep right on going."

"Good to see you too." Cole stuck out his hand, but Greene failed to shake it. "We have two pics for you to possibly identify."

"Why didn't you show them the other time you were here?"

"Didn't have a reason then."

"Nothing more?"

"No." Cole scrolled through his phone until he came to Franc Lawd.

"Never saw him."

Then Jose Aznar's pic.

Greene claimed not to recognize him either. He dragged his tongue over his lips. "Should have told you this the other day. I was scared with my record and all. But Moore called me right after the bombing of one of his oil rigs. Said he wanted me to follow someone."

"Who?"

"Ann Krantz."

Anita. "Did you agree?"

"Yep. She and I work the same hours, so it was easy. I kept an eye on her until the day he was killed. All I saw was she stayed to herself."

Nathan had suspected Anita of being dishonest about something, so he hired a man he could trust. Hadn't kept Nathan alive.

❋

Tori grabbed the grilled chicken salads from the front seat of her car and made her way to Mom's door. Time they talk like mother and daughter, discuss the tragedies of their family, and move on. With everything that had happened over the last eight days, she'd vowed to treasure every moment with Mom, beginning now.

The case had nearly exhausted her, and she didn't sleep well at Sally's. This afternoon, she, Cole, and Max planned to reread every report since the bombing. Brainstorm. Find what they were missing. Piece together snippets of conversations.

Before Tori rang the doorbell, Mom opened the door.

"We are about to have a first. My daughter here for lunch on a weekday at eleven thirty."

She groaned and hugged her. "Mom, am I that bad of a workaholic?"

"Not today. Come on in." They moved into the kitchen.

While Tori unpacked the salads and set a separate bag in the freezer, Mom placed silverware and blue-flowered napkins on the table. A frosted pitcher of iced tea rested between them.

"What's the monumental occasion?" All lightness vanished from Mom's face. "Are you okay, honey? Is your arm infected? Max doing all right? Cole?"

If not for the serious reason why she was there, Tori would have teased her about being a helicopter mom. "I'm very good. I admit to having an ulterior motive for lunch, but it's nothing bad." She planted a kiss on Mom's cheek.

Mom touched her heart. "Okay, Victoria, curiosity stole my appetite. Best tell me."

"Have a seat. This will come as a shock." She took her mother's hand. "Before Kevin died, he made me promise I would seek God. I agreed only because I loved him. My church attendance has been every other week out of respect for him. There've been Sundays I've listened and Sundays my mind has wandered. The past few days have proved to me God exists and is looking out for me." A thickening in her throat brought reality to watering eyes. "I could have been killed on Saturday when Cole and I were attacked by the gang for hire."

Mom covered her mouth with her free hand. "I try not to think about the danger you're constantly in because it's your job. I realized the seriousness of the shoot-out on Saturday when I saw you and Cole." She stopped. "When did you make the decision?"

"In the ER waiting room before y'all arrived. No harps or trumpets, but I feel like a bag of rocks has been lifted from my shoulders."

Mom swiped at a tear. "Kevin asked me to search for God too, but I couldn't make the commitment. Now I will."

"So glad, Mom. This doesn't mean the next time I'm in the middle of a firefight, I'll walk away alive. This proved to me who Kevin trusted." Tori smiled. "Now let's eat."

"If Kevin were here, he'd pray."

"I will." And she did. "For dessert, I brought cookies and cream ice cream—with gold sugar sprinkles." Kevin's favorite mode of celebrating.

The hour and a half she'd taken for lunch passed quickly—a

rarity. Mom wanted to attend church with her this weekend—a first. They hugged good-bye, and Tori promised to call later.

"One more thing," Mom said. "Is the US Marshal a special guy?"

"Why?" Warmth crept up her neck.

"I saw the way you two were looking at each other."

Laugh it off, Tori. "So you've turned detective?"

"In this instance, I have the facts." Mom giggled and covered her mouth. "I like him. Go for it, Victoria."

58

ALBERT TRIED TO REACH James for the third time Wednesday evening. Where was he? Desperation and the ticking clock for Erik kept him pacing the hospital room. He threw a paper cup of water against a wall.

Erik slept, his breathing a pitiful wheeze. After Erik was diagnosed with bacterial pneumonia, his doctor had admitted him to the hospital, but the antibiotics weren't doing the trick.

Albert watched his son sleep. If only he'd waken and be healthy and ready to go home. How much longer would his precious son be able to fight the disease taking over his body?

"Albert?" James answered on the fourth ring. "What's going on?"

"Erik's in the hospital—St. Luke's." He explained his son's condition. "I have only one option to save him."

"Then do what you must to rectify the damage done to your son years ago."

"I plan to this evening. If I fail, I want to thank you for supporting me."

"You've been a good friend. If need be, I'll be there for Erik."

"Thank you." He drew in a heavy breath and ended the call. Staring at his dear son, he kissed his forehead. Hot tears fell onto Erik's face, and Albert brushed them away. "For you," he whispered. "My love, my heart. Any sacrifice."

Albert left the hospital and got into his car. His plan had been rehearsed for days, and yet he regretted what must be done. He'd given Sally an opportunity to handle Nathan's obligations, but she'd refused.

He contacted her on his cell. "Mrs. Moore, this is Albert Weiman. I'd like to stop by and chat for a few minutes. Erik's in the hospital with pneumonia, and I'm not getting the answers I need. I thought with your nursing background, you could help me understand the medical terms."

"Mr. Weiman, I'd be happy to do what I can. My skills are a little rusty, though. When would you like to stop by?"

"Now, if you're home. I'm about to leave the hospital."

"That's fine. I just baked banana bread."

Albert chuckled at the irony of it all. Serve him banana bread while he held her and those boys at gunpoint. He patted his pants pocket to ensure the slip of paper with his bank account number was intact.

He pulled a .38 from the glove box and placed it in his jacket pocket. He'd stop at Starbucks for all four bodyguards and Sally Moore. The bodyguards' drinks would be laced with a generous dose of Erik's sleep medication. Those cups would be marked with *Thanks*. How could armed guards refuse an old man who brought coffee? He wasn't worried about Sally Moore's sons. With their mother as hostage, they'd behave.

At the Moore home, he delivered the coffee to the man and woman guarding the exterior. "I appreciate what you're doing for Mrs. Moore," he said and smiled at their gratitude.

He returned to his car for the remaining coffees, carried the cardboard container to the front door, and rang the bell. Sally answered the door. She'd lost weight since he'd seen her. She was about to lose more than a few pounds.

"Good evening, Mrs. Moore."

"Call me Sally. Come on in." She stood aside for him to enter.

"I brought coffee for the adults. Here are the ones for the inside security."

"How considerate. They'll appreciate your kindness."

"Theirs have a *thanks* on them. Yours has an *M* for Moore and mine has an *A* because I added sugar and cream. Oh, there's an extra one in case anyone else in the house would like one."

"My boys don't drink coffee." She took the cardboard container. "I'll deliver these. Have a seat in the living room, and I'll be right with you."

He inwardly sighed relief. She soon returned and sat in an adjoining chair with her coffee cup in hand. She removed the lid, and steam circled from the top.

"Where are your sons?"

"Upstairs watching a movie in Lance's bedroom. They're doing a Star Wars marathon."

He smiled. "Nothing better than brothers being together."

Erik typically responded to the sleep medication within ten minutes, but Albert estimated it would take fifteen for the bodyguards. He and Sally talked on about Erik's problem with bacterial pneumonia.

A crash startled Mrs. Moore, filling him with anticipation.

"Excuse me," she said. "I need to check on that noise."

He set his cup on an end table. "I'll go with you." He stood without waiting for her to object.

In the kitchen, two men were sprawled on the floor about six feet apart. One must have fallen asleep and the other had attempted to assist him before the drug hit.

Albert pulled his weapon from his pocket and aimed it at Sally. "Don't say a word. You and I have a little business to take care of. It's time you took care of your financial obligations."

59

TORI CROUCHED on the steps and listened to Albert demand Sally sit in the living area. She'd heard the crash and started down the stairs, but the man's threats stopped her. She made her way down the hallway and peered around the corner. Albert and Sally weren't positioned in front of a window for anyone to take a shot.

Tori clutched her weapon. Why hadn't Sally told him that Tori was in the house too? Too late now. Sally's back was to her, and a shot at Albert could prove deadly to her friend. The two bodyguards lay on the floor, hopefully not poisoned.

The boys' safety took precedence. She crept back up the stairs, then texted Cole from outside Lance's door.

Albert Weiman has Sally hostage in kitchen. Protection detail in house unconscious or dead.

The boys?

Safe @ moment. Impossible 2 get 2 Weiman from my angle.

Sit tight.

She rapped lightly on Lance's door. "Boys, please, we have to talk now," she whispered. When Lance opened the door, she touched his mouth and shook her head. He let her inside, where she told them about the situation downstairs.

"Cole is handling it. In the meantime, I need your word you'll not move from this room."

"You're talking about our mom," Lance said, his nostrils flaring. "You can't ask us to do nothing."

"There's something you can do, and it's what Cole would recommend. Pray." She secured their attention. "Lock the door behind me. Promise?"

The two frightened teens agreed, and she slipped back downstairs. A SWAT team and negotiator would be in place within the hour. But she feared it wasn't soon enough. Albert must have a specific agenda. As she'd concluded the morning he knocked on her door, the man must be mentally ill. His voice rumbled low from the kitchen.

"Nathan Moore destroyed my son's life, and now you're going to pay his debt."

"I have no idea what you're talking about. Tell me what happened." Sally's gentle tone might talk Albert down.

"You know the story. Why lie? Erik and Nathan had been friends since high school. Competitive with sports and grades. Didn't you question why they parted ways?" He waved the gun in her face.

To Sally's credit, she remained calm. "I asked Nathan about Erik. He said they fought because both had feelings for me."

"Why did you stop seeing my son? He loved you. Would have done anything for you."

"Nathan told me Erik was interested in another girl, and I saw them together."

"That's a lie. Erik met with her to discuss what to buy you for your birthday."

Sally sighed. "Then I'm guilty of believing Nathan."

"What was his excuse for stealing Erik's patent?"

"What?"

Albert huffed. "Don't act like you weren't aware of Nathan's underhanded business dealings."

"I'm confused. Please explain what you're talking about."

"He stole Erik's patent to more efficiently conduct fracking."

Tori cringed. Nathan had made millions with his method of fracking. Had he really stolen the design from Erik?

"I have no knowledge of this. I swear to you. Did you kill my husband?"

"He deserved it for refusing to pay Erik for his design. With the money owed my son, he could receive treatment in Germany for MS. But Nathan refused, even after he learned Erik was facing death."

If Tori could only get a clear shot at the man. All she could do was listen and pray SWAT arrived soon.

"Mr. Weiman, I'm so sorry for Nathan's actions. I'd never hurt or steal from anyone. I want to make this right, so tell me what to do."

Smart move, Sally. Your sympathy may be what keeps you alive.

He pulled a slip of paper from his pants pocket. "Transfer three million dollars into this account."

She took the paper. "Of course." Strength and resolve resounded in her words. Her cell phone rang.

Albert grabbed it. "No way are you stopping me."

"Mr. Weiman, would the three million take care of Erik's treatment in Germany?"

"Yes."

"I need my phone to make the transfer." He pushed it back and she appeared to type into it. "I would have given you the money if you'd explained the situation." She lifted her face. "I loved Nathan with all my heart. He never displayed anything but devotion to me and his sons. But since his death, the things I've learned have convinced me I didn't know the man I married."

Good, Sally. Keep talking and stalling for time.

Sally continued. "He obviously lied to me about Erik years ago before we married. He cheated your son out of countless dollars, and he set up an office in London without bothering to inform his family." Her fingers touched his wrist, the one holding the gun on her. "We've both been deceived and hurt. Please, put the gun away. You now have the money."

Sally, be careful. The transfer will take a few days, and he may know the protocol.

Albert swiped at a tear. Then another. "I couldn't figure out what else to do. All I ever wanted was Nathan to pay what he owed so Erik would have another chance at life. I never wanted your husband dead. I . . . I don't even remember doing it."

His finger rested on the trigger, stopping Tori from moving forward.

"If one of my sons was that ill, I'd do whatever I could to seek treatment."

"Murder?"

Tori envisioned her offering a sad smile.

"I honestly don't know."

He swiped at his nose. "The idea of hurting you and leaving those boys without a mother makes me as evil as Nathan."

"I've put the money in your account. All you have to do is leave and take care of your son."

"The cops will be after me for what I've confessed to you. Never dreamed I'd stoop this low." He pressed his lips together. "And I can't now." He pushed himself from the table and aimed at his head.

Sally lunged forward and shoved the weapon aside. The gun went off, and he stumbled.

Tori rushed into the room, noting the blood flowing from Weiman's thigh. She wrestled the weapon from his hand while he clutched his wounded leg.

Sally grabbed a blanket from a chair and joined her. "Mr. Weiman, we'll get you help," she said.

The poor man needed physical and mental care.

"I can't even kill myself so Erik could have the insurance money. Stay with me, will you?"

"Yes." Sally knelt beside him and took his hand. She glanced at Tori. "Please don't restrain him. He isn't going anywhere."

"I heard the entire conversation."

"So very sad . . . and needless."

Sounds from the front door indicated law enforcement had burst in.

"We're in the rear," Tori called. "Mr. Weiman needs an ambulance."

The thud of boots on the hardwood floor grew louder.

Tori texted Lance upstairs. **Ur mom is ok. Man wounded. Meet me @ stairs.** Neither boy should see this blood. Cole rushed in and gave her a grim nod.

"Finally," he whispered.

Tori met his blue eyes and walked to the foyer. The boys were pale, just as she'd left them. "Everything is under control. Your mom handled herself like a soldier. The shot came from Albert Weiman. He fired the gun and shot himself."

"We have to see her," Lance said.

"Not yet. Mr. Weiman needs medical attention. There's blood on the floor, and the investigators will need to sweep the area. I'm sure your mom will be with you shortly."

"Why did the old man pull a gun on her?" Lance said. "He's been here before and acted okay."

"I'll let your mother tell you." Like Tori, Sally would have to weed through Albert's story for facts. A little bizarre, but with the new information surrounding Nathan, she shouldn't be surprised.

60

COLE AND TORI entered Katy's Memorial Hermann emergency room, where Albert Weiman had been treated. His pants were torn to his thigh so the bullet could be removed and the leg bandaged. The doctor excused himself.

Albert's hands shook, and Cole questioned his mental condition.

"Mr. Weiman, we have questions regarding the hostage situation at the Moore home," Cole said. "Special Agent Tori Templeton heard your confession, which has been corroborated by Sally Moore's statement. We'd like to record this interview."

"I don't care anymore. And it's all the truth." He rubbed his face. "I also threw a rock at Mrs. Moore's house and threatened her once on the phone. Can you give me an update on my son?"

"Mr. Weiman," Tori said, "I'll need your code word at the hospital to check on Erik. I called for an update while you were being treated, but the nurse couldn't give me details. I took the liberty of passing along a message from you to keep fighting and that you love him."

Tears welled in his eyes. "Thank you. He's not going to make it much longer without special treatment."

"Erik was always a strong man."

"Except when it came to MS. None of the drugs have helped. Do you suppose Sally might see him? He still cares for her."

How very odd to request Sally in light of the circumstances. "I'll talk to her," Tori said. "Sir, Cole and I need details on how you hacked Nathan's pacemaker."

His face tightened, and he gripped the bandage on his leg. "I got the idea from a TV show. Looked around until I found a greedy hacker."

"Who?"

"Walt Hanna. I have his phone number and address." While Albert spoke, Cole typed the info. "He charged me $8,000, then wanted more. A greedy punk. Took all I had to pay him." He glanced up with reddened eyes. "I must have been drinking and given him the go-ahead. I was such a fool to believe Nathan might have left money for Erik."

"We all want the best for those we love." Cole heard a difference in Tori's voice, more than compassion or friendship. "I'm really sorry. The weapon you had this evening—it isn't registered to you."

"Bought it off the street. One thing about delivering mail in bad neighborhoods, I met all kinds of people."

Cole cleared his throat. "Were you involved with the Moore Oil & Gas rig bombing near Texas City?"

"No, sir."

"Is Anita Krantz a familiar name?"

"No."

"The murder of Preston Ustach?"

"No, sir."

"The attack on Tori and me at the oil rig, led by the Hermanos de Pistoleros?"

"No."

"Are you acquainted with a man by the name of Jose Aznar?"

"Never heard of him until I saw he'd been killed."

"Have you been working with Franc Lawd?"

"He's a friend. And he spied on the rig for me."

"You're telling us these are the only crimes you've committed."

"Yes. Would you check on my son? He'll be worried."

Tori spoke up. "I'll call the hospital before we leave. Remember I need your code word."

He gasped and seemingly held his breath. The pain meds must not have taken effect yet. "The word's *healthy*."

The old man had *beaten* written into the lines on his face. "Thank you. Always thought you were a good girl. I never wanted to hurt Nathan or his wife. In fact, I wish it all hadn't happened. At least with Nathan alive, he might have changed his mind and helped Erik."

Cole read over Walt Hanna's background before interviewing him. Authorities had picked him up at his address. "He's in the system," he said to Tori. "A family man with a daughter, infant son, and a wife. He works in sales at a computer company."

Cole and Tori observed him through the one-way glass of an interview room. Just an average-looking guy. But bad guys seldom wore T-shirts announcing their criminal intentions.

"We have a court order to image his devices," she said.

Cole refused to rest until he fulfilled his vow to end the crime spree. "I'm more than ready to put all the pieces together."

They stepped into the room. Cole introduced himself and Tori. "Mr. Hanna, we need answers. Tonight."

Not a muscle moved in Hanna's face. "I have no idea what this is about."

"Do you know a man by the name of Albert Weiman?"

"No, sir. Never heard of him."

What did Cole expect? "Mr. Weiman signed an affidavit in which he claims to have paid you $8,000 to hack Nathan Moore's pacemaker. That makes you guilty of murder."

Hanna shifted and his breathing increased.

"Are you ready to start over, Mr. Hanna?"

"I . . . I took the money, but I'm not a killer."

Cole frowned. "I'm confused."

"Weiman never gave me the okay to hack the pacemaker." Hanna inhaled sharply. "I realize he's dead because of a hack job, but I didn't do it. I have proof, and it's on my laptop—"

Cole waved his hand in front of the man's face. "You're telling federal agents you had the ability to kill Moore, took the money, but never got a green light?"

"That's the truth. Look, I give you permission to access my laptop. You'll see I'm innocent. I was out with my wife and friends when the murder took place. They'll vouch for me. In fact, I left my phone and laptop at home in case this ever came back to bite me."

"We're holding you until evidence proves your claim."

61

LATE WEDNESDAY NIGHT, Tori and Cole received word that Walt Hanna had not hacked Nathan's pacemaker. Or at least his devices hadn't been used to initiate the murder.

So first thing in the morning, Tori met Cole at Memorial Hermann to further question Albert Weiman on his plans to eliminate Nathan Moore. The big gap in his and Hanna's stories said a possible third party was involved.

"I'm tired of the run-around in this case," Tori said.

Cole gave her a thin-lipped smile. "We both are. Would you mind leading out with Weiman? With your history, I think he'll respond better to you."

"I'll do my best. I remember him from college days, the supportive dad—kind and gentle. That man is still there. Did you receive his employment records and history?"

"Just got them." Cole read from his phone. "Solid worker. Dependable. Above average aptitude. Here is a man who valued hard work and never rose any higher in his job as a postal worker. He seemed to live for Erik, and nothing else mattered. Hard for me to think he arranged to kill Nathan."

"But he did, Cole." She turned to him. "We talked about this late last night, actually early this morning. Someone else had to know Albert's plans, a person who finished what Albert refused to accomplish. The question is who?"

"That's what we need to find out."

They approached his hospital room. "Good morning, Mr. Weiman," she said. "We have a few more questions."

He appeared to be in pain. "I told you everything last night. There's nothing left."

His white, thinning hair gave him a lovable grandfather appeal. Not the case.

She sighed. "We interviewed Walt Hanna. He has the skills to hack Nathan Moore's pacemaker, but he said you didn't instruct him to do the job."

Bewilderment settled on his lined features. "You're not making sense. Nathan's dead."

"Did Erik have a part in this?"

His gaze darted around the room. "He has no idea what I've done."

"Who else knew about it?"

"I can't tell you. My friend would never intentionally hurt anyone."

"I understand loyalty, but what kind of a friend betrays another?"

"What do you mean?"

"He could have potentially executed a murder and set you to take the fall."

"You're wrong." Albert pressed his hands onto the table. Mixed emotions and a spark of fear flashed from his eyes.

"Mr. Weiman, we've verified his claims," Tori said. "Give us the man's name, and we'll get the matter resolved."

"Impossible."

Tori focused on him. Pity moved her. "Some people pretend to be our friends when they have their own agenda."

"I can't give you his name. Leave me alone."

Seeing Weiman refuse to incriminate anyone, Tori and Cole left the hospital room. "I have to talk to Erik. He may have evidence his father refused to give. Sally wants to see him, and I promised to go with her. The man's dying, and he may not be as bitter as Albert. It's worth a try."

Tori and Sally checked in with the ICU nurses' station at St. Luke's for instructions regarding Erik.

"Mr. Weiman is very weak," his nurse said. "Please don't stay longer than ten or so minutes. He's due for meds soon, and that will help him rest this afternoon."

They walked toward his room. Tori stopped and focused on her friend. "Are you sure you want to go through with this? I can talk to Erik alone."

"I have to see him. This nightmare started with Erik and me when I believed he was seeing another girl. According to his father, he loved me, and I broke his heart."

"Sal, it started in high school with them. You entered the picture much later."

They lingered outside his door. Sally lifted her shoulders. "It's about time a Moore took the initiative on righting a wrong. Ever since Nathan died, my sons and I have endured tragic news, horrific things that have devastated us. Our lives will never be the same. How will we ever be able to trust anyone again? I can't help but keep reliving last night with Albert. If he'd stopped to consider that I couldn't have transferred so much money with a keystroke, I'd probably be dead. Still, I feel horrible for the way Nathan treated Erik."

Tori wanted to mention God, but she held back. Sally had voiced her disinterest in spiritual matters, and moving her friend toward faith would be as tough a journey as her own.

Sally took deliberate steps into Erik's room and Tori followed. The monitors—steadily beeping—showed indicators of heart rate, respiration, oxygen level, and blood pressure. Oxygen flowed through his nasal cannula.

"Erik," Sally said, "are you up for a visit?"

His brown eyes fluttered open, and a feeble smile widened. "It's you."

She giggled lightly, probably out of nervousness. "And I brought Tori."

Tori waved. "Hey, Erik. How are you feeling?"

"Good now that the two prettiest girls in Texas are here." His words sounded like the old Erik but were fragile compared to the once-robust man. "A nurse and an FBI special agent. My lucky day."

Sally took his hand. "It's been too long."

His smile stayed, but his cloudy eyes were marked by the medications flowing through his body.

"Dad said he'd seen you. Met your sons." He drew in a ragged breath. "Sorry about Nathan."

Sally blinked. "Thank you. The ordeal has been difficult for me and the boys. According to the nurse, we can't stay long. So let me talk and you listen, okay?"

The anguish of his lost love could not be denied.

"Your dad told me about the girl I saw you with all those years ago at the coffeehouse. He said she was a friend. You tried to explain, but I refused to listen. I apologize."

His eyes pooled.

"I loved Nathan, but I regret our relationship began with a lie."

Erik continued to stare at Sally, his face filled with pure adoration.

"There's more. I've been informed that Nathan stole your patent. He told me your friendship ended because you had feelings for me. Another lie."

He exhaled his apparent discomfort. "Nathan was my friend—"

"Hush. I'm talking." Sally's tenderness reminded Tori of when the boys were babies. "Your dad says there's a treatment for MS in Germany that's been successful. I want to help. Nothing I can do will make up for the past."

He lifted his hand, the one with the IV. "Please. It's not necessary. Look at me. At most I have six months."

"More of a reason to fund the treatment."

"Did Dad ask you for money?"

How could Sally respond honestly? "He made me aware of the problem when I asked about you."

"No way would I take your sons' inheritance."

Sally tilted her head. "There's plenty for them. Your objections have no consequence, Erik. I plan to make the financial arrangements."

But who would escort him to Germany when his father would be in jail for murder? Why hadn't Sally discussed this with her before announcing it to Erik?

He started to speak, his jaw quivering. "I'm embarrassed. When Dad gets here, I'll ask him to leave you alone. Not sure where he is this morning."

How soon before he learned the truth? A TV was anchored on the wall, and the remote sat on his nightstand. Time for Tori to handle the critical aspect of the visit before a nurse chased them out.

"Sally, I have to take over," Tori said.

She glanced away. "I understand."

"What's going on?" Erik attempted to push himself up. "Has Dad been hurt?"

"He'll be fine," Tori said. "He shot himself in the right thigh, and he's been treated. He's really worried about you."

"Shot? Why? How? What are you not telling me?"

Tori despised questioning a dying man—who was also a friend. "I'm sorry about what I have to ask. But it's my job. Were you aware of a conspiracy to kill Nathan?"

He frowned. "Is that what you think? While I'm dying of pneumonia and MS, I hacked Nathan's pacemaker?" His head sank onto the pillow. "Tell me Dad's not a person of interest."

Sally kept a firm hold on his hand, while Tori continued. "He confessed to hiring a hacker."

Erik moaned. "He despised Nathan, even blamed him for the MS. What has he done?"

"Your dad confessed to arranging Nathan's death, but the person he hired didn't follow through. We're trying to find the responsible party. Do you have any idea who else could have been involved?"

"No." Weariness settled on his face, pinching his features. "Can life get any worse? Dad needs a solid attorney."

"The court will appoint one."

He shook his head. "I have no idea what's going on. My dad's not a killer. There must be a mistake."

Tori swallowed the thickening in her throat. "I'm doing my best to learn the truth. Did you develop the fracking method that Nathan claimed as his own?"

"Doesn't matter anymore."

"Your dad said he stole it."

He peered at Sally. "Is this the only reason you came, to see if I'd planned Nathan's murder? Of course. I shouldn't have asked."

336 // DEEP EXTRACTION

She held on to his hand. "Tori promised your dad she'd see if you were okay, and I asked to come along. I had no idea about your illness until your dad told me."

"Okay. Tori, tell Dad I love him and I'll do whatever I can to help."

Most likely Albert would spend the remainder of Erik's life in prison. "Of course. We need to go so you can rest."

Sally kissed his forehead. "I'll be back. I promise."

"Excuse me, Erik. I should have checked to see if you had visitors. You doing all right?"

Tori whirled around. Franc Lawd stood in the doorway.

COLE AND TORI entered the FBI interview room where Franc Lawd awaited questioning. Contempt swept through Tori at the way he lustfully eyed her. He denied all dealings with the gang, the bombings, the shootings, and the murders of Nathan Moore, Preston Ustach, and Jose Aznar.

No surprise.

Cole approached Lawd. "The sniper who killed Preston Ustach rode a motorcycle. Was that you?"

"I don't own a motorcycle. Told you I had nothing to do with any of those things."

Tori was tired, and this jerk made her angry. "You obviously are on a first-name basis with Erik Weiman."

"We nurses like to make friends with our patients."

"Mr. Lawd," Cole began, "were you aware of the initial bombing of the drill site prior to Nathan Moore's death?"

"It hit the news, so the answer's yes."

Cole had taken over the interview, and that was fine with Tori.

She refused to believe Lawd's hands were clean. "Who killed Preston Ustach and Jose Aznar?"

"We're back to zero. If I had any idea who killed Moore, Ustach, or Aznar, I'd tell you."

Cole closed the file. "Mr. Lawd, you're a person of interest in three murder charges, assault, and an accessory to various crimes."

"You have no evidence."

"Mr. Lawd," Cole said, "you claim to be a member of the medical community, which means saving lives, not taking them. It is in your best interest to come clean. The only thing going for you at the moment is I don't see a tat signifying the Hermanos de Pistoleros."

"I'm being detained illegally, needlessly, and I have a job to get to."

Cole rose from the table. "I'm holding you in custody until you're ready to talk."

Tori wasn't about to barge in on the interview. Cole had the upper hand, and the twitch under Lawd's right eye indicated he might be ready now.

Lawd swore.

"Is that language you use with your patients? What will the publicity do for your career?" He nodded at Tori. "He's not worth our efforts. Let's go."

"Okay, what do you want?"

"Answers to the same things we've asked you before, plus a few more. How exactly are you involved with Albert and Erik Weiman? What do you know about the murders and other crimes? Are you affiliated with the Hermanos de Pistoleros?"

Lawd held up his hand. "I'm ready."

Cole took a seat and pulled out his phone. "Do you have a problem with this being recorded?"

"No. Go ahead. I haven't done anything to be labeled a criminal." He scratched the back of his neck. "My career is too important."

Tori couldn't hold back any longer. "What have you done, Mr. Lawd?"

He took a deep breath. "I became acquainted with Erik and Albert Weiman during one of Erik's many hospital stays. As his day nurse, I often talked with them, and we became friends. I liked the father and son, valued their closeness. A few months ago, I walked into the room while Erik was sleeping to find his dad emotionally upset. He'd spoken to Erik's doctors, who offered him no hope for the MS. I offered to do a little research and discovered the experimental work done in Germany."

"You made him aware of the MS treatment?" Cole said.

"Yes. In private, I relayed the information to Albert, but he said the trip was impossible because of the cost. Then he told me what Nathan Moore had done to Erik. I suggested he visit Moore and explain the situation, which he did. But Moore refused to help. Albert asked me to snoop around his rig in Texas City. See if there was anything Albert could use to persuade Moore to pay. I agreed. You know what happened there. I was thrown off the site. Didn't learn anything derogatory about the man. When someone bombed the rig, Albert voiced his concern about Erik's inheritance being devalued. Wanted me to take another look. I was to head that way when a shooter killed Ustach. You two showed up at my apartment, and I let Albert know I could no longer be a part of whatever he'd arranged."

Cole leaned back in his chair. "Did Albert kill Nathan?"

Lawd shook his head. "I doubt it unless he'd been drinking and out of control."

"Have you witnessed him drunk?"

"Yes. Watching his son die drove him to alcoholism."

Tori and Cole left Lawd in the interview room. She sorted through what he'd said. "We're back to the original question that started this case. Who killed Nathan? Albert doesn't remember his actions. We've proven Hanna didn't hack the pacemaker, and Lawd's role appears to be friendship." She held up a finger. "And the Hermanos de Pistoleros are hired killers, not techies." She fumed. "Why can't we pick up César Vega? He can't hide forever."

"I'm going to call Manny. See if he remembers anything from the bar we could remotely use."

She rubbed her aching neck muscles. "I'm heading over to Sally's. She wants me to help her put away photos of Nathan used for the funeral. A part of me says it's a waste of time."

"No more of a waste than the three of us sorting through college stuff tonight."

"Max says every detail solves a murder."

63

SHORTLY AFTER 2:30 P.M. Thursday, Tori followed Sally to her and Nathan's master suite. Sally carried a large manila envelope containing the photos used during Nathan's funeral. Tori understood the hesitancy of putting the pics in their resting places, as though burying Nathan one more time.

"We'll put these away and sit by the pool," Sally said. "We haven't had a poolside chat for a long time. Maybe I'll have the document from Mr. Farr's office by then."

"I'm available for a short while." She smiled into Sally's thin face. "I can put the photos wherever you want—or do you store them in special albums?"

"Most have designated places, but I don't have the energy to organize them."

"We'll do it together, and the job will go faster. Should I brew us some tea?"

"Since when do you drink tea?"

Tori wanted to break the edge on the solemn occasion. "Only when I have a cold, but it sounded like a plan."

"Fresh ground coffee beans brewed to perfection when we're finished, and I baked ginger cookies earlier."

Sweet Sally. She'd get through this yet.

Inside the huge suite decorated in turquoise, cream, and accents of brown, Sally gestured to the sitting area, where photo albums lay strewn across the floor. "See what I mean? It's a mess." She tilted the envelope, freeing the pics. Picking up one of Nathan holding Lance as a baby, she shook her head. "We were so happy then, or so I thought."

"Hold on to the good times, Sal."

"I'm trying." She handed Tori a leather album and the photo of Lance and Nathan. "This one goes in there, but I have no idea what page."

"I'll find it."

Sally picked up her wedding album, soft white leather with two gold rings embossed on the cover. She leafed through it with soft moans. Tori continued to search for the empty page for the photo in her hand.

The doorbell rang and shortly thereafter, one of the bodyguards called Sally's name. "There's a delivery requiring your signature."

"Thanks. I'll be right down."

Nathan, please don't announce more tragic news to your family. "I'll be here waiting," Tori said.

In a few minutes, Sally returned with a sealed envelope. She sank onto the floor beside Tori and gingerly opened it. "It's a letter from Nathan written to me and the boys. His own handwriting." She focused on its contents. With a sob, she lifted a tear-glazed face to Tori. "Can I read this to you?"

"Of course." Could it lead to the killer?

"*Dear Sally,*

If you're reading this, then I'm dead. I hope the cause was my heart and not a murder. Threats were mounting from those who wanted me gone, but I couldn't figure out who despised me enough to really murder me. The ironic reality is I'd angered enough people in my life that the list is extremely long.

Apologizing for what you've learned about me is useless. Perhaps an explanation will help you understand my family was not at fault.

When I discovered Lance had been in my computer files and he'd likely learned about my indiscretion with Anita, I escalated my plans to open a second office in London. I'd purchased a flat shortly after making financial arrangements for two North Sea wells, and thought it would be an escape if you and I needed space. Or even for us to put our marriage back together. I didn't despise my habits or myself enough to end my affair and tell you the truth, but I wanted to be a better man. Truly.

Leaving you financially secure is the best way for me to apologize for my unfaithfulness and deceit.

If Erik Weiman is still alive, would you check on him? He's the best friend I ever had next to you. At the writing of this letter, he's very ill with MS. I owe him an incredible debt. At the bottom of this page is a bank number for him to collect eight million dollars, tax free. I should have taken care of it myself a long time ago. His father asked for help, but my pride got in the way. I stole a patent from him and never had the guts to admit it. There's a hole in my heart where selfishness resides. I always fought to be the best at everything and hurt far too many people in the process.

Lance, you're a fine young man. If you learn anything from my life, it's the danger of thinking more of yourself than others. Life is an uphill climb, but running over good people is not the way to peace of mind.

Jack, you have your mother's heart. She loves unconditionally, and I took advantage of her. Keep her values but look deep into yourself before making commitments.

Sally, you're so much better off without me. I hurt you and loved you at the same time. Honestly, I fail to understand my own actions.

One thing I've always recognized is my love for all of you. Move forward and hold your heads up high. You are the courageous ones. Survive to live.

Love,
Nathan"

Sally folded the letter. "The boys need to see this. Maybe it will bring closure."

Or he'd lied again. Tori kept her thoughts to herself.

The letter still offered no clue to who'd killed him. Quite the contrary, he had no idea either.

64

TORI, SALLY, AND COLE assembled in the dining room of the Moore home Thursday evening to talk through what Nathan had revealed in his letter about how he treated Erik. Max had wanted to offer his assistance, but he and Janie had previously arranged a meeting with their adult children. His new commitment to family took priority.

Tori suggested rummaging through the stacks of high school yearbooks and college memorabilia in Sally's attic to jar memories of events and activities that took place in Nathan's and Erik's lives. Tori helped her gather the books, photographs, pamphlets, and miscellaneous material and scattered them the length of the sixteen-foot wood-and-metal table. The musty smell overpowered Tori's senses, but she'd get used to it, especially if it meant answers.

Lance stood in the entranceway, his hands in his back jeans pockets. "I've never seen any of these. Can I help?"

Sally declined. "We're looking for information that could point to your dad's killer. The discussion could be . . . inappropriate."

"I was the first to discover the . . . stuff."

A boy trying so hard to be a man.

Sally studied her son. "Not everything about your dad was deceitful. There were admirable qualities, plenty of them. But in the course of our searching, some things will have to stay among the adults."

"Please, Mom. I'll find out sooner or later anyway. I'm mature, nearly fifteen."

Any other time, Tori would have found his comment funny, but any humor was smothered in reality.

"Where's Jack?"

"Doing a world history report for the tutor."

Sally hesitated, then pointed to a chair beside her. "All right. But at my discretion, you may be asked to leave the room. We're looking for connections between your dad and an old friend. They went to high school and college together."

"Erik Weiman, the son of the man who tried to kill you, the man you and Tori went to see at the hospital."

Sally sighed, no doubt regretting all Lance had been exposed to. "Yes. How much can you handle?"

"Don't shelter me, Mom, 'cause it only makes finding out the truth harder to accept. Actually, good things about Dad would be an okay thing."

"I hope I'm not making a terrible mistake. Do you agree to my terms?"

He saluted her. "Got it."

Once they were all seated, Cole flipped open the lid to his laptop. "I'll document the highlights of what we find. Am I correct the four of you attended the same high school and college?"

Sally picked up a high school yearbook. "No, Tori and I met

Nathan and Erik as freshmen at the University of Texas. The guys went to Bellaire High School here in Houston."

"What do you know about Nathan and Erik in high school?" Cole said.

Sally stared at the wall and appeared to think back. "Both of them told me the same stories. They were highly competitive for awards, grades, and sports. I have no idea how it began." She peered at the senior year pic of the class officers. "Freshman year, Erik was president and Nathan vice president. For the next three years, Nathan held the office as president, and Erik vice president." She lingered on the Spanish club pic. "They alternated roles here for presidency and vice prez." She traced her fingers over Nathan's face. "If the two kept score of their accomplishments, Nathan won by a narrow margin. He graduated valedictorian and Erik salutatorian.

"Erik told me by college he was finished with the competition. He wanted the friction to go away. Hard for me to understand how they were good friends." She paused, the puzzle evident in the lines around her eyes. "Nathan thrived on being the best. Always has. After we started dating, he and Erik continued their friendship, but I noticed a lot of sarcasm between them that I hadn't heard in the past. I thought it was because Nathan caught Erik cheating on me. I should have asked."

Cole's typing continued, and Tori appreciated him documenting portions of the conversation and not her.

"Did Erik attend your wedding?" Cole said.

Sally reached for Lance's hand. "He was best man. Considering what we've learned, I wonder why Nathan insisted Erik be a part of the ceremony."

"Spite," Lance said.

Sally tossed him a disapproving stare.

Tori recalled the wedding . . . Erik's toast to the couple. How difficult that must have been for him.

The four browsed through the yearbooks and memorabilia together, beginning with Nathan and Erik's freshman year of high school.

Lance examined pictures of his dad as though seeing him for the first time. "Jack really looks like Dad. Sorta weird."

Sally leaned over the yearbook page and covered her mouth. "Look at the resemblance. We'll put these aside for Jack."

A time of healing in the midst of chaos.

Sally sorted through a box of college souvenirs and picked up a photo of the two men at a frat party. They toasted beers to the camera. "Both majored in geology. Both received their master's degrees after we were married. Erik never said a critical word about Nathan. Their goal was to one day open an oil and gas business together."

Cole handed various other loose photos to Sally. "What happened then?"

"They put together a business model. Nathan didn't want his parents contributing to the venture. I'm sure they'd have called the shots, and Nathan wouldn't have been able to handle their interference. He'd always complained about them dangling money in front of him so he'd comply with whatever they wanted. They weren't fond of me. Nathan said it was because I didn't have the right pedigree. Their relationship was rocky while we were married. His parents passed within a year of each other when Lance was a baby. When they died, it was hard for Nathan to attend their funerals." She breathed in deeply. "So back to Nathan and Erik. One day Nathan announced Erik had decided to form his own company. He'd admitted he was still in love with me and thought it best to distance himself. The two parted. Nathan appeared to mourn the loss." Her countenance fell, and Tori wanted to make everything in her world right. But that was an impossibility.

Cole lifted his fingers from his laptop. "Is there anything else you remember from those days?"

"Nothing, except I wish I hadn't been so naive. I sound pitiful. Sorry."

"It's fine. Any other friends?" Cole said. "A person or persons we can talk to?"

"Perhaps I'll think of someone while going through these pictures and keepsakes."

Tori picked up more college photos. "They spent a lot of time with a professor who . . ."

"Are you referring to Professor Howard? He taught computer and business classes."

"Right. Did Nathan keep in touch?"

"For a while, until he and Erik ended their friendship. Professor Howard advised them in the start-up of their oil and gas business."

"Which didn't happen," Tori said. "Why break it off when he was an asset for Nathan?"

"The professor and Erik had been friends since Erik was a little boy. The two enjoyed the outdoors, hiking, fishing."

"I can see how backing away from Professor Howard made sense in light of his long-term relationship with Erik."

"Let's see what he's doing now. Do you remember his first name?"

Sally hesitated. "James, I think."

Cole typed *University of Texas* into his Google search and scanned the faculty list for Professor James Howard. "He's still there, head of the business department. I'll call the university in the morning. See if Professor Howard remembers Nathan. If he spent years with Erik, then he could offer insight into the case. Any information is a help at this point."

"Tori told me you two interviewed Albert Weiman last night and earlier today," Sally said. "Can you give me an update? Erik was extremely upset over his dad's actions."

"Physically Albert will be okay. But he needs counseling. He swears he had nothing to do with the drill site bombing, the murders, or hiring a gang to carry out shootings. I'm inclined to believe him—his priority is Erik, not an elaborate revenge scheme. Albert appears to have acted out of desperation and an unstable mind, not as a man who calculated a series of crimes."

"He exhibited the same tendencies when he held me at gunpoint. Both times he came here, he'd been drinking. Do you even think he has the intelligence to put it all together?" Sally said.

"Yes, but not the heart," Cole said. "We have a friend who vouches for his story. So who was calling the shots?"

65

EIGHT THIRTY FRIDAY MORNING, Cole pressed in the cell phone number for Professor James Howard. When Cole had contacted the University of Texas, he learned Howard was in Houston speaking at a business conference. When the man didn't pick up, Cole left a voice mail.

"This is Deputy US Marshal Cole Jeffers, part of a joint task force with the FBI in a case involving the death of Nathan Moore and other crimes related to Moore Oil & Gas. It's imperative we talk to you as soon as possible. We understand you're attending a conference at the Omni Hotel on the west side of Houston. We are on our way there now." He disconnected the call and texted Tori and Max to meet him at the rear of the FBI building.

As Tori drove to the Omni on the Katy Freeway, Cole grumbled about how much better he felt. Hated to have a woman provide transportation, especially when she'd been wounded too. Max couldn't drive with the intense meds he was taking, which meant they were a pitiful team. Just when Cole swore off the pain meds at night and the mounds of Aleve in the day, his shoulder throbbed. Weak and bordering on ineffective, but he still had his US Marshal attitude.

The hotel parking lot brimmed with vehicles. "With the crips in the car, we could try the handicap area," Max said. "But the car'd get towed."

"Rich," Tori said. "FBI agents cited for parking in a handicap zone."

She found a spot in the rear, and they made their way to the hotel's entrance.

Inside, Cole phoned Professor Howard again, and the call went to voice mail. He shook his head. "Looks like we find him."

At the front desk, Cole greeted the clerk and flashed his badge. "Federal agents. We need to talk to a gentleman by the name of Professor James Howard. We believe he is attending the business conference."

The young man handed Cole a brochure about the three-day conference. "We have a leadership session going on currently. I imagine Professor Howard is in attendance."

He was listed as a speaker at 10:00. Cole turned to Tori and Max. "According to the schedule, Professor Howard has half an hour until he takes the podium. That should give us time to pose a few questions."

"Pull him out of there," Max said. "Let's get this done."

The young man at the desk made arrangements, and within ten minutes, Professor Howard appeared, an older version of the professor in Nathan's college memorabilia—tall, trim, with thick white hair and a matching mustache. His navy pin-striped suit fit perfectly.

Tori approached him first and extended her hand. "Professor

Howard, not sure if you remember me, but I was in the same graduating class at the University of Texas as Nathan Moore and Erik Weiman."

He smiled broadly. "Yes, you were good friends with Sally Arnold. How very unfortunate to hear of Nathan's passing. How is his widow doing?"

"She's taking one day at a time." Tori introduced Max and Cole. "We're investigating Nathan's death."

Professor Howard gave Cole his attention. "I apologize for not returning your call. With so much spam and annoying telemarketers, I thought you were just one more."

Cole bristled at the comment, but he'd let it slide for now. He directed the man toward a corner table in the lobby where they could have privacy. "We have a few questions, sir."

Professor Howard lifted a brow. "I don't think I can help you. This conference is demanding, and I have a speech to give."

"Shouldn't take long."

Once seated, Cole requested Tori explain how they'd stumbled onto the professor's relationship to Nathan and Erik. "The photos were a reminder of how close you were to them. Is there anything you can tell us that could lead to finding Nathan's killer?"

Professor Howard folded his hands in his lap. He wore a Rolex, and Cole made a note to find out what kind of car he drove on a college professor's salary. "That was a long time ago, and many students have come and gone. Such is my career. But what I do recall about Nathan and Erik was their competitive nature. Are you implying Erik Weiman caused his death?"

"No, sir." Tori stopped while a staff member picked up a newspaper lying on a table nearby. "Erik is seriously ill with MS."

"I'm sorry. He was a fine young man." He shook his head. "I first met Albert decades ago, when his son was not quite two."

"And what is your relationship with Albert Weiman today?" Tori said.

Professor Howard sighed. "I wish I hadn't said a word. In truth, I've been in contact with him over the years. He has a drinking problem."

Tori nodded at Cole, and he took over the interview. "Why were you hesitant to mention your friendship with him?"

"The few times we're together, he's inebriated and talks freely. I sincerely apologize for not being straightforward."

Cole watched the professor's body language, confident, and yet his eye twitched. "This is a federal investigation and withholding information is a federal offense."

The man stiffened. "Yes, I understand the legal implications, even if Albert is an acquaintance." He swallowed hard. "He told me Nathan Moore had stolen a plan for fracking from his son, Erik. Nathan used it to make millions. When Erik's health deteriorated, Albert talked to Nathan about helping out with the rising medical costs, and he refused. Albert told me he wanted Nathan dead and would do anything to make it happen."

"How did you respond?" Cole said.

"I encouraged him to seek counseling and an attorney, but I have no idea if he took my advice. Albert believed if Erik was doomed to a premature death, then Nathan deserved to die. Albert also thought Nathan might have left him something in his will. His plan was to hire a hacker to interrupt his pacemaker."

"For a distant friend, Mr. Weiman revealed quite a bit of information."

"He'd been drinking."

"Why did an intelligent man like yourself encourage the relationship?"

"Simple. I enjoyed the man's company, so refreshing from academia."

"Mr. Weiman and the supposed hacker have been questioned," Cole said. "Mr. Weiman is in custody."

Lines deepened around his eyes. "What happened to him is inequitably wrong."

"Do you mean the situation with Nathan?"

The professor clenched his fists. "I was referring to the unfairness of his son dealing with MS. There's treatment for him in Germany, but it's expensive. Excuse me, but it's nearly time for my presentation. Do you have any other questions?"

"Professor Howard, is there anything else you can tell us that might help our case? Anything you remember? We have bombings, murders, and shootings. Who would Albert Weiman have hired to further these crimes?"

"When he's drinking, he talks nonsense."

Irritation nipped at Cole's patience. "Did he mention a specific name?"

Professor Howard nodded. "Franc Lawd. Albert had met him at a hospital where Erik is often under a doctor's care."

Max coughed. "Professor Howard, you've helped us tremendously." In the next breath, he excused himself as the gut-wrenching effects of the cancer gripped his body.

Cole peered at the professor. "We'll need a signed statement."

"Absolutely. I can drive to your office once I've concluded my speech this morning and the Q and A following."

Cole checked the time. "We have several minutes before your presentation. This can be handled now."

Once the statement was completed, Tori thanked the professor. "We appreciate your time and input."

Cole's impression was the professor had a shady side. First he seemed reluctant to talk about his relationship with Albert, then he recalled conversations with the man and shared dinner with him. "Professor Howard, we have evidence the man Mr. Weiman hired did not complete the contract."

"You mentioned the hacker had been questioned. Didn't he kill Nathan?" The professor appeared taken aback.

"No, sir," Cole said. "What restaurant do you and Albert frequent?"

"Chili's on the Southwest Freeway. When I'm in town, I have work near there."

The investigation was by no means over.

66

EN ROUTE BACK TO HOUSTON, Max asked Cole if he could handle the rest of the day with Tori. He'd become nauseous at the hotel.

Cole agreed but shook his head. Max's surgery couldn't come soon enough.

At the jail downtown, Cole and Tori discussed Professor Howard while they waited for a police officer to escort Albert Weiman from his cell. The older man had been transported there upon his release from the hospital.

"Doesn't it seem unlikely the professor and Albert Weiman were friends?" Cole couldn't wrap his brain around the unlikely pair.

"Not if you knew Erik," Tori said. "So full of life and loved everything about the outdoors. Professor Howard enjoyed those things, while Albert preferred a more sedentary lifestyle. The professor and his wife were childless, and Erik could have filled the role."

"What about Erik's mother?"

"She left when he was a baby."

"Unfortunate circumstances."

"Cole, what are you thinking?"

"Erik is the center of Albert's life. How did he feel about the professor's interest?"

"Never thought about it. But if Howard acted more like a father to Erik, I doubt that was ever said in front of Albert."

Cole weighed her words, mulling over the relationship between Erik and Professor Howard. "Everything appropriate in the friendship?"

"I never heard otherwise." She studied him. "You don't care for Professor Howard."

"That obvious?"

"Like a book. I see the professor is conducting a keynote after dinner tonight. I'd like to hear him."

Now she had Cole's attention. "Mind if I tag along?"

"Sounds good to me."

"And I'm running a background on him."

"He's the—" She stopped. "My reservations aren't based on an investigator's mind-set. Yes, by all means get a history. I respected him in college, but that has nothing to do with this case."

The door opened, and Albert limped into the small room used for questioning. He winced as he lowered himself onto a chair.

"Mr. Weiman, Special Agent Templeton and I have had a few interesting conversations with friends of yours."

"Who?"

"Franc Lawd, who admitted to keeping an eye on the oil rig for you."

"He's always taken good care of Erik."

"Earlier today we spoke with Professor James Howard."

His hands trembled. "Why?"

"His name came up in your son's and Nathan Moore's friendship. Claims you and he are friends."

"We are. Have dinner when he's in town."

"He says you often meet at Chili's on the Southwest Freeway."

"Right. What does James have to do with why I'm under arrest?"

"He said you threatened to kill Nathan by hiring a man to hack his pacemaker."

Albert dragged his hand over his face. "You know the truth. I planned the murder and paid for it, but it didn't happen the way I expected."

"I see. What about the other crimes connected to Nathan Moore?"

"Told you before, I have no idea about them."

"Who else besides the professor was aware of your scheme?"

"No one."

Cole wanted a connection he couldn't find. He tried a different tack. "Why did you visit Special Agent Tori Templeton at her apartment last week?"

He glanced away. "She was getting too close. I . . . I had chloroform to drug her."

"You planned to kill me?" Tori's words were low.

He glared into her eyes. "I don't know. . . . Scared me when I saw you were on the case and still friends with Sally. But . . . I'm tired of fighting."

Tori shook her head. "Murder is never an alternative to justice."

"I understand." Albert folded his hands on the table. "We're finished. Those other crimes belong to someone else."

Once the door closed, Cole turned to her. "How about lunch at Chili's?"

❧

At the popular restaurant, a hostess estimated it would be about fifteen minutes before they could be seated. Tori frowned. She and Cole had more than food on their minds.

"Do you have seating at the bar?" she said.

The dark-haired young woman grabbed two menus. "We do. Right this way."

Water for Cole and a Diet Coke for her arrived in short order. The middle-aged man serving them was preoccupied with a purple-haired young woman dressed in black at the bar. . . . She could have been his daughter.

"Sir, we have a few questions." Tori laid her phone on the bar, and when he turned, she gave him her brightest smile.

"About the menu?"

"When you have a moment. We're federal agents investigating a murder."

"You're serious?"

"Yes, sir." She introduced herself and Cole. "Would you be willing to take a look at a couple of pics? We've been told persons of interest frequented this restaurant."

"Certainly."

Tori showed him Albert Weiman's and Professor Howard's photos on her phone.

He stared intently at them.

"Do you recognize those men?"

"Yes, they meet here at least twice a month."

That was more than Professor Howard had indicated. "What can you tell us about them?" She smiled to keep his attention on her.

He pointed to Albert and handed her the phone. "The older man has a problem with alcohol. Often drinks too much. The younger man takes care of him when it happens."

"In what way?"

"I think he drives him home or calls a taxi. Gotten to be a habit."

"Do you ever overhear their conversations?"

He shifted uncomfortably. "I've heard a few things from the older man when he was drunk."

"What was said?"

He glanced away.

"Sir," Tori said, "we have a series of murders to solve."

"The older man hated another guy, wanted him dead. And somebody was sick." He shrugged. "All I know."

"Did his friend ever comment?"

"Not that I heard."

Cole slid his phone onto the bar. "I have another photo for you to see." He showed the server a pic of Anita Krantz.

"Yes, she's been here with one of the men."

"Which one?"

"The younger man."

"Were they involved?"

The server sighed. "I'd say yes. They were real regular. Then it stopped."

Cole took his phone. "When did it end?"

"Less than a month ago." He rubbed the back of his neck. "I really should get back to work."

"Oh, sure." Cole's sympathetic tone was comical. "Anything special about their last meeting?"

He offered a thoughtful stare. "They must have had a doozy of an argument because she stomped out. The guy stayed here and finished his meal."

"Thank you," Cole said. "Were the two men and the woman ever here together?"

"No."

Cole nodded at Tori. "Agent Templeton, anything else?"

"Not right now." She flashed the server her thanks. No reason to burn bridges if they had more questions.

She gave him her card and left the restaurant.

As soon as the door closed behind them, Cole reached for his phone. She knew he was contacting Anita. "Ms. Krantz, this is Marshal Jeffers. Would you kindly return this call as soon as possible?"

"She might be shopping on a Saturday," Tori said. "Should we have her picked up?"

TORI AND COLE waited in an interview room while HPD drove Anita Krantz to the FBI office. She'd been picked up leaving a nail salon close to her apartment.

Various scenarios with Professor Howard nibbled at her brain. They had a surveillance team keeping an eye on him at the Omni. They'd also had Anita Krantz followed since she was first named as a person of interest. Although she kept to herself, the series of crimes could have been planned with accomplices.

"Where are you on this?" Cole said.

"Anita's refusal to have the paternity test," Tori said.

"As in, the baby belongs to the professor?"

"Exactly," Tori said. "She could have been angry enough with Nathan about something to pull off the bombing and murders. Where she obtained the funds and what she hoped to gain is another mystery."

"I'm curious about the argument she had with the professor at Chili's prior to Nathan's death. Was it the pregnancy tossing a wrench into their plans? My mind is speeding with what-ifs that might head to a dead-end road."

"I'm on the same path. Unplanned babies have a habit of interrupting lives. If she was with the professor and Nathan, who does her baby belong to? Maybe she doesn't know."

Their phones alerted them to a message. "Professor Howard's background came at the right time." He read the report. "I noted a red flag earlier with his personal financials, so I requested more info. A couple of recent large withdrawals raised suspicion."

"How much?"

"Fifty grand ten days ago, and sixty-five more three days afterward."

Tori swung to him. "Quite a hunk on a professor's pay."

"His wife inherited family money. But her name isn't on this account."

"We'll ask him when we attend his keynote tonight."

A text alerted them—Anita had been brought in.

�֍

At 4:30 p.m., Cole held the door for Tori to enter the room where a nervous Anita Krantz sat at a table. She greeted them with professionalism and wore composure as fitting as her navy-blue slacks and stylish jewelry.

But her lips quivered.

"Why am I here?" she said. "I haven't done anything to warrant such humiliating treatment."

Cole and Tori sat across from her. "We have evidence otherwise," he said. "Why don't we begin with what we know, and you can fill in the blanks." He drew in a breath to manage his impatience.

Terror creased her features. "I doubt I can contribute anything more than what you already have."

"We could begin with your affair with Professor James Howard. Or would you like for me to clamp the cuffs on your wrists for the murders of Nathan Moore, Preston Ustach, and Jose Aznar? But wait, there's more. We have bombings, attempted murder, and concealing evidence in a federal case."

She buried her face in her hands, but her dramatics soured him. How many times had he and Tori faced her when all the while she knew how to end the carnage? He cleared his throat. "Are you ready to sign a confession?"

Anita lifted her makeup-smudged face. "I had nothing to do with those crimes, but I know who's responsible."

Cole seldom resorted to swearing, but the words still tramped across his brain. "Your choice—arrest or a name."

"He'll kill me like he did the others." Anita wrung her hands. "I'll do anything to protect my baby."

"Choose."

"In telling you this, I'm signing my death certificate."

"We'll do all we can to keep you safe," he said.

She moistened her lips. "My baby belongs to Nathan. I refused the paternity test because his killer would have turned on me. Five months ago, Professor James Howard met with Nathan at the office. All traces of what transpired are missing from the security footage and other documentation because Nathan had them deleted." She took a breath. "Like he did with Preston Ustach's second visit. Shortly after the two started talking, Nathan requested my presence. Later I learned he was afraid of Professor Howard, and I was supposedly a safety cushion. The things James revealed about Nathan shocked me—how he'd lied to win Sally from Erik Weiman. How he'd stolen plans from Erik regarding the fracking method that made him millions. Refused to help with Erik's medical needs. I couldn't believe the accusations, but Nathan didn't deny them. Professor Howard demanded five million dollars for Erik. Nathan called him stupid. James said he deserved to die for what he'd done. Again I heard another vile accusation. James said when Nathan stole Erik's plans for fracking, he also destroyed the paperwork naming the two as partners."

Anita took a deep breath. "The truth hit me very hard. The man I loved couldn't possibly be such a monster. Once James left, Nathan begged me to see his side, said Erik gave him the plans and the accusations were lies." She massaged her temples. "The rest is inexcusable. James called me at work and asked to have coffee. I was angry with Nathan and agreed. We met a few more times afterward and became . . . intimate. One night he revealed a plan to destroy Nathan's business, to blackmail him out of several million dollars. He wanted to help Erik and ensure he received the money due him, and he wanted my assistance. He said, 'Anita, he's used you all these years. You deserve better, and I'll make sure you receive 10 percent of what we get.'"

"What were you supposed to do?" Cole said.

"Look through his records for incriminating information."

"And?"

"Nathan kept impeccable files. I never found a thing to use against him. Then in working with him every day, he made his way back into my heart." She touched her stomach. "I ended the relationship with James and asked him to stop his plans, or I'd go to the police. He became furious, violent. He told me to watch what happened. I warned Nathan about him. Then I learned about the pregnancy. The bombing occurred. Nathan's murder, and all the other crimes. James threatened to kill me if I went to the authorities. When the media released news of my pregnancy, he contacted me and wanted to know if the baby was his. Out of fear, I said yes."

Up to this point, Tori hadn't said a word. "You claim Nathan destroyed the record of Professor Howard's meeting, but did you keep a copy?"

"For insurance," she said. "The moment I witnessed the atmosphere in Nathan's office, I recorded their conversation separately on my phone to protect Nathan. I also recorded the threats made the last time I talked to James. When Nathan was killed, I placed a thumb drive with the audio in a safe-deposit box in case the investigation stumbled onto James's part. If he were arrested, then I was safe."

Now he understood why the woman had kept the truth secret. Fear held her back.

Suddenly Cole remembered the dying words of the gang member who tried to kill him: "Pra" for *professor*.

"I'll sign your paperwork if it means stopping James. For some reason, he's obsessed with Erik."

He looked at Tori. "Looks like we have another date with the professor."

68

TORI BRAKED in front of the Omni Hotel at the same time FBI agents and US Marshals arrived. Professor Howard wouldn't have an opportunity to deliver his keynote.

Cole had been texting since Anita Krantz had been taken into custody. "What are you doing?" she said.

"Working on closing this case," he said without glancing up. "Verifying information on Professor James Howard and César Vega."

"From whom?"

"US Marshals." He opened the car door. "Got a hunch. I'll explain later."

They hurried inside and were directed to the huge conference room where dinner was under way. She and Cole entered from a side door near the speaker's podium. Law enforcement opened the main doors.

The movement caught the professor's attention, and he bolted through the rear service entry opposite her and Cole. She chased him down the hall where servers carried trays with soiled dishes to the kitchen. The professor pushed through a pair of swinging doors into the kitchen with Tori and Cole close behind.

"Stop! FBI." She drew her weapon.

The professor wove through the kitchen staff. They scattered as she raced after him, gaining ground amid crashing trays, broken glass, and metal clanging against a concrete floor.

Cole passed her in pursuit. The professor stumbled beside a stove. He grabbed a large pot by the handles and tossed boiling water at Cole. He dodged the scalding brew.

The professor picked up a knife and whirled around. He grabbed a man attempting to clear out of the fight and held the knife to the man's throat.

"Put your gun down, or he's dead." A trickle of blood dripped from the frightened man's neck.

Tori eyed Howard. "This place is crawling with law enforcement ready to take you down."

"Not while I have a hostage."

From the corner of her eye, she saw Cole inch toward the professor.

"You won't make it out alive," she said.

"I'll take my chances."

"Why all the deaths and destruction?" she spoke softly. "Do you think Erik wants this?"

The professor swung toward Cole. "Stop now, or I'm cutting his throat. You know I will."

Cole held up his hands and stepped back. "Sure. Tell us more about Erik. Why the interest all these years?"

"I didn't have a son. He filled the gap."

"I think it's more," Cole said. "Erik's your son, isn't he? You loved him the best you could, and when MS attacked his body, you vowed to do whatever it took to save him. But your wife had no idea. If she learned the truth, the money would end."

"What are you saying?"

"You and Albert's wife were lovers. All these years, he thought she'd left him, but you killed her."

"Where's your source?"

"I took a look at the police records when Albert reported his wife missing. He gave them everything to locate her. Seemed odd she simply disappeared."

The calls and texts occupying Cole earlier now made sense.

The muscles in the professor's face tightened. "Smart man, aren't you?"

"Authorities never found her body," Cole said. "You betrayed Albert. You befriended him so you could be near your son. Then you set him up while paying the Hermanos de Pistoleros to do your dirty work. Am I right, Professor?"

"You're crazy. You must have been listening to drunken Albert."

"Don't think so. What about threatening Anita Krantz?"

The man's eyes seemed to burn. "I'd do anything to save my son."

"Really? What about that Rolex? Looks to me like you'd do anything as long as it was with someone else's money."

Tori seized a moment of hesitation from the professor and slammed into his lower right side, knocking him off-balance. He dropped the knife and it slid across the floor.

Cole rushed into place. Pushing aside the hostage, he sent the professor sprawling.

"Cuff him," she said. "Do the honors. You figured it out."

Once the man was restrained, Cole jerked him to his feet.

"Nathan deserved to die. He stole everything from Erik. I wanted him and his precious oil company destroyed."

Tori struggled to unload her fury—the personal toll on friendships and the deaths and destruction. "What about Preston Ustach and Jose Aznar, the bombings, and attacking federal officers?" Tori said. "What's your excuse for that?"

The professor's face twisted. "If Nathan had taken care of Erik, none of this would have happened. It's his fault. The Hermanos de Pistoleros created trouble at the oil rig."

"But you paid them, right?" Tori said, attempting to control her fury.

"Prove it."

Cole snorted. "We will. César Vega has been picked up by the US Marshals. I'm sure he'll name you in exchange for a lesser charge."

69

AFTER ELEVEN THAT NIGHT, Cole sat in Tori's car and stared at the Moore home, lit up with their friends inside and protected by bodyguards. The satisfaction of ending a crime marathon slowed the adrenaline that had kept him going.

"It's finally over," he said. "Professor Howard's confession demonstrated a man whose selfishness knew no boundaries."

"Yet he planned Nathan's murder because of Nathan's self-centered personality." She touched her head to the steering wheel, then faced him. "Poor Albert. I was afraid he'd have a heart attack when he learned the truth about Erik's father and about his deceased wife."

"At least Professor Howard told us where her body is buried." Cole recalled the shrieking grief of the old man and the corresponding call for an ambulance. "Albert will face charges for attempting to kill Nathan while dealing with how the professor manipulated him."

"All those years, Albert thought his friendship with Professor Howard was real. It's as though the professor took out his bitterness of not being able to raise his son on Albert and Nathan."

Tori's words sailed into his heart. Bitterness . . .

"What are you thinking?" Tori said. "You went silent on me."

"Big-time realization. Remember the guy who shot me and left me for dead?" When she nodded, he continued. "I forgave him, but I didn't get rid of the bitterness. I allowed my pride to take over, fear, even thinking I'd be avenged when he was caught."

"And?"

Cole reached for her hand. "Time to get past it."

"Then do it."

With Tori's hand clasped firmly in his, he bowed his head and got himself right with God. A few moments later, he pointed at the Moore home. "If any of them are watching, they're wondering what's going on. They need answers to Nathan's murder. My guess is they know Professor Howard has been arrested but not the whole story."

"You texted them we were coming, right?"

"Yes, ma'am."

"Oh, I like that. Can I hear it again?"

He tugged on her hand, and she leaned toward him just close enough for a light kiss. "There's more for the future."

"Promise?"

"Promise." He opened his car door, feeling the impact of his shoulder wound. Taking her hand, he walked with her up the sidewalk.

Sally answered the door before he rang the bell. "Does Professor Howard's arrest mean the crisis is over?"

"Yes," Tori said. "We'd like to tell you about tonight."

"What about the boys?"

"I think it best you hear the story first. Later you can decide how much Lance and Jack should know."

"Good." Sally gestured them inside to the kitchen, the familiar meeting spot. Once seated, Tori asked Cole to begin.

"Professor Howard had a history of violent behavior. It began when he had an affair with Albert Weiman's wife. Erik was the result. When she told the professor she was finished with him, and she'd not tell Albert the truth about their son, he killed her and staged it to look like she'd left her family. The professor entered Albert's and Erik's lives as a friend, acting as a mentor and bene-factor for Erik. Over the years, he slipped money into a private account to help his son as needed. The professor's wife is wealthy, but if she ever learned about her husband's affair, he'd be penniless. The professor put Albert up to approaching Nathan for money and encouraged planning the murder when Nathan refused."

"Then murder wasn't foreign to Professor Howard." Sally pressed her hands together. "Did he cause Nathan's heart attack?"

Cole nodded. "He knew when Walt Hanna was scheduled to hack into the pacemaker and monitored it. When Hanna didn't follow through, the professor had the skills to take over."

Sally stared at him. "He masterminded it all?"

Tori took her friend's hand, a trait Cole had come to recog-nize as her way of showing compassion. "Sally, Professor Howard orchestrated every detail and used his wife's money to fund it. He also enlisted Anita Krantz to help him, but nothing came of those efforts except her fear of him." Her gentle tone wafted around them. "He sent threatening notes to Nathan and hired the Hermanos de Pistoleros to create trouble any way they wanted. Before we arrived here, César Vega confessed to the gang's part. They bombed the oil rig, targeted Preston Ustach in a shooting, eliminated Jose Aznar because he refused to do any more dirty work, and attacked Cole and me, along with killing the guard at the security shack."

"I respected the man, and this is what he did? Tori, he attempted to murder all of us. He's a coward, afraid of claiming his own son." Sally stiffened. "What will become of him?"

"That's for a jury to decide, but I'd say life in prison."

Cole captured Sally's attention. "The important thing to remember is you have answers, and those responsible for the tragedies will never hurt anyone again."

Sally's eyes watered. "I can't believe it's finally over. Thank you. Thank you so very much for not giving up, for sacrificing your time, for pursuing the killer even when you two were injured. I can never repay you, but I love you both. Because of you, my sons no longer have to walk in fear. We have our lives back."

Tori glanced at Cole as their friend dabbed her eyes. He offered her a grim smile. Yes, Nathan had left behind a string of questionable choices and actions, but Cole felt confident that his friend's family would stand strong and carry on the man's legacy of hard work. Cole had his life back too—one that seemed brighter for Tori's presence in it.

EPILOGUE

THREE MONTHS LATER

Tori fastened her helmet and swung her leg over the bicycle. Cole laughed and commented on her awkward stride. "Are you sure you want to follow through with this?" he said.

"Absolutely. I'm one determined FBI agent pitted against a gritty US Marshal. I know who the winner will be. I've been training for six weeks."

"We could still race your Charger against my new truck."

"This will be more fun. I plan on enjoying a free steak dinner."

He gave her a pitying look. "I'll treat you to a steak—you name the restaurant."

She lifted her chin, feeling the helmet's strap rub against her neck. "You're afraid to lose?"

"Trust me, I won't."

She and Cole had bought racing bikes as a way to spend time together. Hers was blue, lightweight, and sleek, while he referred to his black racer as aggressive.

The two took off on a country road west of Houston. Though

she'd biked it many times during her prep for the race, she wasn't so sure she'd win. But she'd give it her best.

She pedaled hard to keep up with him. He made the process look entirely too easy, but who'd be ahead at the end of the ten miles?

"You're sweating," he said. "And it's only six in the morning."

"What do you expect for mid-July?"

"We US Marshals live for endurance."

"Don't bet on it giving you the edge."

Cole had recently been assigned to witness protection, and she was working a murder linked to a drug cartel. Max had retired and seemed to be happy with Janie and their kids and grandkids. With his lung removed, he was responding well to treatments. His renewed interest in life caused him to fight the effects of cancer positively. Janie even had him in church.

Only a half mile left to go, and she'd kept pace with Cole. No reason why she couldn't win this race with a spurt of energy that would send her over the finish line.

"I talked to Sally yesterday," she said in an attempt to slow him down. "She's taking the boys to Hawaii for a break, snorkeling and deep-sea diving."

"Good. They've worked hard to support each other. She seems happy."

"The company is doing well under her leadership. Who would have thought she'd take over Moore Oil & Gas with such confidence?" Tori smiled. "And loving it."

"Has she seen Erik since he returned from Germany?"

"A couple of times. Nathan's funding of his treatment and Sally paying for a nurse to accompany him helped her heal. His prognosis is still grim, and he hasn't been well enough to visit Albert in prison."

"We need to visit both of them. By the way, I'm taking Lance and Jack fishing next weekend. Wanna come along?"

"Can't. Sally and I are having a spa day with Mom."

He pedaled ahead of her.

"Hey, you just think you're going to beat me."

"Know what? You sure are cute when you're all sweaty and losing," Cole said with no indication of being out of breath.

"I'm always cute."

"Which is why I love you."

What did he say? "I don't think I heard you."

"I said, 'I love you.'"

"How can you say such a thing in the middle of a race?"

He glanced at her while she fought to keep from falling over in a puddle of sweat. "It's easy when a woman makes you crazy because she's crazy beautiful, crazy smart . . . and crazy to win." He added an extra bolt to his speed, then stopped six feet short of the finish line.

"What are you doing?"

"We're finishing this race together."

Tori smiled into those incredibly sky-blue eyes. "I love you too."

A NOTE FROM THE AUTHOR

Dear Reader,

Deep Extraction is more than a romantic suspense tale about solving a man's murder. This novel shows how people can grow and become better people from their circumstances or sink into the depths of degradation. We are all seeking something, and I pray your search is a quest for truth.

In my story, Tori longed to please her beloved brother, even when he was gone. When she found God, life finally held purpose and meaning.

Cole struggled with bitterness when he nearly died in the line of duty for the US Marshals. Later, when he reached out to God, the things of the world that had stalked him held less importance.

Nathan was a man to be pitied. Despite his worldly success, he failed as a husband and a friend. Unfortunate but true.

All of the characters were faced with choices. Some decisions met with positive results, and others resulted in challenges. Just like us.

The gift of love is powerful. Tori and Cole accepted the joy it offered with gratitude and hope. Can we all meet its zeal with the same commitment? Do we have the courage to reach within ourselves to love and face what *unconditional* means?

Be blessed, my friends, and may your journey lead you to God.

DiAnn

ABOUT THE AUTHOR

DIANN MILLS is a bestselling author who believes her readers should expect an adventure. She currently has more than fifty-five books published.

Her titles have appeared on the CBA and ECPA bestseller lists; won two Christy Awards; and been finalists for the RITA, Daphne du Maurier, Inspirational Reader's Choice, and Carol Award contests.

DiAnn is a founding board member of the American Christian Fiction Writers; the 2014 president of the Romance Writers of America's Faith, Hope & Love chapter; and a member of Inspirational Writers Alive, Advanced Writers and Speakers Association, and International Thriller Writers. She speaks to various groups and teaches writing workshops around the country.

She and her husband live in sunny Houston, Texas. Visit her website at www.diannmills.com and connect with her on Facebook (www.facebook.com/DiAnnMills), Twitter (@DiAnnMills), Pinterest (www.pinterest.com/DiAnnMills), and Goodreads (www. goodreads.com/DiAnnMills).

DISCUSSION QUESTIONS

1. At the beginning of the story, Tori Templeton wrestles with the idea of a good God in a world plagued with sickness, hurt, and unrest. What would you say to her in those moments? Have you ever had similar thoughts? What truth does John 16:33 tell us?

2. Cole Jeffers struggles to get past a defining moment that led to the end of his career as a US Marshal. What prevents him from moving on? What convinces him to take the next step? Do you think he's able to set the incident aside entirely, or will it continue to dog him?

3. Max Dublin steps on plenty of toes in what could be his last case. How well is his behavior handled by the FBI? By Tori? By Cole? If you encountered someone equally as curmudgeonly without knowing what factors might be contributing to their attitude, would you be more inclined to give them the benefit of the doubt? Why or why not?

4. Tori and her friend Sally are seemingly blindsided when details about Nathan Moore's secret life are uncovered. While Tori is confused by the disparate qualities in the man, Sally continues to champion her husband, though she denounces Nathan's inappropriate actions. Is Sally simply being naive? Or is it right for her to stand by her man?

5. Albert Weiman is consumed with seeing his son, Erik, get the justice he deserves—and the medical help he needs. What measuring stick do you use to determine how far you should push to get your way? What happens when you push too far?

6. When Cole and Tori get into a theological discussion, Tori tells him she needs evidence in order to believe, even when it comes to proving her friend's innocence. Do you think Tori really needs tangible proof for the case, or does she, deep down, believe Sally? What would you say to someone who asks for physical evidence of God's existence?

7. Officer Richards tells Tori, "Things are rarely only as they seem. Your case, the people in your life, even your thoughts and fears have a purpose." In what ways does Tori see this play out? Describe a time when this has been true for you.

8. Several characters in *Deep Extraction* have moments of great anger: Tori with Max; Lance Moore over his father's indiscretions; Sally with Tori and Cole for not keeping her informed about the investigation; Cole at the Hermanos de Pistoleros. How well do they each handle their emotions?

What happens when you get angry? How do you respond
to someone who is angry with you?

9. Tori worries quite a bit about cancer and feels she lacks the
   other big C: courage. What advice does she get from the
   people in her life? How does she find peace? When you're
   afraid of something, what do you do?

10. Were you surprised by the twists and turns in the story?
    Which one shocked you the most?

SATURDAY MORNINGS were Stacy Broussard's escape, especially when life slapped her with stress. No better way to unwind from the week than to ride her quarter horse on Houston's airport trail and enjoy nature. This morning promised to be the perfect distraction from a truckload of problems, from the anniversary of the death of her sister to seeking custody of a twelve-year-old boy. She looked forward to a lift in her spirit.

She pulled her truck into the Aldine Westfield Stables. As usual she was the first one of the airport rangers to arrive. Chet's pickup wasn't parked beneath the moss-draped oak, and he normally arrived before dawn. Strange since he took his responsibilities as stable manager seriously.

Finishing her latte, she grabbed her wallet and keys and stepped outside her truck to admire an incredible purple-and-gold sunrise. Not even an early morning aircraft landing disturbed her. She walked slowly to the stables, taking in the singing robins and the familiar humidity. The smell of horseflesh and straw tickled her nose.

"Good morning, boys and girls," she said. "Your friendly veterinarian is on the scene."

If anyone heard her, they'd declare her insane. Maybe so when she reflected on how much she preferred an animal's company to a human's. Except Whitt . . . the most fascinating twelve-year-old on the planet.

Stacy ambled past each stall until she reached Ginger's, greeting the horses by name, touching velvety soft noses, and visibly checking to ensure they were okay. Her pets looked healthy. Spending a few extra moments with Ginger eased the knots in her shoulders that no massage could ever eliminate.

She led Ginger into the stable area and grabbed a pitchfork to tidy up her stall. A strong horse smell and a little manure on her boots never hurt anyone. Being prissy was not one of her traits. When finished, she retrieved her mare's blanket and bridle from her tack box. Her cell phone alerted her to a text.

Sorry, Stacy. Got a sick baby. Won't b there.

No problem. Take care of her and give a hug 4 me.

She'd miss her friend this morning. The idea of a sick child sent a pang of loss and melancholy through her—and not just for what she didn't have. Who was she fooling? Reaching the age of thirty-five without a husband and children hadn't been her idea of the future. A quote sailed into her mind: *"Want to make God laugh? Tell Him your plans."* Not going there. Not today.

Checking her watch, she pondered the whereabouts of her other partner and Chet. She saddled Ginger, adjusting the cinch twice. Another text landed in her phone.

Stacy, my in-laws arrived late last night. 4got 2 call.

After a soft sigh, she typed, **Enjoy the visit.**

Airport ranger guidelines stated volunteers were to ride in pairs or threes. This kept the rider safe if a situation arose on the trail, like in the event a rider fell or encountered a difficult person.

But what choice did she have? Chet hadn't made an appearance either. Who would ever know she made a solo ride? She closed Ginger's stall door and hoisted herself into the saddle. No point in abandoning this beautiful morning because of a single guideline.

"Let's go, Miss Ginger. We'll see if we can shake up a few squirrels."

She crossed the road and made her way to the entrance of the wooded area where the north trail around IAH began. An aircraft broke the sound of chirping birds and the peacefulness that had settled upon her. Right on time. The moment she turned Ginger into the brush area, another aircraft announced its departure. So much for the quiet.

She rode the inside perimeter of the fenced area. Nothing eventful to report—not even a piece of trash. As she made her way into a clearing, a squirrel scampered across her path. A ray of morning light filtered through the trees.

Ginger reared, catching Stacy by surprise. She pulled fast on the reins. "Easy, Ginger."

Her mare crow-hopped and reared again.

What had startled her? A snake?

Then she saw it.

A pair of legs stuck out from a bush approximately fifteen feet to her right.

Her heart hammered, and Ginger had to feel it. She struggled to control her own fear and the horse beneath her while her sights were glued to the man's lower extremities.

"Hello, are you okay?" When only the quiet met her, she dismounted and moved closer to where the man lay. Eyes open and vacant. Stacy had seen scowls like this before, but not on a dead man. He appeared to have defied his attacker in one last fit of anger before surrendering to death.

Blood pooled on his chest and trickled over his abdomen and left side. One—no, two horrible holes. The wounds looked fresh, perhaps within the last hour or so.

Terror rose, and she thought she'd be physically sick. She swung her attention in every direction, expecting someone to emerge from the tangled green terrain along the north section of Houston's Intercontinental Airport. She yanked her only permissible weapon from her jeans—a pocketknife—and opened it as if it would ward off a killer.

Why had she chosen to ride alone?

A yellow Lab snuggled near the body, her head resting on the dead man's chest. A leather leash from the dog was wrapped around the man's fingers. Five feet to the right, a blood-spattered motorcycle stood at attention. Securing the pocketknife in her palm, she lifted her phone from inside her jeans pocket and pressed in 911 while she continued to look over her shoulder.

"What is your emergency?" the operator said.

Stacy swallowed the acid rising in her stomach. The morning's heat didn't help. "I've found a dead body on the north trail that runs along the FM 1960 side of IAH. The nearest entrance is on Farrell where a sign designates the Houston Airport System equestrian security trail. My name is Stacy Broussard, and I'm an airport ranger volunteer."

"You're sure he's not alive?"

She bent beside the body and felt the side of his neck for a pulse. Nothing. "Very much so. He's lost a tremendous amount of blood from his chest and abdomen. I'm assuming gunshots."

"Do you know the man?"

"No, ma'am."

"Are you all right?"

"Shaken. I'm alone except for a dog lying next to the body. The animal's right front paw is bleeding, and I'm a veterinarian. She's not protective or aggressive." Stacy drew in a ragged breath. The dog rose from the body and limped to her side, while the leash stayed fixed in the man's hand. She rested her head on Stacy's knee.

"You're doing fine," the operator said. "I'll keep talking until the police arrive and I'm assured you're safe. How did you happen upon the body?"

Keep your head. You can get through this. "I'm a volunteer for the airport rangers. We ride horseback to patrol the outer perimeter of IAH and report any problems to the Houston Police Department. The man is in a clearing. I checked for a pulse, and I'm sure of his condition." She removed the leash from his hand and examined the dog's bleeding paw, a wound that would require a few stitches. The man wasn't as fortunate. "How long until officers arrive?"

"Only a few more minutes. You're a brave woman."

"I don't feel brave. How awful for this poor man." The victim's eyes would haunt her for a long time, maybe forever.

"Tell me more about the airport rangers," the operator said. "I wasn't aware Houston had such a service."

She's trying to calm me, divert my attention from the blood-coated body. "We're not highly publicized. Normally we find evidence of drugs or kids' inappropriate behavior. Never anything like this. And we aren't supposed to ride alone, but the other two volunteers canceled at the last minute. Our stables are close by." Stacy avoided staring at the body and instead concentrated on the injured dog. Her collar didn't have an ID. Had the animal been hurt while protecting her master?

"Are there any signs of a struggle?"

She peered around for what seemed like the hundredth time.

"There's a motorcycle, a Kawasaki. I suppose the plates won't be hard to trace." A strange object captured her attention in the shadow of the bushes. Boots? Shoes? "I see something unusual, but I can't make out what it is."

"Be careful. The police can investigate it."

No need to caution her. She was already frightened out of her wits. Sirens grew closer. "I hear them."

"Stay where you are until the officers arrive. They'll take over the situation."

"I'm sorry, but it might be another body or someone hurt. I have to see if someone needs help." She bolstered her courage and moved toward the questionable object. The dog followed her to the edge of the clearing, where a type of drone with four propellers was lodged in a fallen tree branch and bushes. A churning panic swirled through her. Had the dead man stopped a potential crime of blinding a pilot? "What happened here?" she whispered, more to herself than the 911 operator.

"Talk to me, Stacy."

"I've found a drone. A clear dome is attached underneath, and it's pointed toward the northwest end of the runway."

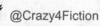